Antiphon

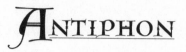

TOR BOOKS BY KEN SCHOLES

Lamentation

Canticle

Antiphon

ANTIPHON

KEN SCHOLES

A TOM DOHERTY ASSOCIATES BOOK
NEW YORK

This is a work of fiction. All of the characters, organizations, and events portrayed in this novel are either products of the author's imagination or are used fictitiously.

ANTIPHON

Edited by Beth Meacham

A Tor Book
Published by Tom Doherty Associates, LLC
175 Fifth Avenue
New York, NY 10010

www.tor-forge.com

Tor® is a registered trademark of Tom Doherty Associates, LLC.

ISBN 978-0-7653-2129-9

First Edition: September 2010

Printed in the United States of America

0 9 8 7 6 5 4 3 2 1

For Ray Bradbury,

who showed me what I wanted to be when I grew up

ANTIPHON

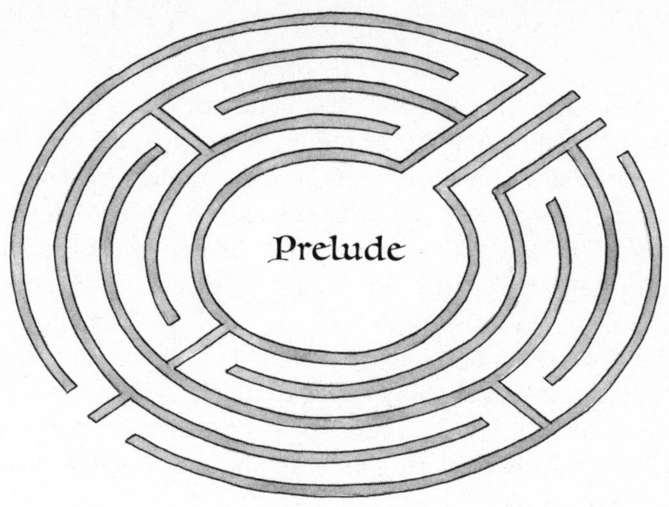

Prelude

A rising full moon washed the calm sea in brighter tones of blue and green, bathing the shoreline as well as the robed figures who stood upon it in dim aquamarine light. Overhead, stars danced and guttered in a warm night sky.

Rafe Merrique leaned on the gunwale of the longboat and scanned the shore. Behind him, the *Kinshark* lay at anchor in the shallow bay, unmagicked for now in these abandoned waters. Ahead, he saw a small gathering of men amid their wagons and horses.

"They have the look of Francines," he whispered to his first mate.

The man grunted a reply as he worked the oars. Rafe kept his attention on the beach. There were four figures in view, their backs turned and their hoods up so that he could not see their faces.

But why are they so far from home? Merrique was a veteran of the horn, seasoned at bringing his ship and crew through the Ghosting Crests and into the Churning Wastes. He'd spent half his life running the Order back and forth on one secret venture or another. At first, he'd done it for the bits of magick and technology they'd offered him. Later, the money had been enough of an incentive.

And now, with the Order decimated and the Ninefold Forest assuming guardianship of Windwir's holdings, the Gypsies were his customers.

Until the moon sparrow found him, that is.

He'd just landed a fresh company of Gypsy Scouts to assist with the work at Sanctorum Lux and was turning his vessel west when the bird fell from the sky to perch on the railing of his forecastle. It was small and made of a silver metal so bright that the sunlight reflecting from it burned Rafe's eyes. It hopped twice, regarding him with emerald-jeweled eyes, before cocking its head and opening its tiny beak.

A reedy voice whispered out. "Rafe Merrique," it said, "the light requires service of your ship."

And if it weren't a bird he'd seen so many times before, bearing a message he'd also heard many times, he might not have yelled for a pencil to scratch down the course heading and coordinates it suddenly chirruped before closing its beak and lifting into the summer sky to speed northeast.

Now, three weeks later, he approached by sea and studied the beach where the robed figures waited. The wagons were loaded down with supplies, but there was no sign of a camp. No welcoming fire, no tents, and no sound but the gentle lapping of the water and the whisper of oars.

"Ahoy," Rafe called out as they ran the longboat into the shallows. He stood and hopped over the side with a splash. The acrid scent of ozone and salt struck him. "You are a long ways from anywhere," he said.

The robed figures shuffled by their wagons, and an odd sound reached his ears. A wheezing—like a bellows—and the slightest metallic clacking. It was oddly familiar, though he could not place it at first.

"You are Captain Rafe Merrique of the *Kinshark*," a flat, inhuman voice said. One of the robed figures separated from the others.

Rafe's men were out of the longboats now, hands reaching for knives and cutlasses. He frowned. "Yes," he said. "I am—"

But when he saw the eyes, he could not finish his sentence. A sense of wrongness flooded him, and his mouth suddenly tasted like iron. He felt the hairs rise on his arms and the back of his neck. The eyes were amber jewels, dimly glowing in the recesses of the hood. Steam whistled out from the back of the robe, and as the figure approached, Rafe saw the metal hands and the metal feet. "The light," the metal man said, "requires service of your ship."

He stepped back slowly and whistled for his men to do the same. "What is this about?"

The metal man cocked its head. "You are not authorized to know. Archived data indicates that your vessel has been hired on seventy-three occasions to assist in various matters of transport and recovery for the Androfrancine Order."

Rafe glanced to the other robed figures. He saw the faint glow of their eyes and the gleam of moonlight on their metal hands. There were four of them. He'd seen the mechoservitor Isaak—he'd even conversed with the mechanical over breakfast during the voyage back to the Delta. Truly one of the Order's greatest wonders. And he'd heard bits of rumor and gossip among the men he'd transported—Charles, Aedric and the others—about the hidden library, Sanctorum Lux, reduced to ashes by mechoservitors now fled to unknown quarters.

"You're one of the mechanicals from Sanctorum Lux," he said.

But the mechoservitor ignored the statement. "Your arrival is the salvation of the light," the metal man said, stepping forward. "We have urgent need of your vessel in the formulation of our response."

Rafe Merrique prided himself on knowing which jobs to take and which to turn down. This one, he realized, was the latter. *I should not have come here. I should not have heeded the bird.* His mouth went dry as he found the words. "My vessel," he said, "is not for hire after all."

"The *Kinshark* is a Tam-manufactured galleon sailing with a complement of forty-seven men," the metal man continued, again ignoring Rafe's words. "Stealth oils are applied routinely for concealment, and scout powders are administered to the crew in three shifts to maximize effectiveness and minimize adverse health impacts. The vessel boasts comfortable passenger accommodations and various holds—concealed and plain—for the transport of sensitive goods. Minimum seagoing complement is four men."

The other three robed figures were converging on them now, walking slowly, metal frames clicking and gears whirring beneath their plain gray robes.

"We're leaving now," Rafe told his men as he turned back to the longboat.

But as he moved toward the boat, a metal hand came down firmly upon his shoulder. Rafe spun, reaching for his cutlass, but another hand gripped his wrist and he cried out at the strength of it. Around him, his men surged to life, but the mechoservitors were faster and stronger. Struggling, he twisted against his captor and saw his first mate collapse beneath a hand on his windpipe. "You will be adequately compensated," the mechanical said, "upon our return."

Firm hands pulled him quickly toward the wagons. "Analysis

indicates that with proper rationing the provided supplies will allow forty-seven men to survive fourteen days in this environment. The nearest intact Androfrancine supply cache is twelve days' march at a pace of thirty leagues per day. A map and lock ciphers have been provided for you. We will summon you by the bird when our return is imminent."

Rafe opened his mouth to speak, but the hand had now moved to his throat, and spiderwebs of thin, white light filled his vision as the pressure increased.

"My deepest apologies," the mechoservitor said, "for this violence and deception."

Then his world went gray.

When it came back into focus again, Rafe was bound to the wagon with his landing party. His crew of forty-six cursed and sputtered in the surf, so recently extricated from their vessel by the unexpected speed and force of its metal boarders. Underneath the clamor of their cursing came another sound: a hot night wind catching the *Kinshark's* sails as she left for points unknown.

Eyes fastened upon his departing vessel, Rafe Merrique added his own curses to those of his men and shouted for someone to untie him.

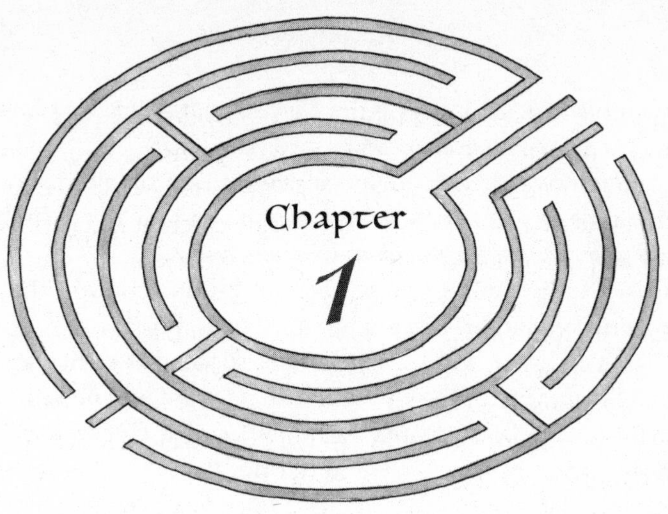

Rudolfo

Rudolfo urged his stallion forward and laughed with his son as the wind caught his turban. Overhead, the afternoon sun blazed in a sky so blue it burned the eye. Around them, a warm wind stirred the Prairie Sea, golden waves rippling across the vast, rolling expanse. Ahead and around them, on the horizon, the Ninefold Forest rose up to meet the sky.

"He takes well to the ride, General," a voice shouted to his left above the pounding of the hooves.

Rudolfo looked to Aedric, the first captain of his Gypsy Scouts, and grinned. "Aye. He does." Then, he leaned forward and whistled the horse faster as Jakob squealed with delight. They'd ridden long enough now for father and son to both grow comfortable with the riding harness that held the swaddled infant snug against Rudolfo's chest.

The same that bore me upon my father's steed. Rudolfo felt the slightest stab of loss. Those knives were different upon him now that he himself was a father. The cut upon his soul took a different turn as the moments with his new heir brought back hazy recollections of his own rides with the man he'd named his son for—the man Rudolfo had watched die in his twelfth year. And those memories came with others—wrestling with his brother in the shallows of the Rajblood River, singing in the forest with his mother, learning the *Hymnal of the Wandering Army* with Gregoric, Aedric's father, now nearly two years dead.

Those memories had brought sadness to him many times before, but now, alongside the grief, he found hope and joy in remembering. *This child helps me find the good in it,* Rudolfo realized.

A whistle to his right brought his head around. Low in the saddle and laughing herself, Jin Li Tam pulled ahead of him.

"You're slowing down, old man," she shouted over her shoulder. Her red hair, shining in the sunlight, caught wind and flowed behind. She wore the rainbow-colored riding silks of a Gypsy queen, and though they were unnecessary and did not match her chosen outfit, she also wore the scout knives that had once belonged to his mother.

They'd been on the move for two months now, visiting each of his forest manors, introducing a jubilant people to the heir they had longed to see. Of course, so soon on the heels of their wedding at the Seventh Forest Manor, each stop simply continued the celebration as each of his towns rallied to honor both his bride and his boy.

And they honor me as well. They always had, even back to his days as a boy king. But until recently, like those losses in his life, it had meant something different to him. Now, it was a kind of amazement tempered by a gratitude he'd never felt before.

Paramo had been their last stop—a logging town that now stretched itself into a city as refugees settled in to work the old-growth forest, milling the wood and shipping it south by river for the library Rudolfo and Isaak built. Tonight, they would rest easy in their own bed. And tomorrow, Rudolfo would approach the waiting tower of paper that no doubt threatened collapse as it dared gravity there in the basket on his desk. Still, it had been a good respite between the first rains and the last of the sun.

A flash of white on the horizon caught his eye, and Rudolfo slowed his horse at the familiar sight. It shimmered and blurred in the heat of the day, moving in a straight line toward them, low to the tops of the grass. When the bird struck Aedric's catch net, Rudolfo matched his pace with that of his first captain and watched as the man stripped the note, read the knotted message in the blue thread and unrolled the scroll.

Behind them, the rest of their caravan slowed. Ahead, Jin Li Tam turned and doubled back in a wide and sweeping circle.

Aedric frowned and turned, looking to the northwest. Rudolfo followed his gaze. In the distance, the Dragon's Spine rose up, gray and impenetrable, above the Prairie Sea and the Ninefold Forest that spread like ancient islands across it.

Rudolfo laid his hand upon Jakob's cheek. Aedric's grim look in the direction of the Marshlands told him the source of this latest news. "What are they up to now?"

It had been six months since the Council of Kin-Clave. Half a year since the woman Ria had announced herself as the Machtvolk queen and saved his son's life before slipping back into the north and vanishing behind her closely watched borders. The Named Lands had slid into madness and disarray, though of late there had been a brooding peace of sorts.

Aedric's voice brought him back to the moment. Already, the young captain was inking a response and twisting knots of reply into the blue thread of inquiry. "They've breached our borders again, General."

Rudolfo sighed. "Where now?"

"Glimmerglam."

He felt his stomach sink. Jin Li Tam had slowed her horse to a trot and joined them. "We were just there three weeks ago."

Aedric nodded. "Two evangelists this time. Preaching their so-called gospel in the streets openly. The house steward has them locked away for now. I'll deal with them once we're home and I've seen to the men."

Rudolfo stroked his beard. This had started not long after the council there on the plains of Windwir. Initially, they had found Marshers wandering the Prairie Sea or the more isolated parts of the Ninefold Forest. These they turned back—even chased back—to the low hills that served as a border between his lands and the woman who called herself Winteria the Elder and claimed the Wicker Throne. Later, the ragged preachers had shown up in the towns surrounding his forest manors. These, his militia beat and delivered back to their border. It was less violent than what his father would have done, and still it made Rudolfo wince. Lord Jakob would have placed them on Tormentor's Row, and after a day or two under the knives of his Physicians of Penitent Torture, they'd have seen the value of keeping their beliefs within their territory. If they'd returned, he'd have had them killed and would have buried them at the border.

The beatings had seemed a reasonable compromise when reason failed.

But still they persist. Rudolfo sighed. "I think a new tack is in order," he finally said, glancing down at his son. "Have them brought to me."

Aedric's face registered surprise. "You want to see them?"

Rudolfo nodded. "I do. I want to speak with them. Question them."

He glanced to Jin Li Tam. She regarded him with a face he could not read, but her hands moved with subtle grace along the reins. He admired the care she took to be sure none saw but him. *Are you certain giving them voice is the answer?*

He smiled, though it was brief and felt out of place. He'd just started teaching her the subverbal language of House Y'Zir last month, and she was nearly proficient. Of course, she'd already known eleven other subverbals. Rudolfo's fingers moved over Jakob's shoulder and head as he formed his reply. *I'm not certain.*

Rudolfo felt the power of his words even as his hands made them. He truly wasn't certain, and it was foreign to him. "I think our old strategies are no longer serving us well," he said, keeping his gaze steady on her blue eyes.

Then, he looked away from her, toward Aedric. "Be certain they're well cared for, Aedric. I intend to return them *whole* to their bloodletting queen."

He did not wait for Aedric to speak before he pushed his horse forward. He wondered if Jin Li Tam would follow him but secretly hoped she wouldn't. He needed this time for himself and his son.

Two years ago, he'd ridden these same plains, Gregoric at his side. A shadow had moved over the light of that second summer day, and he'd looked up to a pillar of smoke on the sky. He marked it now as a day when his life—and his world—changed utterly. From that moment, so many other changes had flowed out to him, sweeping him away with the force of their current, including his betrothal to Jin Li Tam and the birth of their son.

He felt the warmth of his son against his chest and thought about the new shadow passing over the light that remained. Six months earlier, at the edge of spring, he'd watched Ria bring Petronus back from the dead with her blood magicks and had watched his betrothed beg for their son's life as a result of it, the culmination of a grand manipulation. With relations already strained, the events on the Plains of Windwir had driven an even deeper wedge between his houses and the other nations of the Named Lands. Pylos had broken off kin-clave entirely, and Turam was close behind. The Delta remained a loose ally, but it was a paper kin-clave as they wrestled through the upheaval of political reform. And now, adherents to this new Y'Zirite Resurgence brought their sermons into his lands, preaching them to his people and pointing to his son as their so-called Child of Promise.

As he whistled his horse to a gallop, Rudolfo wondered what path he would take. His own words came back to haunt him: *I am uncertain.* It was a strange sensation, not knowing the best path to take.

He felt the sun on his face and savored the wind that pulled at his silk clothing and his scarf of rank. Silent for a time, Jakob gurgled and laughed again.

When Rudolfo placed his hand over his child's chest he felt strength there. His fingers moved, and he tapped a message there. *Whatever I do, I do for your future.*

He could not bring himself to laughter now with the gravity of that thought. Instead, he kept his hand there and urged his stallion faster, finding delight in the voice of his son and purpose in the heart that beat lightly beneath the palm of his hand.

"My best and truest compass," Rudolfo said in a quiet voice.

Then, he turned his horse toward the line of old-growth forest and raced homeward to his waiting work.

Neb

Holding his thorn rifle loosely, Neb lay still and studied the dust cloud that moved across the shattered landscape of the Churning Wastes. The afternoon sun baked the ground beneath him, and from his vantage point in the hills, he watched heat waves rising from the sand and rock floor of the valley below. There, against the backdrop of that shimmer, a figure ran under cover of magicks.

This was the third time they'd encountered magicked runners in the Deep Wastes in as many weeks.

Shielding his eyes, he chewed the black root and watched. Using fixed patches of scrub or outcroppings of rock to mark distance, counting silently beneath his breath, Neb ciphered out the runner's speed as he had with the others. He moved too fast for the scout magicks Neb had trained under during his short time with the Gypsies. Faster even than the black root would allow.

Neb had a theory but didn't want it to be true.

If his theory was correct, the scout below would not only be fast—he would be strong, too. Stronger than four men. And he would be dead in three days' time, once the blood magicks burned their way through his organs.

Neb shuddered. A sudden memory of Rudolfo's Firstborn Feast

gripped him—the sudden clamor of third alarm as the doors burst inward, the invisible wall of iron that pushed through the Gypsy Scouts as if they were made of paper, assassinating Hanric and Ansylus. It had been a dark night of violence throughout the Named Lands.

Blood magicks. Forbidden by kin-clave in the New World and the product of older ways—the way of the Wizard Kings with their cuttings and bloodlettings and bargains made in the Beneath Places.

He glanced to his right where Renard lay, also scanning the landscape below. The Waste Guide wore the tattered robe of an Androfrancine and the sturdy boots of a Delta scout. He lay with a spyglass to his eye, his own thorn rifle within easy reach. Renard's mouth was a grim line.

"Three now," Neb said in a whisper.

Renard's eyes narrowed as he pulled back from the glass. "More are coming, I suspect."

But from where? And more importantly, why?

After Renard's leg had healed from his brutal encounter with the mechoservitor at D'Anjite's Bridge, they'd spent months in the deeper Wastes. By day, Neb learned not only how to survive, but how to thrive in the harshness of the blasted lands. He'd learned how to trap, how to hunt, and how to find the scant pockets of life that sprang up hidden in the Wastes. Renard had shown him the secret gun grove nestled in an arroyo at the base of the Dragon's Spine and had taught him how to harvest both the rifles and their thorn pods from the tangled thicket they grew in. Then, he'd taught him how to use them.

At night, Neb held the silver crescent to his ear and listened to the strains of the song that trickled out from it, trying to find his way into the dream he knew lay beneath that haunting music. Even now, he heard it faintly, though the crescent was wrapped tightly in thick wool and buried in his pack. He'd deciphered bits of the code within the song—series of numbers without meaning to him—but so far, he'd not been able to interpret what response the canticle required.

It chewed him, not knowing.

But somewhere out here, he knew there were metal servants who *did* know the response. Yet in months of searching, there had been no sign of the metal men themselves, only evidence of where they had been. Carefully concealed digs. Empty supply caches. He and Renard moved from place to place, tracking them as they could.

Between them and the song, Neb already had two Whymer Mazes to solve. Now the runners presented him with yet another.

Already, the figure below had disappeared behind a massive outcropping of fused glass and stone, and Renard tucked the spyglass back into his pouch as he pulled himself up into a crouch. Neb did the same.

Renard scratched his close-cropped salt-and-pepper hair. "You say the blood magicks will kill the user in three days' time?"

Neb nodded. "That's what Aedric told us." Even the scout magicks that Neb had trained under could eventually kill a man if he hadn't been raised up in them from an early age and if he didn't exercise caution and moderation in their use.

Renard backed away from their vantage point and bent to pick up his pack. "It makes no sense," he said. "We're weeks from anywhere—at least two from the coast and three from the Keeper's Gate. Three days wouldn't get them very far."

Neb chewed his root and pondered this. His Franci training took hold, and he remembered their seventh precept. *The simplest path is most often the best to take.* "Perhaps it's a different kind of magick, then. Or"—here, the root became more bitter in his mouth "—perhaps they've found a way to prolong their exposure to the magicks."

Renard stood upright now, his eyes to the north. "That seems likely. We should get word to the Gypsies. One was an oddity; two was a problematic coincidence." He looked to Neb. "Three is a pattern."

Neb pulled his own pack on and cinched the straps tight on his shoulders. "Rudolfo will want to know what these runners are up to."

"Yes." Renard's voice sounded far away.

When Neb looked up, he realized the man watched him carefully. He'd run with Renard for long enough to read him and could see the discomfort in his eyes now. "I think we need to find that out, too," the Waste Guide said. "Something tells me it can't possibly be good."

Neb felt the slightest tickle of fear in the deeper part of his stomach and at the base of his spine. "What are you proposing?"

"There's still a Gypsy camp at Sanctorum Lux," Renard said. "You know the way. And you can handle yourself in the Wastes, Neb. You've taken to it like a kin-wolf cub." He nodded to the north. "I can track our new friend for a bit, see what he's up to. You bear word to the Gypsies and meet up with me at the Dreaming Well in three weeks' time."

Neb blinked and felt the fear spreading farther into him. No longer a tickle, now it was as cold and pervasive as the Second River in winter. He'd spent months in the Wastes with Renard and certainly had known at some point they'd part company, even if only for a season.

Still, now that the moment stared him down, his mouth was dry and his feet felt rooted. "Are you sure—"

Renard offered a grim smile. "You're ready, Nebios." He dug about in his pouch and pulled out a smaller cloth sack tied shut with a bit of twine. He passed it over to him. "You know how to use the powders. Be wary of mixing them with the root for too long—they burn harder and will wear you down faster. If you run into anything you can't handle use the magicks."

Neb opened his mouth to protest but couldn't find the words. Renard was right, of course. He *could* do this. And it made sense that one of them should track the runner—and that Renard, being the most experienced, was the best candidate for that work. Still, Neb felt the hesitation in both his mind and his body. During his time in the Wastes, Renard had been a constant, and the thought of striking out alone, even for three weeks, frightened him.

Renard's eyes were on him, and the man raised a hand to place it on Neb's shoulder and squeeze it quickly. Then, he dropped his arm. "You're ready for this. Hebda would be proud."

His father's name settled the fear in his stomach. Or maybe, he thought, it gave him the resolve he needed to face that fear. "Three weeks then . . . at the well."

"Three weeks," Renard said with a final nod. Then, he turned and ran north along the ridgeline, dust from his boot heels rising behind him as the root took hold and his speed increased.

Neb watched him run until he could no longer see him, then took a deep breath. Cinching the straps of his pack even tighter, he willed his legs to carry him southward.

As his feet found their way, he turned his mind back to the song, and not for the first time, he wondered if he would ever hear within it what the mechoservitor assured him lay beneath the notes.

Those few times he'd discussed it with Renard, the Waste guide had simply shrugged. "You'll hear it when it's time to hear it."

Neb had wondered what the man knew that he wasn't saying.

He'd run twenty leagues before he finally placed his pondering on a shelf in the hidden corners of his mind. Tonight would be soon enough for those questions, when the moon was up and the song was at its loudest. Alongside it, he shelved his questions about the magicked runners and instead tried to turn his mind westward toward Winters, the girl he loved. The girl who had first pointed him toward his purpose in the days before that purpose had sundered them.

But when he could not remember her face, he set that aside as well and gave himself over to the warmth of the sun on his neck and the fingers of wind in his long, flowing white hair. He blessed the solid ground beneath his feet and the steady rhythm of each breath moving in and out of him, keeping time with the pounding of his heart.

As the sky moved into twilight, a kin-wolf howled in the mounded ruins of a city to his east. In his ears, it was a cry of praise and despair.

I would join you in your song, Neb thought.

But instead, he simply ran and gave himself to the running.

Jin Li Tam

The Seventh Forest Manor stirred to life when the sky was still pink from dawn. Servants bustled, laying fires to heat water and cook breakfast, all under the watchful eye of Lady Ilyna. Jin Li Tam moved quietly among them, smiling at each member of the staff that she passed on her way to the back door near the kitchen.

It was unusual for her to awaken before Rudolfo. Typically, he rose first and it was his rising that started her slow journey to wakefulness. But these last several mornings, even while camping on the Prairie Sea or staying in another of his nine Forest Houses, she'd found herself waking first. This morning, she received it as a gift. She had much to do.

Besides, she told herself as she stepped into the cool morning, this was better than the dreams she'd been having of late. Their frequency and intensity had let up since Jakob's healing there in the midst of the Desolation of Windwir, but when they did visit her, the darkness and terror in them was smothering.

Lately, they'd been about the children.

She walked quickly through the back gardens, past Rudolfo's Whymer Maze, nodding to the Gypsy Scouts who stood at the small, rear gate of the manor. The younger of the two men opened the gate for her and she passed through. She followed the trail until the forest swallowed her; then she broke into a gentle run and left the path, letting the wet ferns slap at her as she built speed.

She wore loose trousers and a looser shirt for these excursions, trading her low, sturdy boots for a pair of doeskin moccasins that protected her feet without encumbering them. And of course, she wore the knives Rudolfo had given her for their wedding—blades she'd already helped herself to and had even wetted in battle in the days of violence that had culminated in the blood magick that spared her son.

Like the manor, the forest also came to life around her. Birdsong echoed beneath a dark canopy, and foliage shuddered and whispered with the movement of wildlife slipping back into dens to sleep out the day. Mist clung to the ground, lending the wooded terrain an ominous beauty. She ran through it, leaving the familiar path in favor of making her own.

She built speed until she felt the sweat trickling down the sides of her breasts, until she tasted iron in the back of her mouth, until her breathing deepened with effort. Then, she held that pace.

As she ran, she thought about the day ahead of her.

First, she would see to Jakob. And after feeding him, she'd dress him and take him to see the other children. Isaak had tasked one of the mechoservitors with basic education and childcare, drawing on theories from the vast tomes of Franci thought they now re-created for the new library. They had built a school for the children at the base of the hill where that massive structure slowly took shape. She'd wanted to bring them into the Seventh Forest Manor, but there had simply been too many of them; in the end, her father had suggested that this would be more in their best interest.

Memories of the nightmare tugged at her and she increased her speed slightly, as if the extra effort might exorcise the iron knives and the children's screams from her nightmares.

Y'Zirite monsters. It still closed her throat to think about it. Somewhere southeast of them, in the Ghosting Crests, her father worked with a small remnant of their family to learn what he could about the Blood Temple that had so recently cut most of House Li Tam out of the world.

To save my son, she realized, by making from the blood of others a magick so powerful it could raise the dead, or cure the deathly ill.

She felt the heat of her shame and transmuted it into anger, forcing her legs to bear her rage, savoring the slap of the foliage across her skin as she ran.

I am the forty-second daughter of Vlad Li Tam, she thought as she ran. *I am the queen of the Ninefold Forest Houses.*

But another voice whispered inside of her—the voice of that so-called Machtvolk queen, Winteria the Elder—calling her by a title she still did not fully comprehend: *You are the Great Mother.*

She felt the woman's feet again within her grasping hands, saw the woman standing above her blurred by tears of terror and hope as she begged for her son's life. She heard again Rudolfo's cry of surprise and saw him, too, also trapped behind her curtain of tears, standing in the doorway of the massive tent in the last of winter, upon Windwir's blasted plain.

She turned east and pushed harder, but the run could not strip away the image of her scarred and broken father and the compound of scarred and broken children, cut with the mark of House Y'Zir over their hearts.

As she ran, the forest took on a gloomy silence that weighed heavy on her. But just as she noted the silence, a sound that did not belong there reached her ears.

It was the slightest high-pitched whine, so slight that it tickled her ears, barely discernible over the sound of her pounding heart and feet. Then, another sound—the guttural cry of a bird of prey, the muffled flapping of its wings.

By instinct, she turned toward the noise and slowed. Her right hand moved toward a knife handle even as her left moved out ahead of her to slow the slapping branches.

The whine shifted into a staccato burst of chirps just as Jin Li Tam moved into a small clearing. There, at the center, an enormous bird pecked and clawed at a rotting tree trunk. The chirping rose in volume as if fear fueled it. She drew her knife slowly.

The raven was weathered, its feathers mottled and its large head scarred. It turned as she approached and regarded her with one midnight-colored eye. Its beak opened, and a static hiss leaked out as it cocked its head at her.

I've seen you before, she realized. She remembered the dream vividly. "What are you hunting, kin-raven?" she whispered.

And how do I know what you are called? The kin-raven was a bird from older times, from the Age of the Wizard Kings. Though some claimed to have seen them in the skies of late.

In the dim gloom of morning, she thought she saw a flash of silver behind the bird. Something twitching in the hollow of the trunk, just out of the larger bird's reach.

Jin Li Tam balanced the knife in her hand and crouched. When she threw it, the blade flew straight and struck the kin-raven with its handle. The bird flapped and shrieked at her as she drew her second knife.

"Begone, kin-raven," she said in a low voice.

It turned its head, casting a long glance at the tree stump. Then, as if understanding her, it launched itself into the sky to speed northwest.

Jin Li Tam recovered her knife and approached the stump. There, huddled in the hollow, a tiny bird shivered and chirped. It sparked and popped as it moved, the flashes illuminating its delicate, silver form.

The chirps slowed slightly, and she suddenly realized they were much more than the sound of fright and panic. The numbers were clear despite the speed with which they streamed from the tiny beak.

She knelt and stretched a hand into the hollow but did not take hold of the small mechanical bird. Instead, she flattened her hand in the way her father had shown her when she was a little girl standing with him at the open cage of his golden bird, which had been at least twice—maybe three times—larger than this one.

"Where have you come from, little sparrow?" she asked it, forcing calm into her voice. "And where are you going?"

The numbers ceased, but the beak remained open. A metallic voice leaked out. "Mechoservitor Number Three, Seventh Forest Manor, Ninefold Forest Houses," it said. "Message follows."

It sparked again.

Jin Li Tam withdrew her hand and sat back. Mechoservitor Number Three? She knew that title: It was Isaak's designation before Rudolfo had named him there in the Desolation of Windwir, where they had all first met nearly two years ago.

The numbers started up once more, and she regarded the small and huddled form. Again, she stretched her hand out. "I am Jin Li Tam," she said, "queen of the Ninefold Forest. I can take you to Isaak"—she corrected herself—"Mechoservitor Number Three."

But even as she said it, she wondered if the tiny mechanical could possibly understand her. Her father's bird—now caged in Isaak's office in the basement of the Great Library—had understood basic commands but did not have even a fraction of the range that a larger mechanical like Isaak had when it came to memory, speech and analytical function.

Still, her musing was cut short when the chirping abruptly ceased and the bird shuddered one last time. A final pop and spark, and it lay still within the hollow. One tiny jeweled eye went dark.

Biting her lower lip, Jin Li Tam stretched out her fingers and carefully pulled the delicate bird from its hiding place. Its tiny feathers were of a silver so intense that it threw back the reflection of her eye as she studied it and wondered if it could be fixed.

Isaak had repaired her father's bird. Charles, the man who had built Isaak and the others, surely had similar skills. He was the last of the Androfrancines in the Ninefold Forest, the rest of the remnant having followed Petronus east into the old Pope's exile in the Churning Waste.

They would know what do, she told herself.

Cradling the silver bird in her hands, Jin Li Tam cut short her morning run and let this new mystery wash away her rage and shame for the moment. As she turned toward home, she wondered what word this tiny messenger carried to Isaak, and why.

Whatever it carried, the kin-raven had brought it down just short of its destination, and she knew of a certainty that there was intent behind that hunting. That the dark bird of prey had sped west and north did not surprise her at all.

As the sun rose behind her, the tiny bird in her cupped hands took on the mottled shading of a red morning sky as light pierced the forest canopy, and Jin Li Tam felt cold fingers moving over her skin.

It was the color of blood.

It was the color of her dreams, as well.

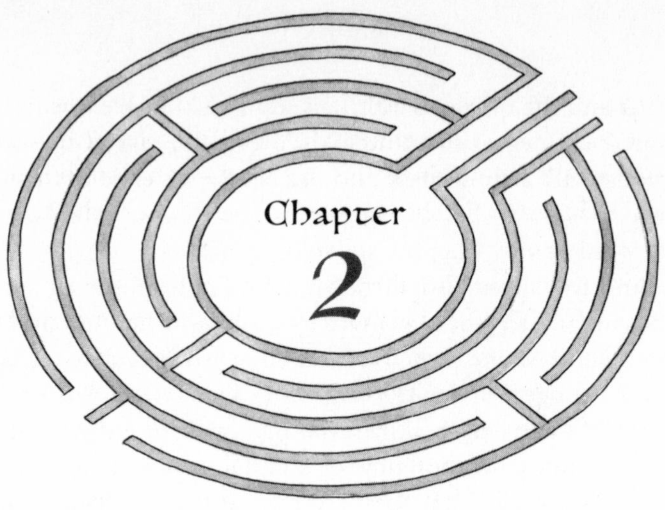

Chapter 2

Petronus

Petronus awoke, shivering in sheets soaked from his own sweat. He kicked them away and sat up, his hand moving instinctively to the scar that burned at his throat.

Again.

Eyes closed, he gulped in the warm night air and listened to the kin-wolves howling in the distant Wastes. His hand moved along the rough skin of his neck, then moved to the scar over his heart that burned even hotter. Forcing his eyes open, he reached for the cup of tepid water on his nightstand and drained it with one long gulp.

Outside, the Gypsy Watch on the Keeper's Wall whistled the last *all's clear* before dawn. Standing, Petronus groped for his robe and pulled it on.

The dreams were harder now, more urgent in their demand to be heard.

But I can't hear them. They were all light and shadow without sound, vague moving images, ending finally in one burst of sudden noise that drove him awake, shouting and sweating ahead of the dawn.

Walking to his cabin's door, he cracked it open and looked out on the small compound he and the other Androfrancines shared, huddled against the Keeper's Gate where Rudolfo's Gypsy Scouts could watch over them. Of course, the only true threat against them lay within the

Named Lands, on the other side of the locked and guarded gate that barred entrance to the Churning Wastes. But still, what remained of the Gray Guard took their turn at the watch, and a makeshift wall of tall pine logs stood nearly finished around the perimeter of the Androfrancine camp.

Petronus moved out into the predawn morning. Cool air from west of the Keeper's Wall stirred his wet, tangled hair, which he pushed out of his eyes as he moved forward, barefoot.

"Chai's nearly ready," Grymlis said in a low voice when Petronus approached his watch fire.

Petronus chuckled. "You're expecting me now."

Grymlis shrugged. "You come each morning at the last whistle. How were they this time?"

Petronus moved to a round stone near the fire and sat, noticing the two mugs set out within reach of the boiling kettle.

How were they? He closed his eyes and let the memory of that light wash over him. He winced at it, his hand moving again to his breast as if it were enough to quell the heat that rose from his scars. Then, the roar of cacophony—the voice of many waters—and the terror it raised within him as he clawed his way shrieking for wakefulness. He swallowed and opened his eyes, forcing them to meet Grymlis's across the fire. "About the same," he said.

"I wonder what your Franci dream mappers would say about these?"

Petronus wondered the same. He had at least two dozen volumes scattered around his small cabin, books he'd asked Isaak to send with the regular supply wagons. But dream interpretation relied on knowing enough of what was dreamt to identify the images and archetypes within it. Still, he parroted what he did know. "They'd say it was brought about by the trauma of the event, that it was a deeply planted anxiety response that will work its way out in time as my body and mind gradually accept what happened to me."

Grymlis chuckled. "And what do you say?"

His eyes went to the edge of the watch fire's light. "I'd say it was most likely a side effect of whatever blood magick they used to bring me back."

It's what he told himself. Because in truth, he felt no trauma from the act. The memory of it unfolded for him upon request—her hand moving slowly up, the cold ache of the blade as it opened him, the added layer of cold when the winter air touched his open wound. He could smell the blood, could hear the heavy indrawn breath of the surprised room, the slow wail of Rudolfo's son Jakob, and could feel his need for reckoning pulsing out onto the sawdust floor with his blood after his legs gave out and he fell.

Then, there was a consuming light and then nothing and, just beyond, a choking, gasping return.

But no trauma. A miracle, to be sure, and certainly not a comfortable one. But apart from the discomfort—and the dreams—his life felt normal enough.

Still, Petronus had not expected his life to go in such a direction.

To be a testimony in their blood-loving gospel. And more than that: to be used to compel Jin Li Tam, daughter of his old friend, to beg their aid for her dying son.

A new voice joined them, and Petronus jumped. "You would not be far from the truth," it said. "Exposure to blood magick had a similar effect upon the boy."

Blood magick? Boy? He looked up, but Grymlis no longer sat across from him. And he no longer sat at the fire. Instead, he sat in his study. The windows were open and afternoon sunlight poured in. He looked out of one window and saw the massive spires of Windwir's Great Library. He looked back to the speaker but did not recognize him.

He rubbed his forehead. Where had he been just now? "I'm sorry? Which boy?"

"Nebios," the man said. He was an Androfrancine but not one Petronus recognized. His crest of office was unfamiliar to Petronus as well, which surprised him. He thought as Pope he'd known every office under his shepherd's staff. "He did not become sensitive to the dream until after he was exposed to the blood magicks at the fall of Windwir."

He remembered the dream the boy had about the Marsh King riding south, remembered also the dream about his proclamation of Petronus as Pope there in the ruins of the garden of consecration and coronation. His throat and chest itched. The light around him grew brighter. "Is this a dream?"

"No," the man said. "This is not the dream. This is about the dream. You are resisting it." Their eyes met. "Don't."

"I don't intend to resist," Petronus said. The scars burned now.

The man shrugged. "Intentions aside, learn to hear what the dream has to say. You've been chosen to hear it."

Outside, the light built and the sound of a metal voice, singing, reached Petronus's ears. There was a mighty roar building beneath it, a voice of many waters and—

Petronus blinked and it was dark again but for the dancing of the watch fire.

Something different, he thought.

Grymlis looked up as if he'd spoken. "Father?"

"Nothing, Grymlis," Petronus whispered, closing his eyes. The white light of Windwir still blazed behind his eyelids. Something different indeed.

One last kin-wolf howled as the sky moved from gray to purple. Then, the water hissed and burbled in its kettle, announcing that a new day could begin in the Churning Wastes.

Winters

The city outside her office window, now being called Rachyle's Rest by the refugees from the south, stirred to life as Winters sipped her second mug of tea and looked at the day's work that stretched ahead of her. She'd initially been provided quarters at the manor, but after that first month she'd chosen quarters in one of the completed sections of the new library, near Isaak and the other mechoservitors. Truth be told, she'd also spent her share of hours sleeping near the book makers' tents while the mechoservitors reproduced volume after volume through the warm summer nights. Somehow, their proximity soothed her.

And their simplicity, she thought, though she knew it was a misconceived notion. There was nothing simple about Isaak and his kind, though they presented a childlike innocence, a simple obedience to task, that made her envious.

She reached for the next report in her stack and paused, noting the back of her hand, her slender wrist, her long slightly tanned forearm. After all of these months, it still felt unnatural, and she still started when she saw her face in the mirror. She did not seem herself without the mud and ash of her father's faith—her own former faith—upon her.

And it goes deeper, beneath the skin. Once her dreams had ceased—both those pleasant dreams of Neb and home and those darker, more violent dreams of blood and iron—she'd discovered something hollow within her that she filled with work. And when she did not work, she read or helped Lynnae in the refugee quarter. Until they'd set out to ride the Nine Forest Manors, she'd spent a goodly amount of time with Jakob as well. It was the life she could forge for herself in this new home she'd chosen.

At least until Neb returns. She'd cried the day Aedric returned without him, though she'd kept that hidden and secret from the others. The first captain had pulled her aside as soon as he'd made his report to Rudolfo, and she'd read the message on his face before he gave it. *Tell her I am called to find our home.* That was all; nothing more. No words of love, no promise of a swift return. It had been yet another loss on top of so many others, and though she'd sent a dozen birds telling him that the quest was fruitless, that the dreams had misled them all, each had come back with her coded note untouched.

She heard the solid thud of metal feet in the corridor and took comfort in the gentle wheeze of pumping bellows, the whistle of steam, the whir of gears that accompanied it. She looked up at the tap on her door. "Yes?"

The door swung open, and Isaak's jeweled eyes blinked at her as the shutters opened and closed over them. "Good morning, Lady Winters."

At one time, he'd called her Winteria. All of them had, but in the days since her supposed sister's return to the Named Lands, bearing the same name, Winters had insisted she be called by her less formal nickname. And when she thought of the woman who supplanted her—a woman who looked too much like her to not be kin—she forced herself to think of that usurper as Ria, though part of her knew that along with everything else, even her very name was lost despite the clever shell game she played with it.

"Good morning, Isaak," she said. "How was the night's work?"

"Two hundred twelve complete volumes," he said, eye shutters flapping. "We will bring the work into the western basement at the end of the week in preparation for winter." They had used the manor last winter, she recalled. The house staff had hidden it well, but she'd seen the traces of that work when she visited with Hanric for Rudolfo's Firstborn Feast.

The first of those losses had arrived that night, and Hanric's funeral was the last time she'd seen Neb in the flesh. "And is Rudolfo still dedicating the wing this week?"

Isaak nodded, steam whistling from the exhaust grate set in his back. "Yes."

Winters smiled, wondering if Isaak felt proud. After eighteen months of construction, the lowest basements were in place and the first wing stood ready. Ornate shelves, built in Paramo and sent by barge, housed the first volumes brought back from the Desolation of Windwir. Thick carpets from the finest silks of the Emerald Coasts lay atop polished wooden planks. She'd wandered the wing at night, alone, her lungs pulling in the heavy smell of paper, wood and ink. It intoxicated her and made her wish she'd seen the Great Library that made up such an important part of Neb's childhood before they met in the midst of its ruins. "Let me know if I can help," she told him.

Isaak's eye shutters flashed. "I will, Lady Winters. Good morning to you." He inclined his head slightly, then turned and pulled her door closed as he left.

Winters tried to force herself back to her work but found herself restless. Instead, she turned to her office's small bookcase and pulled down a volume of collected legends of the Age of the Weeping Czars and the Year of the Falling Moon. She turned the pages slowly, savoring the words she found there. She found the Last Weeping Czar, Frederico, the most compelling. Love out of reach, a lost throne, the end of a way of life. The resonance gripped her.

A rapping at the narrow window in the corner startled her, and she looked up to a muffled cry from outside. She'd seen the kin-ravens before, both in dreams and in the sky, but never one so close. It stood outside, filling the small window in its size, and pecked again at the thick glass. Then, it hopped back and cocked its head, regarding her with one blood-red eye.

The bird had seen better days. It was singed and missing feathers. One eye was closed over with scar tissue.

Her first inclination was the bell. Her eye darted to it and she raised her hand. Swallowing, she tasted the copper of fear in a mouth gone suddenly dry.

I should call for the guards. But something else asserted itself within her, and instead she stood slowly. "What business have you here?" she asked the kin-raven in a quiet voice.

As if hearing her, it hopped forward and pecked again at the glass. Then, it waited and watched.

Approaching slowly, she stretched up on tiptoes to reach for the window's latch. Then, she paused as her fingers found it. *What am I doing?* she asked herself.

But a certainty grew within her that this bird at her window was there with intent, that it had come for her and bore some note that she must read, though she saw no colored thread tied to its foot.

Holding her breath, she worked the latch and pushed the window up. A cool morning wind wafted scents of wood smoke and evergreen into the room, but under the surface of those smells was a darker, older smell of carrion and dank earth.

For a moment, the kin-raven regarded her and then tipped its head to one side. Its beak opened, and a familiar voice whispered out from it.

"Winteria bat Mardic, my younger namesake, I send you greetings," her sister's voice said. "It grieves me that our meeting was not better orchestrated and that you are not now by my side working with me to establish our new home by the grace of the Crimson Empress." Winters watched as the beak remained open and the kin-raven pulled in a deep breath. "But it is fortunate that you have remained with the Great Mother and the Child of Promise. Even now, my ambassadors approach to seek audience with Lord Rudolfo, but I fear he will not hear the dark tidings I bear. The Child of Promise is in grave danger. I have sent my kin-raven to you that you might bear word to your hosts and entreat them to take heed and accept my offer of aid in this matter."

The bird paused again, and Winters felt the words taking root within her. Certainly, she knew she could not trust this woman who claimed kinship with her. If Lord Tam and Rudolfo were correct, her entire faith was a fabric of lies created by Jin Li Tam's grandfather to bring down Windwir for reasons they were only just beginning to understand. She'd heard their speculation, late at night, of a foe beyond the borders of their New World.

The bird continued. "We are kin, you and I, and despite our differences I bear you nothing but deepest love. Bear this word to Rudolfo. Bear this word to the Great Mother: The Child of Promise was not saved to die at the hands of wicked men."

The bird's beak closed and it hopped back, away from her. For a moment, she thought she might leap up, reach out, grab it, hold it and cry out for the guards to assist. But even as the thoughts formed, the bird leaped up and unfurled its wings, pounding at the quiet morning air.

She watched it as it sped west, and then she went looking for her boots so she could climb down from Library Hill to seek out Aedric and Rudolfo.

Winters had no reason to trust this message or messenger, but the dark, cold pit of fear in her stomach was a feeling she'd learned to trust over these last years.

As she let herself out into the morning, Jakob's tiny face and hands flashed across her memory; Ria's words followed: *The Child of Promise was not saved to die at the hands of wicked men.*

Winters hurried her pace and wondered what new darkness awaited them now. As she walked quickly down the cobblestone road that led into town, the morning sun kissed the back of her neck and the top of her head with a warmth she could not feel.

Vlad Li Tam

The setting sun washed the clear water in a purple so deep that it was nearly black. Overhead, the first of the stars struggled against a sky that was still too bright for them to shine in, and Vlad Li Tam sighed.

Of late, he'd taken to fishing again, though he knew that it would be more effective if he went out in the boats with those sons and daughters of his working that particular shift. Rod and tackle from the high dock was not nearly as efficient as their casting nets. Still, Petronus had taught him as a boy that the art of it was to love the act of fishing more than the act of catching. And moreover, it gave him time alone to think.

Don't fool yourself. It also gives you time to watch the water. Yes, he thought.

Behind him, the dinner bell sounded out from the halls of the Y'Zirite Blood Temple he and his family now called home. Rudolfo had rescued what few remained of House Li Tam from this place in a chaotic night some six months past. Vlad Li Tam had returned weeks later to take revenge on the Resurgence that operated the island temple, but they had found it abandoned.

Still, they spent months scouring the building for any clue they could possibly find. They'd dived into the wreckage of the ships Rafe Merrique and his men had scuttled in the harbor. They'd dug through the mass graves and refuse pits. They'd wandered every last span of the island to gather what little they could about the people who'd occupied this place. They'd even established regular scouting expeditions deeper into the Ghosting Crests in search of vessels he knew must be out there—vessels that did not match the line and trim of the New World.

And while they searched, Vlad Li Tam allowed each stained stone in the temple to remind him of the last words of the children and grandchildren he'd lost beneath the cutters' knives while Ria whispered love into his ear and left her own scars upon his flesh and soul. He remembered each cry, each stanza of every poem they screamed to him while the Machtvolk queen extracted agony from him along with his blood and the blood of his family. Blood used for magick-making, to resurrect Petronus and heal Vlad's forty-second daughter's son. All to establish a gospel and a strategy that his own father had helped design in a grand betrayal that left Vlad filled with rage and despair at once.

He shifted on the dock and looked to his rod and line. He'd taken no fish this evening, but it was fine. There would be plenty of food. Some of his children harvested the plentiful island while others hunted or fished, and supply ships from the Delta, financed by the Ninefold Forest, kept them well stocked with other provisions.

No, he did not care so much about the catching. Or the fishing for that matter, if he were honest. His eyes went again to the water.

You want to see it again.

He closed his eyes and tried to conjure it up. It had happened in the midst of pandemonium and madness. Rudolfo, magicked, had freed Vlad's children from the holding cells in the tower's basement and had taken the woman Ria hostage. He'd loosed Vlad, and they'd fought their way down the hill to the docks.

When his first grandson, Mal Li Tam, had threatened the youngest children, he'd given himself over in exchange for their promised safety, and when he'd seen his opportunity, he'd taken it. Sometimes, at night, he still dreamed it.

The solid thud of Mal's head striking the railing. The warm immersion chased quickly by the pain of salt water in his open wounds. His hands clutching at the throat of his first son's first son as they went deeper and deeper.

And the light. It was blue-green, and it filled the deeper waters with song. He'd named his forty-second daughter for the d'jin that swam the Ghosting Crests without having seen one. But to behold it—if that indeed was what he saw there—was stunning. Buried in the pain of loss, he'd felt love from it, and when strong hands pulled at him a part of him wanted to be released, allowed to drown in that love.

Footsteps sounded on the dock behind him, and he knew them instantly. "I heard the bell, Baryk," he said. "I'll be up soon."

The large warpriest sat down beside him. "How's the fishing?"

Vlad chuckled. "The fishing is fine. The catching, not so much."

Baryk also laughed; then his voice turned serious. "It's good that you're here," he said. "I'd hoped to talk with you alone."

Vlad turned and regarded the man. Baryk had married into his family, and though he'd always relied on the older warpriest, in the months since his daughter—Baryk's wife—had died, writhing in agony as the blood magicks consumed her, he'd grown to see the man in a new light. He suspected that the 'Francis would say that the trauma of the loss they experienced together bonded them in a deeper way. With most of his oldest children now dead and buried here on the island, Vlad had learned to lean on Baryk for strategy and wisdom.

Now, the old warpriest looked worried and worn. "What's on your mind, Baryk?"

He sighed. "I don't think we're going to learn any more from this place."

Vlad nodded. They'd gone over every last bit of it. They'd found the bargaining pool and the blood-distillery within it, though the Y'Zirites who had fled Tam's return had poisoned it somehow before leaving. "You think we should leave," he said in a flat voice.

"We have four ships. We could hire more, step up our forays south and east."

His eyes went once more to the water. "What about Merrique's ship?"

Baryk shook his head. "Still no word."

The old pirate had been out of touch a goodly while now, House Li Tam's birds unanswered for nearly two months.

Vlad looked from the water to the island behind him. "This would be a logical point on the map to operate from," he said. But before Baryk spoke, Vlad knew what he would say.

"It would," the warpriest said, "but I think your family is restless. I think this constant reminder of loss is no longer sharpening your blade." He paused. "It may even dull it."

Vlad turned from the man and looked back to the water. "You may be right, Baryk. I'll consider it."

Baryk inclined his head slightly. "It's all I ask, Father."

He calls me father now. It stirred something in him, and he savored the meaning in it. He remembered the first time it had happened, the day they'd buried Rae Li Tam in the frozen plain of Windwir. Baryk had not done it in front of the other children, though. No, he reserved the title for the times they were alone, and Vlad understood that very well. He looked to his daughter's widower and forced a smile. "You are a good man, Baryk."

Baryk stood and returned the smile. "Shall I tell them you're coming soon?"

Vlad nodded. "Soon."

As the warpriest's footfalls faded across the wooden dock, Vlad pulled in his line. The man was right, of course. They *had* learned everything they could from this place. And it was a reminder, a constant reminder.

One that I need, he thought, though as he thought it he also knew that perhaps what little remained of his family did not need such reminding.

I will grow my pain into an army. They were the words that had carried him through the worst of the cuttings, the worst of his children's screams. And they were the words that his daughter had later given him with her final breath.

Perhaps it was time to leave after all.

He sat with the rod across his lap while the sky darkened and the harbor stilled. He sat until he lost track of time, and when a flicker of blue-green danced across the waters he felt his heart catch in his throat. He could hear the song, too, if he listened for it. If he could just *listen* for it. And somehow, that ghost could soothe him, could save him. But in the end, it was not the catch he longed for. No, it was simply the moon, rising up to lend its light to those quiet waters he contemplated daily.

Victorious, the stars at last poked through a dark velvet veil of sky, and Vlad Li Tam sighed at them. Perhaps tomorrow, he thought.

He rose, turned his back to the Ghosting Crests and made his way up the hill.

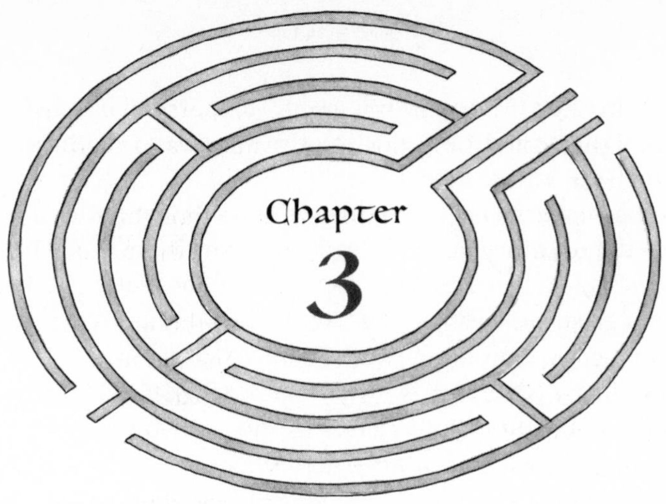

Charles

Charles spun the gears and listened to the low groan as the mirrors around his workroom moved on their tracks and bent more light onto the object upon his table.

The moon sparrow lay disassembled, its various pieces laid out for examination with the magnifying lens he held before his eye.

When Jin Li Tam and Isaak had awakened him just after sunrise, he'd thought perhaps one of the mechanicals had broken down during the night's work. He'd pulled on his robes and met them at the locked door of his subbasement workroom.

He wondered now, hours later, if they had seen his face grow pale when he saw the little messenger. Or if they had noticed a catch in his voice. Or the trembling in his fingers as he sought the tiny reset switch beneath that one small feather that felt slightly rougher than its other silver companions.

Fortunately, their questions had been few and he'd managed to deflect them under the guise of getting to work to find answers for them.

Charles lifted the tiny firestone that powered the bird. It was the size of a grape, burning white but without heat that he could feel through the thumb and forefinger that gripped it and held it beneath his eye. With his thumbs, he carefully pressed it into the bird's silver chassis and used tweezers to carefully hook the long golden wires that led from it to the memory scroll casing. The casing had been punctured by what he assumed must be the kin-raven's talon or beak. It was a small puncture—and precise.

Where have you been off to? Biting his lower lip, he found the switch and moved the bird's wings and feet farther from its torso and head, as if somehow it might reattach them itself when it saw that it could not flee. When his callous fingertips found it, the bird's tiny red eyes flickered open and it started humming in the palm of his hand.

When the hum reached its highest pitch, Charles held the bird even closer to his face and whispered into its small audio receivers. "Authorize, Charles," he said, "arch-engineer, School of Mechanical Studies." He listened to the chirruping and waited until it subsided. "Report, scroll unwind five oh three. Backtrack flightpath to point of origin for confirmation of navigational accuracy."

The small beak opened, and a voice trickled out. It was his own, from years ago, and it caught him off guard. Though certainly, he remembered the days he'd spent speaking to the little birds they'd found within their little cages, giving them a language they had not previously known. "Report unavailable," his own voice told him, tinny and sounding far away.

"Confirm authorization," he said, feeling his brow furrow and feeling his curiosity melting into something more pronounced, more anxious. These birds had not required much in the way of maintenance. Androfrancine archaeologists had dug them out, still functioning in their cages, from the ruined subbasement of one of the Wizard King's palaces in the Old World. But still, they were complex mechanicals of a time that dated back beyond even the Age of the Wizard Kings. He'd learned what he could of them and had even found obscure reference to them in Rufello's notes on the golden birds that ancient scientist had managed to bring back into the world.

It had taken Charles years, but he'd learned enough about them to eventually offer them up to the Office of the Holy See as an improved means of communication, particularly in the Churning Wastes where the living message birds lost their magicks and their direction.

"Authorization unconfirmed."

Unconfirmed? Charles let his held breath out through his nose, watching the force of his exhalation move the moon sparrow's soft silver feathers. He could remember establishing the authorizations for these particular messengers. He'd updated them just months before his apprentice betrayed him and destroyed Windwir. He paused a moment, trying to reach back into his memory to find the correct query language. "Emergency protocol, unwind scroll four, six, two: Destination?"

With the slightest pop, his voice vanished and another—this one reedy and metallic—slipped out of the bird's open beak. "Mechoservitor Three, Ninefold Forest Houses, Seventh Forest Manor, Library."

He thought about asking again, thought even that perhaps he could find other hidden paths within the Whymer Maze of its tiny memory casing. Some back path that might tell him where the bird had come from. They'd used moon sparrows as a part of the Sanctorum Lux project, along with other similar endeavors that required something more reliable than an organic bird or a person. The birds were small, fast and—until now—had not encountered anything that could successfully stop them.

Charles heard the heavy footfalls outside his door, heard the slightest wheeze of bellows and hum of gears from where the mechoservitor waited. He put down the small mechanical and stood from his stool, stretching the muscles that threatened to knot his shoulders and neck.

He was opening the door just as the robed mechoservitor raised a metal hand to knock. "Good afternoon, Isaak."

Isaak's eye shutters flashed open and closed. Steam slipped out from the back of his robe, where he'd carefully cut away the fabric around his exhaust grate. "Good afternoon, Father."

Father. Until recently, Charles had never considered himself truly a parent. Certainly, he'd joked often enough about his mechanical creations and re-creations being his children, but he'd come to the Order as a young zealot from the Emerald Coasts. At that age, with the precepts and gospels of P'Andro Whym so near his tongue and matters of the flesh so far out of mind, he couldn't even comprehend the act that might lead to fatherhood. And throughout his tenure in the Order, he'd stayed that course.

Now, however, a machine he had built, assembled based on Rufello's *Book of Specifications,* had grown unexpectedly into something capable of regarding him as its father. The notion of it staggered him, though if he were completely honest, there were also days he still doubted it despite his own experience.

"Good afternoon, Isaak," he said, inclining his head toward the metal man. He'd told him many times that he could call him Charles or even Brother Charles if he preferred. Each time, Isaak had suggested that his preference was to call him Father.

For a moment, Isaak stood still and the awkwardness of the moment played out. Finally, his amber eyes flashed again. "May I speak with you?"

Charles motioned for him to come in. "I'm nearly finished with our little friend."

Isaak entered and waited while Charles closed the door behind him. Then, he followed the arch-engineer back to the workbench and watched over his shoulder while he took up the magnifying glass once again. The bellows filled, and Isaak's reedy voice resonated in the room. "Were you able to learn anything about its point of origin or the message it bears?"

Charles shook his head. "I'm . . . unauthorized for those things." The word felt distasteful in his mouth. "But Lady Tam is correct: Its message is for you." He looked back to Isaak.

The mechoservitor blinked, turning its head slowly to the left and right. Charles had noticed that Isaak did that when he was accessing deeper lines within his memory scrolls. "There was a matter of authorization prior to your arrival in the Churning Wastes," Isaak said. "At the bridge where we encountered the mechoservitor that later ended his operational effectiveness."

"This is the instance where the boy, Nebios, was authorized access but you and the Waste guide were not?"

"Yes, Father."

Charles moved the magnifying glass, shifting so that the metal man could see him but also so that the towering figure did not block his light. "More of the mystery," he said. "But we've had a triple helping of mystery. Do you want to hear your message, instead?"

Amazing, he thought, how easy it was to see the mechanical as a child of sorts. He heard a child's hesitation now in the whine of the mouth flaps as they opened and closed. He waited until Isaak finally spoke. "I would like to ask you a question first."

Charles put the bird down and turned to face the metal man. "Ask, Isaak."

"What level of malfunction would be necessary for a mechoservitor to practice active deception, and can it be corrected?"

The spell again. Rudolfo had briefed him early on about it, of course, and Charles understood why. The spell trapped inside of this device could, in the wrong hands, bring down the world around them. It had razed Windwir. Two thousand years earlier, Xhum Y'Zir's death choir of similar mechanicals had sung the spell and brought about the Age of Laughing Madness and the end of the Old World. And as much as he understood why Rudolfo had made him the third person—the fourth if they counted Isaak—to know that the spell had survived, he also understood why Rudolfo had warned him to let Isaak bring the knowledge to him in the metal man's own time.

Charles sighed and wondered if real children had better-timed curiosity than their mechanical counterparts. "I think it depends upon the deception. Not all deceptions are a result of malfunction. Some may be a highly analytical outgrowth of careful thought regarding the better choice when *no* choice is truly optimal."

He watched Isaak now while the metal man thought about this. "But wouldn't that contradict a mechanical's scripting?"

Charles shrugged. "It could. But other scripting could call for that contradiction—or untested circumstances could alter the scripting in some way." He paused. "And I know it seems incorrect on the surface, but sometimes deceptions are carried out for love, for safety, for any number of noble purposes."

"I can see logic in that," Isaak said, his tinny voice taking on a matter-of-fact tone. "Still, it perplexes me."

Tell me. He bent his will toward the metal man. He would not ask the reason why. But in the end, he did. "What brings this question about, Isaak?"

Now watch, Charles told himself.

A gout of steam shot from Isaak's exhaust grate. Deep in his chest cavity, gears whined and springs clacked with enough violence that his metal plating shook for a moment. A low whine built, noticeable, but quieter than the last time Charles had heard him lie. "I was simply curious."

Charles bit his tongue and turned his gaze back to the moon sparrow. He attached first one wing, then the other. "Well, I hope your curiosity is satisfied."

The next sound from Isaak made Charles jump. It sounded unnatural, but it was obvious. Isaak had *chuckled*. "I doubt my curiosity shall ever be satisfied, Father."

Now it was Charles's turn to chuckle. "I think you may be right." Then his thumb found the switch beneath that out-of-place feather. "But for now, let's bend our curiosity towards your message."

The bird fluttered to its feet. Its small beak opened, and the tinny voice of a faraway mechoservitor echoed into the workroom. "Addressee," it said, "Mechoservitor Three, Ninefold Forest Houses, Seventh Forest Manor, Library."

Charles looked to Isaak. "I am Mechoservitor Three, also called Isaak," the metal man said in a quiet voice. "Chief Officer of the Forest Library."

The tiny bird twitched slightly in his cupped hand, and when the stream of numbers hissed out they were too fast for Charles to identify them. Their pitch and tone warbled, and the old arch-engineer was impressed with what that told him. *Numeric code with inflection markers to show emphasis and vary definition.* When he was younger, if he'd had the luxury of months, he might've parsed out the code with a forest of paper and an ocean of ink. And yet, he watched Isaak's flashing eyes and saw his fingers spasm as he deciphered the code as it was given.

It was a mighty thing, Charles decided, to watch something he had made with his own two hands do something in seconds that he would need most of a season to accomplish.

Isaak looked to the bird and then to Charles, his mouth flap opening and closing as if he meant to say something.

Then, the metal man snatched the moon sparrow from Charles's fingers and fled. In his haste, he tipped over a chair and forgot to close the door behind him. All the while, he whispered to the bird, cupping it near his mouth.

Charles leapt to his feet and ran into the hall, his heart hammering in his temples. The last mechanical he'd seen move this fast was the one he'd scripted to escape from Erlund and bear his message to the Order. Both times, he tasted fear at the daunting machinery he had constructed. "Stop him," he cried.

But before anyone could react, Isaak had thrown open the doors and flung his silver messenger into the sky.

Then, Isaak turned to Charles, bellows chugging with grief and surprise.

"I'm sorry, Father," his metal child said.

Neb

Neb ran though the rest of the day and long into the night before he made camp to give his body at least a few hours of sleep away from the black root that fueled it. As he ran beneath the moon, he heard the crescent's song increase in volume, and he bent his mind to that cipher. As he slept beneath that same moon, he cradled the sliver of silver to his ear to dream music and numbers and light.

At one point, in his deepest dreaming, he thought he heard his father's voice calling to him beneath the melody of the canticle. He stirred, cast about for some memory of Winters with her long, dirty brown hair, her muddy face with its big brown eyes. But when he found nothing, he let the song enfold him and carry him back down into sleep.

By noon on his second day alone, he skirted the ruins of Y'leris, a scattering of mounded wreckage and glass that had melted and then cooled in twisted, razor-edged hills.

He would have kept south if it weren't for the commotion.

At first, he thought it might be kin-wolves hunting, but that made no sense. They hunted only at night and slept by day unless something disturbed them. Renard had shown him—very carefully—how to look for the spoor and avoid the dens of these fiercely territorial predators of the Churning Wastes. And with the sun at its highest point and the sky ribboned with waves of heat, he knew they could not be hunting.

He stood at the edge of the ruins and listened to the howls and snarls warble through the glass-and-steel Whymer Maze. He hefted his thorn rifle and felt the bulb for freshness. He frowned at what his fingers felt and quickly wet a small cotton wad with water, then pushed it up into the bottom of the thorn bulb. Then he dug into his pouch to find one of the vials of kin-wolf urine he and Renard had traded for last month.

Their snarls intensified, and one kin-wolf yelped.

What are they up to? He counted four distinct wolves. And they were perhaps a league or two into the heart of the city. Neb tried to shake off his curiosity, bending his mind to the south, where the shell of Sanctorum Lux and Rudolfo's expedition of Gypsy Scouts awaited.

But the girl's scream, blood-chilling and long, clinched his decision. Neb swallowed the bitter root juice, raised his thorn rifle, and ran into the ruins toward the sound.

His feet moved easily over the debris and scattered stones. Overhead, the sun beat down; and within the city, the varied colors of twisted glass threw a rainbow of light against the shadows, lending it an unearthly quality. Even as he increased his speed, Neb's nostrils flared and his eyes moved over the ground ahead of him, looking for sign. Still, he didn't need it. The noise of the commotion deeper in the city was enough to guide him true.

When he came upon the makeshift camp, strong with the scent of kin-wolf urine, he stopped and drew his vial. It took only a few drops, but once this new aroma found the wind, it proclaimed a rival wolf laying claim to this marked territory. He sprinkled the drops and moved forward slowly.

The camp was in shambles. The blanket was shredded, the small cooking pot overturned and the remnants of a smallish fire scattered. Quickly, his eyes took in what they'd been trained to take in. A sling lay discarded amid a scattering of silver bullets, and a knife belt, its sheaths empty, lay near a pair of small boots made from the skin of some kind of lizard or snake.

No time to linger here. Neb skirted the camp, the snarls louder just to the west of him. As he drew closer, he also heard the ragged rasp of labored breathing.

Now, he moved slowly, the rifle up and ready. A hot wind picked up behind him. It would carry his scent forward to the pack, but this didn't alarm him much. It would also bear the markings of the white kin-wolf.

There were four of them—one male, two females and a pup. They circled a low mound of rubble, growling and snapping at it. Beneath the rubble, Neb saw occasional flashes of light as a knife blade darted out. Just as the kin-wolves stopped and looked in the direction of the breeze, Neb raised his thorn rifle and sighted in on the largest of them. He flexed the bulb and heard the slight cough as the needle-sized thorn launched from the long lacquered tube to bury itself in the right shoulder of the male kin-wolf. He squeezed again and put another in its side as its yelp became a snarl and the wolf launched himself at Neb.

Fire and flee. Renard's words from months of hunting the Wastes came back now, and Neb embraced them. The snarl of the wolves and the sudden smell of them, heavy and sour, brought the taste of copper to his mouth and threatened his balance. Still, he moved as quickly as the root would allow him, all the while counting the seconds. Spinning, he fired another thorn at one of the females now also in pursuit, but the shot went wide and the thorn clattered off a bent wave of purple glass.

He saw a mound ahead and gathered speed to leap for it, glancing quickly over his shoulder. Behind him, the male was already faltering as the thorn's sap worked its way quickly into his bloodstream. And only one of the females pursued; the other stayed near the pup and cornered prey.

Neb leaped to a round boulder of black glass, then scrambled onto the mound of rusted steel and spun around. The female was close behind him. Firing blindly, he put three thorns into her face and breast as she pounced for him. Behind her, the male had collapsed into a whimpering, twitching pile of matted fur.

Yelping, she scrambled over the glass, then onto the mound itself, her teeth bared. Neb smelled the carrion on her breath. Kicking out with one booted foot, he discarded the rifle and drew a single scout knife from his belt. He felt his hands slick with sweat, and though the black root increased his strength and stamina, he could hear his own ragged breathing as it reverberated through the desolate city.

The kin-wolf threw back her head and howled, eyes wild, and launched herself at him anew. She caught his boot in her mouth and wrenched his leg, knocking him over with enough force to drive the wind from him, but even as she climbed over the top of him, he slid the knife into her soft underside and twisted, forcing her snout away from him with a forearm against her matted throat.

Neb withdrew the knife and stabbed again, the sharp teeth closer and closer to his face as the sheer weight of the beast crushed him. He felt the claws moving over him, tearing his clothing and skin, as the kin-wolf scrambled to regain advantage. Eyes wide, Neb felt his bladder threatening to cut loose and felt the sticky wetness of blood. Still, he stabbed again and willed the sap to do its work.

Finally, the kin-wolf slowed and then became still, her wheezing and whimpers all the fight that remained in her. Neb crawled from beneath her, recovered his rifle, and climbed down to what had once been a street. Quickly, he checked himself, and when he saw that most of the blood was from the wolf, he released a sigh that felt more like a sob. Then, he tipped back his head and voiced the howl that Renard had taught him. The sound of it raised the hair on the back of his own neck.

When he reached the other mound, the remaining kin-wolf snarled at him, sniffed at the blood upon the wind, and turned suddenly to flee with her cub following after.

"They're gone now," he told the mound. "You can come out."

He heard words, quiet and mumbled, but could not understand them. Drawing closer, he lowered his rifle again, pointing it loosely toward the mound. The Wastes were not a place for trust.

"You're a long way from home, whoever you are," he said again. This time, there was silence.

Moving in, he saw a still form wedged tightly into a crack in the mound. A long, slender arm hung loose, a bloody knife dangling from limp fingers. Crouching, he approached until he could see the rest of the woman. She wore tattered silk clothes and was barefoot. Her left arm was bloody and mangled from the shoulder to the wrist where the wolves' teeth had ravaged her in an effort to drag her free. And her high cheekbones and close-cropped red hair carried a familiarity that he could not place immediately in context. Her small breasts rose and fell with her ragged breathing, and her eyelids twitched.

Neb noticed all of this, but he also noticed more, and it both surprised and frightened him with its sudden intensity after so long away from home.

She was beautiful beyond measure.

Kicking her knife aside, he set himself to pulling her out of the shadows and into the light of the afternoon sun, where he could better see her wounds.

There, the light did its work and Neb gasped at the fine lattice of scars that spiderwebbed her alabaster skin.

Old scars forming old symbols more terrifying to him than an ocean of kin-wolves.

Rudolfo

The invitations went out quietly, and one by one, Rudolfo's guests slipped into the private dining room of his Seventh Forest Manor. It was a comfortable room, paneled in dark oak offset with silk tapestries from the Emerald Coasts and carpeted with the finest Pylosian rugs. The fireplace lay unlit but ready. The long table filled as Jin Li Tam, Aedric and the others took their places at it. Most, including Isaak, were frequent guests here—nights spent with laughter and wine—but tonight was a night for quiet conversation.

The moon was up, and if the windows had been open, they'd have heard the frogs of second summer. But they were closed, as were the doors, and Gypsy Scouts had been posted to assure that no ears could hear this private dinner.

Rudolfo waited until the house servants replaced the cheese platters with bowls of steaming roast duck, wild rice, forest mushrooms and fresh carrots. Then, after the wineglasses were refilled, the servants left and pulled the doors closed behind them. He looked to Winters and then to Isaak. "We have guests coming from the west *and* from the east?"

Isaak's eye shutters flapped. "Not guests as such, Lord Rudolfo—"

Before he could finish, Rudolfo raised his hand, cutting him off. "I'm being facetious, Isaak." He looked to the metal man and let the frustration show in his voice. "And you released this so-called moon sparrow without first consulting me?" He'd never felt disappointment toward the metal man before now. Still, alongside that disappointment, a suspicion nudged him. Something about the code in the message had brought about this reaction in Isaak. It had to be so. Isaak would not do such a thing of his own volition.

A machine with volition. After two years of . . . what? He struggled to find the word. *Friendship.* After two years of friendship with the mechoservitor, Rudolfo was surprised. Regardless, once he'd turned the bird loose with his reply, the metal man had immediately sought audience with his Gypsy King.

"I did. I do not know what came over me. I felt compelled." Isaak hung his head. "I'm sorry, Lord Rudolfo."

Rudolfo felt a stab of guilt at the sight of the metal man's remorse and looked to Charles. "Could the code have compromised his scripting somehow?"

The old man nodded. "A code within the code, I suspect. Something to compel response if the message was received."

Rudolfo stroked his beard. A message, given by a metal bird to a metal man, that could compel behavior? This was alarming. And equally alarming: Some or all of the mechoservitors who had fled Sanctorum Lux were even now approaching from the east, requesting his aid. He imagined them moving across the Churning Wastes, steam billowing from their exhaust grates as they ran at top speed, amber eyes bobbing like fireflies in the night. "What do they seek?"

He'd asked the question more to himself, though he knew their stated purpose. But Isaak still answered. "They seek sanctuary and safe escort to the northwestern edge of the Ninefold Forest," he said. But he rattled and hissed when he said it, and Rudolfo glanced quickly toward Charles. The arch-engineer stared, tight-lipped, at his creation, and Rudolfo noted that he would need to ask about that look when he and Charles were next alone.

"And from our western neighbors?" Rudolfo looked to Winters. He'd seen enough of her these last few months that the mud and ash she once wore upon her face was a faded memory. Now, she was a young woman of coltlike awkwardness and uncomfortable silences, pretty but unaware of her prettiness at this intersection between childhood and womanhood. "Your kin-raven prophesies danger against Jakob and claims Machtvolk ambassadors are en route to warn us and offer aid?"

She glanced to Jin Li Tam and Jakob in the corner of the room. "It's what the bird said. Yes." She dropped her eyes. "I do not trust it."

Rudolfo chuckled, but there was no humor it. "I suspect none of us do. Trust is not a commodity we can afford in our present economy."

Machtvolk ambassadors, renegade mechoservitors and Y'Zirite evangelists in the Ninefold Forest. Rudolfo felt the stabbing ache of a days-old headache revisiting his temples. "What are we doing to prepare?" As he asked, he took up a piece of warm bread and broke it open, finding no satisfaction in the smell of it, and turned to the first captain of his Gypsy Scouts.

Aedric cleared his voice, putting down his wineglass. "I've tripled the watch on the manor and stepped up scout recruitment. We've been thinned by war, by maintaining the gate, and now this work in the Wastes. Have you considered calling up the local regiments?"

Rudolfo nodded. "I have . . . and will if necessary." But he did not wish to if he could avoid it. Twice in as many years, his Wandering Army had surged forth from their forest homes. Fathers, sons, brothers all leaving their families behind to serve their king.

And their queen, he thought. While he'd scoured the sea to find her family, Jin Li Tam had become the second queen in Forester history to raise the Wandering Army and lead them into war. "I would prefer not to call them if it can be avoided. They've spent too many months away from home and hearth these two years."

Rudolfo looked to Lysias and saw the storm brewing on his face. *He wants to speak but is choosing not to,* he realized.

In the past months, the man had proven invaluable to the Ninefold Forest. Initially, Rudolfo had felt skeptical about the man's loyalties, having fought against him in the war that followed Windwir's fall. But the general's daughter, Lynnae, had served as Jakob's nursemaid during his illness, and from the time Lysias first sought asylum with the Gypsies, he'd given himself fully to whatever task fell to him. Most recently, he'd organized the Refugee Quarter and had devised a system of employing and housing the sudden influx of residents in the various towns of the Ninefold Forest and had created a constabulary among them. "What are your thoughts on these matters, Lysias?"

Lysias looked around the room. Rudolfo watched the older man make eye contact with Aedric before speaking.

When he looked back to the Gypsy King, his eyes were hard. "I intend no disrespect, Lord Rudolfo, but your world has suddenly changed, and you have not changed quickly enough to keep up with it."

Rudolfo raised a glass of chilled pear wine and paused midway to his lips. "Explain."

Lysias glanced around the room and put down his own glass. "The days of riding your forest circuit of houses have passed. Your seventh manor is now your capital, home of the new library and the center of the Named Lands. The days of being overlooked and unnoticed are behind your people. Refugees roll in from neighboring lands in disarray and you do not turn them back. Laborers and students and wayward scholars follow them, hoping to build a better life near this new light you cast—you do not turn them back, either."

Rudolfo swallowed his mouthful of wine. "We will *not* turn them back," he said, feeling his earlier frustration build toward anger. "The Ninefold Forest has ever been a haven for those who've sought it."

Lysias locked eyes with him now. "You could not turn them back even if you wished to, Lord. You have no real control of your borders. Scouts on broad patrol, scattered watch posts poorly manned. These evangelists slip in through the gaps. These metal men"—here he looked to Isaak—"they will come and go as they please as well. As will anyone else who wishes." He lowered his voice. "You have enemies, Lord, who can place their so-called Blood Scouts any place at any time, and as good as your men are . . . they are not good enough. More than that, you've heard it from Tam himself and that fox Petronus—there's more trouble on the rise, and I fear it's looking for us. We're being hemmed, Rudolfo, with wolves on the prowl beyond our ken." Lysias reached for the bread and tore off a piece, holding it up. "And already, your resources are stretched like a thimble of butter over a mountain of rye."

Aedric's face was red with anger, and he started to stand. "You can't—"

Rudolfo raised his hand. "It's fine, Aedric."

He knew the words were true. Certainly, his Wandering Army was the fiercest group of fighters in all the Named Lands, but these were men with homes and farms and families to tend. They were never intended to maintain borders or operate in a constant climate of vigilance and conflict. He looked at Lysias now with narrowing eyes. "You would not say this if you did not also have a solution."

The old general nodded. "It is time," he said, "for the Ninefold Forest to join the rest of the Named Lands." And Rudolfo knew the words that were coming; he dreaded them and winced as Lysias spoke them.

"It is time for you to outfit a standing army and establish a firm and permanent presence both within the forest around your assets and along your borders."

Rudolfo glanced to Jin Li Tam where she sat. She looked away, but not before he saw agreement in her eyes. She'd suggested the same to him not long after they'd returned from the Council of Kin-Clave, and it had led to the first strong argument in their marriage. Her mouth was tight now.

He looked from her to the child in the built-up pine chair beside her. He, too, wore his green turban of office and his rainbow-colored scarves of rank.

Change, he remembered, *is the path life takes.* But at what point did that change rob life of its value? A standing army in the Ninefold Forest? A kept and guarded border? It was far beyond the life he'd inherited from his father and his father's father before him. It smacked of everything they'd disdained about their joyless neighbors, everything they'd vowed they would leave in the Old World when they'd left its ashes and madness behind them.

What are you inheriting, my little late-coming prince?

Rudolfo sighed and finally spoke. "I do not wish it—and I do not accept that it is the only answer." He paused, stared at the food on his plate that he knew he would not eat. When he looked up again, he glanced first to Aedric. In the young captain's fuming, Rudolfo saw the boy's father, Gregoric, in the tightly clenched jaw and the narrow eyes. Then, he turned to Lysias. "Draw up the plans for it. But it is to be kept secret at all costs. Our kin-claves are tenuous at best, and this is not the Gypsy way." Even as he spoke, his hands moved in the sign language of House Y'Zir. *Work with him, Aedric.*

Aedric did not answer at first. Then, his hand moved, though with reluctance. *Yes, General.*

Now Jin Li Tam's face was troubled. *Do not ask me,* Rudolfo willed, but she did it anyway, her fingers moving along the side of her wineglass. *Are you certain, love?*

Rudolfo stood and looked to her, hoping his eyes would not betray his answer. "I beg your forgiveness," he said. "Please excuse me."

Then, turning, he left the dining room. He stepped quickly past the Gypsy Scouts assigned to guard him, ducked around a corner and slipped into one of dozens of passages kept hidden for just these reasons. He walked at a brisk pace along the narrow corridors and slipped through a hidden door into the garden.

His Whymer Maze towered in the moonlight, and the frogs raised their voice to the blue-green moon. Looking over his shoulder to be sure none followed him, he moved past the maze and into a copse of trees he rarely visited these days.

There, near a white stone marked simply with three names, he sat upon a marble meditation bench that none had sat upon for decades. After a long silence, he finally spoke, and it was the voice of a frightened boy.

"Father," he said to the stone, "I do not know this path."

Then, in silence, Rudolfo sat still and begged answer from the ground of Jakob's Rest.

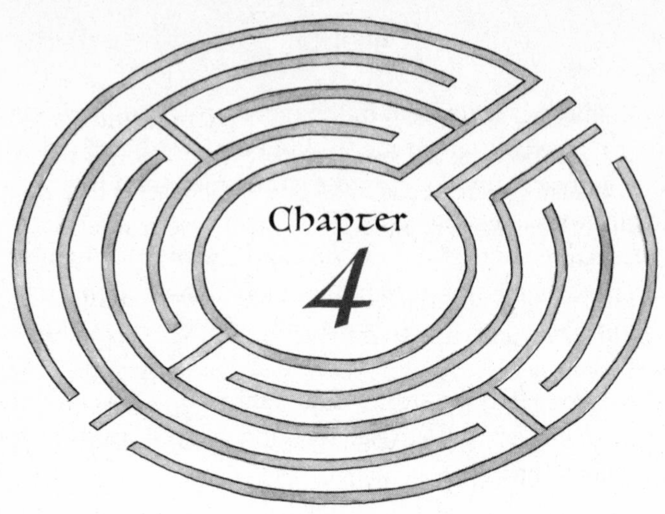

Petronus

Petronus raised his eyebrows and looked at the man who rocked to and fro before him. "So what you're proposing"—he glanced to the report from Grymlis in his hands, looking for the name once more—"*Geoffrus*, is it?" At the man's hurried nod, Petronus continued. "What you're proposing is that you and your company of men supply our entire outpost with hunting, trapping and scouting services for—" He scanned the report again, but the numbers ran together into a blur. "Well," he finally said, "for significant barter, primarily in metal goods and fabrics from the other side of the gate."

Geoffrus nodded. "Yes, Luxpadre. I—or I should say *we*—are prepared to execute on a time-is-of-the-essence basis, immediately, that is, to give you and your Ash-Men the best our Madding Lands can offer."

Petronus sat back in the wooden chair and rubbed his eyes. Here in the shade, the afternoon sun still kept the day warmer than comfortable for his tastes, accustomed more to the cool seaborne breezes on Caldus Bay than the hot wind of the Churning Wastes. Already, his robe was damp from sweat, though the man across the table from him looked dry and comfortable.

The Waster was a slight man, dressed in tattered clothing shored up with patches and bits of leather. He'd sought audience at least three times before over the past several months, and Petronus had managed to hold the meeting at bay. But finally, he'd relented and agreed to see the man when it became obvious that this Geoffrus was not going to pick up on the subtle social cue of disinterest Petronus had attempted.

Petronus offered a weak smile. "I'm certain your offer is very generous, Geoffrus."

The man beamed, the black root stains showing on his teeth. "You will not find more generous terms and conditions, Luxpadre."

Petronus went back to the report and found Grymlis's scribbled note. "Yes, I'm sure of it," he said, "but there is the matter of *what* game you intend to provide us? As you no doubt know, the Ninefold Forest keeps us well provisioned, to include game."

Geoffrus nodded again, this time with added vehemence. "Yes, yes, the contract is flexible in that regard, of course, to provide you and yours with the finest selection our *significant* and *highly desirable* skills might provide. Such succulent tasties as the Rainbow-Men could not imagine."

Petronus knew better, of course. He and Grymlis had gone over his report earlier that morning. The men he'd sent into Fargoer's Station had gathered every bit of information they could on this part of the world, including what scraps could be found on this Geoffrus and his small band of Waste thieves. He already knew the rumors. People who trusted these particular men tended to disappear. He wondered what further information Isaak might be able to send him from the archived records of the Office of Expeditionary Unction—but also knew that that knowledge wasn't necessarily worth the effort when he already knew his answer. "I'm certain that you are highly skilled," he said. "Though to be perfectly honest, we do not require your services at this time." Then, he smiled. "However, I am deeply gratified by your proposal. I recognize that you've gone to enormous efforts on our behalf, with nothing but our best interests in mind."

Geoffrus grinned again. "Aye, we have. Aye, we have," he said, repeating himself quickly.

Petronus returned the smile. "Therefore, I am pleased to offer you and yours tokens to assure you of our gratitude." He motioned, and a young Androfrancine approached, carrying a haphazard pile of folded fabric.

As the tattered Waster took in the armful of cloth his eyes went wide along with the smile. "This is indeed most generous of you, Luxpadre."

"Ask him about the runners in the Wastes."

Petronus looked up at the nearby voice, recognizing it but not placing it. "I'm sorry?"

Geoffrus said nothing. Beside him, the young man with the cloth also remained silent.

Petronus looked around to see who else could have spoken, but other than these two, no one else stood close enough. Still, the voice was one he knew. When had he heard it last?

He felt the blood drain from his face when the memory found him. *You heard it yesterday, old man.*

Suddenly, he wanted very much to leap up from the table and flee but forced himself to stay. A new smell filled his nose, driving out the acrid scent of the hot wind and the dried sweat of the unwashed man before him. No, it was roses and lavender he smelled now, as a summer breeze caught the aroma of his gardens and wafted them into his office window, and—

Petronus blinked, forcing himself back to the conversation. "These," he said, "are a gift. But I can offer you something even finer in exchange for a bit of information."

Geoffrus looked to the stack of cloth and then back to Petronus. "What *finer*?" he asked. "What *information*?"

Petronus drew in his breath. "What do you know about runners in the Wastes?"

Geoffrus's eyes narrowed. "Ash-Men do not run. Rainbow-Men run. *Renard* runs." At the man's name, he spit in the dirt. "And Geoffrus runs." He licked his lips. "What *finer* for me and mine?"

Petronus closed his eyes, only for a moment, but when he opened them the world had bent and twisted away. Once more he sat in his papal office. Outside, the smell of summer was heavy from the gardens below.

He looked back to the table, and now, across from him, sat the man he'd seen the day before. He was bent over a large map that was spread out, and Petronus saw it was a map of the Churning Wastes. "Intelligence is problematic, of course," the man said, "but we're aware of runners here, here and *here*." Each time, he pointed to a different section of the map with a chewed pencil. "They are magicked. We suspect blood magicks, though they do not appear constrained in the same way that the Marshers have been."

Petronus blinked again and tried to recall where he'd been just now. There had been heat. And smell, though nothing quite as lovely as roses on the wind. "Who are you?" he asked.

The man looked up, his eyes hollow. "We suspect they're looking for the same thing we are, but it could be worse than that."

"And what are we looking for, exactly?"

The man studied Petronus before answering. "We're looking for the mechoservitors," he finally said.

Mechoservitors. The word held meaning for him, but in this context he could not find it. Still, something the man had said registered with him suddenly, and a new question spilled out before he could stop himself. "And if it's worse?"

"If it is worse, then they're looking for the Homeseeker."

Another familiar word that he could not place, and Petronus glanced back to the map. *Here, here and here.* He felt something like an ocean swell pulling him back, and he closed his eyes against the sudden feeling of vertigo that seized him.

This time, when he opened them again, he was lying on his back while hands held him down and still. He struggled at first until he saw Grymlis's worried face as he knelt over him.

Somewhere in the distance, he heard Geoffrus ranting and hooting. "Luxpadre has the madness," he cried. "Luxpadre has the madness."

Petronus opened his mouth to speak but found no words, but the Gray Guard captain must have read the questions in his eyes. "You're fine now," Grymlis said. "You fell over." Here, his brow furrowed with worry. "You were convulsing, babbling. Nothing coherent." His voice lowered. "I think it was glossolalia."

Petronus winced. *Ecstatic utterance.* Taking a deep breath, he forced himself to lie still and recollect himself.

Where had he been? He vaguely remembered a voice and a map. *Here, here and here.*

He dug at the memory, pried at it, and found nothing but noise that hurt his head and made the afternoon light unbearable. One final tug and he found the recollection he sought.

"Runners in the Wastes," he said, his tongue heavy in his mouth. He nodded to Geoffrus. "Ask him. Pay him."

Grymlis squeezed his shoulder. The firm hand felt reassuring to Petronus. "I'll see to it, Father. After we get you to your cot."

Petronus wanted to protest, wanted to insist that he not be carried to bed as if he were a child. But as he opened his mouth, he suddenly felt the dampness of his robes, and the heat of shame flushed his face. His bladder had cut loose during the fit.

Hoping no one would see that he'd wet himself, the Last King of Windwir let his ragged men lift him and carry him to his cot.

Vlad Li Tam

Vlad Li Tam awoke from too little sleep and sat up in his narrow bed. The windowless room offered no light, though he blinked and rubbed his eyes as if it might if only he were patient.

When they'd returned to find the island and its Blood Temple abandoned, he'd gone through the massive building assigning quarters to his family. He was careful to be sure that this room became his once again, though he wasn't sure exactly why. Perhaps it was an anchor to the pain of that time, something to keep the memory banked like a fire.

His recollection of those months was a blur of agony and terror. Nights spent huddled in the corner, sleeping fitfully, open-eyed with his back against the wall. And underlying those memories, Ria's voice—filled with love and comfort—as she worked her knife or as she sat at his table and conversed with him while he lay twitching upon the floor.

Other voices joined hers. The voices of his children beneath the knives, offering up their last words to him as he watched, echoing long after their final breath as he waited here for the next day's cutting.

My room.

He'd memorized it during his clearer moments, and that served him well now as he stood and pulled on his light cotton trousers and shirt. Barefoot, he padded to the door and let himself into the empty hallway.

He'd spent another day on the dock, fishing but not catching. At the end of the day, he'd discovered his bait had been taken at some point without his knowledge.

Still, he'd not been fishing for fish.

This afternoon, he'd force himself away and back to the paper-strewn table in his room. Back to the book his father had written and passed to Vlad's first grandson, a secret history devised to bring down Windwir and establish a lasting Y'Zirite resurgence in the Named Lands. The plot was as carefully conceived as any Tam intrigue—perhaps even more so given that the network of conspirators stretched far beyond his family, into other families, into the Marshlands, and even into the very heart of the Androfrancine Order itself.

Vlad had spent his life weaving a web he'd thought was his own design, only to learn it was a carefully crafted manipulation by the man he'd respected, feared and loved above all others.

A man who had conceived of this plot, knowing full well that the price of it would be the near extinction of his own bloodline.

Somewhere out there, other conspirators continued this work. He'd seen their ships at harbor here—ships unfamiliar to the Named Lands' most skilled family of shipwrights. Even now, his children scouted for them.

And yet all I can think about is the ghost.

He moved through the hallway slowly, listening to his feet as they whispered over the marble floor. When he reached the wide double doors, he pushed one open slowly to slip out into the moonlit night.

A young man separated himself from deeper shadows, silent on feet trained for scouting. "Good morning, Grandfather," the man said.

Vlad looked at him and tried to remember his name but couldn't. Before the cuttings, before his time here, he'd remembered every child, every grandchild and great-grandchild. Even those he lost along the way. He'd known their walk, their mannerisms, every little detail that might help him sharpen and fire them at the heart of the Named Lands as arrows for his hunting.

But since his time here, he'd found that his memory faltered. *As if I don't want to know.*

"Good morning," he answered. "How goes the watch?"

The young man shrugged and smiled. "Quietly."

Vlad nodded. All of their watches had been quiet upon returning; still they set them. He looked down to the harbor, where one of his iron vessels sat at anchor. "I'm going fishing," he said.

The guard inclined his head and slipped back to where he'd waited before.

Vlad looked to the moon—it was high but not full yet, though its light still cast shadows. He looked to the water below and saw its reflection dancing upon the surface.

Following the wide stone stairs down to the docks, he collected his tackle in the bait shed at the bottom and nodded to another guard.

I've become obsessed. The thought struck him, and Vlad felt some part of his old self stirring to life to examine this new realization. Standing apart from it, he saw clearly how unlike him this fixation was. He'd come here every day for months under the guise of fishing when he knew—and suspected his family knew, too—that he really was searching for ghosts in the water.

No, he thought, *one* ghost in particular. And today, after so many days of sitting and watching, it was time for a new tack.

Bucket, rod and tackle clutched tight, Vlad climbed down the wooden stairs to the lower docks and paused to take in the stillness of the predawn water. There, at the end of the lower dock, a skiff lay tied and ready. He walked to it, laid his tackle within, and climbed into the small boat.

As a boy on the Emerald Coast, he'd learned to sail at a young age. But growing up in House Li Tam left little room for those luxuries in the face of a first son's training. In the end, he'd picked up most of his nautical experience fishing with Petronus and his father during the year he'd spent with his family in Caldus Bay. Of course, these memories lay over sixty years behind him now. Still, his feet remembered themselves, and as he found his place upon the rowing bench, his hands found the wooden oars and knew their work.

"Grandfather?"

Vlad looked up toward the whispered voice upon the dock. "Yes?"

In the dim moonlight, he saw yet another guard emerge now from shadow. "May I find someone to row you?"

Vlad smiled to himself. It was a simple inquiry, but the statement beneath it was clear to him. *You are Vlad Li Tam, lord of House Li Tam. You should not be rowing about the sea alone in a tiny skiff.*

"No need," he said. He pointed to the mouth of the natural harbor. "I'll not go far out of sight." Still, he knew that once he put his back into the oars, a bird would flash back to their watch captain, who would in turn inform Baryk.

Protocol, of course, would be followed.

Dawn was hours away yet when the cracking of his back and shoulders joined the whisper of the oars into water and the creaking of the wooden boat. Overhead, stars throbbed heavy in a velvet sky and the slice of moon lent the faintest blue-green limn to the warm water. Careful to stay beyond eyeshot of the anchored iron ship and its own watch, Vlad took the skiff around the edge of the harbor and savored the feeling in his arms.

It wasn't until he cleared the mouth and turned south along the shoreline that he finally paused and blinked at the empty night around him.

Why am I here? He'd started slow. First, an hour at the dock. Then eventually, half of a day. And lately, it had been the full day. Baryk and the others were handling the investigation and patrols, and Vlad knew they noted his increased withdrawal from that work. He even suspected that Baryk's desire to leave was driven in part by Vlad's gradual descent into this obsession.

Now, in the middle of the night, he found himself at sea. Months on the dock were no longer enough to satisfy his longing to see it again.

"Where are you?" he asked the waters in a quiet voice that frightened him.

And as if in answer, the water suddenly shimmered around him with a blue-green glow that stopped his breath.

Bringing the oars into the boat, Vlad carefully gripped the gunwale and leaned over the side. There, in the deeps, he saw it and felt the rush of joy and relief flooding him at the sight of it.

Ribbons of light twisted around an undulating, pulsing being that slowly ascended toward him. One tendril, long and slender as an arm, reached upward to float just beneath the surface, and Vlad felt the boat tip when he stretched out his own arm to let his fingers move across the water. The light withdrew, and he felt a pang of panic seize him.

Don't go.

And even as he thought it, that older part of him stirred again. *What is this that you feel?* It was deeper than memory, stronger than instinct, and it pulled at him with a gravity he had not expected. Still, he set it aside for now.

He forced his arm still, the hand dipping into the gentle waves, and beneath his skiff, the ghost moved in a widening circle, rolling as it did, before it shot southeast—a streak of light within the water.

Vlad opened his mouth to speak, but his voice caught in his throat. More than that, he realized—it was more a sob than a gasp, and that knowledge rattled him.

Don't go.

Fast as it had fled, the light returned, wavering beneath him again, and for the faintest moment, he felt the cool electric tingle as one tendril brushed his hand. It pulsated more urgently now, and a new compulsion seized him.

Hooking his foot under the rowing bench to anchor himself, Vlad stretched over the side of the boat to dip his face into the water, forcing his eyes open to take it all in.

Its song was everywhere around him, and the light drew nearer for a moment before fleeing again.

Vlad raised his head, drew in a deep lungful of air, and reimmersed himself.

He counted to five, and just as before, the ghost was back and all around him. *I could give myself to it,* he thought. *I could let go of the bench and join it here and never leave.*

But even as he thought it, he knew it was not the path for him, despite deep longing. That part of him that had ruled House Li Tam with iron resolve, making and breaking the leaders and houses of the Named Lands, knew with certainty that something suspicious and ancient and more powerful than any compulsion he'd ever known now gripped him, and rather than being satisfied by at last finding what he sought, he was instead more curious and more compelled by this longing.

Withdrawing his face from the water, Vlad watched as the ghost once again fled southeast only to return. *It means me to follow.*

But he knew that for now, he wouldn't. For now, he had learned what he needed to and would return to the Blood Temple, take his breakfast, and meet with Baryk as soon as the warpriest was awake.

Tomorrow, he would return alone. He would do the same each day after. And in a week's time, he would gather what remained of his family and would sail southeast . . . though it made no sense to do so.

Yet I will do this.

It broke his heart open to set himself firmly again on the rowing bench. He felt that pulsating ache moving and twisting across the deep, dark waters of his recent losses and was surprised at the tears that now coursed his cheeks.

It is as if I am in love, Vlad Li Tam thought with a rising panic that threatened to capsize his understanding.

Winters

The young Gypsy Scout stationed near the door ushered Winters into Rudolfo's audience chamber just ahead of the prisoners, and she slid quietly into the chair provided for her in the corner of the room. Already, her stomach knotted at the thought of this afternoon's meeting. She'd sat through hours of interrogation that morning, breaking only for lunch. Rudolfo's questioning was skillful, even courteous, but what she heard from her people—what she saw upon their faces as they proclaimed it—chilled her.

She smoothed her plain dress and forced herself to watch when the women were brought in. Their hair was cut short, and the lines of ash and mud upon their faces were drawn in a more deliberate pattern, like the woman who claimed to be her older sister. Their feet were bare beneath the robes they wore. They walked with their heads held high and their shoulders back, and they met Rudolfo's eyes with their own, and with the confident smile of peers. They inclined their heads slowly and sat in the chairs he waved at.

"I hope," Rudolfo said to them, "you enjoyed your lunch."

They nodded, and the one who had kept silent through most of the morning session spoke. Winters stretched for her name. *Tamrys.* "We are grateful for your hospitality, Lord Rudolfo."

Winters watched him nod slightly, watched his eyes slide to Aedric and then glance up toward her. "I am grateful for your cooperation," he said. "These are curious times."

"These are the times foretold," Tamrys assured him, and Winters heard the faith in her voice. It gave her pause.

How long had this resurgence cooked slowly among her people? How blind had she and the Council of Twelve been? Thinking of the council, she looked across the room and saw Seamus sitting quietly. When their eyes met briefly, she saw sadness in them, and she tried to find a similar sorrow within herself.

Tamrys continued. "We know that these are but the labor of a difficult birth. With the Child of Promise delivered, the road is made straight for the Age of the Crimson Empress."

All morning, as Rudolfo gently probed them with questions, Winters had listened to fragments of gospel and references to prophecy she had not heard before. And with each spoken word, she'd heard the belief in these women's voices and felt something stirring in her that heated her face and forced her hands into white-knuckled fists.

She forced her attention back to the conversation.

"Yes," Rudolfo said. "You have shared that with us. And I'm certain that you believe this to be so—I can see why one might. But it remains that bringing this"—he paused, and his brow furrowed as he looked for the best word—"*faith* into the Ninefold Forest is unacceptable."

Winters watched both of the women blink in surprise, then recover with knowing smiles and sly glances to one another. "It just hasn't been revealed to you yet, Lord Rudolfo." She heard love and conviction in their voices. "When it has, you'll understand your great part in this gospel and the tremendous grace visited upon your son and your line."

Rudolfo looked to her again, and Winters saw cunningness in his dark eyes. His hands moved, and she read the words quickly. *Do you wish to speak to them?* He'd asked during the morning, too, but she'd declined. Once more, she shook her head, and as she did, she saw Tamrys staring at her from the corner of her eye.

"You are Winteria the Younger," she said, starting to stand. "We did not recognize you without your markings of Home-longing." Gypsy Scouts slipped in from the edges of the room until a glance from Rudolfo and a whistle from Aedric stood them down. The other stood, too, and both bowed deeply. "We bear word to you from your sister, the Elder."

Winters felt the blush rise to her cheeks. "I do not recognize her as my kin."

Tamrys smiled, and it was warm, genuine even. "You do not need to as yet. These things take time." She looked to Rudolfo. "May I approach her?"

He looked to Winters, and she wondered how wide her eyes had become even as his narrowed. He must have seen something there, because his voice was cautionary. "I'm not certain—"

Winters found her voice. "You may approach."

Under the watchful eye of the scouts, the Machtvolk evangelist walked slowly across the room. As she did, Winters stood and faced the woman.

The woman was tall, and when she gathered Winters into her arms, Winters felt the strength of the embrace and smelled the sweat and earth and ash of the woman. She felt warm lips upon her forehead, and then the mouth moved to her ear as the voice lowered to a whisper. "Little sister," Tamrys said, "come home to me and to joy."

Unexpected, the words—and the love within that voice—raised goose bumps upon her skin.

Then, with the message delivered, the evangelist inclined her head and returned to her seat.

The conversation continued beyond that. Rudolfo asked questions, and the answers, circular and cryptic, followed. She heard references to schools and shrines built; to an expansion of the Machtvolk presence into what had once been Windwir; and candid discussion of evangelists moving out across the Named Lands in their robes and mud and ash, preaching their new gospel.

But gradually, the words drifted someplace out of reach to Winters. As hard as she tried to, she could not escape that whispered voice and that firm embrace.

Little sister, come home to me and to joy.

And yet, this same woman—her older sister supposedly—had sent assassins out in the night to murder Hanric, the man who had raised her. And now, this new queen and her kind transformed her people into something that frightened Winters though she did not fully grasp why.

She remembered that day in the tent at the edge of spring and felt the rage washing through her as she surged forward with upraised axe. She felt shame rise to her cheeks at the memory of being so easily restrained and subdued. And she realized suddenly that she'd spent these last six months avoiding the truth of what had happened to her and how she'd responded, hiding in the basement of the new library pretending she was only a girl. Sudden tears threatened her now, and Winters felt her face grow even hotter as she resisted.

I gave up on my people.

She remembered Tertius and the nights he often read to her. One of her favorite stories had been "Jamael and the Kin-Wolves." He'd suggested it to her one night and had then been subjected to reading it again and again to her. *And one day Jamael came home from the fields to find a kin-wolf in her sheepfold. . . .*

She looked at the two women again. The light in their eyes. The deep sense of passion in their voices. How many more were out there, even now, sharing this gospel and feeding this resurgence? They had brought down Windwir to bring this faith out of the shadows. They had butchered and resurrected Petronus to create this belief. They had cut their mark over the hearts of innocent children. And they had healed Jin Li Tam and Rudolfo's dying son with the blood of thousands.

She knew from her talks with Rudolfo and Jin Li Tam that this resurgence had been engineered, but now, for the first time, she saw that her people were also victims of this dark movement. They were being bent and twisted into the servants of this so-called Crimson Empress, and the thought of it awoke anger in her. These people were in her care, and she could not hide here and pretend otherwise.

Wolves in the fold, Jamael cried.

"Wolves in the fold," Winters whispered softly to herself.

And as if she heard, the evangelist Tamrys paused, turned to the girl and smiled at her.

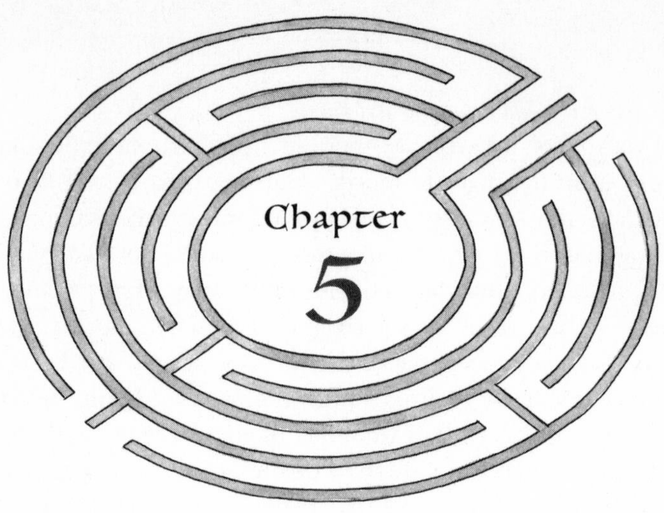

Rudolfo

Rudolfo looked up as Jin Li Tam and Jakob entered the back of the room, suddenly apprehensive about the decision they had made over lunch. He looked from his wife to the two Machtvolk evangelists and last, to Winters. The girl had been quiet, and he had been unable to read the emotions that washed her face. Something had happened when the woman Tamrys had embraced her and passed on her older sister's message.

Something to be mindful of.

His eyes locked with Jin Li Tam's, and the shrewdness he saw there bolstered him. "Ah," he said with a flourish, rising to his feet. "May I present the Lady Jin Li Tam, daughter of House Li Tam and queen of the Ninefold Forest. And our heir, Lord Jakob."

The two evangelists first went very pale, then blushed as they scrambled to stand and turn.

They are surprised. Perhaps, Rudolfo thought, *this is the right path after all.*

They bowed deeply, and he did not need to see their faces in that moment to read the adoration written there. "G-great Mother," Tamrys said, stammering, "this is an unforeseen honor."

Now, the other spoke as well, and Rudolfo heard the sob catch in her throat. "And behold, the Child of Promise—hearty and hale by the grace of the Crimson Empress."

Or by dark design and blood sacrifice. Rudolfo felt himself frowning and forced a smile to his mouth. "Please join us, Lady Tam," he said, motioning to a chair nearby.

Jin Li Tam gave the evangelists a quick look, her face a calm mask. But underneath it, Rudolfo knew that rage seethed there. Certainly, the Y'Zirite blood magicks had saved Jakob's life, but it had cost countless others, her sisters and brothers lost upon the cutting tables while Jin's father was forced to watch the murder of his children and grandchildren on the island Rudolfo had rescued him from. He knew Jin's shame, but he knew that if he had been there, holding their gray and gasping son, he too would have fallen to his knees and begged for that cure once he knew it worked. He could not fault her.

But like her, the shame of it would chew him.

Now, he admired her placid, regal tone. "Thank you, Lord Rudolfo. We would be pleased to join you."

He waited until the women seated themselves. Their eyes kept moving to the child, adoration painted clearly upon their faces.

They truly do believe he is their Child of Promise. Rudolfo noted this and set it apart to consider later. Then, he put his attention back upon his unusual guests. "I can see that my son is important to you," he said.

Their nods were enthusiastic, their smiles wide. "He is our promise that the Crimson Empress will soon come," Tamrys said. "The First Gospel of Ahm Y'Zir teaches us that clearly."

First Gospel. It piqued his curiosity. "I'm unfamiliar with it. Enlighten me."

Tamrys's eyes did not leave Jakob as she lowered her voice and recited it from memory. "And in the shadow of the Usurper's Pyre, a child of great promise shall be given as light in darkness, as hope in despair, and he shall make straight the arrival of his Crimson Empress as a bridegroom prepares for the feast." She glanced back to Rudolfo. "There are other passages," she said. "I would be happy to share them with you."

Rudolfo smiled. "Perhaps later." Then, he leaned forward. "As you can imagine, Jakob's safety is of great importance to me. I've word from your queen that he is in danger and that her ambassador approaches even now. What do you know of this?"

Tamrys looked back to the baby, then to her companion. Rudolfo watched the knowing glances pass between them and waited. "There have been prophecies of late," she finally said.

Rudolfo opened his mouth to ask for more detail but closed it.

Something suddenly felt wrong, and the hair rose on the back of his neck. He smelled something—it was earthy and rich with just a hint of apples. And the slightest breeze whispered against his cheek. He glanced to Aedric and opened his mouth again, then felt fingers pressing into the back of his neck.

Be still. Say nothing.

Rudolfo waited. The fingers were warm and small. He felt the slightest scraping of a nail against his skin, and gooseflesh broke out on his arms and back beneath the soft silk of his shirt.

The fingers moved again. *I assure you that you are safe in this moment, Lord Rudolfo. I bear urgent and private word for you and the Great Mother.*

Rudolfo's mind spun its calculations. It was a woman, magicked and well versed in the subverbals of his House. The smell of earth and ash, along with her reference to their gospel, betrayed her as a Marsher.

Magicked and in my home. He felt anger rising within and alongside it, a feeling he was not accustomed to: fear. Still, the interloper assured him of safety, and if she was capable of concealing herself within his manor with such relative ease, capable of placing herself in such close proximity to his person and to his family, then surely if she had wished to cause harm, she would have done so already.

Jin Li Tam and Aedric were both looking to him now, and he could see by the look on their faces that they knew something was afoot. "My apologies," he said in a careful voice, "but I fear we will need to postpone this audience." He started to rise out of courtesy and felt the hand move from his neck as he did. "My Gypsy Scouts will return you to your quarters, and we will continue our conversation at a later time. I'm very interested to learn of these . . . prophecies." The word felt distasteful in his mouth, but he smiled around it anyway.

Already, his hands were moving. *Keep them under close watch.* He looked to Jin Li Tam. "I would speak with you, Lady, when we are alone."

He watched the scouts as they escorted their guests from the room. He watched Seamus and Winters as they followed, and last, he watched Aedric pause at the door. "Is all well, General?" he asked.

Rudolfo inclined his head. "It is, Aedric. But stay nearby."

After the door closed, he expelled held breath and let slip some of the anger that had coiled around his spine. "You come into *my* house under *magicks*? You insert yourself into the affairs of the Ninefold Forest?" He felt his voice shaking from it, though he was careful not to raise it. "You have much explaining to do."

Jin Li Tam looked at him, her mouth slack. "What—?"

But another voice cut her off. "You have my deepest apologies, Lord Rudolfo, for this deception." There was a brief pause. "It was necessary that I travel quickly and quietly."

The woman's voice sounded familiar, despite being thickly muffled by the magicks, but Rudolfo could not place it. Still, he felt the anger prickling his scalp as he white-knuckled the arms of his chair. "What you deem necessary is your own concern. You've violated my territories—my very *home*. This is unprecedented."

"We live," the woman said slowly, "in unprecedented times."

And in that moment, he placed the voice and looked up to lock eyes with Jin Li Tam. Her own face, he saw, had gone pale. Jakob gurgled in his sleep and waved a tiny hand.

"You are a long way from the Marshlands, Ria," he said.

"I am far from the Machtvolk Territories," she conceded. "But the news I bear merited personal and prompt attention. You and your family are in grave danger."

His eyes narrowed, and he willed the pounding to slow behind his temples. "Go on."

Now, her voice was from another corner of the room. "We've word of a growing threat against your household."

"And how exactly have you come by this word?" he asked, tipping his head slightly as if he might somehow hear her move.

She did not answer at first. When she did, the words were carefully chosen. "As you no doubt have surmised, we have an active network in place."

And, he remembered, the ability to somehow divert their birds and decode their messages. For the last six months, Isaak and his mechoservitors had been busy scripting new codes nearly as fast as they were broken. He paused, uncertain, and then took a risk. "We also know you have access to our birds and codes."

She hesitated, then answered. "Yes. We do."

Honesty, then. How refreshing. Rudolfo sighed. "Continue."

"There are spies in your house, Rudolfo, and there are enemies in your forest." She paused. "And I can assure you, they are *not* my overzealous evangelists. Though I will deal with them once you've concluded your own audience with them."

Spies in my house. "I want specific details."

"When I have them," she said, "you will have them." He sensed more hesitation in her next pause. "Meanwhile, I wish to extend aid to you. Already, my network is scouring the Named Lands for more substantive evidence of this threat. With your permission, I can widen my investigation to include the Ninefold Forest, and I can also send you a hundred of my Blood Scouts."

Rudolfo's mind reeled at her suggestions. Blood Scouts in the Ninefold Forest? The Machtvolk Y'Zirites investigating his people. But three of her words snared him fastest. "With my permission?"

She chuckled. "I know you think us monsters. The Desolation of Windwir. The kin-healing of House Li Tam and the night of purging. But we are not monsters, Lord Rudolfo. We are the servants of House Y'Zir, and by bonds of kinship, we are your servants as well." Her voice drifted across the room now from the other side. "My deception this day notwithstanding, I have the very best interests of your son at heart, and I would not easily violate the trust or sovereignty of your Ninefold Forest Houses."

Then why not come in open dialogue? Why sneak in, magicked? But even as the questions formed in his mind, he knew the answers without asking. If there were spies in his house, the arrival of the Machtvolk queen would not go unnoticed. Her strategy was sound . . . if she was indeed being truthful.

He glanced at Jin Li Tam. Still her face retained its calm expression. But when their eyes met again, he saw the rage there. "I appreciate your offer of assistance," he said. "But we will handle these matters within the Ninefold Forest without Machtvolk assistance. If you truly have my son's best interests at heart, you will respect our borders and will share your intelligence with my people as you receive it."

For a moment, she said nothing. Finally, when she did speak, she was near him again. "Think carefully, Rudolfo," she said, "and you will see that at no time have we raised a finger to harm you or your family. We are allies."

Rudolfo pondered this. He could still remember the voice on the night Hanric was killed. *No, not him.* And Rudolfo had been cast aside without even a bruise. Later, when Jin Li Tam had taken the Wandering Army to field, she'd challenged a Blood Scout single-handed, and when the Marsher had known it was his so-called Great Mother, he'd refused to fight. Still, these cultists left a forest of bones on the plains of Windwir and had murdered thousands of others in their faith.

"You have done enough harm to others to merit my suspicion," he said.

"And I have saved your son's life," she reminded him. "What does that merit with you?"

Rudolfo nodded slowly but found no words to accompany it.

Her voice became even more muffled, heavy with emotion. "Your son will be the salvation of our world," she said. "We have pledged blade and heart to his well-being and to the well-being of his parents." Her voice was moving across the room. "I will ask you to reconsider my offer of aid. You have many enemies in the Named Lands, and your borders are not secure. Allow me to assist you or, if you can not abide a Machtvolk presence on your soil, send your wife and child to me and I will watch over them until this threat has passed." Her voice was near the door now. "It *will* pass, Rudolfo, and when the Crimson Empress arrives, she will make all things right."

He squinted but could not even make out the ghost of her. *She will make all things right.* That would be quite a trick. He considered his next words carefully, tasting them like iron shavings in his mouth before he spoke them. "Ria," he said in a quiet voice, "do not come to me in this way again, and do not broach my borders without announcing yourself."

The door handle moved beneath a hand he could not see. "I will do what I must to preserve the life of this Child of Promise," she said, and her next words stung him though he knew she meant them to. "The question remains, Lord Rudolfo, as to whether or not *you* will do the same."

Rudolfo heard Jin's swallowed gasp and looked over to see her face red in wrath she could no longer conceal. Still, Jakob slept on.

As the door swung open slowly, Aedric looked in. "Was there someone—?"

When Ria moved past him, the first captain leaped back and reached for his knives, his lips puckering to whistle third alarm.

"Let her go," Rudolfo said, hearing the weariness in his own voice. Even as he said it, his fingers were moving. *Do you believe her message?*

Jin Li Tam sighed. She had not spoken through the entire exchange, and he could see that her lips were a tight, pale line. *I believe her, but I do not trust her.*

Yes. "I concur," he said.

Then, he reached for his glass of chilled peach wine but found that his interest in it had passed. Instead, Rudolfo fixed his eyes upon his sleeping son and pondered the darkening paths that lay before them both.

Neb

Neb sat in the shadowed opening of a glass cave and watched the dark bird moving high across the sky. He'd seen more of them in the last day, and unlike the messenger birds, these seemed to fly with purpose and direction in this desolate place.

Renard had called them *kin-raven*, but he'd also told him that they were supposedly extinct . . . until approximately two years ago, when the first of their kind had migrated back to the Named Lands. Though they flew too high for him to tell, he wondered if it was the same species he used to see in Winters's dreams.

Once the kin-raven passed, he went back to lacquering his thorn rifle and wetting the bulb for another night of guarding the woman.

She'd stirred but had not awakened since he pulled her from the rubble and washed her wounds. He'd mixed the herbs and powders as Renard had showed him, adding extra kalla for the pain she'd feel if the wolf venom took. Then, he wrapped her with bandages torn from a clean cotton shirt he'd found in her bag.

Last, he found the cave, twisted into a wall of glass, where they could wait out the worst of her wounds. He marked their territory, shaking drops from his phial of kin-wolf urine though he doubted it would work with the girl's blood on the wind. Then, he rolled large rocks in front of the opening, leaving just enough room for him to squeeze through if he needed to. And so, he forced himself awake, chewing the root for focus.

He put away his rifle brush and lacquer pot, then crawled back to check on the woman again. She moaned in her sleep from time to time, twisting in the blanket he'd wrapped her in. Neb found himself trying hard not to look at her. Her chiseled features and the gentle curves of her pulled at his eyes. He forced them to her scars.

The cuttings were clearly intentional, forming symbols that he recognized from his years in the Franci orphanage in the shadow of the Androfrancine's Great Library. It was the language of blood magick; the cuttings of House Y'Zir and its Wizard Kings. He could not read the runes from that former age, but he knew there was dark meaning behind them.

He crouched beside her now and placed a hand upon her forehead. She was cool and clammy to his touch and she stirred again, the blanket falling aside to reveal another curve. When he averted his eyes, they fell upon her pack.

It was small, made for traveling fast and light, not dissimilar to those the Gypsy Scouts wore. Apart from the clean shirt he'd shredded, he'd not gone through it other than to be certain there were no weapons. Her dark iron scout knives were safely tucked away, out of reach and out of sight.

He stared at the pack for a full minute, biting his lower lip. But in the end, he did what he thought Rudolfo or Renard would do; he reached for the pack and retreated with it to the mouth of the cave.

Neb eased the contents out onto the fused glass floor and used his hands to spread them out. He felt his cheeks grow warm when he saw her undergarments and toiletry kit.

He pushed them aside and picked up a compact, thick book. It was old, and he opened it, not recognizing the language within it. But he saw that it was marked with notes, including an inscription in the front. A few of the letters looked familiar but none registered. He set it aside and next looked to the tarnished silver flask. Holding it to his ear he shook it gently.

Half-empty. He hesitated, then unscrewed the top to sniff the contents. The rancid smell turned his stomach, and he glanced back to the woman again. His initial thought was that these were blood magicks—that perhaps she was one of these runners—but he thrust the thought aside. The blood magicks he'd seen lasted three to five days and, in the end, killed their users, consuming them from within before the effects had worn off. And apart from her wounds, the girl showed no signs of other discomfort.

Unless. The other runners had also seemed to defy this fate. What if this was a new blood magick?

Or, he thought, a new people? Certainly the cuttings suggested that.

Tucking the flask into his own pouch, he went to the next object that caught his attention. It was an oddly shaped sliver of black stone. At first he thought the shape held no meaning, but he quickly saw the wings and the beak. It was a crude carving, but clearly a kin-raven. He reached out for it, and when his finger touched it he felt warmth rolling through him, tingling along the bones of his arm, up into his shoulder. Even that brief second, a dozen images flooded him and he felt the nausea of sudden vertigo, as a sound like mighty rushing water swept him.

Neb jerked back his hand and blinked.

He put a finger on the carving, this time forcing himself to keep it there to a count of ten.

The images were there again, spinning about him, and he reached for one, though he wasn't sure how he did it. And as he laid hold of it, it wasn't so much that his own sense of space vanished as it was a new space falling into place around him. He pulled at it, drew upon it like a thread.

It was a darkened place that smelled old and closed off and cold. In the distance, water dripped. Neb did not know how he could pick out that single sound beneath the roar around him, and yet he did. He also heard the gentle wheeze of bellows behind him and turned around.

When the golden eyes fluttered open, his breath caught in his throat. "Nebios Homeseeker," the metal man said, "you should not be here. How have you circumvented our dream tamp? I charge you by the light to leave quickly." The eyes flickered on and off as the mechoservitor worked its shutters and looked from left to right. "We are being listened to."

Neb opened his mouth to ask who was listening but suddenly found himself standing in the courtyard of the Franci orphanage. Brother Hebda stood before him, gaunt and hollow-eyed, now these two years dead. "Neb?"

There was surprise in his voice.

"Brother Hebda?" Certainly, it wasn't the first time he'd seen his father since Windwir's fall. Hebda had warned him that the Marsh King rode south back in the gravediggers' camp in what remained of Windwir, and he'd also told the boy that he would proclaim Petronus Pope and King and that eventually Petronus would break his heart. Both had come true. Still, how was it possible that the small black carving could do this?

Brother Hebda's face paled even as it began to fade along with the crisp blue winter skyline of the great city of Windwir. "Runners in the Wastes," his father said. "Beware of them, Son. I fear they—"

Then, Neb fell out of the scene and into the roaring once again. Spinning, he found himself at the center of a Whymer Maze beneath a graying sky. There, upon a marble bench, a girl sat quietly with her hands folded in her lap. There were evergreen wreaths upon a grave there, and he remembered this place very well. He'd stood here what seemed so long ago and kissed Winters good-bye after Hanric's funeral rites.

The girl wore a plain dress, and her prettiness made his heart hurt. Her long hair was held back from her face by wooden combs, and a light dusting of freckles speckled the bridge of her nose. He rubbed his eyes and looked again. He knew her, though he'd never seen her without the mud and ash of her people's faith. "Winters?"

She looked up. "Nebios? How—?"

And he was gone again, falling away to land upon a jagged sea of razor-edged glass. "He's wandering in the aether," a woman's voice said. "Awake and casting."

"Yes," another said from the eastern end of D'Anjite's Bridge.

Then a third spoke, and Neb saw the locked well she camped near. The very place he'd found the silver crescent. And this time, he saw the woman who spoke. Her close-cropped hair was blonde, and the cuttings upon her flesh were similar to those upon the woman he watched over.

"We know you see us, Abomination, despite our magicks," she said as her smile widened. "And we see you as well, there in your glass cave."

It is the stone. Somehow, the count had escaped him, and he still held his finger to it. Neb yanked back his hand and scowled down at the carving.

What had he just seen? And was it real? Mechoservitors in dark, forgotten places who spoke of dream tamps. The ghost of his dead father warning him of runners in the Wastes—something Neb already knew, in an uncharacteristic prophetic failure. And a Winters who no longer wore the mourning hope of her promised home.

And what had the woman in the Wastes called him? *Abomination.*

He tucked the book into his pouch alongside the flask, but for the longest time he sat and stared at the carving, suddenly unwilling to touch it again.

Finally, he scooped it up into a bit of cloth and tipped it into his pouch as well.

Then, he settled back against the wall, his thorn rifle across his lap. Beyond his cave, a kin-wolf bayed beneath a rising moon. Behind him, the scarred woman whimpered and cried out in her sleep at whatever darkness rode her dreams.

Jin Li Tam

Jin Li Tam sheathed her knives and wiped the sweat from her face and neck. The evenings grew cooler now as the winds picked up, sweeping south from the Dragon's Spine. With the sky still purple from the setting sun, she felt that breeze now as it kissed her wet skin.

Taking in a great lungful of lavender and roses, she tested herself to see if the evening's knife dance had settled her.

Yes, she realized, *I feel better.*

After the audience with Ria and her evangelists, Jin had left Jakob with Rudolfo and stormed away to rage privately for an hour. But it had not been enough. In the end, between breaks spent feeding Jakob, a run and a dance or two with the knives had dulled the anger as she suspected it might. There was a time when she would not have known that about herself, but there was also a time when she wouldn't have realized that she went to anger first when she became afraid.

She was there in the room with Rudolfo for hours biding her time. How long had she hidden there? How much had she heard? And had she hidden in other rooms, too? Was she here now, watching? She felt another stab of anger.

Jin Li Tam took another breath. Then, she looked to the house. The windows were lit now, beckoning, and she found the one she knew belonged to Rudolfo. No doubt, he sat in his study and took dinner in the midst of reports and messages to digest and respond to.

She set out for the manor and paused near the edge of the Whymer Maze. Faint footfalls reached her ears, and she saw a young woman emerge from it. Winters, she realized, no doubt returning from Hanric's Rest at the center of the maze, near the Whymer meditation bench.

There is much to meditate upon.

Jin whistled the low, soft note of a Gypsy Scout on alert.

Winters looked up, startled. "Lady Tam," she said.

Jin stopped. The look upon the girl's face was consternation and fear. To a degree, it made sense—Ria claimed to be her older sister, thought dead in infancy, and certainly by now Rudolfo had told her about their magicked guest. Still, she had to ask. "Are you okay, Winters?"

The girl shook her head, and for a moment, Jin thought she might burst into tears. "I don't think I am. I failed my people. And I think I saw Neb."

Neb? Jin Li Tam looked around. "You think Neb is home?"

Winters took a deep breath. "No, not like that." She swallowed. "More like a dream. He was in a cave made of glass. There was a woman with him. Only, he didn't look like himself. His hair's too long, and he's too gaunt. He looked at me and said my name, and then he was gone."

Jin knew the two of them had somehow shared dreams together before he'd entered the Churning Wastes. Until recently, Jin hadn't put much thought into Marsher mysticism with its glossolalia, prophecies and Homeseeking. But she'd also not believed there was a magick strong enough to bring back the dead or heal the mortally ill. She felt her eyebrows furrow. "It's been a long time since you've shared dreams with him, hasn't it?"

"Seven or eight months," Winters agreed. "But this was not a shared dream. It was like a dream, but I was awake." She looked away and Jin read the discomfort. "A . . . vision, I think."

She knew the girl was no stranger to such things and wanted to ask more to get to what part of this made her uncomfortable, but then it struck her. *There was a woman with him.*

She thought about telling her that she should not concern herself with it or leap to any specific assumption about the woman, but instead, she changed the subject. "And you feel you gave up on your people?"

She watched the discomfort melt into sadness. "I did. I did not have to give up on them. But I did. I came here and hid myself underneath a mountain of books."

Jin Li Tam chuckled, and it was sardonic. "You've not failed them yet, and I don't think it's fair to say you've given up on them, either." She watched the girl's eyebrows knit together. "Maybe you don't remember, but you had few choices left on that day, and you needed time to absorb that great loss and craft an appropriate response to it. You came to your only kin-clave in the Named Lands and took asylum. This is not failure or abandonment."

She saw a bit of hope spark there, but it went out too soon. "I can't even fathom an appropriate response to this."

Jin Li Tam nodded. "For now. But you will." She locked eyes with the girl, willing courage and hope into her that she did not herself have to give. "Give it time. Meanwhile"—here she hefted her knife belt, dangling the sheathed blades—"it's time for you to get back to your knife lessons."

They'd started practicing together in those early days after Winters had first settled into the Forest life, but they'd stopped for the wedding and the royal family's tour of the Ninefold Forest. Getting back to the knives—and out of that basement—would be good for the girl.

And, Jin realized, it was good for her to have someone to teach. "So tomorrow morning, then?"

Winters offered a weak smile. "Tomorrow morning."

Jin Li Tam inclined her head. "Good. And don't fret about the boy."

Inclining her own head, Winters turned and moved in the direction of Library Hill. Jin Li Tam watched her go. Then, she set out for the manor.

She had told Winters that in time, the young, deposed Queen would find an appropriate response to what had happened to her last winter. On that day that Winters lost everything, Jin Li Tam had bargained with a devil and saved what mattered most to her.

Like Winters, she could not fathom what her response might be, and now, with the anger burned away, her fear moved toward sadness she could not afford to feel, and she tried to keep it at bay. *Focus on what you have gained,* she told herself. *Life for your son.*

She paused at the hidden entrance and the series of narrow passageways that would take her to Jakob's room and then to her own bathing chambers, and turned again to take in the nightfall.

She tried not to think of her father and the scars that covered him, or of the mass graves she'd never seen upon that distant island, or of the orphaned children now nearby who bore the scar of Y'Zir over their hearts. She tried not to think of them and failed.

For all that I gained, I've lost as well. And for that, a response was certainly called for. But what response?

Wiping a stray tear from her cheek, Jin Li Tam begged an answer from the first star that poked its light through the dusky canopy of sky.

Then, she slipped into her home and pushed her fear once more aside.

Winters

Winters undressed by moonlight, her bare skin noticing the slight chill of her basement bedroom. She hurried into her sleep shift and then scuttled into bed, pulling the covers up quickly and gasping at the cool of the sheets.

Lady Tam had surprised her; she'd thought she was alone in the gardens but for the scouts who patrolled it. But she was glad to have seen Lady Tam and spoken with her, however briefly. She'd missed her and Jakob especially while they were off touring the Ninefold Forest. Rudolfo had offered to bring Winters along, but she had preferred the library.

Hiding underneath your mountain of books. Perhaps, she thought, but no more. Now, she knew that something had to be done. The light of blind, loyal faith in those evangelists' eyes. And the self-assured tone that masqueraded as love, dripping from their voices. Her people were beset by wolves, and it seemed Rudolfo's were now, as well.

He'd told her of Ria's visit, and she'd felt her own mouth drop open in surprise. Then, he'd shared her message of the impending threat. Now she understood something that had perplexed her.

Ria had been in the Ninefold Forest when she sent the kin-raven. The violation of Rudolfo's borders and home were handled with discreet precision. She'd even kept it from Winters, having her dismissed from the room with the others. If it had not been for Rudolfo's trust in her, Winters might never have learned of her sister's visit. Something about that bothered her.

Because of the message. Come home to me and joy. If she felt so, why not ask herself?

She felt the slightest breeze and started. The hand fell over her mouth quickly before she could cry out, and a calm voice whispered at her ear. "Be still, little sister."

Winters struggled against the hand, then stopped.

"Much better," Ria said, lifting her hand.

Winters waited, surprised at how unafraid she suddenly felt. She simply breathed, in and out.

"I wanted to see you before I left," the woman said. Winters lay still, unable to find words. *I must say something.*

Winteria the Elder continued. "You would not recognize the Marshlands. Towns and schools are being built—each with its own Council of Twelve. Children are being taught the oldest ways and taking the mark. Settlers are moving into the river valleys around Windwir, and shrines are being built in the villages that were already there."

She thought of the Tam children and their scars and imagined the same upon the mud-and-ash-rubbed skin of her people. Finally, she found her words. "You savage my people with heresy."

"I restore *our* people to their prideful place as servants of the most high. And I meant it, Little Winteria: Come home to me and share this joy. Home is for the taking, and the advent of the Crimson Empress is at hand."

Winters wanted to rage. She wanted to scream at this woman, lash out at her with fists and feet, but once more calm asserted itself in her and she poured herself into each breath she drew in, each she pushed out.

Winters said nothing.

After a minute, she felt the breeze again and saw the window open. Ria's voice drifted across the room to her. "I've brought you a present. It's beneath your pillow. Perhaps it will change your mind."

Winters resisted the urge to reach beneath her pillow. Instead, she waited a full three minutes. Then, she crawled from the bed and closed the window, locking it. After, she lit her lamp and carried it to the table beside the bed. Reaching out a tentative hand, she lifted her pillow.

A small book lay beneath it, bound in leather. The cover bore no title, but it did look old. She put her pillow down and took up the volume.

Opening the book, she saw the title and remembered it instantly from the audience earlier. *The Gospel of Ahm Y'Zir, Last Son of the Wizard King Xhum Y'Zir.*

She read the first paragraph. The print was too consistent for a scribe and the pages too small for a printing press. Still, it was a familiar style to her, though the age of the paper made it seem highly unlikely.

This gospel, she strongly suspected, had been scripted by a mechoservitor.

Intrigued, she went back to the place her thumb marked and continued reading. Hours later, when she finished it just as her lamp guttered, Winters understood why her people had been so easily swayed. There was a beauty and a power to the story, made even more compelling by the miracles clearly predicted that she herself had borne witness to.

This gospel, she realized, was carefully crafted. A snare carefully set for her people. She had talked with Rudolfo enough to know about House Li Tam's involvement in this, the secret network Vlad's father had put into place, operated by his grandson.

Not just my people. The realization struck her hard, though she wasn't sure why she hadn't realized this all along. This snare caught them all. It took down the Androfrancines. It shattered the trust between the nations of the Named Lands. It created a strong, unbeatable army on the flanks of the New World and set Rudolfo and his family apart.

The age of the Crimson Empress was indeed at hand, and it was not a gospel that required faith. It was a message of something dark and terrible coming regardless of whether or not she believed it.

Tomorrow, she would take this book to Rudolfo. He would understand the rune marks of House Y'Zir, she suspected. And he would want to know what was coming. He would want to do what he could to prepare for it.

When Winters did finally slip into light slumber, she found her dreams were full of Neb, though he would not look at her or acknowledge her when she called out to him.

"He is in grave danger," she thought she heard a voice whisper into her dream.

Alone in the Churning Wastes, her white-haired boy fled just ahead of those ravening kin-wolves that hunted him.

Powerless to help, Winters watched.

Petronus

Petronus paced his study and tried to shake the sense that something terrible was coming on the wind. Each time he looked out the window at the spires and towers of the Great Library and the massive city that spread out from there, he saw brief flashes of a plain littered with skeletons and felt the bite of blisters in his hands. He heard the distant sound of pickaxes and shovels working frozen ground and vaguely remembered a boy beside him, one with hair shocked white at the desolation he'd witnessed. But what desolation? Where?

Why can't I remember?

There was a knock at his door and he looked up. The gaunt Androfrancine stood in the doorway. "The time for subtleties has passed," he said. "The boy is in grave danger."

"Which boy?" But Petronus already reached into his memory, and a name drifted into reach on the tide of that vast ocean of things he could not remember. "Neb?"

The man nodded. "Aye, Father." He walked farther into the room, and Petronus noted that he carried a rolled-up chart beneath his arm. "There was an incident earlier. He broke through the mechoservitors' dream tamp—something he should not be able to do without a conduit. Still, he's done it and he's announced himself loudly. He's also revealed the canticle." The man did not wait for Petronus's invitation. He went to the sitting area, spread his chart upon the table there and took a seat near the wide fireplace. "Sit with me, Father."

Petronus walked to the empty chair facing the man and sat. "Do we have any expeditions nearby? Do we have time to get a contingent of the Gray Guard to him?"

The man sighed. "You are disoriented still. The stone has that impact. We're still new to it and haven't learned the more subtle nuances of using it."

Nothing this man said made sense. Petronus leaned forward. "Stone?"

His companion nodded. "I'll show you." Then, closing his eyes and furrowing his brow, he groaned and Petronus felt the vertigo seizing him. His study fell away, as did the city of Windwir, and a chill took him. He stood on the shore of an underground lake of quicksilver, and at the center of the lake, set into the silver water as if it were a setting in a ring, rose a large, smooth black stone. A man lay sprawled over it, facedown, and in the distance, Petronus could see the man's lips working in a whisper.

But the voice was clear in his ear. "We do not know exactly what it is, and we are only now discerning exactly what it can do. Some artifact of the Younger Gods buried and forgotten in the Beneath Places."

Petronus looked around the cavern, trying to memorize it, but before he finished, he was once again in his study, sitting across from the man. "I will not remember this when I . . ." He could not find the right word and finally settled for the closest. ". . . return?"

"You'll remember more than the times we've spoken when you were awake," the man said. "It seems to work better when the receiver is asleep. We think the Younger Gods intended it to affect dreaming."

Petronus nodded though it made no sense to him at all. An island that let a man speak into the dreams of another? "And this boy you speak of, he somehow is using it, too?"

"No. Neb isn't using it. The stone is under constant guard, and the boy is *here*." The man lowered his finger to the chart, and Petronus saw it was a map of the Churning Wastes. "The runners are here, here and *here*." More pointing. "And to the best of our knowledge they are under blood magicks."

A question found Petronus. "How are you tracking them?"

The man looked as if he wanted to say more but then thought better of it. "It is best not to share too much with you. Regardless of how Neb has accessed the aether, all of the blood-affected are vulnerable when he does."

Blood-affected. A distant memory of an earlier conversation pried at him behind his eyes. "You said the blood magicks made me sensitive to the dream, like Neb."

The man nodded, his face tightening with worry. "But we will not discuss the dream here now, Father. Circumstances have changed, and the dream is in jeopardy until Neb is safe."

"And who exactly is hunting him?" Petronus was certain that any answer provided would slip away from him, but he asked anyway.

"Enemies of the dream," the man said. "Enemies of the light."

Petronus willed his eyes to harden along with the line of his jaw. "That is no answer."

The man regarded him and sighed. "We are still uncertain beyond that, Father. But they are behind the fall of Windwir, ultimately, and behind the Y'Zirite gospel that called for your execution and resurrection. We know the Tams were involved, but not to what extent."

Execution and resurrection. Fall of Windwir. These sounded familiar to him, just as the boy's name did, but he could not place any of them within proper context. But he did know the name Tam, though he could not fathom why Vlad's family would be involved in something like this.

But how could Windwir be fallen if he sat within that great city now?

As if to reassure himself, he looked around his study and took in another lungful of the summer scents that drifted in from the open windows. He looked back to the map and to the chart on the table. "Nothing you say makes sense to me."

The man nodded. "I know it seems that way. I'm still unsure of the casting. Finding Neb is far simpler. At least it was before the dream tamp. But he's different. He—" But the man cut himself off now, looking away. "When you go farther into the Wastes, I won't be able to reach *you*, either. But it seems Neb can reach *me*. Don't let him try until the threat is dealt with, Father. Too much is at stake."

A hundred questions swam his mind, each looking for access to his tongue. Finally, one broke through. "What do you expect me to do?"

"Enlist the aid of the Gypsy King. Find Neb. Do not fail, Father, or the light is gone forever."

Petronus opened his mouth to speak again, but the vertigo gripped him and that roaring took him yet again, pulling him into a brightness that burned as it penetrated him. He forced his eyes to stay open, and though it took every bit of effort, he kept them upon the map, memorizing the geography nearest to the man's pointing finger. He opened his mouth again and pulled in a great lungful of the white, hot soup he now swam in. "Who are you?"

He could no longer see the man. He could no longer see the chart. But a distant voice reached him even as the roar died out and the light faded into the quiet midnight he suddenly found himself in.

"I am Arch-Behaviorist Hebda," the man whispered, "of the Office for the Preservation of Light."

That voice still whispered in his ear when he leaped from his cot, pulled on his robes and went out into the moonlight to find Grymlis and ready a bird for Rudolfo.

Yes, Petronus thought. *I remember.*

Charles

Charles cocked his head and bent the light from his reflector deeper into the mechoservitor's chest cavity. He stretched nimble fingers up and in, reaching for the slipped memory scroll.

"He should be fine now," he said, withdrawing his hand and firing the metal man's boiler as he did.

"Thank you, Father," Isaak said.

Charles chuckled. "You don't have to thank me, Isaak. It's my responsibility."

Isaak's eye shutters opened and closed. Gears inside whirred and clacked. "I suppose it is a part of parenthood."

Now it was Charles's turn to blink. *Yes, it was.* "And you provided this care before I turned up, didn't you?"

They'd been discussing the various aspects of love for the better part of an hour. Isaak had brought it up, and lately it was less and less surprising to Charles. The mechoservitor was full of questions, and it seemed that the more Charles answered, the more Isaak asked. Now, Isaak hissed steam as if surprised by his answer. "I did provide that care. But I was instructed to do so. By Lord Rudolfo, of course."

Charles's fingers found the sequence of hidden buttons and switches and pushed them. The mechoservitor he'd been repairing shuddered to life. "Be still," he murmured, and it did. He looked up to Isaak. "Yes, he did instruct you to. But if he hadn't instructed you to do so, would you have done it anyway?"

Isaak shrugged, and Charles chuckled. *He even learns our gestures from us.*

Isaak's voice lowered. "I do not know."

"You would have."

Isaak's amber eyes glowed brighter. "How can you know this?"

"Because," Charles said, "I am your father and I made you to be logical. It is logical to preserve your kind."

Isaak nodded. "It is." Then, the metal man did something surprising. He hesitated. "Father?"

Charles looked up. "Yes?"

"You made us. I want to ask you a question about how we were made." His tone betrayed how serious his question must be.

"I built you from Rufello's *Specifications* and from scraps dug out of the Wastes," Charles said.

"No," Isaak said. "Not how we were made."

Charles leaned in to the mechoservitor on his worktable and whispered into its ear. "Return to task, Mechoservitor Twelve."

"Returning to task," the mechoservitor said as it stood and left the room.

Charles turned back to Isaak and wiped his hands clean on a nearby rag. "What do you want to know, Isaak?"

Isaak paused, and a wisp of steam leaked out from the exhaust grate in his back. "I want to know why we don't dream."

Charles scratched his head. "I don't think you were meant to dream," Charles said, picking his words carefully. "The Franci believe that dreams are where the basements of the brain work out the hidden fears and hopes of a man's life."

Isaak blinked. "Surely women dream, too? The library certainly references—"

Charles laughed, interrupting him. "Yes. And children. And dogs, even."

"But not mechoservitors?"

Charles did not like the direction the conversation moved in. Even he was unsure of Isaak's status—he was clearly sentient. And he was learning. *At a rapid pace.* But what was he? "I don't know," Charles said. "It wasn't in Rufello's *Specifications.* I suppose a dream could be fashioned. It's not much more than a memory scroll, though the random nature of dreaming would be hard to—"

Isaak's next question ambushed him. "Is it dangerous?"

He felt his eyebrows raise. "Is what dangerous?"

Isaak lowered his voice. "Dreaming."

Charles thought about this. "No, not especially. Though not all dreams are pleasant."

"So were I to have a dream, it would not be harmful?"

"No," Charles said with another chuckle. "I don't believe it would."

Isaak moved toward the door. "Thank you, Father."

Charles watched him leave. "You're welcome, Isaak."

He'd just settled back into work when there was a knock at his door. "Back so soon?" he called out. It didn't surprise him.

But when the door opened and Rudolfo entered, he *was* surprised. The lord of the Ninefold Forest rarely put in appearances in his shop. But now, the man walked in, his eyes haunted by the circles of sleeplessness beneath them. The Gypsy Scout behind him took up a position outside the door as Rudolfo closed it. "Forgive my unannounced visit, Arch-Engineer Charles. I have matters to discuss with you."

Charles put down the wrench he'd been using. "No forgiveness required, Lord Rudolfo. Shall we retire to a more comfortable room for conversation?"

Rudolfo shook his head. "No, I would speak with you here. These are matters of great discretion."

He looks worried. And he should be, Charles reckoned. In the span of two years he'd inherited a lot of orphans and had taken on a tremendous labor on behalf of the light. And while he did, the Named Lands came apart around him. "You have my ear and my silence, Lord."

Rudolfo moved to a stool near Charles and sat upon it. He looked out of place in his silk jacket and green turban, surrounded by bits of broken mechanicals and scattered tools. "There is a type of steel so silver that it gives back a perfect reflection. The Marsh King's axe is made of such a metal. Are you familiar with it?"

Charles nodded. "Firstfall steel. Legend has it that it fell from the moon along with the Moon Wizard and his armies at the end of the Age of the Weeping Czars."

"Yes. Can you work with this steel?"

Charles paused to think. He could, but it was a rare metal. More rare than gold or platinum. "I could work with it," he said, "depending upon what you needed it worked into."

"The metal's reflective capacity exposes stealth magicks—even those built from blood. We learned this last year during the attack on the Firstborn Feast." When Rudolfo said the words, Charles saw his eyes darken.

Charles prided himself on anticipating needs and already, he started nodding. "Some kind of device that would take advantage of those properties, then?"

Rudolfo offered a tight smile. "Yes."

Charles started to wonder why and stopped. *We've already been breached.* It was the fear and doubt upon his face, the sleeplessness in his eyes. "I would need the metal. It's extremely hard to come by. A handful of the wealthiest families in the Named Lands might have a few pieces of it. There's more, of course, buried at Windwir."

"Windwir is out of reach to us now," Rudolfo said. "But my procurement agents are quietly in place and at your disposal. See Isaak for a fresh code book."

Charles hesitated, then offered up the truth he wanted to withhold. "This could take time, Lord."

Rudolfo sighed. "We don't have time, Charles. Just do your best."

"I will do my best, Lord." Already, he was thinking of the design and whether or not lenses could be fashioned using the mirrors to reflect back through them in a type of spectacle that could be worn. He looked to his drawing pad. "While we look for the metal, I'll give thought to some design specifications."

Rudolfo stood. "Excellent. Two final things and I'll leave you to your work."

Charles waited, taking in the slight man. *He's frightened now, but this will only add fierceness to him later.*

"As you know, I am considering the potential of a standing army."

Yes, Charles thought. He'd been in the room that night, and he'd seen the teeth that consideration had brought to Rudolfo's soul. Change was certainly the path life took, but it was never as simple as it sounded. "It may become necessary, Lord."

Rudolfo nodded and looked away. "It may indeed. If it does—and if it has any chance of standing against this Y'Zirite threat to the west—it will need magickal and mechanical assistance."

Yes. And yet all of the war-making knowledge had been burned out at Windwir. *All but what I carry in my head.* Charles sighed. "I do not wish to make war engines, Rudolfo."

Rudolfo's eyes snapped back onto Charles, and there was a fire suddenly ignited there. "Nor do I, Charles, but I will not lose all that we build here. I will guard it whatever way I must."

What had they called the Gypsy King? Charles stretched his memory back to the conversations he'd overheard on the return journey from the Blood Temple. *Shepherd of the light?* But he knew the man meant more than just the library and its mechanicals. He meant the boy, too, who had appeared here in the middle of his life. Charles wasn't sure what to say. "I will give it thought. Most of what we kept hidden is lost now."

"Consideration is all I ask," Rudolfo said. "Work with Lysias and Aedric. I am only interested in protecting the Ninefold Forest."

Charles could see that on the man's face. But now, even as he read it there, it vanished, hidden behind a smile. "Thank you for your time, Arch-Engineer."

Rudolfo moved toward the door. He put his hand on the latch, and Charles remembered something. "Lord Rudolfo?"

He turned. "Yes?"

"There was another matter you wished to discuss with me."

Rudolfo thought for a moment, his brow furrowing. "Oh. Yes. I'm . . . concerned . . . about Isaak. He's asking a lot of unusual questions and seems preoccupied. And this matter with the message bird is worrisome." He paused. "Keep good watch over him, Charles."

Even Rudolfo's noticed it. Charles nodded. "I will, Lord."

Then, Rudolfo slipped from the room and Charles turned to his drawing pad.

He sketched for an hour, laying out specifications for a type of heavy spectacle, then tried a spyglass and a handful of other variants, but his mind kept coming back to his metal child and his ten thousand questions. When Rudolfo had asked after him, he'd seen the concern on his face. It was a type of love, Charles knew, and he wondered at it.

Why do I not feel love for my metal children? He could not answer that question without following more threads backward in time than he could afford in this moment. The Franci certainly could tell him after a few hours upon their analyst benches. They could give him many theories, not the least of which was that they were machines, designed for a purpose and powered by a sunstone, running scripts written by men.

But I have made a machine who wishes he could dream.

And even with that thought, he did not feel anything beyond pride and curiosity. Nothing quite as strong as affection, yet enough for him to do what needed doing for their care and to sometimes enjoy their company.

Perhaps, Charles thought, it was enough for now.

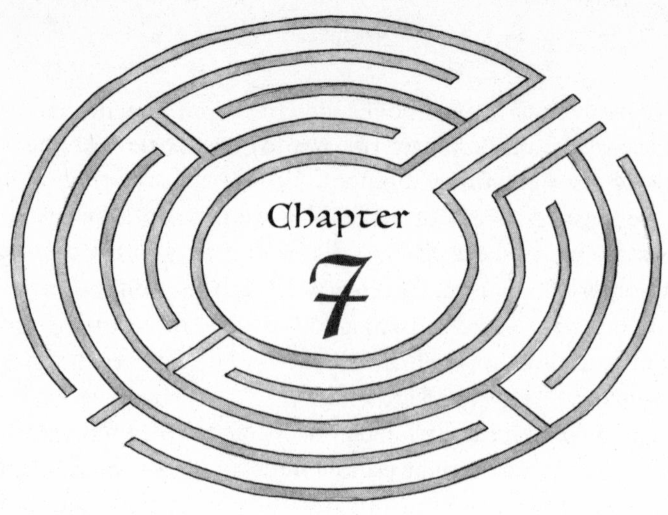

Chapter 7

Jin Li Tam

The courtyard on the south side of the library was a mad press of people as Foresters and refugees alike gathered for the dedication of the west-facing wing.

Jin Li Tam stood between the pillars of the western patio and bounced on her heels to keep Jakob amused while Rudolfo talked quietly with Aedric and Isaak. Jakob had been fussy of late after being so long a quiet baby, but she suspected that his first teeth were coming in.

I will ask Lynnae for teething powders. The girl had spent the last few months working with the River Woman and seemed to have an aptitude for the work. The River Woman herself had referred to her as an apt apprentice at least twice, both times bringing a blush to the girl's cheeks.

Thinking of Lynnae, she glanced around the front lines of the crowd to see if she could find her. When she singled her out, standing between the River Woman and her father, Lysias, Jin Li Tam flashed a smile that was quickly returned. Then, she turned back to Rudolfo and the others.

"It's time, Lord Rudolfo," Isaak said.

Ahead of them, the crowd built. This first wing was small, but in these times, small victories had to be celebrated as they were achieved. There at the base of the stone steps, wagons of food and wine stood ready for the feast to follow. After eighteen months of construction and a near-constant stream of books flowing from the mechoservitors' pens, they'd reclaimed some tiny part of what had been lost at Windwir.

And today marks two years.

She stepped to the side of the podium and felt pride as her husband stepped forward. He held a single sheet of scribbled notes in his hand and glanced to her and Jakob as he placed the paper on the flat, wooden surface. Then, he looked to Isaak and Aedric before clearing his voice.

"Two years ago," he began, "we all watched the sky and lamented that loss of light that was Windwir's pyre." He glanced to Isaak again, and Jin saw how carefully he chose his words. "Evil men with terrible intent used the Androfrancines' knowledge against them, and in doing so, changed our world."

She heard the timbre in his voice as he projected it over the crowd. Watching them, she could see the rapt attention upon their faces as they listened to their king. *They love him,* she realized. And she knew he and his family had earned that love over two millennia in this place. She'd seen that love poured out—even extended to her, especially since Jakob's birth—since she'd first come to the Ninefold Forest nearly two years ago.

She could remember pondering that charismatic Gypsy King and what one of his young Gypsy Scouts had told her in those early days. *He always knows the right path to take . . . and he always takes it.*

Not so anymore. She could see the doubt in his eyes, and sometimes, in their late-night murmurings, he would whisper his fears to her while she held him close. And though she did not say it, she felt it, too. The world had changed with the Desolation of Windwir and had kept changing from there.

People were applauding, and Jakob stirred awake in her arms. She felt a stab of guilt and looked up. Had he finished so soon? She looked to him and he appeared to be paused, finger raised to make another comment. She scanned the crowed, glancing again toward Lynnae.

She paused.

Just left of Lynnae stood a young man with close-cropped hair, and in a sea of smiles and clapping, his face was sober and his hands were at his sides. He was staring at the central pillar of the portico.

Rudolfo continued speaking, and she followed the young man's eyes. Something shimmered there, and she opened her mouth to shout.

The light was white and followed by a hot fist of wind and sound that shattered her ears. Something large and metal and fast impacted her and the world spun as she felt long metal arms encircling her, pulling her and Jakob close as heat billowed around them. She heard cracking as the pillar collapsed and the roof followed. She heard rock hitting metal and bellows rasping. She choked and sobbed.

The dust and smoke settled, and Jakob's wail rose up to join the screams and cries of the wounded and bereaved.

A reedy voice whispered in her ear. "Safe," he said. His voice had an odd lilt to it, and she heard popping and grinding deep in his chest cavity.

The world wobbled around her, and she fought its graying, forcing herself to move as best she could, shifting Jakob. "Isaak?" she asked.

But the metal man did not answer.

Neb

Outside the cave, kin-wolves slunk about, casting shadows by the light of a blue-green moon as a warm wind moaned down the canyons of the ruined city. They'd been out since the sun dropped, though they'd not approached as yet. Still, when the wind dipped, he could hear their claws upon the ancient, decimated street.

Odd. They do not howl.

Behind him, the woman stirred, and he turned to face her. Her fever had broken early in the day, telling him that his poultice and powders were doing their work. More and more, she moved and mumbled, her eyes moving behind closed lids. Neb went to her now and drew his canteen, unscrewing the cap.

He'd found three sources of water on the quick scouting runs he'd allowed himself since securing them in the cave. In the morning, he would need to make another run if she kept taking the water.

Placing a hand beneath her head, he lifted it and put the mouth of the canteen against her lower lip. Her lips parted by reflex, and he tipped the water into her mouth. The skin on the back of her neck felt cool and smooth now in his hands.

Her eyes fluttered and opened. They went wide, and he saw that they were a light green. She started to struggle, her mouth opening as she pulled in the breath to shout. When she did, it was a hoarse sound but in a language he did not recognize, and her wrestling was too weak for any kind of effectiveness. He waited, holding the canteen to her mouth once more.

"I can't understand you," he said, keeping his voice low and quiet.

Her eyebrows furrowed, bending the scars on her forehead. "Understand?" she asked.

He heard the snuffling outside now and pressed the canteen into her hands. Lifting his thorn rifle, he moved back to the mouth of the cave in time to see a large shadow retreating from the stones he'd piled at the front of the cave. He took aim and squeezed the bulb, listening to the hiss and cough of the thorn as it exited the rifle and closed the distance between them. He could not tell if the poisoned missile clattered off against stone and glass or if it found its mark in the flank of the kin-wolf.

He turned back and saw the woman pulling herself weakly from the blanket. She wasn't getting far, but the fear on her face was unmistakable. Neb moved slowly toward her, crouching nearby as she tried to pull herself up with trembling arms. Her clothing, wet from sweat, clung to her, and once more, Neb found himself averting his eyes. He thought perhaps the scars upon her arms and neck and face would snare his eyes, but in truth, each line of images pulled toward the curved parts of her he sought to avoid.

Neb swallowed. "You understand Landlish?"

She stopped, her eyes going wide for a moment. She turned to him. "Yes." She paused, and when she spoke again, her voice was hesitant and uncertain. "But . . . it has been a very long time."

She settled back now, still eyeing him with suspicion. But when he extended the canteen, she took it and drank from it. He watched as her eyes broke contact with him here and there to take in her surroundings. Each time, he knew she marked some detail.

She is a scout of some kind. Keeping his voice even and low, he asked her the first question that came to mind. "Where are you from?"

"Far away," she said. "But that doesn't matter." Her eyes narrowed. "Are you the Abomination?"

The other woman called me that. He did not know how to answer, but the questioning look on his face must have been sufficient. She continued. "The one called Nebios Homeseeker?"

He felt the blood leave his face as the hair on his arms and neck rose. "I'm Neb. How do you know my—?"

She leaned forward, interrupting him, her eyes suddenly wide and wild. "You're in grave danger. My sisters hunt you even now, and through you, the mechoservitors. You must go."

Neb blinked, his memory pulling him back to his encounter with the carved kin-raven and the woman in the Wastes who had spoken to him. *We see you there as well in your glass cave.* He thought of them, magicked and racing across the Wastes, and then he recalled the phial of blood magicks this woman had in her pack. "And what of you?" he asked. "Are you here hunting me as well?" *And how is it you can use the magicks and not be killed by their potency?*

Their eyes met. "I was not hunting you, though it is what I was sent to do." She looked away. "I have other matters to attend to."

He looked to her bandaged shoulder and saw the fresh blood seeping through. "I don't think you'll be attending to those matters any time soon."

Even as he said it, he could see the pain and weariness registering on her face. She settled back into the makeshift bed. "You must leave," she said again. "My sisters will tend to me."

Neb glanced toward the mouth of the cave. The kin-wolves had gone quiet, and that meant it was time for him to take up his post. He looked back to the girl. There was urgency in her voice and written into her furrowed brow. "Why would your sisters wish me harm?" Another question dug into him with the sharpness of an Entrolusian cavalry spur. "And why do they call me *Abomination*?"

"They do," she said, "because of what you are. But they need to stop the metal dreamers first, and only you can find them."

"And why are you telling me this?"

Her eyelids drooped, and her voice faltered. "So that you will listen to me and leave while you can."

She closed her eyes now, and her breathing became heavy. He looked once more to the mouth of the cave, then set himself to changing her dressing and rebandaging her wound. She stirred twice and tried to push him away, but he easily held her in place long enough to finish his work.

Then, he slipped back to the mouth of the cave. He fished the cloth-wrapped icon from his pouch and studied it, careful not to touch it. He had no idea what it was or how it did what it had done, but he did not doubt for a moment that it had shown him one of the mechoservitors who had fled Sanctorum Lux, and that he'd seen Winters, though she looked foreign to him, cleaned and dressed like any other woman in the Named Lands instead of wearing the dirt and ash of her people. The strange carving had even reached beyond the grave to his father Hebda. And he'd seen the women who hunted him, too.

More importantly, they'd seen him. And if this girl spoke the truth, they wanted him to help them find the metal dreamers.

He put the wrapped image away and thought for a moment about pulling out the plain box and the silver crescent that lay within it. The moon was up, and the canticle would be clear. He could taste the code buried in that song, could feel the equations and formulas within the numbers it hid. He knew it lay there, ancient and beguiling, and that somehow the mechoservitors had found a dream within it.

The metal dreamers.

The idea of the metal men dreaming intrigued him. He'd spent a good deal of time with Isaak during their early days at the Seventh Forest Manor. He'd found him different from the others, somehow set apart after his experience with the blood magicks at Windwir. Of all his kind, Isaak seemed the most advanced, and Neb had watched fascinated as the metal man became more and more human each day.

He had passed Isaak the scroll from Sanctorum Lux, and he believed that it was a copy of the metal dream. He wondered if the metal man had run the script. If he had, what had he seen?

And what about it brings these strangely carved women, hunting us in the Wastes?

His eyes went back to the box, and he glanced to the sleeping girl. He craved the song in its fullness, but knew if he used the crescent, the woman might hear it as well. And he could not trust her. Not yet. Certainly she'd seemed sincere in her effort to convince him to flee. And he believed her—believed his own ears, having heard them say so—that her sisters hunted him. Some small voice in the back of his head assured him that he did not want to be found by them.

Still, how could he leave?

It was a question for another time because there *was* time. Tomorrow, he would check her wounds and reassess.

He closed his eyes and called up a map of the Wastes by memory and recalled what geography he'd seen when he saw and heard the Blood Scouts. The closest had been the one at the well—at least a week by the root. But he could not be certain that the blood magicks didn't cut that time drastically. Regardless, there was time. He could not afford to panic.

"Panic," Renard had told him again and again, "is the Waste's swiftest killer."

They do because of what you are.

Her words were cryptic. How or why anyone could see him as an abomination eluded him, but nothing he'd experienced these past two years had made any kind of sense. Rationally or not, it was happening.

Even his very father—dead now these two years—had cast his own warning.

Neb shook his head and moved his focus to the song. He could hear the crescent in its lockbox, and again he resisted the urge to open it and cradle it against his ear.

Outside, the kin-wolves broke their silence and bayed as the swollen stars guttered overhead. The canticle was indeed loud tonight.

Settling into his dark corner, thorn rifle laid carefully across his knees, Neb watched the night and listened for the dream beneath each note.

Rudolfo

They burned bonfires in the courtyard to illuminate the rubble, and Rudolfo paced and cursed as the rescuers dug the last survivors and bodies from the wreckage.

He stung from a dozen cuts and burns; he ached from the same number of bruises. His right arm hung broken in a sling, and his stomach clenched and unclenched as rage and anguish washed through him.

Be alive.

Twice, he'd tried to move past the Gypsy Scouts set to keep him from the wreckage. Both times, their hands upon his chest had been enough to subdue him, though the first time he'd raised fist to them before he caught himself.

Be alive, he willed again.

Once more his mind veered into that place he could not bear it to go. His first thought was of them when he first stirred to wakefulness in the medico tent, and he'd felt the world shift and slide when Aedric, battered, burned and bleeding himself, told him that they still hadn't found his wife and child. Or Isaak.

How long ago had that been?

Hours.

A white bird flitted back from the blast zone and was caught in the catch net. He'd seen it happen three times now this night and had watched the medicos race out. He heard shouting, and a team set out even now at a sprint, carrying a stretcher between them.

He saw Lysias barking orders to teams of refugees as they moved books by wheelbarrow around to the entrances of the subbasements.

He'd been told that the general's men had extinguished the flames quickly, forming a bucket brigade within moments of the blast, even as the Gypsy Scouts took up a perimeter and rescuers began pulling out survivors. Of course, he'd been unaware of this, and he still felt the knot on the back of his head. As close as he was to the explosion, he had no idea how he had survived.

He also had no idea how it could have happened. After Ria's infiltration, he'd doubled the watch. And still, somehow, someone had done this terrible deed. There were over thirty dead now and three times that number of wounded.

And still they dug. The entire roof and front portion of the wing had collapsed in the blast.

I did not listen to her. Ria had warned him, and he'd not listened. Certainly, some part of him wondered if she herself hadn't instigated this attack. And yet even as he thought it, he knew it couldn't be. She would not put him at such risk. Despite everything, she had still spent tremendous resources to concoct Jakob's cure—and he'd heard the reverence in her tone when she spoke of the Child of Promise, the Great Mother in their gospel. The very book itself lay open upon his desk, and already he'd marked passages that seemed to speak prophetically about his wife and son.

He looked to the pile of rubble, the devastated front third of the wing, and wondered again what kind of device could do this and how it could come to be here, in his forest.

A scout approached at top speed, his rainbow-colored uniform torn and smeared with ash. He inclined his head to Rudolfo and to Aedric, his face lined with worry. "We've found the mechoservitor."

Rudolfo felt his heart race. "Isaak?"

The scout nodded. "He's . . . nonfunctional."

Rudolfo's stomach fell away, and his head suddenly ached. "Nonfunctional?" He glanced to his left, where Charles labored under a makeshift tent, moving between two of the most damaged mechoservitors. Over half had been damaged in the blast, though most superficially. "Take the arch-engineer. Tell him it's Isaak."

The scout nodded and took off at a run.

Rudolfo sighed. "Gods," he muttered.

"Or devils," Aedric answered. "I have magicked the scouts, and they are scouring both town and forest, General. I'll wager that Machtvolk bitch has something to do with it."

Rudolfo shook his head. "I don't think so, Aedric."

But who? Whoever it was, he would find them and—

Another scout approached at full sprint. "We have them, Lord Rudolfo! They're alive!"

Rudolfo felt the wind go out of him. The world slid away, and his legs went to water. Gravity pulled him down and he went to his knees. *They're alive.* The building rage slipped from his clenched fist for just a moment, and he felt his face flush as tears threatened. He blinked them away and realized Aedric's hand was upon his shoulder, firm and much like Gregoric's had been so many times before.

He heard himself breathing, and each gasp seemed a sob. He swallowed against it and forced himself to his feet. "Take me to them." He stared at his first captain, his grief suddenly frozen into resolve and anger.

Aedric opened his mouth and closed it. "Yes, General."

They made their way around the edges and then down a makeshift path through the debris. As they walked, Rudolfo fixed his eyes ahead.

I did not listen. I did not protect them. It was sharper than any scout knife, and it twisted in him. She'd proven to him how vulnerable he was when she snuck into his forest, into his home, into the very room where he met with her evangelists. Before that, she had sent her kin-raven, beseeching her sister to bear warning to him.

Another path that eluded him.

He found his footing and increased his pace as Aedric guided him by his good arm. Ahead, he saw the men and women gathered around Isaak. The metal man's head was twisted at an impossible angle, his chest cavity crushed and his left jeweled eye dangling free on gold wire. He felt another sob shake him. Then, he saw them lifting his wailing boy from the ruins, and Rudolfo faltered in his run.

The cry was wrong; it was agonizing pain. And the blood on Jakob's blankets wrenched Rudolfo at some deep place in himself that he did not know existed until now. He pulled away from Aedric and then sprinted ahead.

Now hands were lifting Jin Li Tam from the rubble, and when she looked to Rudolfo, he saw wild panic and grief upon her face. Two medicos intercepted Rudolfo. "No further, Lord."

"My son," he shouted, pushing against them.

"A ruptured eardrum, I'll wager," the River Woman told him, placing a hand on his chest. "Lord Rudolfo."

"I need to see them," he said.

"They will be fine. They need to be cared for, and you have work to do." Her voice was firm and it surprised him, though it shouldn't have. She'd pulled him from his mother and into the world when she was a younger lass.

Rudolfo looked past her and the medicos. Jin was being forced into a stretcher, her hands stretched out for Jakob. The River Woman followed his eye. "Give the child to his mother—she'll better soothe him until we can get the powders on him." She gave the Gypsy King another stern look and went back to her waiting work.

Rudolfo looked to Isaak. Charles had arrived and was running his hands over the metal man's chassis and head, checking the limbs. He saw the matter-of-fact manner with which he did his work and marveled at it. *If I were to look at it as such,* Rudolfo thought, *how would I behave now?*

He pondered for a moment and looked up to Aedric. "Bring Lysias over," he said.

Aedric gave him a puzzled look but heeded. He whistled to a scout and sent him careening through the rubble. Rudolfo knew the younger man wanted to ask—his father, Gregoric, most likely *would* have asked. And would've privately let Rudolfo know in clear words his opinions on the matter.

I miss you, Gregoric. Still, he saw his fallen friend in the face of Gregoric's son, and he knew that the father's strength was in Aedric.

Rudolfo looked to Aedric now. "How long to muster the West Brigade of the Wandering Army?"

Aedric's eyebrows furrowed. "A day, maybe two."

Rudolfo nodded. "Good. You'll call them up tonight after I speak with the two of you."

Even as he said it, Lysias approached. The general's eyes were filled with worry and red from smoke. "Lord Rudolfo? Are they safe, then?"

Rudolfo shook his head. "None of us is safe, Lysias." He paused. "*General* Lysias."

He saw the look of surprise in the old soldier's eyes. "Lord?"

"Swear fealty to me and mine, General, and serve my family and my people well." Something caught in Rudolfo's voice, and the words sounded foreign to him as he said them. "Build me an army to keep my borders," he said.

"You have my oath, Lord," Lysias said.

Rudolfo looked to Aedric. "Lysias will raise them up; the Gypsy Scouts will train them. Bear witness, First Captain."

"Aye, General Rudolfo."

"Until they are ready, the Wandering Army will watch out for us. I want the Western Brigade on the line in three days' time." Rudolfo wanted to close his eyes for these next words, but he knew he could not. It went against everything his people had believed these two thousand years in the forest, and he had to look them each in the eye as he said it.

"The borders of the Ninefold Forest," Rudolfo said, "are now closed to passage. Send birds at dawn to all, kin-clave and foe."

Aedric and Lysias exchanged glances. Aedric spoke first. "Are you certain, Lord Rudolfo?"

Am I certain? He heard the wailing of his son and the cries of the frightened and wounded around him. He heard Charles cursing and grunting as he manhandled Isaak onto the stretcher with the help of two scouts.

He remembered the anguish in Jin Li Tam's eyes.

"Yes," Rudolfo said, letting the wrath show in his voice. "I *am* certain.

Vlad Li Tam

The sun rose behind him as Vlad Li Tam rowed the skiff into the harbor. Already, the scant remains of his iron armada built steam as they prepared to leave. Even in the dusky rose of morning, he could see the remnant of his family as they scurried along the upper and lower docks, moving the last of their lives back onto the ships.

Six months and so little to show for it. Yet, even as he said it, his heart felt full. These last nights, rowing out to where the ghost awaited, had added something indefinable to him—something he'd lived without for too long. The compulsion of it was frightening, especially given that this love he felt was for a twisting, writhing mass of tentacled light. Not for the first time, he wondered if perhaps something had happened to him those moments when he first encountered the d'jin, so fresh from his time beneath Ria's knife, with his hands upon the throat of his first grandson.

He sighed and worked the oars, his shoulders creaking with his increased activity of late.

They'd found nothing here, but there were sure to be clues elsewhere.

After all, there had been those ships. And unfamiliar, dark-robed men. And now, though his heart drew him to sea for other purposes, his brain saw clearly that whoever was out there was not coming back to this place. And despite the strange feelings that now pulled him, relentless as a tide, Vlad knew that discovering the nationality of those ships and those men meant discovering the true hands behind the fall of Windwir.

And behind the surgery that cut my family from the world.

It wasn't that these new sensations trumped that loss—or even mitigated it. No, the loss was there, and if his soul went to it he could feel the hollow ache, like a tongue to the socket of a lost tooth.

He slowed his rowing and watched the sun lift up from the ocean.

Then, he looked back over his shoulder to the docks, adjusting his pull on the oars to line up with where Baryk stood waiting.

As he slid alongside, the old warpriest grabbed the rope Vlad tossed and tied the small boat off. "We'll be ready to sail in two hours," he said. His brow furrowed. "Is it still called 'sailing' when there are no sails involved?"

Vlad shrugged and stood carefully, grasping the edge of the dock as he climbed out of the boat. "How are spirits?"

"Fine. Nervous. Excited." Baryk's chuckle was more of a bark. "Should I ask *you* that question?"

He'd told the warpriest about the ghost, uncomfortable with the telling but even less comfortable with leading his family off to follow such a flight of fancy without speaking to someone first. Someone he trusted; someone who would not think him utterly mad. And Baryk was a metaphysick, though moderate in his beliefs. The city-state he hailed from—Paltos—was one of few in the Named Lands that not only allowed but encouraged a religious system, the people worshiping a loose pantheon of the more benevolent Younger Gods. When the Androfrancines had been in power, they'd avoided that corner of the Outer Emerald Coast and had encouraged others to do the same.

"We know their ghosts are in the waters," Baryk had said. "I've not seen them myself, but I've heard the sailors tell of it. Your own daughter is named for them." Then he'd offered a reassuring smile. "Who am I—and who is anyone else—to question what you've seen or experienced?"

Vlad had been comforted by the man's response.

Now, he returned the chuckle. "It was a good night. But she was restless. I think she's eager to leave."

She. How did he know this? He blinked at his own words and bit his lower lip. He did know it. And not for the first time, he realized there were many ways of knowing a thing. He stood and stretched on the dock.

Baryk studied him. "You know that some of the older children are whispering about this. They know something is afoot. They've watched you watching the sea, and now these midnight rowings."

Vlad nodded. He did know this and he'd expected it. "Let them whisper. They will still follow."

"Aye," Baryk said, "they will, though they may quietly think you mad."

I think myself mad. But he didn't say it. He held that in and turned it over and over like a Rufello puzzle. It was possible—even likely—that he saw nothing at all there in the sea. Perhaps something had broken in him during his time of captivity and kin-healing. Perhaps he'd concocted a beautiful singing spirit to pull him away from his pain and into the deep waters where he could find some kind of peace. Perhaps he was in love now with the notion of forgetting beneath the waves. Regardless, he knew the power of perception, and if somehow he was wrong in what he saw and experienced, that would work its way out as he pursued it. He vaguely recalled a Francine arch-behaviorist who'd written a slender volume on the subject of hallucination as a means of the psyche healing itself.

"What they think," Vlad Li Tam said, summoning firmness to his voice, "is what they think. We leave as soon as the ships are loaded."

Baryk nodded. "I've seen to your things. They're in your cabin on the flagship."

Vlad forced a smile. "Thank you, Baryk. I'll be in the temple until we leave."

Baryk clapped Vlad on the shoulder. "I'll see to the ships."

Vlad left his son-in-law and climbed the stairs slowly, inclining his head to those members of his family who passed him. He reached the top of the low bluff and climbed the marble steps up into the white building.

Once inside, he made his way to the top of the building, entering the large domed observation room on the fourth floor.

He walked to the railing and looked down, expecting vertigo and a memory of screams to overtake him and drive him to his knees.

Neither happened.

Vlad Li Tam stood still and listened. Outside, he heard the first whistles of those ships that were loaded and ready to depart.

"I'm sorry," he said quietly to the ghosts of his family.

Then he stood silent and listened for absolution in the stillness of the room. He waited, not even able to find his tears, until Baryk's runner found him and told him that the last longboat awaited him.

Then Vlad Li Tam turned his back upon those ghosts and gave himself to the chasing of another.

Winters

In the first days following the explosion at the library, the city of Rachyle's Rest was awash with panic, and Winters did her best to stay out of the way and help where she could.

Most of that help was filling in for Isaak to keep the work of the library moving forward while at the same time launching repairs.

Charles had hidden himself away with the broken mechoservitors, rarely leaving his workshop. The metal men that remained were already doing what they could to replace the volumes lost in that brief blaze, and fresh crews of refugee laborers had already cleared the rubble and begun repairs to the damaged wing.

Of course, it did not surprise Winters at all that even as they worked, the skies above the Ninefold Forest broke open and the first of the rains began to fall.

And it also did not surprise her that her first summons to the Seventh Forest Manor after the blast came in the midst of that first deluge. Careful of the gathering puddles of water and the mud sucking at her boots, Winters ran through the downpour in the gray of midmorning.

As she ran, she watched the city around her. Soldiers from the local brigade of the Wandering Army stood at key locations or patrolled the streets. And as she approached the manor, she saw a half-squad of scouts administering their powders, fading into the wash of water as they raced for the woods. They were running the forest day and night now, she knew, enforcing Rudolfo's new edict and looking for any clues as to who caused the explosion.

The rainfall lightened as Winters approached the gates to the manor, and she nodded to the guards as she passed. The massive house loomed ahead, rising above the rooftops of the city. Five minutes later, she was barefoot, dripping wet and standing outside the door of Rudolfo's study, catching what water she could with a rough cotton towel.

The Gypsy Scout at the door ushered her in.

Rudolfo and Jin Li Tam waited in the sitting area with Aedric. Between them, a pitcher of wine and a platter of cheeses sat untouched. They stood as she entered, and Rudolfo gestured to an empty armchair near the fire.

She shook her head. "I'm soaked," she said. "I'd better stand."

"Nonsense," Rudolfo said. "It's only water. Join us, Winters."

She paused, suddenly mindful of their faces. All of them were bruised or cut, and each had dark circles beneath their eyes. Rudolfo's arm was in a sling, and he held the Y'Zirite gospel in his free hand.

Winters sat and looked to Jin Li Tam. "How is Jakob?"

She watched a mother's sorrow flush the woman's pale face. "He may lose some hearing from the ruptured ear, but otherwise, he's fine."

Winters nodded slowly and wondered why she'd been summoned. She suspected the book in Rudolfo's hand had something to do with it.

Rudolfo cleared his voice and she looked to him. "We are at a difficult intersection," he said, "and desire your input." He held the book up. "You've read this?"

Again, she nodded. "I have, Lord." She glanced quickly around the room and noticed with a start the look of subdued anger on Aedric's face.

Rudolfo continued. "It appears that my wife and my son feature heavily in this elaborate mythology."

"They appear to, Lord," she concurred.

Rudolfo started to move his broken arm, winced, then put down the book. He stroked his beard. "I've new word from your sister," he said. "A renewed pledge of aid and a . . . *difficult* . . . request."

"Not difficult," Aedric said, interrupting with uncharacteristic anger. "Unheard-of."

Winters watched as the two men made eye contact, exchanging silent words between them. Aedric looked away first.

"Difficult," Rudolfo said again with more firmness in his voice. He paused. "I've read it through three times and have reached the conclusion that if your sister truly believes this book she can in no way intend harm to me or my family."

Now Jin Li Tam interjected. "Still, they could have engineered this event merely to convince us of this. They provide Winters a copy of the gospel along with a warning. And then shortly after they supposedly leave our forests, this"—Winters watched her reaching for the right word—"*attack* takes place."

Rudolfo's eyebrows raised. "This attack would have killed you both if Isaak hadn't intervened."

Winters started, looking up. "Isaak?" She'd known he'd been damaged heavily—perhaps irreparably, she'd heard—in the attack, but she'd not heard this.

Jin Li Tam looked away, her voice quiet. "He put himself between us and the blast, then shielded Jakob and me from the falling stonework." When she looked back to her husband, her eyes were hard and narrow. "But it still could be a clever machination. Something intended to bring us to this very moment."

"This is my concern, as well, Lady," Aedric said.

"We are *all* concerned about this," Rudolfo said, "and yet." He paused, took a deep breath. "I think she is sincere. Gods know I might be wrong, but I suspect this new threat rises in the south, not the north. Esarov and Erlund have honored kin-clave with investigations of their own, cooperating fully with our own intelligence efforts. Pylos and Turam have not responded to our requests, but we did not expect them to. And Ria's newest message claims her scouts have taken three prisoners, magicked and fleeing across our Prairie Sea."

Machtvolk scouts in the Prairie Sea? She studied Rudolfo's face, knowing this could not possibly please him. Still, all she saw was a wash of weariness and something she thought might be resolve. Winters blushed when she realized their eyes had met and held for a moment. But when she looked away from his, red-rimmed and dark-shadowed, she realized in hindsight the other emotion she'd seen there. *Fear.*

The room became silent and Winters shifted uncomfortably in the chair, still feeling the water from her hair as it traced its way down her shoulders and back underneath the dress she wore. She wondered if she should say something, but even as she pondered, Rudolfo spoke again.

"We've called you here to ask two questions of you, Lady Winteria."

He speaks formally to me now, she noted. "Yes Lord?"

He took a deep breath. "I know your people have changed; I know your sister is a largely unknown factor. But I need to know: Do you believe she or her Machtvolk would do harm to my family?"

Winters thought about it, remembering the look of adoration upon Ria's face when she first laid eyes on Jakob those months ago, and the same look upon the evangelists' faces when their Great Mother and Child of Promise entered the room during Rudolfo's audience with them. Then, she pondered the words of the gospel. When she looked up to meet Rudolfo's eyes again, she hoped her answer was true. "I do not believe they will harm you or your family, Lord Rudolfo. In this matter, I think their attempts to help are genuine. But I could be—"

He raised his good arm. "We all could be wrong," he said. "I only look for your sense of it. Of all here, you understand the more . . . *metaphysical* . . . aspects of your people."

She heard Aedric shifting and looked over to him. The man's knuckles were white on the arms of his chair, and she could see the care with which he guarded his facial expression. She looked back to Jin Li Tam and then Rudolfo. "Why do you ask, Lord?"

More furtive glances between the husband and wife. "Because," he finally said, "they've invited my wife and child to participate in a diplomatic mission behind their borders until such time as this new threat is identified and eradicated."

She felt the color drain from her face as her stomach lurched. "You're going to send them?" Now, Aedric's anger made sense to her, and she saw clearly how much more grave this moment was.

Rudolfo sighed. "If Lady Tam concurs. I've read the gospel. And though your people have been twisted into something very different from what you've known, I trust your judgment of them." He looked to Aedric, then Jin Li Tam again. "And we are uncovering evidence of a new, less careful network emerging from the war-ravaged south."

"I still believe this is folly, General," Aedric started, but Rudolfo cut him off with a hard look.

"Can you keep my son safe *here*, Aedric?" he asked, leaning forward suddenly. "*Can* you?" Winters heard the anger rising in the Gypsy King's voice, and it startled her. When the first captain said nothing, Rudolfo settled back into his chair. "I do not doubt for a moment that the Machtvolk are a threat to the Named Lands. But they do not at the moment appear to be a threat to us. Somehow, my house is tangled in their house and in their so-called gospel of a new Y'Zirite age." He paused. "And," he said, "their borders are secure. Their blood magicks are formidable."

Jin Li Tam looked to the two men. "It could not hurt for us to have a better sense of what is happening behind those borders."

As the woman spoke, Winters saw the careful mask she wore. *She is mistrustful.* "Then you will go?" she asked, her breath catching for a moment in her words. "You will take Jakob with you?"

Jin Li Tam nodded. "Aedric, too, along with a company of Rudolfo's best and strongest scouts."

Winters felt fear for them, cold as the rain that soaked her clothing despite the fire's warmth.

"This brings me to my second question for you, Lady Winteria," Rudolfo said. "I will be frank. Your sister has asked that you accompany them. I believe you would be invaluable to them, but I could never command such a thing of you."

And now she felt the fear herself, remembering that day Seamus made his sobbing confession to her and revealed the mark upon his breast. And that later day when she raised the Firstfall axe to Ria, losing it and her people. *He wants me to go.*

"I concur with my husband," Jin Li Tam said. Winters looked up. The woman inclined her head, her red braid shifting across her shoulder. "Your aid would be indispensable. You know the territory, the people."

Winters took a deep breath, feeling the weight of this new information as it settled onto her shoulders. It brought back memories of the Wicker Throne she'd carried to the Spire the day she had announced herself as the Marsh Queen. She remembered its weight, remembered the blood she'd shed for it through those biting leather straps.

In the end it was not hard at all for her to decide. That memory pulled her shoulders straight and she sat up. Her eyes met Rudolfo's, and she inclined her head slowly toward him.

"Of course I will go," Winteria bat Mardic, queen of the Marshfolk, said.

Petronus

Petronus whistled his horse faster and blinked the sweat from his eyes. They'd pushed the beasts to keep up with Geoffrus and his ragged band of root runners, remagicking the horses at least twice now for speed and stamina as they rode east in search of Neb. If they didn't slow soon, they would kill the beasts.

He watched the ease with which Geoffrus took the terrain in a long-legged lope, wondering how long the man could run like that.

The scattered platoon of Gray Guard rode hard with the half-company of Rudolfo's Gypsy Scouts, the rainbow uniforms of the scouts contrasting with the ash-colored guard against the drab desolation of the Churning Wastes. The sun was high now, and it glistened off the glass hills and razored dunes of the decimated cities that once covered this land. It approached winter just two hundred leagues east, and here, the sky blistered at noon.

It had been years since he'd been in the Wastes, and there was a tragic beauty in it that he did not miss. It was a stark reminder of the Wizard King's wrath but also a reminder of the strength of those scattered survivors, gathered together under the leadership of P'Andro

Whym to dig what could be saved from the ruins and ride west with it to the New World behind the Keeper's Gate. Both human achievements—a penchant for self-destruction and a tenacious will to survive that penchant.

He heard a whistle and looked up. Geoffrus was slowing and motioning for them to do the same. He pointed north as he did.

Petronus slowed his horse and looked. There, across the landscape, four robed figures moved, tossing dust or steam up behind them as they went. They moved fast, faster even than the root moved Geoffrus and his men. They were perhaps a league away, and he realized suddenly where he'd seen that loping run before.

Mechoservitors. Running in the Churning Wastes. Running toward the Keeper's Wall.

Instinctively, he raised an arm, but they paid him no mind.

He'd read the preliminary reports on the findings at Sanctorum Lux and knew about the metal man who had deactivated itself—the remains had been gone when the landing party of Tam survivors and Gypsy Scouts reached that burned-out ruin. And he'd heard about their so-called dream, though he wasn't clear exactly what they meant by it.

Somewhere in the Wastes, Charles's first generation of mechoservitors worked at something secretly, and he suspected that this strange figure, Hebda, knew more than he'd revealed in the hallucinations Petronus had experienced. As Pope, Petronus had made it his business to know every office and every ministry beneath his sanctioned oversight, and he'd heard nothing of this Office for the Preservation of the Light.

But he'd known Hebda's name, though he could not remember why he did.

The farther he moved away from the Wall, the more clear his memory became, though it still confused him. And even as his memory cleared, the dreamlike episodes ceased. He'd experienced neither vision nor dream since leaving their camp. Still, he knew enough. They'd charted his course, and something inside of him strongly believed that Arch-Behaviorist Hebda spoke the truth—Neb was in danger, and Petronus was compelled to act.

He'd not talked to the boy since that last day he'd seen him, there in the crowded silk pavilion of the last Androfrancine Council, Neb shaking with rage as Petronus called for an Androfrancine to take Sethbert's life and thus claim the ring and robes of office. He'd known the boy would've stepped forward—the Overseer had killed Neb's father when he brought desolation to Windwir—and Petronus had taken lengths to spare him that vengeful path. He winced as he recalled the day he excommunicated Neb, after months of faithful service leading the gravedigging of Windwir with the grace and care of an academy general.

It broke me to break him. Petronus swallowed the pain of that memory, trusting that he was right in the end—that the boy was made for more than backward dreaming.

Geoffrus and the others were speeding up now, and Petronus felt the heat of his horse between his thighs. Still, he whistled the roan forward and leaned low into the saddle.

As the landscape flashed past, he wondered what exactly they would find in the far east where these mechoservitors had run from. He wondered about the runners and he wondered about the mysterious man who doled out hallucinations and dreams like candies from a dark and hidden pocket.

And most of all, Petronus wondered if they would reach Neb in time for whatever it was that he smelled coming on the dead winds of the Churning Wastes.

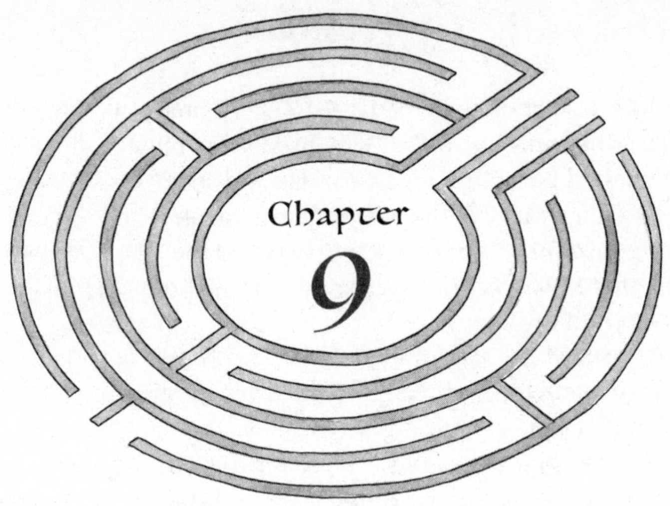

Charles

Charles blinked into his magnifying glass and bit his tongue as he worked the tweezers, inwardly cursing the clumsiness that age brought to his fingers.

He'd lost track of time now, these past days blurring into scattered hours of sleep here and there and meals taken hurriedly to the side of his workbench and the metal body stretched out upon it. Rudolfo occasionally stopped in to ask after Isaak, and at least once, Jin Li Tam had also snuck in, magicked scouts warbling the air around her as they shadowed her every movement. He remembered that they'd asked questions of him, faces lined with worry; but he couldn't remember what those questions entailed now, nor could he recall the short, sharp answers he'd provided.

Initially, he thought he'd lost the mechoservitor. Now, he was convinced that the metal man would function, though he'd cannibalized the two others in order to accomplish even that much. The gears would whir. The bellows would pump. All of the mechanical parts would do their work.

But would it still be Isaak?

The fine, narrow strips of ancient paper-thin steel that comprised Isaak's scripting scrolls had confounded him with its twisted tangle—along with what else he discovered there.

Somehow, they had fused themselves around the sunstone that powered his boiler, and it was not a new development—it appeared to be the result of past trauma, perhaps left over from the Seven Cacophonic Deaths. That made the most sense. Until now, Isaak had refused Charles—and anyone else—access to his inner workings. He performed his own maintenance, using mirrors and tools from the pouch he kept nearby at all times.

It made sense. *I would trust less, too, if I'd been used in such a way.*

And now, with the work just moments from being complete, Charles wondered if his metal child would be . . . *himself* . . . when he fired the boiler and powered the scrolls. He frowned at the thought, exploring the odd emotion that snared him. He'd spent days bent over this mechanical, his back and legs and arms aching from too long on his feet, hunched over the work. Why? He'd not spent so much time over the others. Indeed, he'd scrapped them as needed to bring back this one.

Because Isaak is . . . special. This machine had wept for a ravaged city and had put himself in harm's way to save the lives of his—Charles reached for the word and found it—of his *family.*

He blinked again and suddenly realized his eyes were wet.

And now, if Isaak truly did still remain in that tangle of metal and wire, he would have to give him difficult news. And pass that same news to Rudolfo and the others.

The fused memory scrolls were functional, though Charles was uncertain exactly how that was possible. But the sunstone they were fused into now pulsed on borrowed time. There was no way to repair the hairline fracture Charles found there. And there was no way to replace the metal man's heart without also replacing the memory scrolls.

Sighing, Charles fired the boiler and waited for the steam to build. When Isaak whistled and hissed, he held his breath and hit the switch.

The bellows pumped, and the amber eyes fluttered open, rolling a bit as the shutters worked. The mouth flap opened and closed and the ear flaps bent. Closing the chest cavity, Charles spun the dial on the Rufello lock he'd installed there. He'd repaired all but the limp, and he'd added nothing extra but the lock. Knowing what this mechoservitor guarded so near his broken heart had compelled him.

He watched the mechanical twitch and listened for any grinding gears or high-pitched whistles that might betray yet more work. "Are you functional?"

Isaak sat up on the table and blinked. "Mechoservitor Three is functional and ready for duty."

Mechoservitor Three.

He felt his eyebrows furrowing. "What is your designation?"

"Designation Mechoservitor Three, Library Archives and Cataloging, Office of—" Isaak closed his mouth flap, then looked to Charles. The metal man shuddered, and he heard a grind within, followed by a popping sound. The jeweled eyes dimmed, then grew stronger. "I am Isaak, Father, but you know that."

Charles released his held breath and wiped his eyes. "I do know that."

Wisps of steam leaked from Isaak's exhaust grate. "Why do you weep, Father?" He looked around the room, saw the two mechanicals disassembled upon the other tables, and turned back to Charles, waiting for an answer.

What do I say? He wasn't sure himself. "I think I'm just glad to see you, Isaak."

"It is also agreeable to see you." Then, another pop, and once more the eyes dimmed and then brightened. Isaak surged to his feet. "The library," he said, his reedy voice laced with panic. "Lady Tam and Lord Jakob—"

Charles put a hand on Isaak's metal chest. It was still cool to the touch but warming quickly. "They are alive because of you." He paused. "And the library is under repair."

Isaak looked to the other two mechoservitors. "And my brothers?"

Charles shook his head. "I salvaged what I could from them to repair you. It was a difficult decision. We'll recover what we can from their memory scrolls, but their damage was extensive."

Isaak blinked now, and Charles saw the water leaking from the corner of his eyes. "They are permanently nonfunctional?"

Charles nodded. "Come sit with me," he said, and motioned his metal handiwork toward the plain wooden chairs near his crowded bookcases and guttering stove.

He pulled his chair close to Isaak and put a hand on the metal man's leg. "I have more unpleasant news, Isaak." *How do I say this?* He tried to tell himself it was merely a machine, but he knew better. "Isaak," he said, then surprised himself with his next word. "Son," he added. And now the water returned to his own eyes, and he sat with it for a moment while the metal man waited. In the end, he came back to science, as he ever had from childhood on. "You are aware of the inner workings of mechoservitor technology and the use of sunstones as a power source for your boiler?"

Isaak nodded.

"And you are aware, I'm sure, of the unusual nature of your own scripting mechanisms?"

Long metal fingers made their way slowly to the door in his chest, found the Rufello lock and paused. Isaak cocked his head.

"I installed that to keep your secret safe. It is a complex cipher known only to the two of us," Charles said, then brought the conversation back to the news he could not bear to deliver. "Because of the fusing, your memory scrolls are inextricably intertwined with your power source."

Isaak nodded again. "Yes, Father. I believe it is a result of the spell."

Charles offered a grim smile. "I concur. You were certainly not designed that way." He sighed. "I will simply be frank with you, Isaak. Your sunstone is cracked and there is no way to know when it will break, but exertion and overheating could bring it about sooner." He waited for the words to register. "I cannot replace it without irreparably damaging your memory scrolls."

Isaak's eye shutters flashed, and Charles watched another shudder take the metal man. "When it breaks I will become nonfunctional."

Charles nodded. "And I will do everything in my power to find a way around that outcome, but as yet there is no clear path ahead of me."

Isaak said nothing for a long while. When he spoke, Charles heard sorrow and resolve in the reedy metal voice. "I do not wish to lose who I have become."

No, Charles realized. *I do not wish it either.* He opened his mouth to offer some kind of additional comfort. He closed it when Isaak stood.

"I wish to ask something of you," Isaak said.

"Ask," Charles answered, and suddenly the thought that this metal child of his might someday run out of questions, run out of curiosity, run out of *life*—it opened a chasm of sorrow in him that he couldn't fathom.

Isaak stood. "I must get something from my room." He looked around. "May I have a robe, Father?"

Charles pointed to where a fresh scholar's robe hung waiting. He watched as the metal man pulled it on quickly and cinched its rope belt. Then, he waited and wondered what surprising question would come back to him.

Isaak was not gone long. When he returned, he extended a hand to Charles, and the arch-engineer reached for it. It was small but easily recognizable—a golden scripting scroll, rolled tight.

"I want to dream before I become nonfunctional," Isaak said.

Charles looked at it, turning it over in his fingers. "How did you come by this?" He recognized it, though at the time he'd thought it merely the work of the apprentice who betrayed him into Sethbert's hands two years ago. It had been fused into the memory scroll of the mechoservitor that he'd sent out last year in search of Petronus, the mechoservitor that had fled into the Churning Wastes. He'd read the numbers and symbols, finding nothing but the notes of an ancient love song.

"It was given to Nebios that he might give it to me. It is what my cousin called the *metal dream*."

Charles felt his eyes narrowing, remembering Neb's report on the other mechoservitor. They'd found nothing when they searched Sanctorum Lux just days after its supposed suicide—its body vanished without even a screw or bolt left behind to show it had been there. That mechoservitor had been dangerous—violent, even, damaging both Isaak and the Waste guide Renard and killing dozens of Erlund's finest Delta Scouts during its escape and flight east. "Nebios gave this to you? You've kept quiet about it for some time."

"I was . . . uncertain."

Charles sighed. "I'm also uncertain, Isaak. I would prefer to wait and study it more carefully." *Perhaps run it on one of the others and—* He caught himself, realizing what he did now. He didn't want to risk losing Isaak again. And if this truly was more than a simple song, if it *was* some kind of coded script dressed like a dream, there was no telling what it might do. Isaak could have done this for himself. He didn't have to ask. He had the tools and mirrors.

He came to me because he sees me as his father. Charles felt an emotion that he could not quite label.

When Isaak spoke next, his voice was a reedy whisper. "I want this, Father."

Charles looked up and studied the amber eyes that stared back at him. Without a word, he stood and went to the worktable where Isaak had so recently lain lifeless and battered. He gestured to it, and Isaak stood and removed his robe, replacing it on the hook by the door. Then, he climbed onto the table and stretched out.

In silence, Charles spun the cipher into the lock and opened Isaak's chest cavity. He reached around and found the spool for incoming scrollwork. Carefully, he started the thin gold strip into the threading, then tightened down the scroll on its spool.

Finally, he closed the chest cavity and spun the lock. "Isaak," he said, "run scroll seven six three."

He heard the spool whir, heard the clacking of the metal strip as it began to unwind. Isaak seized for a moment, his limbs going rigid and his eyes lighting brighter than Charles had seen them. Then, the eye shutters closed and fluttered, the bellows wheezed, and Isaak slept.

Perhaps it is *a dream,* Charles thought.

Then, he went and sat by the fire to worry and wait for his metal son to awaken.

Because, Charles realized, *that's what fathers do.*

Neb

Neb used his scout knife to carve a roasted Waste rat he'd snared in the quiet hour before dawn. The crackling meat smelled sour on the morning air, but Neb's stomach growled at it.

He glanced back at the woman deeper in the cave. She was getting stronger and stronger. She'd polished off an entire rat on her own the day before, warning him between bites of his need to flee her sisters.

He was beginning to believe her. There was an earnestness to her voice that compelled him. So he did the math and factored his best guess of their speed beneath the magicks and hoped that his sense of distance here was accurate.

He speared the hindquarters of the Waste rat and slid it onto the tin plate he'd found in her pack. He carried it back to her and hunkered down to watch her eat.

She tore into the rat, peeling back the crispy skin to find the meat beneath.

He didn't wait for her to start this time. He brought it up himself. "I think we should leave tomorrow," he told her.

She looked up from the meat, her face smeared with grease. Her eyebrows furrowed, bending the symbols carved into her forehead. She finished chewing and swallowing. "Tomorrow will be too late. You've—" She closed her eyes in concentration. "Miscalculated."

Tomorrow. It was possible, he realized. He was not familiar enough with the blood magicks to know exactly how fast they made these women who supposedly hunted him. He'd factored them as faster than a horse, perhaps nearly as fast as a mechoservitor. He wanted to ask, but earlier questions had been deflected in her constant press for him to leave while he still could. If they really could arrive as soon as tomorrow, Neb needed to leave.

But what to do about this scarred woman? He could not leave her. His eyes fell upon her exposed leg, and when he averted them, he saw her boots and her pack. He felt the idea land between his ears like a stone in a well. "It is time for us to be frank with one another," he said. "Where were you going when the kin-wolves waylaid you?"

She looked up but continued to chew her food, her eyes hard.

He continued. "You called me an abomination, and you told me your sisters were hunting me to get to the mechoservitors," he said. "But what about you? You claimed to be attending other matters?"

"They are not your concern," she said in an even voice. "Your concern is to not be caught by my sisters if you love the light."

Her words rocked him back on his heels. "The light?"

"You want frankness, Abomination?" She gave him a hard look, then put down the tin plate. "The Whymers are not the only ones concerned with shepherding the light. My family was set to this work long before the days of P'Andro Whym. I've spent myself for it, even against my will at times, and stand now on the brink of failure because of a stubborn boy."

The emotion in her voice surprised him. It was raw, nearly desperate. And the ambush of her sudden forthrightness made him suspicious. "What happens if they find the mechoservitors?"

She shook her head. "I do not know. I only know that they mustn't, or truly the light is snuffed. And I must not be found, either, until I've finished my work."

He felt the bolt slide free in this particular Rufello lock. "You are working against them," he observed. "But who are they?"

Her words were carefully chosen and did not answer his question. "I had limited time to bear my message before this delay; my work is now jeopardized."

Neb sat back on his haunches, propping himself against the cool glass wall of the cave. He looked at her and felt himself blush as she returned the look. There where she sat, the blankets had fallen around her, exposing her scarred shoulders and the cotton sleep shift she'd changed into that morning after bathing herself from a metal cup of water he'd heated. The memory of that intensified the heat in his cheeks as he recalled sitting at the mouth of the cave, listening to her behind him as he forced himself to watch the ruined city beyond their hiding place.

His eyes moved to her breasts without any effort on his part and he forced them away, hoping she didn't notice. He swallowed his sudden discomfort and forced himself to look at her face. It was regal, despite the scars, and she regarded him with an air that he found familiar.

But I find everything about her familiar. It was as if he knew her or should know her. The high cheekbones, the wide mouth, the long legs. The eyes were the right shape but the wrong color, and her red hair should be long and flowing and—

Neb gasped and wondered how it was he hadn't seen it until now. "You are a Tam," he said.

For a moment, she looked angry. Then, her features softened. "I am the thirty-second daughter of Vlad Li Tam," she said. "I have spent my life for this brief season, and if it is to mean anything, we must not be here when my sisters arrive."

He read earnestness in her face and voice and realized that he believed her. He'd read that Petronus, when he was young and Pope, could read a person's character by the line of their jaw. He wished he had that skill now, and wondered what he would see. She held her head high, the jaw straight and firm.

He looked to her pack and boots again, then looked back to her. "Can you run?"

She nodded.

His decision was made quickly despite knowing it meant he would not be meeting Renard. He looked toward the mouth of the cave, his mind's eye out in the east beyond the ruins where his friend pursued one of her sisters. He looked back to the Tam woman.

Their eyes met, and he willed strength into his, hoping it would lend power to his question. "Where are we running?"

Her nostrils flared, but she did not break eye contact. He watched her make her own choices regarding trust, her lips pursed for a moment. "The Keeper's Gate," she finally said, her voice low and steady. "I bear urgent word for Jin Li Tam, queen of the Ninefold Forest and Great Mother to the Child of Promise."

Nodding, Neb started calculating exactly how much time it would take for them to pack their belongings and leave this place to the kin-wolves.

Seven minutes later, they ran west.

Rudolfo

Cold rain soaked Rudolfo despite the cloak he wore, and he tipped his head to let the water run from his hood. A chill wind found the gaps in the cloak and licked at the bits of skin it could find. He could read the weather here. Winter would come fast and harsh this year, and it made him nervous.

How do I raise an army in the dead of winter? Lysias assured him it would be fine, and his carefully drawn plans seemed to support the general's assertion. And Rudolfo had faced Lysias's men in the War for Windwir—of all the academy-trained officers he'd encountered, Lysias was the most formidable.

Trust, Rudolfo thought, *is an exercise of the will.* And he would trust this man to bring about what Lysias promised he could. By spring, the general claimed, the borders would be sixty percent controlled, eighty-five percent by the next fall. And each of the nine houses would have their own troops, supplemented by the Wandering Army as needed.

The thought of it both pleased Rudolfo and broke his heart.

A white bird, blurred by the darkness and rain, flashed past to land in his second captain's catch net. With a low whistle, they stopped and Rudolfo looked to his right.

Isaak and Charles rode side by side. He'd seen them together before, certainly, but something had changed between them since the events at the dedication. Rudolfo had meant to ask about it but had been buried beneath a mountain of maps and meetings and strategies, the meticulous planning that went into Jin Li Tam's upcoming diplomatic mission to the Machtvolk Territories. It had been as carefully considered as any campaign, and though his stomach knotted at the thought of it, Rudolfo knew it was the best path left to them for this time. His family would be protected—Ria's latest kin-raven had assured him of this, sworn upon the mark of Y'Zir that guarded her heart—and the Ninefold Forest would have eyes in a place no other Named Lander was permitted to go. The army Ria had raised now held a border as far south as the Desolation of Windwir.

So now, with Jin Li Tam and Winters leaving tomorrow, Rudolfo once more could exercise his trust, turning his mind to other matters.

It was not an easy task.

He looked again to Isaak and Charles. The metal man rode high in the saddle, mounted upon the strongest horse they could find for him.

Wrapped in the robe, cloak and hood, he could almost be mistaken for a man. His metal hands were gloved, and his metal feet were booted against the cold and rain. All that betrayed his true nature was the amber glow of his jeweled eyes beneath the cowl and the occasional hiss of steam as it vented through the exhaust grate in his back. Beside him, also wrapped against the rain, Charles seemed small.

Rudolfo looked to his metal friend. "They picked a forlorn and miserable night for this," he said.

Isaak started, his gears whirring and clacking. His head swiveled, and when he spoke, his voice sounded distracted and far away. "I apologize for this inconvenience, Lord Rudolfo."

Rudolfo chuckled. "No apology required, Isaak. It is what it is." *And what it is, is damned curious,* he told himself.

The moon sparrow had returned not long after Isaak's functionality had been restored, urging them north under cover of darkness and storm. Somehow, these metal emissaries had crossed the Keeper's Wall to arrive in his Ninefold Forest, yet they had not passed through the gate his Gypsy Scouts now manned there. The foresters had worked out a new code and retrained a new batch of birds just for these communications, and they sat unused in their coops. "Still, I wonder what they're up to."

Isaak said nothing, and Rudolfo looked beyond him to Charles. The old man met his eyes for a moment, and Rudolfo read something there that he could not quite place. He knew when the arch-engineer quickly broke eye contact that something indeed was amiss. *He knows something that he is not telling.*

Looking back to Isaak, he opened his mouth to speak again, then closed it when Philemus spoke. "They are ahead. Four of them, robed and waiting. Scouts have secured a perimeter around them."

Rudolfo nodded. "Very well. Hold here unless we whistle for you."

"Aye, General," the second captain said.

Then Rudolfo looked to Isaak. "Are you ready?"

Isaak nodded slowly but said nothing.

Rudolfo nudged his horse forward at a walk, and the two followed. The forest around them was alive with the rainfall, and a shrouded moon offered no light between the clouds and the thick evergreen canopy. They rode forward in darkness until Rudolfo saw the amber lights ahead. When he did, he slipped from his saddle and led his stallion into the small clearing.

The four stood together, side by side, and steam rose from the heat of them. They'd run far, he realized, and yet had somehow circumnavigated the only pass across the impenetrable Keeper's Wall. Rudolfo waited until Isaak and Charles were beside him, and then he stepped forward. "Greetings," he said, "I am Rudolfo, lord of the Ninefold Forest Houses, general of the Wandering Army."

One of the mechoservitors broke ranks with the others and raised his hand. "Well met, Lord Rudolfo." The metal man looked to Isaak next. "Greetings, cousin." Then, last, he looked to Charles. "Father," he said, inclining his head.

Charles grunted and returned the nod.

As his eyes adjusted to the night, Rudolfo saw the differences between these mechoservitors and Isaak. They were more boxlike, with harder right angles, and copper in color.

Isaak inclined his head. "Greetings, cousin."

"Do you serve the light?" the mechoservitor asked.

Isaak nodded. "I serve the light," he said. Then, he looked to Rudolfo. "And I serve this man and his family."

The mechoservitor's voice lowered. "Do you yet comprehend the dream?"

The dream? Rudolfo glanced at Charles. The old man looked away, and Rudolfo noted the question that required asking once they finished here. He would ask Isaak first, of course, out of courtesy for his friend.

Isaak's eye shutters flashed, and his voice took on a heaviness that sounded so unlike the metal man that Rudolfo found himself blinking. "I do not comprehend it," he said. "But I know that it requires a response."

"Yes."

Another mechoservitor stepped forward. "Even now the antiphon is being shaped. We are here to aid that work."

Rudolfo was not familiar with the word and set it aside for later conversation. "Return with us to my manor," he said, "and we will discuss this aid."

The mechoservitor looked at him, and Rudolfo saw something in those eyes, in the way the metal man held his head, that spilled uneasiness into him like ink in a pond. "Do you serve the light?"

Rudolfo cocked his head. "I do. I am restoring what I can of it by—"

There was gravity in the mechoservitor's tone when he interrupted. "The dream has shown us that the light cannot be truly preserved in a building of stone and wood. Your aid is not required." He looked to Isaak. "You have tasted the dream and we have come for you, cousin. Join us."

Rudolfo held his breath. He had not foreseen this, and judging by the look on Charles's face, the old arch-engineer had not expected it either. They both stared at Isaak.

Isaak's eyes flashed, bright and then dim, as his working parts clacked and whirred with this new information. "I cannot join you," Isaak said. Rudolfo heard the sadness in his friend's voice. "I have work to accomplish here."

Another of the four stepped forward, repeating the other's words. "The light cannot be truly preserved in a building of stone and wood, cousin. You of all our kind should comprehend this fully."

Rudolfo started. *They know of his role in Windwir.*

A gout of steam burst from Isaak's exhaust grate, and his metal plating rattled. "I cannot join you, but I will aid you as I can." The metal man looked to Rudolfo, and he thought for a moment he heard pleading in his voice. "I believe Lord Rudolfo will aid you as well if you will be forthright with him."

More trust. And Rudolfo had no reason to offer it. Yet.

The last mechoservitor joined them now. "We run for the Marshlands to search the Book of Dreaming Kings." He looked to Rudolfo and repeated his companion's words. "Your aid is not required."

Rudolfo felt his frustration building and wrestled it down. "You are in my forests," he said in a low and even tone. "You may not wish my aid, but you should still desire my grace."

The mechoservitor's eye shutters flashed open and closed. "We will not long be in your forests and require only such grace as will let us pass in peace and secrecy."

Rudolfo looked to Isaak and Charles again. "And you think the Machtvolk queen will grant you access to her book?"

"We will not seek access from her." The mechoservitor dug into his robes, and Rudolfo felt wind nearby as his scouts drew closer. He whistled them to stand down as the mechanical pulled out a cloth-wrapped bundle and passed it to Isaak. "Should we fail," the mechoservitor said, "our task will fall to you or the antiphon will be incomplete."

Isaak took the bundle and looked at it.

"It is the only existing copy," the mechoservitor said, "and it should remain so."

The first mechoservitor spoke to Isaak now, even as Rudolfo opened his own mouth to speak. "If you change your mind the book will bring you to us, cousin. It is glorious to serve the light by way of the dream. We beseech you to reconsider and take your part in formulating the antiphon. We will not send for you again."

Isaak said nothing. And before Rudolfo could find his own words, the mechoservitors turned and sped from the clearing.

Follow them, he signed to the scouts surrounding them. *At a distance, but do not breach the Machtvolk border.*

He heard the faintest clicking of tongues to the roofs of mouths as the scouts set out. As they left, he looked to Charles and Isaak. "It seems we have much to discuss," Rudolfo said.

Isaak nodded absently, carefully unwrapping the book while shielding it from the rain with his cloak. It was an old volume, one that had somehow been spared the destruction of the Great Library.

"What book is it?" Charles asked, leaning in.

Isaak read the cover. "It is Tertius's *Exegesis of Select Lunar Prophecies As Recorded in the Book of Dreaming Kings.*

As if on cue, the rain around them let up as high winds pushed back the clouds enough to leak the moon's blue-green light over the clearing. In the distance, Rudolfo heard the fading clack and clank of the metal men as they ran west, but the metal man before him captured all his attention.

Isaak looked at the book and then raised his amber jeweled eyes as if in prayer. "It requires a response," Isaak said as he gazed upon the moon. And there was such sacredness, such conviction in Isaak's voice that Rudolfo could not help but join his friend in staring at the sky. Above them, that same wind brought back the clouds, shrouding what little light they had as the rain once more began to fall.

Petronus

Geoffrus's men found the shallow grave just west of D'Anjite's Bridge, and only Petronus's insistence kept them from skinning the corpse they found there.

The sun was low and heavy with morning when he saw their quiet commotion in the camp, and he'd known instantly that something was afoot. Whistling for Grymlis and the first lieutenant of Rudolfo's Gypsy Scouts, Petronus had fetched his horse and followed the ragged band of Waste runners to their newest find.

They'd already exhumed the body.

Now, they stood at a distance, muttering and whispering, while Petronus and his men studied it.

It was a woman, her hair shorn and her yellow-gray skin scarred in a way that dropped ice into Petronus's stomach. He knew those markings, had seen them all too recently upon the skin of his childhood friend, Vlad Li Tam. She lay stretched out, her hands folded upon her chest and her eyes closed, dressed in a loose-fitting tunic and trousers of unfamiliar cut, wearing well-worn low boots made for running. Around her lay the scattered rocks that had covered her shallow grave. And though she'd been dead for some time, her body looked more asleep than not.

Grymlis bent over her while Petronus hung back. "There's no

decomposition," he said. His large hands moved her head, revealing the deep bruising around her throat. "And her neck has been broken." He scowled. "It's a clean break. Something strong and fast."

Petronus glanced back to Geoffrus and his men. "Did you find anything else?"

Geoffrus shook his head. "Nothing, Luxpadre. But my men wish to *assert* to you the contractual clause regarding the fair division of *found objects* among our party as—"

Petronus cut him off with a stare to match the hardness of his words. "This is a woman, Geoffrus. Not a found object. You'll not desecrate her corpse."

For the briefest instant, Petronus saw rage on the man's face, and he noted the line of the man's jaw. *He could do me harm,* he realized. And then, the rage was gone, replaced by calm acceptance. "As you direct, Luxpadre, so I serve."

He looked back to the woman. She was young—perhaps the tail end of her twenties. And even before he ordered it, he knew what he would find. The cuttings on her face and arms, the symbols etched into her, told him exactly what he needed to know. "Open her shirt," he said.

Grymlis looked up, surprised, and Petronus watched the light spark in his eyes. He nodded, swallowed, then forced her arms from her chest. Then, he used his scout knife to cut the fabric open.

Petronus's hand moved to his own chest, fingers tracing the skin of his own raised scar through the fabric of his robe. There, just to the left of center, cut into her skin between her breasts, was the mark of Y'Zir. And surrounding it, swirling in line upon line of symbols, was a lattice of scars he could not read, though he caught their meaning well enough.

Grymlis slowly rose and stepped back. "What next, Father?"

Petronus looked to the sun. The day was young, and though they'd slowed their reckless pace somewhat, they had much ground to cover.

Runners in the waste, the man Hebda had said. This, he knew, must be one of them. But something had intercepted her, snapped her neck like dry wood and buried her here in the Wastes, even placing a white stone at her head in the custom of the Androfrancine funeral rites. The lack of decomposition made it impossible to know how long ago, but he suspected it had not been more than days.

He turned to Edrys, the first lieutenant of the scouts that rode with them. "Have the scouts walk the surrounding half league for anything they can find." He gave Geoffrus another firm stare. "You pull back your men, Geoffrus."

The Waste runner did not look at Petronus; his eyes never left the naked chest of the girl, and it was not the scar that caught his eye, not by the way he licked his lips. Disgusted, Petronus raised his voice. "Geoffrus," he said. "Pull back your men. We ride in two hours."

Startled, the Waste runner looked away from the girl and with a word to his ragged band, slunk away with them.

When only Grymlis remained, Petronus sighed.

"That one will be trouble before we're done," the Gray Guard captain said in a low voice.

He nodded. "He will; but for now, we need him."

"Still, he and his would cut our throats in our sleep. And if the rumors in Fargoer's Station have any truth, he'd make a tasty stew of us and our horses."

Petronus offered a grim smile. "You'll not let it come to that, I'd wager."

"Aye, Father," Grymlis said. "I'll not. My eye is on him." The old soldier nodded toward the body. "What do you make of her?"

"She's an Y'Zirite." Petronus looked at her, her arms stretched out and her chest bared, the purple bruising of her neck offsetting the pale Whymer Maze of etchings in her flesh. That one mark, central and larger than the rest, still pulled at his eye, and he felt the burning in his own bosom from the scar Ria had cut into him when he lay dead upon the floor of that tent on Windwir's desolate plain. "But not of a variety I've seen before."

"And these are the runners this mysterious behaviorist was warning us about? The ones looking for the boy?"

Petronus nodded, remembering Hebda's words. "And looking for the missing mechoservitors."

Grymlis studied the body, and Petronus followed his eyes. "She was a tough one by the looks of her, but no match for whatever found her. And likely not much of a match for our men."

Still, Petronus knew there must be more to this than what lay before their eyes. And as if in answer, a low whistle reached his ears from the other side of a low rise of bent and mounded glass.

They joined Edrys where he crouched with his scout. "It happened here," the lieutenant said, pointing with his knife to the bare patch of ground. "She was carried to the place they buried her."

Petronus stared at the ground, barely able to see the marks so obvious to the Gypsy's trained eyes. "They?"

Edrys nodded. "There were three—maybe four of them—not counting the girl." He pointed to another nearby outcropping, blue and yellow and green, with wind-sharpened ridges. "They waited here and took her quickly by ambush, I suspect, without much fight." He stood and stepped carefully out of the clearing. "She ran from the east. Possibly in pursuit. Her stride indicates magicks of some kind were employed."

Yes, Petronus thought, remembering that night so long ago in his shack, when the blood-magicked assassin had attacked him and sent him into Ria's trap there on the Entrolusian Delta. The trap that had laid him out dead for his sins and brought him back in some twisted mercy he still could not comprehend, bending him into a miracle to prove their abominable gospel.

Grymlis must've been thinking in the same direction. "If she were under blood magicks, even a half-squad would be hard pressed to take her so easily—let alone four men."

Edrys stood. "Not men," he said as he looked to Petronus, and the realization dropped into his awareness like a rock in a well. He followed the scout's knife tip and saw the clear outline of a footprint.

"The mechoservitors killed her," he said, and his voice sounded flat in his ears. "The ones we saw moving west toward the Wall."

Edrys nodded. "It appears that way."

"Gods," Grymlis muttered.

Petronus inwardly cursed the broken skies of this place that kept the birds from finding their way. Then, he cursed their already small numbers and gave his orders anyway. "This," he said, "is something new that we cannot overlook. Magick a runner and send him for the Wall. And gather the party—we ride immediately."

Then, as they moved off and away, Petronus turned back and made his way slowly back to the shallow grave and the girl who waited there in it. He was not sure if it was her nakedness or the starkness of the mark over her heart, but something compelled him, and he stooped to pull her shirt closed. With the scar covered, his eyes found the bruises at her neck and he imagined the quick, possibly even painless end she'd met in service to her faith in this desolate place.

Whatever the mechoservitors guarded, whatever they were about, they were willing to kill for it. And that was something utterly against the gospels and precepts that fueled their scripting. It unsettled him deeply.

And at the same time, he found himself quietly rejoicing.

Because if these are the same that seek Neb, he realized, *there's now one less of them for us to deal with.*

Grabbing up a stone in each hand, Petronus set about to bury his enemy. He worked quickly, feeling the sweat that trickled from his hairline and armpits tracing its way down his back and sides. When he reached that final stone, the white one that signified the light inherent in every human life, he hesitated.

In the end, the mechoservitors had more mercy than he himself could muster, despite the cold and calculated murder of their prey.

He remembered Ria's knife, remembered her words, and felt the burning of the scars she'd left upon him. Felt the despair washing over him when he realized just what his death and resurrection had accomplished after a life of service to the light of reason, the light of human knowledge and experience. Then, he looked to the place near the corpse's head, where the light-colored rock had lain before.

Hefting that stone, Petronus cursed and hurled it as far from the grave as his strength would allow.

Then he turned back to find his horse and press eastward with his men.

Jin Li Tam

Cold rain pounded them from a bruise-colored sky, and Jin Li Tam's hands kept moving beneath the rain cloak to where Jakob nestled close against her in his riding harness.

She was grateful that he rode so well, having heard stories from the house staff about the less amenable infants they'd encountered. And she'd been surprised—she'd been prepared for his ear to keep him screaming for the trip. But Lynnae's powders, administered through Jin's milk, seemed to cut the pain, and he'd ridden largely in silence.

Still, after so many days in the saddle she was ready for a real bed and a hot bath and a roof that wasn't canvas. She imagined little Jakob felt the same way, though he seemed content enough to pass the time sleeping and nursing and looking about when the weather was less foul.

Aedric's company of Gypsy Scouts were all around them, a platoon's worth magicked and on the run, maintaining a perimeter that moved around her entourage as they rode for the Machtvolk Territories. They'd sighted the first of Ria's watchtowers the day before, tall and dominating the rugged terrain, and a kin-raven late in the evening informed them that they would be met today by an escort who would guide them into the territories.

It was hard to believe that she'd been here not so very long ago, deep in the winter, riding at the head of Rudolfo's Wandering Army. It had been much colder, but the rain seemed more miserable to her than the snow. Of course, growing up on the Emerald Coasts, where winter was a warmish rain, had made settling into her new northern home a bit of an adjustment.

She shifted in the saddle, sore from the ride and aching still from the blast. Isaak had shielded them from the worst, saving their lives, but she still bore the bruises and cuts. She expected a scar now on her thigh where a long sliver of pine had laid open the flesh.

Memory of that day brought a shiver to her deeper than the wet and cold.

A flash of brown to her left brought her head around, and she saw Aedric fishing a bird from his catch net. He whistled and raised his hand for them to stop.

She reined in, a hand once more creeping to Jakob's stomach to feel the warmth of him.

Just beyond Aedric, she saw Winters sitting tall in the saddle, though the girl's eyes were downcast. She'd been quiet of late, and her work with the knives had taken on a determined edge that felt something like banked anger to Jin's practiced eye.

When Aedric spoke, she met his eyes and returned the anger she saw there with cool aloofness. "The Marsher escort approaches ahead," he said, then corrected himself. "*Machtvolk.* Their queen rides with them."

She inclined her head, keeping her face masked. "Good."

She glanced to her right, where Lynnae rode. The girl had insisted that she accompany them. It had been months since she'd served as Jakob's nursemaid, but the bond between her and Jin and the child was palpable, and the River Woman had sent her with a full field kit of powders and scripts. Now, the woman rode swaddled in a rain cloak twice her size, her face buried in the cowl and her long curly hair spilling out from under it.

Behind them, the rest of the company stopped. Aedric would not move them forward, Jin knew. Instead, he would make their hosts come to them—a subtle message.

They did not wait long.

The procession was larger than Jin had imagined it would be—a long train of horses and footmen—and she blinked in surprise.

The Marshers had never been a uniform tribe. They'd ever been a mysterious, mad and mismatched people, known for their rotting fur clothing and their salvaged or stolen weapons, tools and accessories. They employed no industry and lived lives of subsistence in their hovels, shoved far north against the Dragon's Spine Mountains apart from the nations of the Named Lands. They were known for brutal tribalism, and feared widely through the border towns of the northern forests, where skirmishing had bolstered a reputation they no doubt deserved. But there was more to them, she'd learned through her friendship with Winters. The young queen, now deposed and scrubbed clean of her people's mysticism, had shown her a quieter side to this people with their Book of Dreaming Kings and their longing for a new home to rise through the agency of the Homeseeker they believed would bring them there.

The procession that now approached bore no resemblance to the army she'd seen two years ago upon the plains of Windwir. Crimson banners caught the wind, and the riders and footmen alike wore dark uniforms, accented also in crimson and stark against the careful grays and browns and blacks of their face paint.

Who is supplying them? Certainly not the Delta city-states or their neighbors, Pylos and Turam. As they drew closer, she noted that while the uniforms were alike, they were ill fitting and the men who wore them did not appear entirely at ease.

The woman who led them pulled Jin's attention away.

"Hail, Great Mother," Ria said from the back of her stallion. She wore a long black rain cloak, and it hung open to reveal a silver breastplate. In her left hand, she raised the Firstfall axe. "Hail, Jakob, Child of Promise." Then she smiled and turned to Winters. "Hail, little sister."

The words were bitter in Jin Li Tam's mouth, but she said them anyway. "Hail, Winteria the Elder, queen of the Machtvolk Territories. On behalf of Rudolfo, lord of the Ninefold Forest Houses and general of the Wandering Army, I bear you grace and greetings in gratitude for your hospitality." From the corner of her eye, she saw Winters flinch at the words, and it pained her to see it. In that same glance, she also saw Aedric's tightly drawn mouth and the white knuckles of his hands upon his reins.

"Dark times bring you to us," Ria said in a quiet voice as she walked forward. "But you will be pleased to know that our investigation is bearing fruit. I know it is a tremendous act of trust that you would even consider my invitation, and I assure you that every care has been taken for your comfort and protection during your visit among my people."

Jin Li Tam whistled her own horse forward, and she leaned close to Ria. "Swear it to me," she said, her eyes meeting the deep brown eyes of the Machtvolk queen. She saw Winters in the woman's face—there was no denying their kinship. Jin's eyes narrowed. "Swear to me on your gospel and on the mark upon your heart that we will be safe and that we will be free to leave your domain at the time of our choosing."

Ria smiled, and it was wide, inviting even. She reached beneath her robe and withdrew a slender volume, raising it into the air even as her hand went to her breast. "I swear it, Great Mother. I know circumstance indicates enmity between us. I know the wounds we've inflicted upon your family and upon your world are deep, but know this: They were the breaking of bones not properly set in an earlier wounding that now may be undone by the grace of the Crimson Empress." Her eyes moved to Winters and she repeated herself. "I swear it."

Jin Li Tam watched the girl's face redden under her older sister's gaze. Then, once more she looked to Aedric. The first captain looked resolved but angry. "Very well," she said. "I am satisfied."

And yet, I truly won't be until my son and I leave this dark, mad land you are making.

Ria nodded. "We will feast tonight in my new home." She looked again to Winters. "I think you will be impressed with our progress, little sister."

Winters said nothing as Ria turned her horse. Aedric whistled them forward, and they found themselves suddenly at the head of the procession, with the Machtvolk queen riding now between Jin and Winters as Lynnae and Aedric dropped back. The Machtvolk riders and footmen formed a wall to either side of the Gypsy Scouts, and together they moved at a moderate speed.

They rode in silence now, cutting north and passing between two watchtowers that loomed over a newly cut dirt road now mostly gone to mud. Ahead, Jin Li Tam saw low hills shrouded in mist that brushed the tops of the pine trees, and she thought she heard something from the forest there.

As they drew nearer, she became more sure of it and glanced to the woman beside her.

Ria's face bore quiet delight.

It was the sound of singing on the wind.

The song grew as they approached, and suddenly, the rain let up. Scattered rays of sunlight perforated the cloud cover, though the air was still cold enough for Jin to see her breath.

She heard Jakob's muffled laughter and adjusted her cloak so that his tiny face could peer out. They'd learned early that he loved music, and one of her favorite new pastimes as a mother was pretending to sleep while Rudolfo sang quietly to their son.

Now, all around her, voices sang, and she felt the hairs rising on her skin as the lyrics became clear. And as they entered the forest and climbed into the low hills, she saw the people crowding the sides of the road, their evergreen branches raised high in trembling hands as they sang of a healed home through their Child of Promise, a Great Mother of daunting beauty and a Crimson Empress of infinite mercy who prepared even now for her bridegroom.

The song rose high into the winter sky, and Jin Li Tam realized suddenly that other voices joined in around them as the Machtvolk escort and even their queen lifted up their own voices.

Close against her breast, Jakob laughed in delight, and she realized suddenly that tears coursed her cheeks. But even as Jin Li Tam wept, she did not know if her tears were from the beauty or the terror of the overwhelming hymn that encompassed them.

Winters

Winters arose early and slipped out into cold northern air beneath a predawn sky flung wide with stars.

Of course, she'd not really slept. The events of yesterday had rushed at her all through the night. Even during dinner—a lavish feast of salmon, elk and wild mushrooms—the song echoed through her, punctuated by memories of Jakob's delight by it all and Jin Li Tam's unexpected tears.

She rarely sheds tears. Winters wished she were like that, too. But she wasn't. And what she'd seen and heard since her return to these changing lands had added more sorrow, more remorse to her shoulders.

On the surface, all looked well, but beneath it lay something darker. The watchtowers were up, but they watched both outward and inward. And the children, enrolled now in schools, were volunteering to take the mark as they learned *a more balanced history of their people* through history, poetry, drama . . . and the gospels. They were also training the children now in the blood magicks and scouting.

She'd heard this over dinner when the song wasn't pulling her back to their grand entrance into her former lands. And on that ride, she'd seen the evidence of other changes—there was more lumber being pulled from the forest; there were more houses and structures built and more uniformed men moving to and fro among her people.

Winters heard a sound behind her now and looked over her shoulder. She saw one of her sister's guards following at a distance and behind him, a Gypsy Scout that kept to the darker patches of night.

She let her feet carry her, and somehow, despite the changed landscape, they found a familiar path and bore her to the caves she'd once called home, the caves that stored the Book of Dreaming Kings and held the Wicker Throne. The heavy oak doors were closed now, and when she saw the guard there, she paused. He stood in shadows cast by the watch lamp on its post and stepped forward when he saw her approaching.

She stopped, unsure of what to do or say. Suddenly apprehensive, she glanced over her shoulder again. The men that followed her had stopped as well.

"Is the way to the Book closed, then?" she finally asked.

The guard's eyes narrowed. "Yes."

She studied him, finding him suddenly familiar. He was perhaps ten years older than she was, and though the face paint bent his features, she was certain that she knew him. "You are one of Seamus's grandchildren."

The guard nodded but said nothing. He stepped farther into the light and waved to the guard that followed her. Positioning himself so that her body was between him and the others, his hands moved quickly and her eyes were drawn to them.

Hail Winteria bat Mardic, true queen of the Marsh, he signed to her. *I am your servant, Garyt ben Urlin.*

Winters blinked, his words overpowering her. She opened her mouth to speak, remembered herself, and willed her own hands to move into the house language of Y'Zir. *Grace to you, Garyt.*

"These caves are closed by order of Queen Winteria the Elder," he said aloud. And his hands flashed again. *We may bear the mark on our bodies, but we do not all bear it in our souls.*

She felt the heat in her face before she felt the water in her eyes. She remembered these words—she'd said something similar to Seamus on the day of his sobbing confession. But these were not words of comfort spoken into shame. They were words of loyalty and commitment. She felt a tear break loose. "Thank you," she said.

Turn now, she willed herself. And she did. She turned and took another path her feet remembered. The landmarks had changed, but she still found her way. At last, she stood in a wide, bare patch of ground near the river. It was a place she'd come to when she needed to meditate upon the dreams she'd had until just a few months ago.

She tried to remember those days spent in meditation but found the memory of them elusive. Instead, her mind was filled with the song and the children that took the mark and those doors now closed and guarded where her book of dreams lay hidden. She'd seen and heard so much the day before and had assumed it meant her people had wholeheartedly embraced this new way of life.

But Garyt hadn't, despite the mark he'd taken and the uniform he wore. And now she was certain there were others like him.

Drawing her knives, Winters balanced them in her hands and shifted on her feet. Overhead, the stars wrapped themselves in rain clouds to leave her in darkness. The sound of the river's slow current mingled with the soft and distant hoot of an owl.

Winters drew in her breath and held it.

All is not lost here, she realized.

She brought the knives up, held parallel to her forearms, the edges facing out. She moved her legs apart and slowly released her breath, remembering the form that Jin Li Tam had taught her.

Then, Winters began to dance and in that dancing, laid aside her tears.

Vlad Li Tam

Vlad Li Tam stood in the bow of his flagship and squinted against the fading light. He'd taken to sleeping during the day so that he could spend his nights here, watching.

So far, their penetration into the deeper waters of the Ghosting Crests had been uneventful. And while his children had finally seen the anomaly that their father was so utterly fixated upon, they still did not fully comprehend the depth of his obsession.

Not obsession, he told himself with a sigh as he scanned the waters off his bow. *Love.*

But even as he thought it, he knew it was ridiculous. Yet he felt the mark of it on him as real as the scars that Ria had given him. His heart raced when he stood here, waiting for his ghost to appear. His hands were clammy. His mind was filled with the image of her graceful movement in the water, and when he tossed in his cot and tried to sleep, it was the song that emanated from her that kept him awake. No matter where he went upon his ship, inevitably the sunset found him here. Waiting.

Because she draws me.

More importantly, he suspected that she was aware of her pull upon him and used it now to move him and what remained of his family southeast, farther into the Ghosting Crests than any Named Lander had sailed.

The stars throbbed to life above him as the sky blurred from purple to deep charcoal, and as he watched, the moon lifted itself into the sky—a sliver now but enough to light the water. As the day slipped past, the noise of the crew dissipated and the night noise of wave and clanking engine took over.

Here she comes, he told himself, and he felt it on his skin, in the tiny hairs within his ears, as her song started up beneath the water. A patch of ocean shimmered and undulated ahead, and he clung to the railing, leaning forward.

He watched as she moved through the water, tendrils of light trailing behind like hair. There was a grace about her that he'd never seen before, and once more, he felt his heart aching and felt that compulsion to join her.

I have become a foolish old man. And even as he thought it, he watched as she abruptly changed course and struck south. He raised his hand to the pilothouse behind him and pointed in the direction she raced, waiting for the ship to turn along with their guide. Slowly, he felt the list as the ship bore hard to starboard.

After an hour, she was back and changing course yet again, this time heading due east.

He motioned to the pilothouse again and heard the engines groaning as they increased power and turned the ship. He gripped the railing and let the wind catch hair he'd been too distracted to cut and a beard he'd been too unfocused to trim. Ahead, as the ocean around and ahead grew darker, he watched his ghost in the water.

The d'jin slowed enough for them to keep up, adjusting course here and there as needed, and Vlad Li Tam stood watch and counted the hours as they raced over a placid sea.

The sky was lightening when they finally slowed, and he watched as the blue-green lights swung in a wide circle ahead of them. Squinting ahead, he saw something vaguely outlined in the water, and he called it out for the watchman and pilot.

As they slowed and approached, the d'jin rolled and broke the surface, illuminating the small drifting object with the glowing tendrils of light.

It was a lifeboat.

Behind him, the ship went to third alarm and he heard his family scrambling. Before the flagship's longboat slapped the waves, the d'jin had darted off to the southeast again, and Vlad knew that she would not be back until the next nightfall.

Sighing, he left the bow and moved to the port side where he could watch. He saw Baryk, bare chested and wearing silk sleeping pants, and approached.

"Your ghost has found us something," the warpriest said.

Vlad Li Tam studied the water below, watching as his men, illuminated in the light of their lantern, threw their hooks and drew the drifting boat to their own. "Yes," he answered, though his voice sounded more distant than he'd wanted it to. "She has."

He heard excited voices carrying up and across the water, but he wasn't able to pick out any of the words. He saw them scrambling into the boat and heard their gasps at what they found there.

Two men manned the oars of the lifeboat and steered it toward the flagship. The longboat followed after, and when they reached the lift, Vlad leaned over the railing. "What have you found?"

His fifty-first son looked up. "The boat bears the markings of the *Kinshark*." Lying in the bottom of it, Vlad saw a vague shape that took form as the longboat approached with its lantern, and found himself gasping with surprise as well.

What have you brought us, my love? He blinked at the shape, uncertain of his eyes.

There, stretched out cruciform, lay a broken metal man in Androfrancine robes.

Rudolfo

A light snow fell in the northern reaches of the Ninefold Forest, and Rudolfo shrugged the flakes from where they gathered in his cloak. The morning air was still and heavy with the smell of wood smoke and pine. It was cold, too, carrying his breath away in clouds as he walked his woods in the quietest hour between night and dawn.

Behind him, the camp stirred to life as Lysias's sergeants moved among the recruits with their pine switches, slapping buttocks and thighs as they went about motivating the men to a more eager wakefulness. Already, the Gypsy Scouts were up and loaded—as was Rudolfo—and this morning they would ride ahead of the battalion so that Rudolfo could see their discovery for himself.

Just days on the heels of Jin Li Tam and Jakob's departure, his second captain, Philemus, had brought word of what his scouts had found after days of chasing the metal men. He'd been sipping a pear wine that was nearly too sweet for his palate and pushing his fork through a rice-and-venison dish that seemed flavorless when the officer was ushered into Rudolfo's private dining room.

"We've found where they were running," he'd said. And even in that moment, Rudolfo could see on the man's face that he would be packing and riding out himself. The next day, under the cover of a training exercise with Lysias's army, he and an elite squad had set out for the far northern reaches of his territories.

Normally, Rudolfo relished those times he spent away from the manor. He'd always equated it with freedom, but lately he'd found himself counting security as a higher value than liberty. More and more, his guarded manor and his Gypsy Scouts felt safer to him than the wide open expanse of the forest his forefathers had claimed for their people two millennia ago. And everywhere he went, he carried a knot in his stomach and the dull ache of tension behind his eyes.

Picking his way carefully across the new-fallen snow, he tried to find solace in the morning but found worry instead. True to her word, Ria had welcomed his family into her lands—her entire people had welcomed them, it seemed. And she'd also sent what fruit they'd harvested in their investigation. Scraps of intelligence, cut no doubt from the prisoner they'd taken, that pointed south to the coastal nations. The War for Windwir had begun that strain, and then the events last winter—the assassinations and the resulting Council of Kin-Clave—had further eroded their relationship with those nations. The Delta continued a kin-clave on paper, largely forced by Esarov and his compatriots there in the Governor's Council. But it was becoming clear that the attack upon his family and his library was a well-orchestrated operation by allies now become enemies in the madness of these dark times. And he could see why these friends had become enemies. His family and people were the only ones to have profited from the desolation of Windwir, and the rise of the Machtvolk and their demonstrated kin-clave with the Gypsies surely pointed toward collusion. The clear evidence that it was all the product of a carefully crafted Tam intrigue, right down to the Y'Zirite resurgence with its gospels, shrines and evangelists, was not enough.

Closing his borders and raising the army would not be enough, he realized, and that truth frightened him.

He heard a low whistle behind him and turned. Philemus slipped from a darker patch of the forest. "The scouts are ready, General."

Rudolfo sighed and forced his mind back to their present dilemma. Mechoservitors passing through his lands . . . and what his scouts had uncovered far to the north, at the foot of the Dragon's Spine. "Very well," he said, turning back to the camp. "Let's ride."

They rode out before the sun rose, their horses magicked for speed and strength, hooves muffled by the River Woman's powders. His arm ached with each passing league, and the air grew colder as they climbed the wooded foothills at the base of those impenetrable mountains.

By the time they arrived, the sun was a white disk veiled in gray and the snow had let up. They left their horses behind with a handful of scouts and slipped into a narrow canyon only marginally hidden by drifts of fallen pines and displaced rock.

The lieutenant whose men had pursued the mechoservitors to this place led the way, with Philemus and Rudolfo close behind. The uneven ground and the patches of ice made it slow going, especially with only one hand to steady himself. Rudolfo noted that the officer was careful to match his pace to that of his king. He smiled at this.

As they made their way deeper into the canyon, the walls narrowed, blocking out the white sky above. The ground sloped downward as they went, and the temperature dropped until Rudolfo saw crystals of ice forming and his feet found slick patches. The narrowing corridor twisted and turned until it finally spilled out into a large cave lost in shadow. One of the scouts lit a watch lantern and unshuttered its light.

Rudolfo didn't realize he held his breath until he released it and saw it clouding the cold air. In the center of the cave, he saw something out of place, and it took a moment for him to place it.

It was a large, round steel door set into the floor and propped open. Shattered fragments of granite lay around it, and it was obvious to Rudolfo that the hatch had been closed and hidden away beneath the rock floor of this place until recently.

Moving forward on careful feet, he leaned in and let his eyes follow the limited reach of the lantern's illumination. Stretching below, lost in shadows, a steel-lined well penetrated the cave's floor. Rudolfo squinted at strange shadows, realizing suddenly that they were rungs set into the side of it, vanishing down into shadows.

"Gods," he whispered. And the well swallowed his words, the echo of them drifting back to his ears.

He'd wandered these hills since early childhood and had probably stood on this very spot.

Philemus looked from Rudolfo to the scout who had led them in. "You tracked the mechoservitors here?"

The lieutenant nodded, and in the lantern light, Rudolfo noted the blush rising to the man's cheeks. "We did." His eyes darted to his king, then looked away. "We could not keep up with them. They were gone by the time we reached the cave."

Rudolfo nodded, then stooped to pick up a loose chunk of granite. Stretching his hand out over the well, he released the rock and leaned in again, cocking his ear.

Silently he counted the seconds until far below he heard the muffled clatter. Then, he crouched and looked at the rungs set into the side of the shaft.

Philemus crouched beside him. "Does it lead where I think it leads?"

Rudolfo turned to his second captain. "I suspect it does."

An underground route to the Marshlands. He knew that the Dragon's Spine was laced with caves, but this was different. Someone had built this passage. Someone had hidden it here beneath the stone long ago. The metalwork of the hatch and walls was of a kind he'd not seen before, and he stretched out to touch it. Warm to the touch and pitted from time.

"This," Rudolfo said to Philemus, "may be an unexpected gift."

"It could be," Philemus agreed. "If they really were bound for the Marshlands."

But Rudolfo doubted they would lie about that. Even the book they'd given Isaak pointed to the Marshlands. Tertius was the renegade Androfrancine scholar who had educated Winters.

"I'm certain they were." Rudolfo touched the metal surface once again, surprised that it was so warm despite the cold of the day.

An unexpected gift indeed. But what to do with it?

Suddenly, he remembered the first time he'd discovered one of the many secret passages and rooms scattered throughout the nine forest manors he'd grown up in. He'd been six and playing spymaster with Aedric's father, Gregoric. He'd leaned against a section of shelves in his father's library, discovering a knot in the pine that seemed out of place, one that moved to his touch and unlocked a hidden panel in the wall. He'd spent an entire summer finding every door, every passageway, every hidden ladder and stairwell he could find.

Rudolfo smiled at the memory.

This is not so very different. He looked at the men who stood with him. "This remains secret," he said in a low voice. "I want a perimeter kept at all times and guard stations at and in the cave. Use magicked scouts. Bring Lysias in and show him; I want a training ground for the new army established nearby and two companies of scouts deployed to assist." He slowly raised himself to his feet, his eyes never leaving the well. "I want couriers to the mines in Rudoheim and Friendslip—five seasoned men from each."

Philemus raised his eyebrows. "Miners?"

Rudolfo stroked his beard and nodded. "And I want two of Isaak's mechoservitors brought up. If they do not have cartographic and geological familiarity then Charles should script them for it based on whatever we have in the library catalog."

The Second Captain nodded, and Rudolfo saw the understanding dawn in his eyes. "Aye, General."

"I want a half-squad assigned to each miner," Rudolfo continued, "and I want mapping shifts around the clock. "If this *is* a gift—if it truly does give access to the Machtvolk Territories—I want to know everything about it." He paused. "And I want our neighbors to know *nothing*."

"I'll see to it, General," Philemus said, inclining his head.

The others left first until only he remained, with the scout who bore the lantern.

Rudolfo looked down the well once more, then turned away from it. There was a day, he realized, when he would have stayed and commanded this effort himself. He'd have even climbed down the well and set about exploring what lay below with his men. But something had changed. He wished he could say it was the investigation into the attack on his family, but it would only be partially true.

After half a lifetime of security, I no longer feel safe.

No, he remembered, not quite half a lifetime. He reached back and took hold of that first day he truly felt unsafe, there on the grass as he held his dying father while Fontayne's mob of insurrectionists shouted curses upon his family.

Even then, he'd laid hold of every resource, every possible tool or weapon to root out the insurrection that House Li Tam had sown among his people. He had not stopped until every last bit of that vile weed was eradicated from his forest. And he'd watched every last one of them find redemption beneath the blades of his father's Physicians of Penitent Torture. Each penitent named three more, and in the end, peace and order returned to him and to his father's lands.

Rudolfo had not stopped until he felt safe again.

As he left the cave and started his slow climb back into a snow-flurried day, the Gypsy King knew it would be the same this time as well. Because they'd tried to take his family from him for a second time, and it sparked something deeper than the loss and fear. It sparked anger.

I will not stop until I feel safe again.

And for just a moment, Rudolfo thought he smelled salt and blood upon the wind.

Neb

They ran beneath a crescent moon, its dim blue-green light wavering over ridges of molten glass and gray barren slag. Neb steadied the girl as they forced their legs to carry them, powered by the root they chewed. They'd be out of root soon, he realized. With the two of them chewing it, his supply was running dangerously low.

They ran by night, hiding themselves by day as best they could, finding the ruined pockets in the ground or hills where they slept fitfully before waking to run again.

They pressed westward, zigging and zagging across the landscape.

As they ran in silence, Neb tried not to admire his companion's graceful stride. He'd tried to bring more conversation out of her, but she'd been close-mouthed since that afternoon they'd set out. He'd not even been able to wrest her name from her.

A pack of kin-wolves howled a league or two north of them, and Neb steered them south. He could feel the strain of the run in his feet and calves, the solid jarring of his lower back as each booted foot found its purchase in a long and stretched-out stride. He glanced to the woman again.

She ran with her head up and moving slightly side to side, and if her shoulder pained her, she didn't show it. Her long legs stretched out beside him. She wore her pack high on her shoulders, cinched down for easy running, and if she'd had her iron knives upon her narrow hips, she'd have looked the part of a scout.

They put three leagues between them and the wolves before he whistled them to a stop near a patch of scrub they could use as cover. Neb drew his canteen and passed it to her first, admiring the long line of her neck as she tipped back her head and drank from it.

I cannot take my eyes off her. It stirred something in him—guilt, he thought. He'd tried to hang on to the image of Winters with her freshly scrubbed face and her clean dress, but he couldn't lay hold of that dream. He tried to draw from memory the last time he'd stood close to her, felt her hands and mouth upon him, but it had been most of a year since he'd kissed her good-bye there in Rudolfo's garden. And this thirty-second daughter of Vlad Li Tam was here with him now, her face and form filling his eyes and the sweet smell of her sweat in his nose.

The thought of her made him blush, and he cursed himself for it, hoping she would mistake the red in his ears for exertion.

Behind them, the wolves howled again, and Neb turned his thoughts away from the girl and to their westward flight. There was only so much care they could take along the way. But he'd killed prey and left it where he could, hoping the blood would draw kin-wolves to cover their flanks. He'd also poured taint-salts into the scarce watering holes they passed. Anyone who drank from them over the next three days would find themselves incapacitated by dysentery. Even the girl proved her craft, giving him tips on how to quickly erase the evidence of their passing every ten leagues or so. "But understand," she had said, "that my sisters will also know these tricks and will know to look for them."

He looked behind them, watching the blue-green as it danced over glass and stone. "We should cover our tracks and turn south for a bit."

She passed the canteen to him. "I agree." Her brow furrowed, and when it did, her scars shifted.

He lifted the canteen to his lips and took a long swig of the tepid water. It tasted like copper in his mouth, and he tried to remember that last cool, fresh drink he'd taken. It had been months ago, when he'd been recovering with Renard's people. Even then, it had not been the sweet, cold water of the Ninefold Forest.

They covered their trail a half league behind them, established a false trail northwest and then turned south, chewing yet another bit of the root to carry them forward. As the juice took hold, Neb felt the elation seize him and gave himself to his pumping legs.

When the morning slipped upon them, they hid themselves in an abandoned Waste rat warren tucked in a crevice of pockmarked ancient stonework. The woman curled up and fell instantly asleep, and Neb watched her for a while, pondering her. She wasn't a Marsher, despite her use of the blood magicks. Her accent betrayed her even as her posture and appearance betrayed her kinship with House Li Tam. He dug into his pouch and withdrew the phial, opening the lid and sniffing the foul contents. Somehow, she was able to survive her use of them—unlike the Marshers, if what he'd heard in the Gypsy camp near D'Anjite's Bridge held true.

His eyes caught her again where the blanket fell free, exposing her bootless calf and foot. He forced them away again and tried to conjure up Winters's face.

I cannot remember her. After so long sharing dreams with her, she'd become a constant companion. Yet so quickly, she faded. He found the fickleness of his memory frustrating. He replaced the blood magicks, and his fingers lingered over the cloth-wrapped kin-raven. He pulled it out, careful not to let it touch his skin.

Holding it in the palm of his hand, Neb let the cloth fall away, exposing the black stone carving. He'd thought of it often since his first experience with it but had not let himself even bring it out.

"What are you doing?"

Her voice startled him and he jerked, spilling the kin-raven from the cloth and onto the floor. Without thinking, he snatched for it even as her hand found his wrist.

She cried out. "Don't—"

But the rest of her words fell away as his skin brushed the dark bird. Suddenly, he spun away and found himself in a darkened room that smelled like lavender. Winters stood at the foot of a bed, unbuttoning her dress and lifting it up over her lithe form. Her breasts had grown larger and her hips were more pronounced, and Neb found himself suddenly—

—in a great white tower high above a deep blue sea. An enormous brown moon filled the sky, and beside him, Isaak clacked and clicked in time to the song that surrounded them, his eyes flashing bright and then dull. Neb felt the reverberation of the canticle lifting the hair on his arms and neck.

"Neb?" the startled metal man asked. His eye shutters flashed, and before Neb could answer, he stood on a hillside, looking out over a sea of glass. The thirty-second daughter of Vlad Li Tam stood beside him as winds from the north and east rushed down upon them and—

—his father cried into the black stone he lay stretched out upon. "Hold fast, my son," his voice rang out. "Petronus rides for you."

A sharp pain in his wrist caused him to cry out, and he released the kin-raven. He looked up and locked eyes with the woman, his mouth falling open. Her face was washed clean of any expression, but her eyes were fierce. She twisted his wrist again, and he tried to twist himself with her. As he did, her other hand shot out and snaked the thorn rifle from the loose grip of his left hand.

She moved fast, and he found himself suddenly falling backward as she raised the rifle and pointed it at his chest. He saw her fingers stroke the thorn bulb, and he suddenly realized by the way she held it that she knew the weapon even better than he did. The bulb undulated beneath her touch, and before he could say anything, she squeezed two thorns into him.

"What are you—?" His tongue filled his mouth even as his arms fell heavy to his sides and the sudden weight of his body dragged him to the ground. She blurred ahead of him, her face still a mask, her eyes now shining emeralds so sharp that they could shred him at a glance.

"I'm sorry, Nebios," she said as the venom took hold and pulled him down toward thick, warm darkness.

The last thing he saw was her hand stretching out to take hold of the tiny black token. And the last thing Nebios Homeseeker heard before that dark swallowed him was her voice, low and suddenly sounding relieved.

"I have the Abomination right here for you, my sisters," she whispered to the kin-raven. "Come to me."

Chapter 12

Charles

Charles put down his screwdriver and lifted the tubelike monoscope by its leather harness. Outside, a steady snow fell, and the afternoon light that struck his work mirrors was barely enough to see by.

Of course, he could never tell if it was the lack of light or if perhaps it was just his age finally creeping home after years of squinting over his handiwork or over the words and specifications his order had dug from the ruins of the Old World and the worlds before that.

He pulled the monoscope over his head and cinched down the straps, blinking into the telescoping device as he spun gears to let more light into the tube and to adjust the lenses. He'd polished the Firstfall metal yet brighter before lining the monoscope's interior with it.

He turned to the caged rat and dropped a bit of raw meat, finely coated with a pinch of scout powders, in front of the sleeping rodent. It started, grabbed up the bit of venison and started nibbling.

The magicks took the rat quickly, and unfamiliar with the sensations, it launched itself against the sides of the cage, shaking it with the sudden burst of strength even as it warbled out of focus and then became the faintest blur. Charles tipped his head so that the monoscope was pointed at the cage, aware of how heavy it was as it pulled at him.

They weren't the blood magicks that the Marshers were using these days, but Charles hoped it was a close enough approximation to them. If so, he had accomplished a critical aspect of this work: The rat, now settling down and returning to the meat, was blurry but visible in the reflection cast into the silver of the scope.

Of course, the awkwardness of the device was another matter.

This would be improbable—maybe impossible—for a scout to wear in combat. He would turn himself to solving that problem next. For now, at least he knew it was functional and could be used for observation, even from a respectable distance.

Charles moved across the room and turned back. Closing his left eye, he squinted into the tube. He could no longer tell that it was a rat, but he clearly saw something hunched over in the cage.

Yes. He smiled, pleased with his work.

He pondered his pleasure in it, meditating on the Fourth Maxim of Franci B'Yot, the behaviorist who had influenced P'Andro Whym's thinking. *Examine every turn in the labyrinth of your mind, for your many thoughts are sacred in their truth, and the unexamined mind will be consumed by its fears and desires.*

Why is this work so satisfying to me? It did not take him long to see it. It pointed to a simpler time when he'd made simple *things.*

The days spent working to bring Isaak back from the dead had changed him. When he'd first petitioned the papal offices for permission to build the mechoservitors adapted from Rufello's *Book of Specifications,* he'd had no idea he would someday worry for an actual *person* he had created—a machine that had become human somehow, or something close to it—through the grief of genocide and the blood magick of Xhum Y'Zir's final spell.

The monoscope gave him such pleasure, he realized, because it was a problem he could solve. And because it distracted him from worrying about his metal child.

He'd seen little of Isaak in the past days. The metal man had spent his time locked away with the book by Tertius, and Charles suspected he was replaying the dream. The one time Charles had brought it up, Isaak had said nothing, though the shaking of his chassis, the pop of gears within and the sudden gout of steam betrayed the mechoservitor's discomfort.

Charles tried to turn his mind away from his concerns for Isaak, instead considering modifications that might make the monoscope less bulky and more conducive to scout warfare. He'd just lifted his pencil to make sketches when he heard Isaak's heavy but tentative knock on his door. He put down the pencil. "Come in."

Isaak came in and closed the door behind him. His bellows pumped, and steam shot from the exhaust grate set between his metal shoulders. "I've received a courier from Lord Rudolfo," the metal man said. "I wish to discuss it with you." Isaak looked to him and then looked away. "I wish to discuss the dream with you as well."

Charles nodded and gestured to the heavy stool near his worktable. "Sit with me, Isaak."

Charles sat, too, and waited for Isaak to speak. When he did, it seemed he spoke faster than normal, as if his words were crowding his narrow throat. "Lord Rudolfo has sent word by courier that an operation in the north requires two of the library's mechoservitors. They are required to have scripting or archived holdings in cartography and geology."

Curious, Charles thought. He felt his eyebrows raise. "I wonder what he's found there?"

Isaak's chassis trembled. "I do not know. He has asked me to decide which are best suited and send them north under scout protection in utmost secrecy."

Charles noted the lie Isaak's body betrayed with such subtlety. *Perhaps it was a half lie.* "Regardless, his specifications are clear. It should be easy enough to identify the two best equipped."

"Yes," he said. "But there is more, Father." He paused, his eyes flashing brighter and then dimmer. "I am proceeding further in my comprehension of the dream. Tertius's volume was . . . clarifying."

Charles wanted to ask him about the dream but did not. Instead, he forced himself to wait.

Finally, Isaak spoke, and when he did, Charles heard determination and passion in the metal man's voice. "I must join my cousins in their work," the metal man said, bursting into tears that filled the room with the smell of wet copper. "I must leave Lord Rudolfo and the library in other hands and serve the light revealed within the dream."

Charles felt the weight of the words and reached over to place a hand upon Isaak's shoulder. He wanted to ask him why, but everything the arch-engineer needed to hear was in his metal son's voice. "You're going north, too," he said.

Isaak nodded. "The equation holds true: My work here will not save the light. My work with my cousins may."

Charles had heard less conviction in the voices of fresh acolytes, still red-faced with zeal. He blinked at it. "When will you leave?"

"Three days from now," he said, his eye shutters blinking tears from the ducts set just beneath his jeweled eyes. "I will not run with the others. I will ride with a caravan of fresh recruits."

Charles nodded. It was enough time to set the mechoservitors to their tasks. "And where will you go?"

Isaak's chassis did not shake this time, though Charles was prepared for it to do so. "I will follow my cousins into the Beneath Places and join them in their analysis of the Book of Dreaming Kings."

The Beneath Places. Charles felt his face pale. He'd heard stories, of course. The buried basements of the world—civilizations built by survivors over the top of yet more basements stretching back to the forgotten times, the time of the Younger Gods.

Charles looked at Isaak, already calculating how much time he would need to teach the mechoservitors how to reproduce the monoscopes based on his prototype. After that, he would need time to pack and time to be certain the mechoservitors here could maintain themselves as needed. He did not believe for a moment that he would be gone for long. He also did not believe Isaak would be gone long, either, despite the passion he heard in the metal man's voice.

Still, his metal son was leaving, and Charles needed to be ready to leave with him and stay with him until either Isaak's cracked heart broke or until this strange dream had worked itself out of him.

When Isaak stood and left, Brother Charles watched the door and wondered how a thing that he had made could now be a person he loved. And how that person could compel him to action without answers to his questions, with questions left largely unasked.

He did not know. But he knew he was going and that once he had a plan in place, he would inform Isaak and House Steward Kember of his intentions.

Charles returned to his workbench, pushed aside his sketches and started plotting out the hours of his next three days.

Jin Li Tam

They pulled the heavy pine door closed behind them, forcing the winter wind back. Servants surged forward to take Jin Li Tam's, Winters's and Ria's heavy fur robes. They'd spent the morning in a leisurely breakfast and had then set out on foot to the new school, walking on paths plowed clean of snow by men with mules and sticks.

We are far north this winter, Jin Li Tam thought. At least fifty leagues farther than she'd been with the Wandering Army. She instinctively reached for Jakob's head again, touching his tiny ear. He rode snug and warm in his harness, sound asleep, though she was certain he would be hungry soon.

She wiped the snow from her boots onto the thick towels that had been placed there for them.

Ria did the same, smiling at Winters as she did. "I think you'll appreciate this," she said, "given your love of learning. Father's Androfrancine gave you a taste of what we're doing here." She said the word *Androfrancine* with an unmasked tone of disgust.

Jin Li Tam's eyes went to Winters's face just in time to see the look of surprise there. The girl glanced her direction, and the spark of anger that Jin saw gave her pause.

Ria walked down a carpeted hall to another door. Behind it, Jin heard a voice talking in a measured and gentle voice. Pausing, Ria smiled at her and then opened the door.

The classroom sat thirty children easily, lined up on plank tables and benches facing a teacher who sat at a small table at the head of the room. When they saw their queen, they stood.

"Good afternoon, children," Ria said. "I've brought you a most important guest."

Ria motioned for Jin Li Tam to enter, and she hesitated. Checking Jakob again, she stepped into the classroom.

As one, the teacher and the students bowed deeply. The teacher blushed. "Great Mother, I am honored to meet you. When I heard that you were bringing the Child of Promise to our school, I wept for joy."

Now Jin Li Tam found herself blushing. She couldn't find any words, and she was unable to meet the open adoration in the woman's eyes. She looked instead to Winters, who'd stepped into the room to stand beside her. The anger she'd seen was now tucked away, and Jin Li Tam noted the skill with which Winters concealed it.

Ria went to an empty section of table with three small chairs, motioning for them to sit. Once they had, the children sat, too. "I thought," the Machtvolk queen said to the children, "that we might sit with you and hear what you are learning."

The teacher beamed. "I was teaching them about the Great Promise."

Ria inclined her head. "Please continue."

The teacher returned the slight bow and walked to her table. Sitting down, she picked up the newly bound book. "Join me, children, in the fourth verse of the sixth chapter of the Last Gospel of Ahm Y'Zir."

Jin Li Tam remembered that title and glanced to Winters for confirmation. *Yes. She knows it, too.* It was the book Winters had brought to Rudolfo, the one that convinced him that they would be safe here. He'd translated passages for her, as had Winters, but she wondered how much it had lost through that process.

Now, she listened as the teacher selected a child to read the verse they were to discuss. The little girl stood, looked to Jin Li Tam, her face red, and then she recited from the book. "And at the end of days, a Crimson Empress shall rise from the south and a Child of Promise from the north to reunite a kinship long severed. And their reign shall heal this broken earth and restore the Machtvolk to their rightful home."

Jin Li Tam watched the room as the child read and saw that both the teacher and Ria closed their eyes for the recitation. When she finished, they opened them. "Excellent, Nandi," the teacher said. "So who can tell me what is the rightful home of the Machtvolk?"

A boy raised his hand. Jin Li Tam thought he couldn't be older than eight. When the teacher called upon him, he answered in a loud, clear voice. "Our rightful home is in service to House Y'Zir as hand servants to the Crimson Empress and her betrothed."

"Yes," she said. "Very good."

For the next thirty minutes, the teacher asked questions and various students raised their hands. As they asked and answered questions, she found herself caught up in the elaborate story of their gospel, and it disturbed her. On the one hand, she could see the comfort it would bring to know their station, to hope for a better, healed world and to be connected in some way to that healing through their service. But on the other hand, she saw that they were teaching these things to children. Certainly, adults would also believe it—surely the evangelists she and Rudolfo had spoken with believed with their whole hearts. But those adults would turn quicker to doubt than a child would. What they taught these children, now at such a young age, would stick to their hearts like the snow falling outside. Wizard Kings worthy of worship, kin-healing and magick by the shedding of blood—it would follow them throughout their lives.

Your grandfather created this and fed it, she tried to tell herself. But the more she heard, the less she believed that possible. He'd not created it. He'd *believed* it. And he would not have without good reason.

This also disturbed her, and she found herself pulled into the Whymer Maze yet again.

At the end of the lesson, the teacher invited Jin Li Tam and Jakob to the front of the class. She presented them with a copy of the gospel they'd read from—bound in cured leather and translated into Landlish from the ancient language of House Y'Zir.

After they bundled into their robes, they trudged back through the snow to Ria's lodge, where they were met by a warm foyer and yet more servants to help with robes and boots. While the others moved off to the dining room, Jin Li Tam excused herself to feed Jakob. At home, she would have thought nothing of feeding him anywhere she happened to be. But here, with the way these people looked at her and her son, she craved privacy.

She slipped down the hall and opened her door, turning to close it and suddenly stopping when she was caught off guard by the slight breeze that followed her in. "I'll trust you to turn your back, scout," she said as she went to the bed and pulled Jakob from his harness.

"Apologies, Lady Tam," the Gypsy Scout said in a voice muffled with magick. "First Captain Aedric bid me bring word directly to you."

Jin Li Tam laid her son on the bed and shrugged out of the harness, setting it aside. Then, she checked his diaper and unbuttoned her shirt before raising him to her bared breast. She winced as he took the nipple, feeling the beginnings of his teeth. "What have you learned?"

"We spent today scouting unusual bird migration to the northwest and found something of note. A series of caves outfitted as a messaging station."

She heard hesitation in his voice, despite the magicks. "What else?"

"There is evidence of messages being intercepted and altered," the scout said. "And birds are being diverted here somehow."

She'd known that the birds had become unreliable. She remembered well the forged note she'd received in her sister's hand just before Jakob's healing, telling her there was no cure. Setting her up to turn to Ria's blood magick as her last and best hope.

She closed her eyes against the pull of Jakob's mouth. "Is there more?"

"More evidence of compulsory worship for those who are not quick to convert. Forced cuttings. We think there may be a fledgling resistance movement at work, as well."

She nodded. "Very well. Tell Aedric to keep the scouts out and gathering intelligence where they can. I will figure out how to get word to Rudolfo."

"Aye, Lady."

She looked over her shoulder in the direction of his voice. "Now, stay put until I've finished and I'll let you out on my way to lunch."

She turned her attention back to her boy and found herself wondering how it was that he had become so important in this story that she was only now just beginning to grasp. It was an ancient story that stretched back beyond the Age of the Wizard Kings, if today's lesson was to be believed. And it was a story that her father's father had embraced to such a degree that he had arranged to sacrifice his first son and most of his family in order to heal kinship with House Y'Zir. He'd engineered within the Named Lands the beginnings of the fall of the Androfrancines and, through her father, both Rudolfo's reign and her own betrothal to him. He'd arranged for her, through her father, to bear Rudolfo an heir. And had also arranged the transfer of the library, the Order's holdings, and their own family's vast wealth into the Forester's hands.

She wondered if her grandfather bore the coming sacrifice of his family like a great mountain upon his back. Or did he find joy in it? Or both?

She wondered what it meant to believe in something so completely as to make such choices, to love something so wholly as to give everything for it.

Then Jin Li Tam looked to the face of her suckling son and understood what could bring her to that place.

Still, it did not comfort her to know it.

Winters

Outside, wind rattled the shutters and Winters felt sleep pulling at her even as she turned another page in the gospel she read.

She'd read the book innumerable times now, gleaning what she could from the cryptic passages and prophetic promises. She wasn't sure why she poured herself into it; it seemed the only thing she could do. Somehow, she thought, if she could just understand these new beliefs among her people, she might know how to free them from its hold.

No, she told herself, not new, but old. Some aspects older even than their sojourn in this land.

Still, how long had this resurgence lain in secret, gorging itself on her tribe beneath her and Hanric's oblivious eyes? At least back to the time of her father, she knew. And had he been aware of it? Had he, like Jin Li Tam's grandfather, been an active participant in this faith? She could not believe that, but neither could she believe how wrong his dreams had been, how wrong her own dreams had been, in light of what now happened in their world. Some part of her still wept for the home she was so certain would rise, and for the boy now lost to her whom she'd so completely believed would take them there.

She stretched up a hand to check the knife hilts that peeked out from beneath her pillow. They seemed much more likely than dreams or boys when it came to taking back her land. She'd even found herself considering whether or not she could slip one of those blades between the ribs of her older sister and take back by force what she had lost by apathy. But the moment that violent thought intruded, her stomach clenched and recoiled at the thought of it.

What would Jin Li Tam think of that? she wondered. She knew the woman was capable of killing. They'd danced with the knives each morning, and surely the movements of body and blades could be taught. Already, she felt competent. But could that redheaded courtesan spy turned Gypsy Queen and mother teach Winters how to kill?

It is not who I am. But maybe, she thought, *it is who I need to be.*

She forced her mind back into the gospel.

And in those days the birds of the sky shall betray and the darkness that masquerades as light shall be fully illuminated by the grace of House Y'Zir. The Usurper's city will become a pyre and the Machtvolk will rise from their ashes and mud to make straight a path for the Crimson Empress's advent.

She thumbed the pages forward now, finding a less familiar passage.

And behold, I saw those dwelling in the Beneath Places and heard these making their bargain with devils. Weeping, I watched them summon forth their abomination to damn and desolate the children of men by a song. And I wept not because of the sorrow of this, but because of the grace of the Crimson Empress, for even in this, she would prevail in joy, and heal our broken home.

She read it again, drawn in by the power of the words. She'd read as many books as she could get her hands on—Tertius had been particularly good at smuggling them in. She'd read most of P'Andro Whym's gospels, but his were not so dressed in imagery, parable and prophecy. They were mostly admonitions and stories around the preservation of human knowledge and learning from the mistakes of the past.

But these writings, unlike the reason-based words of the Androfrancines, were not so very different from her own Book of Dreaming Kings, and she knew that this similarity was at least a part of its appeal among those of her people who now believed it. It was specific enough to give something of substance to cling to, yet vague enough to allow for varied interpretations.

And unlike the Book of Dreaming Kings, this gospel was something every family could sit with near the fire, read on a winter's night and feel a part of.

Closing the book, she climbed out of her bed and put it on the shelf as far from her as the room allowed. She couldn't bear to keep it any closer. Then, she settled back into the bed, savoring its warmth in the cool room. She dimmed the lantern and gave herself to rehearsing the steps of tomorrow's knife dance. She'd moved through the dervish twice and started on a third, mentally noting each place she'd put her feet in the muddy snow, trying to block out the book.

When the dream fell upon her after so long away, it jarred her and she blinked at the suddenness of it. Sitting up in her Wicker Throne, she savored the sunlight that somehow found her and bathed her here in her subterranean throne room.

She felt a presence and spoke to it. "Neb?"

The only answer was the faint sound of clicking and clacking that drifted up to her from the tunnels behind her. Rising, she gripped the Firstfall axe tightly in her fists, wishing instead for scout knives, and made her way toward that sound.

Winters descended into the caves, passing her sleeping and bathing areas as she wound her way to the leagues-long cavern where she'd spent most of her life before leaving for the war two years earlier. As she drew closer, she heard the sound of a harp and for a moment recalled another dream from months before. She looked in the sitting area and was not surprised to see Tertius sitting there, his fingers moving over the strings and filling the room with music. The last time she'd seen him in this place, the Book of Dreaming Kings was burning as it was consumed by the light. This time, the dream was different.

Four robed figures stood facing the shelves of volumes that lined the walls, and she watched as metal hands moved quickly over the volumes, pulling down one here and one there. The clacking and clicking was louder, now, and punctuated by massive gouts of steam that burst from vents in their metal backs. And whatever books they pulled down did not get replaced, leaving gaps on the shelves, sockets empty of their teeth. She stepped toward them.

"Careful," Tertius warned her, picking up the tempo of his song upon the harp. "They will consume you, too, my queen."

She looked back to him but could not heed his warning. Instead, she stepped even closer and saw more clearly what they did.

Raising the volumes to their metal mouths, they bit into them with sharpened teeth and chewed the paper down, devouring the volumes as quickly as they could.

Her own voice startled her as she reached out a hand, laying it upon a wool-clad shoulder that was warm to her touch. "No," she cried.

The metal man turned on her, quickly, a free hand suddenly flashing up to grab her wrist even as its eyes went bright yellow with alarm. "You do not belong here." It looked to its neighbor. "The tamp is not holding."

"We knew that it might not," the other said. "Their very blood conducts the dream."

"We may be seen," another ventured.

All around her, the song swelled to a crescendo, and she struggled to look back toward Tertius and his harp, only now she could not see him. The metal men crowded her, their mouths opening and closing, no longer seeking the dream on paper as they instead sought it from her flesh.

As those mouths descended upon her, she heard a great shriek and knew that it was she who made it. She felt the teeth grinding over her skin, felt the hungry hands grabbing to hold her still that they might bite into her. She tried to raise the Firstfall axe in her hands, tried to swing it at the metal men, and suddenly there was another presence with her in this room.

"Neb?" she asked again.

"Peace, Winteria," a voice whispered to her. "The dream tamp is merely failing. And as it is with dreams, this one is not as it appears."

The metal men continued to crowd her, and she fell down to her knees beneath the weight of them. Beyond them, she saw wet bare feet that stood in silver puddles near where Tertius had played. Now, though, the harpist and his song had suddenly vanished. She felt a sob shudder out of her. "Who are you? Why won't you help me?"

She wished she could see the man's face as he spoke, but already her eyes were closing involuntarily against the sudden pain she felt as their teeth rent and sundered her. "I cannot help," the man said. "I can only observe. But you can help yourself. Give yourself back to the dream, child."

I do not know how, she tried to say but couldn't.

As if hearing, he answered her. "Give yourself to it. Lay down your axe."

Taking a deep breath, she forced her hands to release the axe and gave herself over to their grabbing hands and biting teeth. She made herself breathe through it and felt the pain become a cool breeze scented with unfamiliar flowers and warm, salted air.

And suddenly, the hands and mouths were gone from her and she stood with a dozen mechoservitors—no, she realized, at least two dozen, maybe even an army of them—upon a massive white tower overlooking a blue-green ocean so clear that it hurt her eyes. Above her, a brown moon filled the sky far larger than any moon could be, and she remembered it from her dreams.

This is our home, she remembered telling Neb where they lay naked and sweating in an open-air bed that showed them that great moon.

All around her, the song rang out and the mechoservitors danced in time to it, forming a great circle that turned around her.

"It requires a response," they sang in unison.

It was the sound of that great metal choir that jarred her from her sleep and caused her to sit bolt upright in her bed.

Weeping, Winters did what she'd done with every dream she'd ever remembered for as far back as she had memory. She went to her desk and, with shaking hand, lifted up her pen to write it down.

Neb

Neb's first awareness was a throbbing pain that licked at him, gradually building to a fierce, hot light that burned him as he forced his eyes open. A blue sky stared back at him, and he struggled to get out from under its brightness.

"He's awake," a woman's voice said just outside his vision. But when she leaned in, her face eclipsed that piercing sky and the shadow of it prevented him from seeing her. "Hello, Abomination." The booted foot surprised him when it struck his side; he felt the wind go out of him. "That is for our sister." The boot landed again, and this time he saw sparks of light behind his eyes and cried out from the pain. "And there are more to come."

He winced and licked his lips. "I don't—"

Another face eclipsed the sky, and now his eyes were adjusted enough to see the thirty-second daughter of Vlad Li Tam. Only now, her face was puffy and bruised, one eye nearly swollen shut. "And *I* haven't even begun with you, Abomination," she said, her voice low and full of rage. "I will repay you sevenfold for every injustice you dealt me." She leaned closer. "*Every* injustice," she said again.

"You'll have your time, sister," another voice said. "For now, be grateful that you were correct about the thorns. If you'd been wrong, you'd be bound for the Imperial Cutting Gardens."

When the thirty-second daughter spoke, her voice was assured. "I was never in doubt, sister. The scriptures are clear on this matter:

And the thorn shall not sting him, nor the beasts of the beneath rend him, nor the ghosts in the water flee him, for the Abomination shall beguile them all.

Neb opened his mouth to speak, turning and twisting. Only now was awareness leaking into him. His arms were stretched out and his wrists burned from the ropes that bound him to what he assumed must be stakes driven into the hard-packed ground. Similar ropes bound his ankles, and he was suddenly aware of his nudity. He closed his mouth.

Their voices shifted suddenly to a language he did not understand, and their faces withdrew from his sight. He lay there, slowly taking inventory of his senses and his questions.

What could he remember? He'd been holding the tiny kin-raven token, and then he'd been startled. It had made contact with his skin and he'd suddenly found himself pulled away again, similar to the time before.

What had he seen? He'd heard his father's voice at some point, but the words seemed far away now. He'd seen Winters briefly, undressing, and then there had been a white tower and—

It requires a response.

Isaak was there with him and they were surrounded by the song, so loud it lifted the hair on his arms and neck and moved through the air around them.

He felt the hot stab of shame. *I've lost it; I've lost the dream.* The silver crescent was now in the hands of these women, and though he did not know who they were or what they intended with him, he did know they were his enemies. And they were enemies of the dream as well.

Neb tested the rope gently with his left arm, then his right. He did the same with his feet. It was tight enough that he doubted he could slip free, but even if he could, what next? There were at least three—perhaps four—of these women, and each, he assumed, was armed in much the same way as the thirty-second daughter had been when he'd found her.

The thought of her twisted that hot knife in him. He'd trusted her and she had betrayed him, delivering him over to her so-called sisters. He had saved her life, and from everything he could glean from her so far, she'd seemed sincere in her need to reach the Ninefold Forest with her message. She'd readily accepted his help, and then, the moment he touched the kin-raven, she'd turned on him and put him down with his own rifle, summoning her sisters to their location.

Or so it seemed.

Their leader was back now, crouching beside his head and leaning in so he could now see her. She wore dark silk trousers and a matching shirt, unbuttoned near the top to reveal the gentle curve of her breasts as she bent over him. Her face was seasoned by midlife, her hair gray and cut so short that it bristled. And like the other girl, her face and arms were latticed with symbols cut into her skin. Her blue eyes were piercing and cold even in this desert.

"Who are you?" he managed to croak.

She chuckled. "I am one who saves us all from the Abomination and his dream." She held up a long silver knife. "And I'm nearly ready to begin that saving."

He looked at the blade; it wasn't a scout knife. It was more delicate, its edge crusted with salt, and he felt his stomach twist. "What do you want?"

She grinned. "First, I want you to know how serious I am. Then, I want you to tell me where you've hidden the artifact and show me where the mechoservitors are."

Hidden the artifact?

The thirty-second daughter appeared above and behind her, and he squinted through the sunlight to make out the expression on her face. For just the slightest moment, he thought he saw fear there. Then, the mask was firmly in place again and she spoke. "I request the first cut, sister."

The woman with the knife cocked her head, considering Neb. "It is a reasonable request given the price you've paid to bring us to him." She held the knife up, and after the girl took it, she stepped back. "First blood is yours."

The girl moved in to crouch beside him, then leaned over him so that her face was near his. "You've brought this on yourself, Abomination." And as she said it, her hand pressed at his shoulder even as she turned her body so that it was between them and the other woman. It took him a moment to pick out the message in her fingers. *Stupid, silly boy—you left me no choice.*

It was the subverbal of the Gypsy Scouts, a language of touch and hand-signs he'd only barely begun to learn before leaving his training as an officer in Rudolfo's Ninefold Forest.

He tried to mask the recognition in his face, and even as he did, he felt the cold edge of the blade moving over his body, a slender fang looking for the right place to bite. *Be strong, Nebios,* the one hand told him.

Then, the other began its darker work, opening a cut that ran from his collarbone to his navel, and Neb tried with every bit of his resolve to not scream at the sudden, searing pain of it as he bucked against the ropes that held him.

He failed utterly.

Rudolfo

Rudolfo scanned the message again, his eyes finding each smudge, each slant to a letter or space between. After reading it for the second time, he cursed again, this time more loudly.

"When did this happen?" he asked, letting the anger show in his voice.

"Five nights past," the courier said.

Rudolfo could imagine it. Some kind of distraction to get his men to open the gate. And then a quick skirmish. Certainly his Gypsy Scouts had done their best, but they were no match for their blood-magicked opponents and the element of surprise.

I am infiltrated on my most protected border. The Keeper's Gate was the only access point to the Churning Wastes unless one was inclined to sail around the horn—something a few men like Rafe Merrique had been known to do. Rudolfo's men had guarded it since Petronus deeded the Androfrancine holdings to the Ninefold Forest before dissolving the Order. And truly, he'd not expected to be guarding it from that direction. They held the gate to keep the Churning Wastes closed to the rest of their neighbors.

But now, a small band of blood-magicked scouts ran his forests.

Why? And who are they? They couldn't be Machtvolk unless they'd somehow sailed the horn, which he found unlikely.

He'd read Petronus's notes and had talked with Vlad Li Tam about his father's slender volume that outlined a strategy for the fall of an order and the changing of an age. He'd read the new gospel of the

Y'Zirite resurgency, written by Ahm Y'Zir, the seventh son of Xhum Y'Zir, and seen his own family somehow written into this story.

He thought back to his time on the island of the Blood Temple during the rescue of House Li Tam. The remnants of that family had seen unfamiliar vessels in the water there, and that took doing, given that Vlad Li Tam's family had been the premier ship-builders in the Named Lands before turning to banking. If they did not recognize them, then these vessels had not sailed the Emerald Sea of the Named Lands. They were foreign, and this pointed in a direction that piqued Rudolfo's curiosity and whispered third alarm along his spine.

For over two thousand years, they had lived in these lands and believed they were alone in the world but for a few scattered people in the Wastes.

But what if we were not alone?

He forced himself back to the courier scout who stood waiting for a reply. He looked to Philemus. "What do you think?"

"Double the guard upon the Wall and upon the manors, General," the second captain said.

Rudolfo nodded, feeling the weariness settling into him. The command tent was suddenly cold. "I concur," he said. "I will return to the Seventh Forest Manor and continue the investigation."

Philemus blinked. "There isn't much you can do in the investigation, General."

Something stirred in Rudolfo at the second captain's words, and it felt like anger. *He's right, of course.*

And more importantly, Rudolfo realized, Philemus was surprised.

Philemus was a savvy soldier turned scout. He'd held the same captaincy under Gregoric for a dozen years and had personally requested that Aedric be promoted to the position his father vacated. An older man, he'd still distinguished himself in the War for Windwir and wore his scarf of rank knotted to show his accomplishments in battle. But more importantly, he'd known the Gypsy King for most of Rudolfo's life.

"I'll have a squad ready to escort you," Philemus finally said. "And I will keep courier lines open between our new interests in the north and your office in the Seventh Forest Manor."

Rudolfo inclined his head. "Excellent, Captain. I think I will also—"

He heard running feet and an excited whistle outside the tent. They both turned toward the flap as it opened for the officer of the watch. "We've found something . . . *unusual,* Captain Philemus."

The second captain scowled. "What is it?"

The man was breathless, and behind him, the light warbled in just a way for Rudolfo to see the vague form of a magicked scout. "Y'Zirite activity, Captain."

He'd not expected this, especially in this isolated region. There were a few scattered villages, but the nearest major town was his Eighth Forest Manor, at least a hundred leagues south. Rudolfo's eyes narrowed. "Evangelists? This far north and east?"

The officer of the watch shook his head. "Not evangelists, General."

Rudolfo met Philemus's eyes and knew his second captain also saw the grim expression upon the officer's face. Words were not going to suffice.

"Show us," Rudolfo said.

Ten minutes later, they ran magicked through the deep northern forest, tongues clicking against the roofs of their mouths to keep formation. Rudolfo kept Philemus on his right, just behind the young scout who'd brought word of this discovery. Around them, mist lay over the top of the ground, writhing with the breeze they made as they sprinted lightly over the surface of the frozen snow. Over them, the canopy of trees filtered the gray light.

Rudolfo stretched his legs into the magicks, finding it hard to keep his balance with just one hand free. He kept his lips pressed tight against the nausea and the headache that always beset him when he used the scout powders and ran with his head down and his eyes moving to the left and right.

Certainly, it was unseemly for someone of his position to magick himself, though his men had seen him do it before on a handful occasions—most occurring since Windwir's fall. Unlike his scouts, he'd not been raised on the powders. He'd used them only enough to learn how to function under their heady influence. His father and his first captain had understood that sometimes the interpretation of kin-clave must be a fluid thing.

They ran ten leagues, and despite the stamina and speed the magicks lent him, Rudolfo knew his body would feel the run later, after the powders had burned their way out of his body. These powders, drawn and mixed from the various ingredients found in the earth's roots and minerals, berries and herbs could render the user stronger, faster, quieter and nearly invisible. But the scouts who had breached his eastern border there at the Keeper's Gate used magicks enhanced by blood and superior to anything the earth could give. Of course, until Ria showed up under those magicks, Rudolfo had assumed that the Machtvolk advantage was tempered by the fact that these magicks ultimately killed those who used them. They'd found the bodies of the Marsher scouts who'd carried out the attack on his Firstborn Feast. And he'd watched several of the Tam family lay down their lives by taking up the blood magicks to rescue their father, most notably the alchemist daughter, Rae Li Tam. But Ria had not been harmed by them, and now these other scouts—either Machtvolk sent despite his firm words to Ria about breaching his borders, or some new threat—used them as well.

A part of him wished he'd brought back a supply that his River Woman could've studied. He'd been in a room full of these magicks, there in the Blood Temple's armory, and had not thought about it.

It is a formidable advantage in this strange war of ours. A war, he reminded himself, where he could no longer be certain who was friend and who was foe.

Ahead, the clicking shifted to the softest of whistles, and Rudolfo slowed. They were leaving one patch of evergreen and crossing a white clearing. Already, enough snow had fallen to cover the tracks of the patrol who had found this place earlier in the day. If they were fortunate, enough would fall over the next few hours to cover this latest trail.

They walked now, picking their way to the edge of a copse of trees. These were a darker evergreen, growing closely together and choked with more underbrush than was common in these parts. The nearer they drew, the more unusual it seemed until he realized it was because of the type of underbrush. These were the thick, twisted and thorny bushes used to cultivate Whymer Mazes—not a native plant this far north. And it had been seeded in the midst of these darker trees, creating a natural boundary to discourage entrance to this particular wood.

"There is an access point just north," the scout said in a muffled voice that the breeze carried to Rudolfo's ears.

They skirted the line of trees and brush, finally stopping at a small and narrow gap. With more whistles and clicks, the squad of Gypsy Scouts fanned out to establish a perimeter, their breath on the air and the clouds of snow where their feet fell giving them away.

Rudolfo waited until he felt the others slip ahead of him. Then, he followed and saw that the narrow tunnel twisted and turned much like a Whymer Maze before depositing them into a clearing that would have never been expected based on how the copse looked from outside.

There in the center of the clearing stood a windowless building made of white stone and hedged with yet more thornbushes. A large dark door stood closed against the weather. He felt a chill deeper than the winter air and forced his feet to carry him forward.

Even before he reached out to the open the door, he knew what this place was, and it took him no time at all to count the years it would take to hide it so thoroughly here within his Ninefold Forest, or to judge by the stonework, how long this building had stood here.

It was at least as old as he was, if not older.

He pushed the door open and waited for his eyes to adjust to the gloomy single room it opened on. It was round, like the Blood Temple, and in the center lay a stained altar with its carved symbols and its catch-troughs for the blood spilled upon it. Rough wooden benches surrounded it, and Rudolfo slipped into the large room.

He noticed the absence of dust, the faintest smell of smoke and something sweet and cloying on the air.

"It's been used recently," he said in a voice that shook with an emotion he could not identify.

"Yes," the scout said. "Within the last two weeks, though they were very careful to cover their tracks. There is a Rufello chest behind the altar."

Rudolfo picked his way around the room and saw the box there. He'd studied the earlier resurgences enough to know what would be within it. Copies of their so-called gospels—perhaps even this newest by Ahm Y'Zir, the one that spoke of his family as a part of the Crimson Empress's coming salvation. And there would be a set of silver knives wrapped in black velvet. Meditation candles made from wax and fat and blood, certainly, and vestal robes for whichever of his people served as the priest for this secluded shrine.

Shaking, he sat down on a bench and regarded the altar. He felt Philemus's hand on his shoulder and forced himself to decipher the pressing fingers.

This, Philemus said with his hands, *is much worse than we expected.*

"Yes," Rudolfo said in a quiet voice.

Friends now become enemies who sought to bring down his household. An enemy posing as his friend to the northwest, breaching his borders at will and sending their river of tripe into his lands by way of their evangelists. Beyond all of that, a potential enemy abroad—possibly dressed up as this Crimson Empress—and now this.

Evidence of Y'Zirite activity indeed, he thought, but stretching back decades in his Ninefold Forest. He reached up a tentative hand, finding Philemus's shoulder. *I want this site watched night and day. I want a list of every man, woman and child who visits this shrine, and I want to know where they are from.* But even as he issued the orders, he knew that it was just one shrine. How many others could be hidden away from the more populated corners of the forest?

Philemus's response was not quick. There was hesitation in the fingers when they finally moved again. *Aye, General.*

He dropped his hand back into his lap. Then slowly, he stood and turned his back upon the altar. He made his way out of the simple stone building and waited for the others to remove all traces of their passing in this place. Already, his mind spun strategy after strategy, trying to find some way—any way—to deal effectively with this latest discovery.

I am beset without and within, Rudolfo realized. *And there may truly be no victory at the end of this.* It bore all the markings of a carefully laid path, set into place possibly before he'd even been born. "Philemus?"

He felt the wind on his cheek. "Yes, Lord?"

"I will not be riding for the Seventh Forest Manor after all," Rudolfo said. "I will stay north with the army. But I want you ride south and personally command a careful but quiet search of the Ninefold Forest for more of these shrines. We need to know where they are and who is involved."

He felt the hand upon his shoulder again. *You are asking me to use the scouts for intelligence gathering among our own people? With resources already stretched?*

And they *were* stretched. He could only hope that Lysias's recruiting strategies would help. But that was not the larger concern in his second captain's mind. Using magicked scouts to follow his own people was a path no Gypsy King before him had taken. "I am not asking you," Rudolfo said in a measured voice. "I am *ordering* you to."

"Aye, General," Philemus said, and Rudolfo heard the discomfort in his voice.

As they set out for camp, Rudolfo slowed his pace and hung back. With each booted foot upon the snow, he tried to find some kind of hope he could cling to that his position was not as untenable as it appeared.

But deep in his heart, Rudolfo knew the truth. And whatever part of his father that still existed within him felt despair and shame at what he knew must certainly be coming.

Petronus

A hot wind rose from the east and pressed down upon them as they made their way across a sea of razor-edged glass intersected by a road just wide enough for two to ride abreast. Petronus rode with his head low, a straw hat held tightly in place with one hand. To his right, Grymlis leaned forward in his saddle. Behind them, their ragged company of scouts and Gray Guard stretched out across the desert.

There was salt on the air and the dead dust of cities. When he was younger, Petronus had had a certain romance about this place. He'd dug in the woods behind his parents' house as a boy, pretending he was an Androfrancine pulling fragments of the light out of the desolation. That romanticism led eventually to belief in their dream and his decision to join the Order.

Now, though, he saw only stark reminders of humanity's capacity for apocalypse.

Petronus.

He looked around, suddenly aware of a tingling in his scalp and a tickling in his ears.

"Petronus?"

He looked up from his desk and the thick parchment reports that awaited his attention. "Yes?" He blinked, recognizing the man who sat across from him. "You're Hebda."

The man nodded, his face looking frantic despite the relative calm of the afternoon. "Listen to me," he said. "Neb has somehow overpowered the dream tamps."

"Dream tamps?" He'd heard these words, but what did they mean?

"Not just one," Hebda said, his voice rising. "*All* of them."

Petronus shook his head. *Another waking dream.* He'd just been in the Wastes. He still had the smell of dust and salt in his nose. "What does that mean?"

He looked somber. "It means we can't contain the dream. It means they can follow it to the mechoservitors." He leaned forward. "Listen."

Petronus listened, tilting his head. Far away, on the wind, he heard a harp. "I know that song."

"Yes," Hebda said. "'A Canticle for the Fallen Moon,' in E minor, by the Last Weeping Czar Frederico." He pointed to a report on the desk, and Petronus looked down at it. "We strongly suspect that Frederico did not actually compose the piece. We believe he heard it and learned to play it."

Petronus tried to recall the details of that particular bit of Old World lore. These stories were ancient when the Churning Wastes were a densely populated continent under the watchful eye of the seven Wizard Kings and their father. He certainly remembered the myth of Frederico and Amal Y'Zir, how their tragic love brought about the Year of the Falling Moon. He looked to the report and scanned the first page. Something about an artifact found hidden away and the song it played, over and over again. He turned the page and scanned the next. "It somehow *affected* the mechoservitors at Sanctorum Lux?"

"Yes," Hebda said. "Neb, too. His exposure to the Cacophonic Deaths greatly enhanced his sensitivity to it. You are sensitive as well, because of your own exposure to blood magicks, though until now the tamps have kept you insulated."

Petronus thought about this. "But these tamps do not work with Neb?"

"They did at first." Hebda looked around the office, as if expecting to see someone. Then, he lowered his voice. "Neb is special; he had latent sensitivity by nature of who he is and the explosion at Windwir. But he's found something out there. Something similar, I think, to what I'm using now to speak to you."

Special. Latent sensitivity by nature of who he is. Petronus took the words, examined them, filed them away. Instead, he forced himself to think of that massive black rock surrounded by an underground sea of quicksilver. Seen from above, at least in his imagination, it looked like a dark and staring eye.

Petronus looked up and met eyes with Hebda. "How many of you survived Windwir?"

Hebda looked around again. "It would be imprudent to discuss that under these circumstances."

Petronus leaned forward, placing both hands flat upon his desk. "What is the operating mission and authority of the Office for the Preservation of Light?"

"Our authority is Papal by Holy Unction. Our mission is secret."

"I am the Pope," Petronus said, his voice rising.

"No," Hebda answered. "You *were* the Pope." Then he stood. "This is fruitless, Petronus. We do not have any more time for this." He pointed to a map that suddenly, conveniently lay open, covering half the desk. "His last transmission point was *here*." He pointed to a point on the map, and Petronus quickly memorized the surrounding area. "If they capture him, they will use him to find the mechoservitors. He has great reach with whatever it is he's found. And if they find the mechoservitors, the light will be utterly lost to us."

Already, he could smell the salt and dust choking out the scent of lavender and paper. But he had to ask at least one more question. "Who are they?"

"They," Hebda said, "are the Blood Guard of the Crimson Empress. And they're now loosed in the Named Lands as well."

Petronus felt the sharp edge of the rock as he connected with it and watched the world blaze white for a moment. Slowly, it refocused and he saw that he was staring into the sky. It was one of those days when the moon was visible, and he saw it thinly veiled behind high, thin clouds. The horses around him stopped, including his own, and Grymlis dismounted.

"Another one?" the grizzled captain asked.

But Petronus said nothing. Instead, he wondered how he'd not heard it before. Because it was everywhere, he now realized. The song was all around him.

And, Petronus knew, it required a response.

Vlad Li Tam

Vlad Li Tam knocked lightly on the boiler room door and slipped inside, pulling it closed behind him as he did. The heat of the room washed over him, and he felt the sweat rising. He licked the salt from his lips and glanced around the room.

Baryk stood nearby, and beside him, Vlad's forty-eighth son, Ren, covered in grease and wet from sweat. On the far end of the room stood the sunstone vault—a massive steel compartment with Rufello locks to keep the ancient power source secure. Though he wasn't supposed to have them, Vlad had long ago paid very well to acquire the ciphers for the locks, but he'd yet to need them. The boiler stood in the center, a series of pipes leading to and from it carrying steam aft to power the engines. Stretched out on a rack, almost as if hung to dry, the metal man stood, chest plate open, wires spilling out. Ren held one end of a braid of wires that led deep into the chest cavity.

He looked to him. "Are you ready, Father?

Vlad nodded. "Do you think it will work?"

"I think so," the young man said. "Yes."

They'd spent the better part of a day looking over the metal man before Ren Li Tam had been brought over from one of the other ships. He'd studied the mechanicals during a dispensational apprenticeship to the library in his youth and had continued to dabble here and there with what little he could find.

It took him no time at all to see that the mechoservitor's power supply had somehow burned out.

Now, most of a week later, they were ready to reactivate the mechanical using the sunstone that powered the flagship of the iron fleet. Ren had gone over his plan with them quite carefully, and Vlad didn't see a better way to discover how a mechanical could be adrift in the deepest south of the Ghosting Crests in one of Rafe Merrique's lifeboats.

"I'm going to power us down," Ren said, throwing a large switch. "Then I will wire the mechoservitor directly to the sunstone."

The vibration of the ship that he'd grown so used to was suddenly gone, and Vlad looked up. He could hear everyone breathing in the quiet.

He watched as Ren threaded his end of the wire braid through what looked like the eye of a gigantic needle set into the side of the vault. He knotted the braids and then pushed the needle into a slot in the side of the vault, slowly. When he was finished, he wiped the sweat from his hands and threw the switch.

The mechoservitor danced upon the rack for a moment, then settled as its boiler started ticking. After a few minutes, the amber eyes fluttered open as the shutters blinked.

"Are you functional?" Ren asked it.

"I am functional," it answered.

"What is your designation?"

"I am Mechoservitor Number Seven, First Generation, attached to the Office for the Preservation of the Light by Holy Unction of Pope Introspect." The metal man shook violently as he spoke, his bellows pumping wildly as his eye shutters opened and closed fast as hummingbird wings. Then, the shaking stopped and the eyes grew bright and then dim. "My name is Obadiah."

Vlad blinked. "You have a name?" He was familiar with Isaak—though the last time he'd seen that metal man had been at Sethbert's arranged execution well over a year before. Still, Isaak was the only mechoservitor he knew of to take a name.

"I do," the mechoservitor said. "Where am I?"

"You are aboard *The Serendipitous Wind*, flagship of House Li Tam," Vlad said. "What are you doing so far to sea? And how do you come to be in one of the *Kinshark*'s lifeboats?"

The metal man pulled at the chains that bound him to the rack. "Why am I restrained?" He stretched his legs.

Vlad smiled. "I ordered it. To be certain of you. When I am, I will order it otherwise."

The mechoservitor blinked. "You are the captain of this vessel?"

"I am Vlad Li Tam."

The mechoservitor clicked and clacked, its eyes flashing again. "Do you serve the light, Lord Tam?"

An odd question. And one he'd not thought about for a good while. Not so long ago, he might have lied in his answer. But now, he opted for the truth. "I do not serve anything," Vlad Li Tam said.

"The light requires service of you."

How many times had he heard these words? To be fair, at least half the times that he had acquiesced when they called, it had been because of some secondary outcome he could achieve beneath their very cowl-shadowed noses. His eyes narrowed. "What service does the light require, Obadiah?"

"A replacement power source. The twelve vessels provided you by the Androfrancine Order are powered by sunstones and—"

"Six vessels now," Vlad said. "Perhaps we can barter a satisfactory arrangement." He glanced around the room, saw the stool someone had placed for him, and sat in it. "But first, a conversation."

"Time is of the essence, Lord Tam. I do not—"

He raised his hand. "First," he said again, "a conversation." He leaned forward. "Where is the *Kinshark*?"

How long had that vessel been missing now? Two months? Four? He made a mental note to ask Baryk.

"I do not know," the mechoservitor said.

"Were you aboard her?"

The eye shutters flashed again.

Vlad smiled. "We found you in her lifeboat."

"I was aboard. I do not know her current location."

He nodded slowly. "What were you doing aboard the *Kinshark*?"

Nothing.

Vlad changed his tack. "Did you hire Rafe Merrique to transport you?"

The mechoservitor's bellows pumped, and a gout of steam released from the exhaust grate in its back. "The light required service of his vessel. Captain Merrique and his crew were provided for." When it met Vlad's gaze he felt suddenly unsettled by the intense light in those amber eyes. "May we now barter?"

Vlad shook his head. "Not yet," he said. "Not until my curiosity is satisfied. What is your purpose in the Ghosting Crests?"

"You are not authorized to—"

Vlad sighed. "Power him off."

The eyes flashed again, and the metal man began to shake. Ren reached for the switch, and the metal man's mouth worked its way open and then closed three times before it spoke in a quiet voice. "The antiphon will fail if you do not aid me, Lord Tam. My task cannot be accomplished without your assistance."

"Then trust me. There is no Order to support you. There is no Pope to offer Holy Unction. You are aware of this?"

"Yes."

"And you are self-aware. You have a name. Obadiah, yes?"

"Yes."

"You are capable of making choices outside of your scripting, Obadiah?"

The mechoservitor was silent for a moment. Finally, it spoke. "I am."

"Then choose to trust me."

It hung its head, and when it looked up, there were tears welling in its eyes. "But the dream is clear on this matter: You are not to be trusted."

Vlad sat back and blinked. "Me?"

"Your kind."

He glanced around the room and made a quick decision. "Everyone out," he said. "I want to be alone with it."

He watched the surprise register on the faces. As they slowly shuffled toward the door, he caught the sleeve of Ren's shirt. "Stay nearby. I'll summon you."

He waited in silence for a minute after they left. Then, he edged his stool closer to the mechoservitor. "Trust is an earned commodity not easily accrued in these times," he said. "So I am going to trust you, Obadiah, and hope that you, in turn, will trust me." He waited until the mechanical stopped clacking, processing his words, and then continued. "The only reason I found you was because the d'jin we follow took us to you. If she hadn't, you would be lost at sea, nonfunctional, and whatever this *antiphon* is that you speak of would surely have failed. Do you concur?"

"I concur."

"You are adept at mathematics and probabilities. What are the chances of another sunstone-powered vessel finding you in the Ghosting Crests?" When the mechanical started clicking and clacking to work the equation, Vlad raised a hand. "I do not need the exact number. Would you concur that it is highly improbable?"

"Yes," Obadiah said. "I concur."

Even as he painted the image for the metal man, Vlad began to see it for himself. She had known. She had brought him to the metal man's rescue, but it did not appear to be her only destination. Each night, even since they'd brought the metal man aboard, she'd appeared to guide them farther southeast. Something still waited for them out in the waters where none dared sail.

"I do not know why she brought me to you," Vlad said, "but I believe she intended us to find you. Even still, she leads us southeast and—"

The mechoservitor looked up. "You sail for the Moon Wizard's Ladder." He started to tremble again. "The light-bearer is calling you into the dream."

Light-bearer? Vlad had never heard the term before. But he'd heard of the Moon Wizard's Ladder from the mythology of the Old World. He'd certainly heard stories as a boy about the Year of the Falling Moon and the ladder that the first Wizard King had used to return and avenge the kidnap of his daughters, establishing the firm but just reign by blood magick in the now desolate lands north of them. He thought of the ghost in the water, and his heart swelled for her, aching in its intensity, in his need to follow her.

Vlad forced his attention back to the mechoservitor. "Calling me into what dream?"

"The dream we serve to save the light," Obadiah said, his voice reedy and low. He clicked and whirred for a minute, as if calculating how much trust to extend. "The dream compels us. It requires a response."

Yes. Like the ghost in the water. Compulsion to follow, expressed by an intense love. "The antiphon," Vlad said.

Slowly, the mechoservitor nodded.

Then it opened its mouth and sang. The metal voice rose in the metal room, and Vlad Li Tam felt the hair on his arms and neck lift. In that moment, he felt a connection to something he had never felt before. The song was all around him, wrapping him like the warm sea, his scars burning from the salt. Light pulsed and undulated, tendrils waving to him.

"I know this song. She sings it to me."

The mechoservitor stopped singing abruptly and fixed his eyes on him. "Lord Tam, you have heard the dream. You are my brother. The light-bearer chose you. The antiphon is nearly complete. We must clear the Moon Wizard's Ladder or the antiphon will fail and the light will be lost."

Vlad Li Tam stood slowly.

Yes my love, he told his ghost.

"Yes," Vlad Li Tam said to his metal brother, his cheeks wet from tears he did not know he cried.

He could still hear the song beneath his skin.

Winters

Winters moved through the new-fallen snow, her feet carrying her once more along a familiar pathway. Behind her, her two constant companions followed at an appropriate distance.

She'd dreamed for three nights straight now, and it startled her how much the dream had changed. Now, metal men and numbers and white towers overlooking placid oceans filled her. And those skies, that world that hung above them, were the ones she'd seen in the Homeseeker's dream. She knew they were connected just as she knew the song was what made it different now.

And then there was Neb.

She blinked, her eyes suddenly full of water. She could not see him, but she could hear him screaming somewhere far away. Or at least she thought it was him. Still, she'd written those parts down, too, even the words he cried out with such agony, though they were in a language she did not know.

From those nights, she'd amassed quite a stack of parchments. She carried them now in her copy of the Y'Zirite gospel, carefully folded in between the pages.

She climbed the slight incline and paused at the top, looking across to the closed entrance to her throne room. Garyt stood by it. When she was certain it was him, she continued walking.

Her hands moved quickly even as she hoped the fading sunlight was enough for him to see it. *I am dreaming again,* she signed. *I must add the new pages to the Book.*

He inclined his head slightly. *I will find a way to add them for you, my queen.*

She returned his nod and followed the trail down to the river clearing. When she reached it, she saw Jin Li Tam waiting. She stood straight, staring out over the river, hands on the handles of her knives. Her hair was pulled back and tied with a leather cord, and for a moment, Winters thought she was looking at a girl, not the ruthless, formidable forty-second daughter of Vlad Li Tam.

Winters approached. "I'm here," she said.

Jin Li Tam looked at her. She nodded to her hands. "Why did you bring *that*?"

She looked down, feeling the heat rise in her cheeks and ears. She still held the Gospel of Ahm Y'Zir. *I need to say something,* she thought. She looked around, then leaned closer and lowered her voice. "I am dreaming again."

Twice now she'd said it, and it frightened her both times. After so long without the dreams, she'd finally accepted that it must be some strange anomaly. They'd been her constant companion for as long as she could remember, and then the dreams were gone. As if a door had been slammed shut.

And now, suddenly it was flung open.

Jin's eyebrows arched. "The ones you dreamed with Neb?"

She nodded and shivered. He'd screamed so loudly. "Yes, but different now. There are mechoservitors in my dream now." She paused, feeling that sudden rush of water again to her eyes. "And I think someone is hurting Neb, but I can't be sure." She continued at Jin's concerned look. "I think I hear him screaming."

Jin looked over her shoulder, keeping her voice low. "We should dance now. We're being watched."

Winters started to turn, realized she was doing it, and stopped. She looked around the clearing, found a stump and brushed the snow from it. Then, she put down the book and shrugged out of her fur coat.

Jin's knives were already out when Winters turned to face her. Drawing her own, she moved into the first overture. They moved slowly at first, their knives finding the others and clinking in the quiet afternoon. Their feet moved across the snow, breaking it up, as Winters matched her rhythm to Jin's. Gradually, the seasoned knife fighter raised the tempo until it was at a point where Winters had to work. At its crescendo, their knives sparked and rasped as they danced across the clearing.

After forty minutes, they stopped and Winters bent at the knees to suck in great lungfuls of the cold air. She looked up as she did it and saw that this time, even Jin Li Tam had broken a sweat. The red-headed queen smiled at her.

"You're getting better, girl."

She slowed her breathing. "Really?"

Jin nodded. "I'd pit you against any of Rudolfo's scouts. And your reach is exceptional. Better than most *men*. Once you've hit your full height, you'll be unstoppable."

Winters felt herself blushing. "Thank you." She managed an awkward curtsy. "I have an excellent teacher."

Jin Li Tam inclined her head, lifting her coat from the rock where she'd put it. "Tomorrow, then?"

Winters nodded.

She watched as Jin Li Tam and her escorts left. Her own guards still stood out of view in the woods, but she had no doubt they'd seen every step she'd taken in the dance, every thrust and slice of the blades. She went to the stump to get her coat and book.

She pulled the heavy furs over her and lifted the gospel. Something seemed different, and she glanced down at it. Opening it, she thumbed through the pages and heard her breath catch.

The dreams, folded so carefully into the pages, were gone.

She kept her back to her watchers, looking quickly around the clearing to see if somehow the pages had defied all logic and loosed themselves. Then, she looked to the snow around the stump. Only her footprints back and forth to it, though that meant little. A well-trained scout could run at top speed in the footprints of another, leaving little to no trace of their passing.

They're gone. But another page had been left—a note scribbled with a birder's needle on a bit of rough parchment. She read it without removing it from its place in the book:

Hail Winteria bat Mardic, queen of the Marshfolk,
and hail the Homeseeker's Dream. Someone will come to you each
day in this manner. Your dreams will be added to the Book.

She closed the gospel and made her way back up the trail. As the forest swallowed her, she found herself pondering the dreams. Isaak had been there, and she thought that maybe he had even quoted the Book to her, though she didn't know how that could be possible. None but the Marsh King had ever read the Book. And Tertius, of course. It had been the price he'd extracted to abandon the Great Library at Windwir and risk a hangman's noose to educate the Marsh King's daughter.

She thought of the Book and the years spent in the smell of paper, in the guttering light of candles. Mornings spent writing and afternoons spent reading, connecting the various bits that connected. Nights spent seeing the shape of things to come; a home rising for her people.

I am dreaming again.

When she passed Garyt ben Urlin at his post, she watched him stand a bit straighter and she carefully inclined her head to him, mindful of the men who followed her.

Thank you, her hands said upon the side of her coat.

He said nothing, his own hands still upon his spear. But the look in his eye was enough for her. It was something she did not see in the eyes of those around her, something she herself had not felt often in the last year or so.

Still, Garyt had it in his eyes and in the line of his jaw, the way that he stood at the door he guarded.

Hope, Winters thought, is a contagious thing.

And in that moment, she knew what she must do.

Jin Li Tam

Late-morning sun slanted into the windows lining the hall, and Jin Li Tam embraced the warmth and light upon her face. It had already been a full morning.

She'd breakfasted with Winters, practicing the Gypsy subverbal language and discussing the girl's latest dream in quiet voices. After, she'd met with Aedric briefly while walking Jakob in Ria's meditation grove. He'd lost two scouts in the caves where the birds were being diverted and had pulled his men back. But still, the bird station had been disrupted. They'd launched a handful of short-distance birds to bear word of that back to the edge of the Prairie Sea. Still, unless Aedric committed resources to actually eliminate the bird station, it would be up and running again. And though Jin Li Tam was certain Ria knew Rudolfo's Gypsy Scouts were running these operations and tolerated them in an effort to prove her trustworthiness, she was equally certain that she would not tolerate an act of open aggression, Great Mother or not.

Thinking of Ria refocused her. The Machtvolk queen's note had been brief and direct, and Jin Li Tam wondered what was planned for her this afternoon. Another school? Not likely—she'd been asked to come alone. And the children at the school were far more interested in Jakob, their Child of Promise. She was merely the means to that end.

An odd place to be.

The doors to Ria's study were unguarded, and when she knocked, she found the door was ajar. "Come in, Great Mother," Ria said, rising from behind her desk. Her face was grim, and there were circles under her eyes.

Jin Li Tam forced concern into her voice. "Are you well, Queen Winteria?"

Ria offered a brief smile. "I am very well and very tired," she said. "And I've someone to introduce you to."

They found their boots and coats waiting for them at the door, and Jin Li Tam followed Ria as they climbed the low hill behind her lodge. They walked without talking and Jin Li Tam savored it, enjoying the sound of the snow and ice crunching beneath their feet, the whisper of the wind through the trees. The air hung heavy with scents of pine and wood smoke and snow, and for a moment she was able to forget about everything but now.

At the top of the hill, a round stone building awaited. She recognized it as a blood shrine, but the guards at the door told her it wasn't the same as the others she'd seen springing up in the Marshlands.

When they approached, the guards quickly opened the door, and an old man in the long black robes of a priest met them. His sleeves were pushed up past his elbows, and his hands and forearms were covered in blood. He grinned behind a pair of thick spectacles. "My Lady," he said, "our penitent has taken the mark."

Ria smiled, and Jin saw genuine joy in it. "Good," she said. "Brother Aric, this is the Great Mother, Lady Jin Li Tam."

The priest bent from the waist. "Great Mother," he said, "I am honored to live so long as to see your coming."

Something in his voice chilled her. Or was it the way he looked at her? She inclined her head to show respect. "Thank you," she said.

He straightened himself. "I will hope to meet the Child of Promise before you return to the Ninefold Forest," he said. "Though I hope this will not be your last visit to our lands."

She smiled. "I'm sure it won't be."

The priest led them through another door, and Jin found herself wanting to retch from the smell of excrement, urine and blood that ambushed her. "I apologize for the smell," he said. "We had hoped to clean up before you arrived, but we only just now finished."

Jin Li Tam looked into the dim-lit room, suppressing the strong impulse to gasp at what she saw. She'd certainly seen violence—she'd given as much as she'd received. It had never felt right, but she'd learned from her father that feelings were simply the body's way of assuring its survival and should be subject to the rule of the higher mind. She'd assumed all violence should feel wrong. But there was a wrongness to what she saw now that turned her stomach over and broke her heart.

He'd been a man once, she knew, strapped to an altar designed to serve also as a cutting table. Now, he was a red mass of twitching, raw meat. His skin, freshly cut in the symbols of House Y'Zir, had been peeled away bit by bit. Sluggish streams of blood crept toward the catchers. The man wept quietly.

Ria approached, leaned in and whispered to him. "I am back, Jarvis."

A red mouth opened, flashing bloody teeth. "Oh my queen," the man said.

"I've brought Lady Jin Li Tam, the woman you tried to murder." She looked to Jin. "We took Jarvis off the Delta. One of our priests in Turam hosted him for a few weeks and prepared him for us. He arrived yesterday and has been most forthcoming."

The man rolled his eyes, blinking more tears and sniffling. "I am mortified by my sin, Lady Tam," he said.

Ria continued. "Jarvis is a former Androfrancine engineer and was one of Esarov's lieutenants in the civil war. He was hired to create an explosive that could be magicked, and to train a team of former Delta Scouts to detonate it."

Jin Li Tam looked at him and tried find rage for him. She could not, and it bothered her. Instead, she felt curiosity and the question slipped out. "Why?"

"Yes," Ria said. "Tell her why."

He sobbed. "I was paid to do it. I did not realize who you were, Great Mother."

Jin Li Tam forced herself to meet his eyes. "Who paid you?"

"I did not meet him. It was arranged through Governor Rothmir's offices."

Rothmir. She recognized the name and suspected it was someone she'd met during her years as Sethbert's consort, doing her father's work. She looked at Ria. "Was Erlund involved in this?"

She shook her head. "We do not think so. A landed nobleman on the Emerald Coast." She smiled. "He's been sent for."

"I am mortified by my sin," the man said again.

She looked at him and tried again to find anger but could not. *How is it that I pity this man?* He had tried to kill Jakob.

Ria examined the knives that were laid out upon a black velvet cloth. She lifted one and held it up to the light. "We've learned all we can learn from Jarvis, and he's ready to pay for his sin." She extended the knife to Jin. "I wanted you to have this opportunity," she said.

Jin Li Tam blinked. "You want me to kill him?"

Ria nodded. "Of course. He participated in a plot to murder your family." She bent over him, stroking his bloody cheek. "You're ready, yes, Jarvis?"

"I am ready, my queen."

Again, Ria extended the blade, and Jin Li Tam understood the intersection she now faced. The choice she made here had significance beyond her feelings, and she willed herself to be, just for this moment, her father's daughter. This was a test, an opportunity to build trust.

Do not think. Do what must be done. Jin hesitated, then took the knife. She turned and bent over him. "You should not have tried to harm my family," she said in a low voice.

Then she did what needed doing.

When she was finished, she washed his blood from her hands in a silver basin they brought to her. She did so with her back turned and swallowed at the tears that threatened her.

Putting her coat back on, she followed Ria back to the lodge in silence, and when she took Jakob from Lynnae's arms, she crushed him to herself and stifled her sob in his blankets.

We are all mortified by our sins from time to time, she thought.

Rudolfo

Rudolfo paced the command tent and tried to force his anger into something he could manage. Outside, a break in the snow gave shivering recruits time to establish their somewhat more permanent quarters with timber felled by a group of loggers arrived out of Paramo, seat of the Third Forest Manor. It wasn't optimal work for the front end of winter, but Lysias had maintained that war did not wait for weather and neither should an army in training. So now, the sounds of saws and hammers filled the morning air.

And now, the last major wagonload of supplies from the Seventh Forest Manor was arriving. Future supplies would trickle in much more slowly now, though already crews of recruits were dispatched to drag heavy plows over the wagon trails to try to keep them clear.

Rudolfo stopped his pacing and forced himself to breathe.

It had been bad enough sending his wife and child into Ria's lands. Now he had word from Charles that he and Isaak made their way north with that last wagon train to follow the mechoservitors into the ground, and the thought that the most lethal weapon in the known world might stroll casually into Ria's hands raised a panic in him that his mind could only translate into rage.

I cannot let him leave. Isaak carried Y'Zir's Seven Cacophonic Deaths in his memory scrolls—a weapon that could leave the Named Lands desolate if the wrong hands were to lay hold of that spell. For Isaak to so suddenly and without a word make this decision and abandon his work in the library was an ambush Rudolfo had not expected, and everything within him whistled third alarm to this new development. And yet, how could Rudolfo stop his friend?

By forbidding it, he thought.

He heard footsteps approaching and listened for the low whistle at his tent flap. When it came, he returned it and a breathless lieutenant entered. "The caravan is here, General."

Rudolfo nodded. "Very well. Send Charles in first once they've been assigned quarters."

He forced himself to sit at his cluttered table, forced himself to sip at the lukewarm firespice that he'd barely touched, feeling the heat of it as it traced its way down his throat and into his stomach. He'd found himself spending more time with the stronger liquor of late, less interested in the fruit wines that had been his preference for so long before. He told himself it was the cold, but he knew it wasn't. It was the dulling of an edge that had become too sharp for him, and an easy way to find sleep at the end of a long day spent worrying.

He reread Jin's coded message about the bird station and what they had gathered so far about the conspiracy on the Delta. He'd conferred with Lysias about the man Jarvis, and saw with little surprise that there was no love lost between them.

"He was ever of questionable character," Lysias had told him. "Choosing his loyalties based on the size of one's letter of credit."

It was a solid lead in the investigation, but he found himself wondering how deep and wide the conspiracy went and whether or not that weed could be dug out. Of course, his own garden was choked as well. They'd not found more shrines, and though his scouts carefully watched the one nearby, there had been no further activity there since his visit. His borders were breached to the west by evangelists, to the east by magicked runners he still couldn't find and to the south by this latest development.

He moved papers about for the better part of an hour, his eyes burning from lack of sleep and the words all blurring together into one that he finally spoke aloud. "Why?"

Just as he asked it, the lieutenant was back with Charles. Rudolfo looked at the man and saw his own weariness reflected back in the arch-engineer's face and eyes. He gestured to a chair. "Please sit," he said.

"Thank you, Lord Rudolfo." Charles sat, and the officer who escorted him slipped back out of the tent.

Even his voice sounds tired. Rudolfo pointed to the bottle of firespice. "It's been a cold ride north, I'm sure," he said. "Would you like a drink?"

Charles surprised him by accepting, and Rudolfo poured a small metal cup half full of the thick, spice-scented liquor. The old man raised his and Rudolfo followed.

"To brighter times," the old man offered.

"To brighter times," Rudolfo repeated.

They sipped, and the Gypsy King forced himself to wait quietly. Finally, he could wait no longer. "What in the Hidden Hells is happening, Charles?"

Charles blinked, and Rudolfo registered the surprise on his face at the sudden and uncharacteristic outburst. "You mean with Isaak?"

"Yes," Rudolfo said. "With Isaak."

Charles sighed. "I am not certain."

Rudolfo leaned forward, feeling the small table bend beneath his weight. "You *made* him. Surely you have some speculation? He's left the library in the care of the others and intends *what* exactly? And why?"

Charles paled, and Rudolfo was pleased that his tone induced such a response. "He intends to follow the other mechoservitors into the Machtvolk Territories. He is deciphering their dream along with notes hidden in Tertius's volume on the Marshfolk prophecies."

The dream. He'd heard reference to it that night in the forest when the four mechoservitors had approached seeking safe passage. He'd heard other references as well. That it was coded into a song—one he actually sang to his infant son, one his own mother had sung to him and his brother when they were very young. "How did he come by this dream?"

He knew the answer already but wanted to hear it from Charles directly. The man made no excuse and no attempt to cover the truth. "I installed it in him after the explosion at the library."

Rudolfo's eyes narrowed. "Why would you do this without discussion with me?"

Charles raised his eyebrows. "I was not aware that discussion was required, Lord."

"He is the most dangerous weapon in the world," Rudolfo said in a low voice that betrayed his anger. *And he is my friend,* he didn't say. "I have strong interest in his safety."

"As do I," Charles answered.

Rudolfo continued, feeling the interruption in the tingling of his scalp. "Anything that might alter his normal functions is of concern to me. I should have been consulted on this decision. Ultimately, I am responsible for him as the inheritor of the Order's holdings and the Guardian of Windwir."

Charles inclined his head. "I would argue that ultimately *I* am responsible for him as the one who made him. But arguing this point would be fruitless. I failed to consult you; I intended no disrespect by this."

Rudolfo did not expect his fist to come up and then down upon the table. When it did, they were both surprised at the resounding noise of it. "Damnation," he shouted. "This is not about *respect*. He carries the Seven Cacophonic Deaths of Xhum Y'Zir within him, and now this dream that has worked its way into your mechanicals at Sanctorum Lux has worked its way into him." He felt the anger in his scalp again and forced himself to breathe in and out before continuing. "The others exhibited strange behavior as a result of this dream. Now he is, too. That library has been his home for nearly two years, and the work there has been his very soul."

"People," Charles said slowly, "often change direction."

Rudolfo opened his mouth to say Isaak was a machine, that he wasn't a person, but even as he started to speak, he knew it wasn't true. He'd seen Isaak as a person from the very first day he met the sobbing metal man. He'd dressed him in robes. He'd given him a name. He'd welcomed him into his family.

He is my friend.

He remembered the anxious days waiting for Charles to finally declare him functional again. He recalled vividly the sense of overwhelming relief when he'd learned the metal man had somehow absorbed the worst of the bomb blast, shielding his wife and son from an explosion that would have surely killed and buried them without the metal man's intervention.

Rudolfo sighed and forced himself to make eye contact with the old man. In those brown eyes, he saw the same two things that hid behind his anger: fear and love.

Charles stared back and let the silence hang heavy for a full minute before speaking. "I apologize for not discussing this with you, Lord Rudolfo. He asked for this dream, and under the circumstances, I felt it was my duty to grant his request and protect his privacy. I do not know what this dream is up to, but my surest path to discovery is to monitor him—and the others—and learn what I can."

Rudolfo studied the man, trying to keep hold of his anger, but already he felt it leaking away from him. He sighed, and it was loud in the tent. "You intend to go with him, then?"

Charles nodded. "I do," he said. "Though I hope we will be back soon. I'm too old to be chasing after metal dreams."

Rudolfo sighed again. "Very well." He looked up and whistled. The scout guarding his tent poked his head in. "Send Isaak in."

When the metal man walked in, Rudolfo noticed the change in him immediately. He carried himself differently, and when he spoke, his voice was also different—more sure and less accommodating. "Lord Rudolfo," he said as he inclined his metal head.

It is confidence. Rudolfo returned the slight nod. "Isaak."

"I fear," his metal friend said, "that I must take my leave of you. I am grateful for your hospitality and have been honored to serve you and your family."

Rudolfo thought there would be more conversation. That perhaps they would discuss this dream and what it meant and where exactly he went and how exactly he would help his cousins in their response to it. He thought they'd talk and find some kind of compromise. But in the end, he simply looked into Isaak's amber eyes. "You know what you guard, Isaak," Rudolfo said. "Do what you will—but guard yourself well, my friend."

He thought that Isaak would hang his head or that he'd see some spark of grief in the guttering light of those jeweled eyes. But Isaak returned his gaze levelly. "I will always be vigilant, Lord Rudolfo."

Rudolfo nodded. "Very well, then," he said.

He offered no word of dismissal. He simply went back to the papers on his desk until the two left his tent. After they had gone, Rudolfo sighed again and called for the captain of the watch.

"Magick a half-squad," he told the officer. "Follow them. Quietly."

And only after he was alone again, Rudolfo held his head in his hands and wondered at how quickly such fierce anger could burn itself into sorrow and despair.

Neb

Neb swam in pain and tried to find some part of himself that he could cling to as the fire laced his body and his mind lurched from scene to scene.

"Where are they, Abomination?" the woman asked as she traced another cut into his skin with her salted knife. She leaned over him, touching her own small, dark carving to his bloody skin.

He was in a room now, and he recognized it as the one he'd seen Winters undressing in. Now, he stood behind her as she wrote at a small desk, her hand moving across the pages. The knife moved over his skin, and she spun away.

Neb screamed.

A new face swam into his view—one he'd not seen for some time, and it reminded him of the words his dead father had told him what seemed so long ago, before the knives, before the crooning voice and the cold, black stone kin-raven pressed against his skin. It was Petronus.

Petronus rides to you.

"Neb?" The old Pope looked even older now. He'd lost weight, and now he wore trousers and a shirt that was far too big for him. A vicious pink scar ran along his throat, and his hair and beard had become a tangled, unruly mess. "Neb, can you hear me?"

He felt the woman near him now, too, and he quickly averted his eyes, careful not to take in any of the landscape. "Don't let them find you, Father," he said.

And then, the knife was to its work again and he was back to screaming as Petronus also spun away.

"Do not show them what they want to see, son," his father, Brother Hebda said. Suddenly, they were in the park near the Whymer orphanage where he had spent his childhood, there in the shadow of the Great Library and the Androfrancine Order. A summer breeze bent the birch branches.

Now, the woman was there with them, too. Only now she did not wear the dark silks or the close-cropped gray hair. Instead, she wore a simple black dress that hugged her curves in a way that made Neb suddenly uncomfortable. Her hair, now long and the color of ash, spilled down around her shoulders. "He will show us," she said, "eventually." When she smiled, she showed her teeth. She leaned in toward Neb there on the bench they shared. "And after we find the Abomination's hand servants, we'll come and find you as well, digger."

"Hold fast, Nebios," his father told him.

And then he, too, spun away.

"Hold fast," the woman said, repeating his father's words, "and let me hurt you more, Abomination."

Then, the blade was no longer on him. And neither was the token. He lay still, certain that any moment both would be back to spin him into a pain-frenzied, stomach-lurching dervish. When it didn't happen, he risked opening his eyes.

The sun was high and the sky spread out over him, a canopy of fierce blue that stretched beyond his peripheral vision. A breeze moved over him like hot breath on his cuts.

These were the times he tried to sleep, though he had no idea how much time passed between cuttings and how much sleep he actually found. At first, he'd used that time to try to ascertain something about the women who held him. But he'd given up on that some time ago now. The rest seemed more useful to him—it gave his mind the focus he needed, despite the pain, to keep his mind away from the one place they wished him to take them.

And it was working. But it took everything inside of him.

Still, he realized, each hour under the knife, it grew harder and harder.

He heard low voices talking nearby in an unfamiliar tongue, and then, a cool hand was on his arm, quickly pressing words he could not understand into his skin. He turned his head and saw the thirty-second daughter of Vlad Li Tam gazing down upon him. For the briefest moment, he saw concern in her eyes. Then, all emotion vanished from them.

"You will show us what we're looking for eventually, Abomination," she said in a flat voice. Then, she leaned closer, her mouth so close to his ear that none could hear but him. "It will not be long, Nebios. I swear it to you."

When she left, he fell into a light, dreamless sleep. He drifted there, feeling the heat gradually leaking out of his wounds and momentarily forgetting the dull ache of the rocky ground that bit into his back. He'd just reached a moment of oblivious peace when he was jarred awake by the sounds of pandemonium.

He opened his eyes, suddenly alert, but could see nothing but a twilight sky and its tentative moon. Still, he instantly placed the snarling and howling of kin-wolves mixed with the sounds of battle nearby.

Twisting his body, he pulled at the ropes that held him, but the stakes were driven too deep. He felt a light breeze, and a strong hand clamped down suddenly over his mouth. A strong arm snaked across his chest to hold him still.

Neb felt an instant of panic when he could not see the figure that now kept him from speaking or struggling. He felt the hot breath of a mouth against his ear and heard the muffled but familiar voice.

"I followed them to you," Renard whispered. "You've been impossible to get close to until now."

Neb stifled a sob at the sound of the Waste guide's voice and tried not to cry. Relief flooded him, and he felt his body trembling from it.

Renard's hand stayed firm over his mouth. "Listen well, lad," he said. "They'll not kill you until they have what they want from you. I'm no match for them on my own, and I'm not sure the wolf trick will work more than once. Stay alive. I will be back for you." He paused, and Neb felt another hand giving a reassuring squeeze to his shoulder. "I will be back for you," Renard said again.

The hand loosened over his mouth, and Neb felt terror racing through him.

Don't leave me.

He wanted to shout the words, to shriek them, but instead, he swallowed against the fear. He'd watched a small number of blood-magicked scouts cut easily through a room of armed men at Rudolfo's Firstborn Feast. He quickly ciphered the odds and knew that Renard—a far more savvy scout and soldier than Neb—was right. He'd most likely used the urine of a female kin-wolf in heat to draw down a handful of males, but they would be no match for the four women who held him. Renard would not fare much better on his own.

Petronus rides for you. Once more, his father had spoken from his grave in Windwir. As the hand left his mouth and the arm lifted from his chest, Neb swallowed and formed words that he hoped Renard could hear within the raw rasp that his voice had become from days of screaming. "Petronus rides for me," he croaked.

If Renard heard, he did not answer. Already, there was yelping and yowling as the defeated wolves realized their mistake and fled the knives of Neb's captors.

Neb tried to will the trembling from his body, tried to take hold of the sobs that threatened him with a storm of tears.

He failed, but when he wept now, it was from the sure knowledge that he wasn't alone. He simply had to hang on, to keep averting his inner eye and inner ear from the mechoservitors at their work and the song that compelled them.

Neb closed his eyes again, and the next time he awoke, it was beneath the knife.

But this time, Nebios Homeseeker did not scream.

Charles

They rode the last two leagues in somber silence, Rudolfo and Isaak side by side in the lead and Charles behind them. They left their horses at the opening of the canyon, handing the reins over to scouts freshly recovered from their magicks and dressed in robes that matched the Androfrancine and his metal son.

I am too old for this, Charles thought. But it was something he'd thought often since that day his apprentice had drugged him and spirited him out of Windwir. Before his secret imprisonment by Sethbert and later, his nephew Erlund, he'd not considered himself especially old.

Perhaps losing everyone and everything you love in a span of hours changes one's perspective on time, he thought.

Rudolfo led them forward over freshly salted ice until the canyon walls narrowed and the downward slope was sealed away from the white sky as the base of the Dragon's Spine swallowed them.

When they reached the cave, it was crowded with men and buzzing with activity. A wooden frame had been set up over and around a large circular hole in the floor, and a system of pulleys had been rigged to move equipment in and out of the ground. Tables and chairs were strewn around the cavern, and men sat at some of them going over crudely sketched maps. Even as they stood, men started climbing from the well, ducking beneath the frame as they scrambled over the edge. They were followed at last by a mechoservitor—Number Eight, Charles thought—and a heavyset man with thick, curly hair, his face and hands black with grime. The man approached them.

"Lord Rudolfo," he said, inclining his head.

Rudolfo returned his nod. "Turik, how goes our exploration?"

"We've mapped extensive tunnels and chambers six leagues south and east. The western passages have been more difficult—a lot of debris and water—but we're making headway."

Rudolfo turned to Charles and Isaak. "This is Turik, chief engineer of our operation here. He's spent most of his life underground in our mines in Friendslip." He offered a grim smile. "Who'd have thought that for two millennia we've had a Whymer Maze beneath us." He looked back to his engineer. "This is Brother Charles, formerly arch-engineer of the Androfrancine Office of Mechanical Science and Technology and now attached to the new library. And Isaak, of course."

The man studied the two of them. "I received your message, Lord, and hoped to speak with you about it. I don't think it is prudent for—"

Rudolfo raised a hand and interrupted him. "It is *not* prudent. But neither will I prevent them. Isaak is most insistent about his ability to find their destination. I want your men to escort them as far west as you have mapped . . . but no farther." Rudolfo looked at Isaak, and Charles saw concern in the Gypsy King's eyes. "From that point, they are on their own."

On our own. It did not appeal to him, traveling underground passages into unfamiliar territories. But Isaak would go either with or without him, and the same curiosity that had driven him into engineering in the first place so many years ago drove him now. Something had happened to his mechoservitors. He had resisted Introspect's order to send them alone and unsupervised into the Churning Wastes on the Sanctorum Lux project, but in the end, Holy Unction compelled his compliance. He had trained them to maintain themselves, had scripted them each for scheduled visits to the Keeper's Gate for a clandestine escort to his offices in Windwir for routine checkups. And something had happened. Somehow they had stumbled across the data coded into that song and had created a new script for themselves based upon it.

And it changed them. As it was now changing Isaak.

Isaak spoke, drawing Charles back to the present moment. "I am confident of my direction." He reached into the leather satchel he carried over his shoulder and drew out the book that the mechoservitor had given him. "There are rudimentary maps ciphered into the text of this book." He extended it to Rudolfo. "The mechoservitors attached to your operation should be able to decipher at least some of them. When they are finished, the book should be destroyed."

Charles felt his own eyebrows rise. Rudolfo raised his as well, a hand moving instinctively to his beard. "You would destroy a book?" the Gypsy King asked.

Isaak nodded. "I would destroy *this* book."

Charles saw the question on Rudolfo's face but asked it first. "Why?"

Isaak blinked, his eye shutters clicking. "Enemies of the light beset us. They must not be permitted to prevail." He paused, his body shaking slightly as his bellows wheezed. Charles saw water at the lower corners of his eyes, where he'd installed the tear ducts as per Rufello's *Book of Specifications.* "My analysis of your physiological and verbal cues indicates that you are displeased with me, Lord. It was never my intention to—"

Rudolfo raised his hand again. "Isaak," he said. His voice was low, and Charles thought for a moment that he might've heard it crack with emotion. "I am not displeased with *you.* I am displeased with this outcome and concerned by your decision." He waited a moment. "You understand some of my concerns, I think. Those that I have discussed with you."

Isaak nodded. "I will guard it, Lord. I swear. And the library will function adequately without my presence. I have reproduced from my memory scrolls all appropriate holdings contained therein and have left them with Mechoservitor Number One."

All appropriate holdings. Charles had not seen the scrolls but felt confident that all matters regarding the spell and the dream had been carefully expunged from the scripts Isaak had left behind.

"But there is another concern," Rudolfo said, "that I have not discussed with you."

Isaak cocked his head, and Charles was struck yet again at how human his creation seemed. No, he realized, not seemed. *Was.* And becoming more so. "What concern is that, Lord Rudolfo?"

Charles watched the hardness soften in Rudolfo's eyes and watched the line of his jaw relax as the Gypsy King stepped closer. Isaak towered above the shorter man. Stretching himself to full height, Rudolfo embraced the metal man. "That I will miss my friend until he comes home to me."

For a moment—just a moment—the arch-engineer thought there were tears in the man's eyes. There was no mistaking Isaak's tears.

And when he was partway down the ladder, wrapped in the warmth of an unexpected wind that rose from beneath them, Charles discovered his own tears.

Blinking them away, he followed his dreaming son into the Beneath Places and wondered what they would find there.

Winters

The howling of a wolf reverberated through the room, and Winters sat upright, mouth opening to scream. She could still smell the burnt rock of the Churning Wastes mingled with the iron scent of blood, and she could taste salt in her mouth from either sweat or tears.

Neb.

"Petronus rides for me," he had told her, his voice more a croak than a whisper. Still, this time he smiled, and when he did, she saw madness in his eyes.

She shivered, soaked in sweat, and climbed from her bed. The dreams had grown increasingly more disturbing, and she could mark the difference in them now. There were the dreams of the white tower and its surrounding sea, the song permeating the air as the metal men moved about her. And the dreams of the Book, each night devoured by more mechoservitors.

Then there were the dreams of Neb.

She walked to her desk, looked at the paper that waited for her there and felt a knot growing in her stomach. After nights and nights of these dreams, she felt them taking their toll upon her. She no longer sat down eagerly to write them out.

And some of them, she realized, seemed stuck. Like wagon wheel ruts running in a circle. And try as she might, she could not steer out of them.

As if they are not my dreams.

No, she did not want to write these out. At least not now, not with the sweat of the night terrors still wet upon her. Instead, she shrugged out of her sleeping shift and pulled on her trousers, a shirt and a thick pair of wool socks.

Picking up her boots, she eased open the door to her room and slipped into the empty hallway.

She had no destination in mind, but the lodge felt suddenly oppressive, heavy as a wet quilt weighing her down. She needed open sky and cold air. Winters let her feet carry her to the front door, where a guard awaited.

He did not speak to her as she approached, and when he saw that she intended to leave the house, he stepped aside and opened the door. She passed through and into the winter night.

Moonlight washed the snow in blue and green, and stars throbbed above her in a clear sky. As she stepped from the porch, she saw movement from the corner of her eye and smiled. It did not matter the time of day; her escorts awaited.

Winters studied the paths and decided against the familiar trail she'd taken past Garyt, the one that led to the river where she practiced with her knives and the door in the hill that had once been her home.

Turning around, she took the path that led behind the lodge, walking slowly and savoring the night. The top layer of newest snow had frozen, and she listened to the sound of it crunching beneath her boots. Otherwise, the night was silent.

But as the trail twisted and started to climb the hill, another sound reached her ears, faint and coming from above her.

Someone is singing.

The farther she climbed, the more clear it became, until she stood at the top and looked upon a circular stone building. The wooden doors stood open, and from within, a woman's rich alto voice trickled out into the night, singing a song that Winters recognized from her ride though that gauntlet of evergreen boughs with their gospel's Great Mother, Jin Li Tam, and Jakob the Child of Promise.

She stood still a moment and allowed the words to wash over her. Then, curiosity drove her to the open door. Peering in, she saw a small foyer and another open door. Beyond that, she saw a woman kneeling at the altar with upraised and bloody hands. Even with her back turned, her sister was unmistakable.

Winters stepped into the foyer.

A guard materialized to her right, offering a low whistle, and Ria looked over her shoulder.

When she saw who it was, Ria smiled and stood. "Little sister," she said. "Have you come to worship?" A second guard appeared, bearing a basin that Ria rinsed her hands in.

Winters shook her head, hoping her disgust at the notion did not show. "No. I was walking. I heard singing."

Ria approached, drying herself with a towel. "I was just finishing." She laid the towel aside and embraced Winters. Winters returned the gesture though she was sure her sister would know it was false. "Walk back with me? You've been here for days, and we've scarcely seen each other without a roomful."

Winters nodded. "Certainly." It was true—they'd been at meals and on tours together. But she'd not intended to seek out her sister and found it odd that her sister wanted her company.

Still, it is a way for me to learn.

Ria pulled on her heavy coat and blew out the lanterns in the temple. "So you walk when you cannot sleep. I come to the temple." Her brow furrowed. "The dreams keep sleep at bay sometimes, and I'm finding the meditation helps with them."

Dreams? Winters blinked. "You have the dreams, too?"

For some reason, the idea that her sister might share the dreams had not occurred to her.

She nodded. "Some of them. I am our father's daughter, after all. But I've learned meditations and prayers to help with them." She smiled. "So I come to the temple."

To help with them. The way she said it made it sound as if the dreams were something to be treated rather than studied. And she only shared some of them. Which dreams?

They passed through the doorway and into the night.

"I'm told you carry the gospel I gave you everywhere you go," Ria said as they walked. There was a kind of pride in her voice that raised the hair on Winters's neck and arms. And her smile seemed arrogant in the moonlight. "I've studied the scriptures for years under the best teachers. If you ever have questions—or want to read more of them—you only need ask."

Winters wasn't sure how to respond. "Thank you," she said. "I do have questions. But not about the scriptures." She thought she saw the faintest trace of a frown pull at her sister's mouth and returned her eyes to the path. "Not yet, anyway," she added, "though I'm sure I will."

If Ria truly had frowned, she recovered quickly and chuckled. "Very well," she said, stopping on the path. "I will grant you answers where I can. Walk with me each morning and bring your questions. But I would ask something of you in return."

Winters stopped as well. "What would you ask in return?"

Ria smiled. "In a week's time, we celebrate High Mass of the Falling Moon. I want you to attend with me."

She'd read about the Year of the Falling Moon during her studies with Tertius—when the Moon Wizard came down to depose the Last Weeping Czar, destroy a world and establish the Age of the Wizard Kings that P'Andro Whym and his scientist scholars had eventually ended in their Night of Purging. Certainly, the gospel she'd read painted it differently, speaking of retribution for that deicide and viewing the Moon Wizard's advent as the beginning of salvation. Attending the mass was a small price to pay.

"I will attend," she said.

Ria smiled. "Good."

They walked the rest of the way in silence, and when they reached the door, Ria embraced her again. "We will walk in the morning," she said. "Bring your questions, little sister. Any of them."

When Winters was once more in her room, she sat to her desk and took up her waiting pen. She wanted to write out her questions, categorize them as the mechoservitors in the library would do and then write out the answers as she received them. But instead, she wrote out the dream as best she could remember it. She blew the ink dry on each page and folded it carefully into the gospel her sister had given her. And when she was finished, she undressed again and crawled into bed.

For a while, she thought about the questions she would ask in the morning. Then, she thought about Neb and hoped his pain and madness was not real. That it was some twisted part of the dream.

But she knew it wasn't.

After months of no contact, her dreaming boy was back, and something terrible was happening to him—being done to him—somewhere in the Churning Wastes.

Finally, Winters cried herself to sleep.

Petronus

The shrill whistle of third alarm pulled Petronus from a light sleep and he kicked his way out of the bedroll, listening to the muttered curses of those nearby as they scrambled for knives and swords and bows.

They'd set up camp at dawn, the Gypsy Scouts establishing a quiet perimeter, hidden in scrub or the twisted stone and glass, magicked when necessary. After a hasty meal and a brief conversation with Grymlis, Petronus had crawled off to sleep in a hollow carved into an outcropping of fused glass.

It seemed he had just settled into his first dreams when the whistle pulled him awake.

Petronus stayed in the shade and let his eyes adjust to the daylight. From the position of the shadows it was late afternoon, and around him, others crouched at the ready. There was certainly no way to hide a company of their size, though they persisted in trying.

Once his eyes could find the way, he moved to where Grymlis waited with Rudolfo's lieutenant.

A brown bird flashed past to land in the officer's net. The young man pulled it out, fingers finding the knotted message in the string tied to its foot. "We've a man requesting audience," he said, looking first to Petronus and then Grymlis.

"Audience?" Petronus asked, rubbing the sleep from his eyes.

"With the Pope," the lieutenant added.

Grymlis sheathed his short sword. "Is he alone?"

"He appears to be. He holds letters of introduction and credit from Introspect."

The men exchanged glances, and Petronus tried to read the old captain. He saw nothing there and knew Grymlis merely waited for him to give the obvious orders. "Ready the camp to ride," he finally said. "And have our visitor escorted in."

He packed quickly and then waited in the shade. Soon enough, he heard the nasal whine of Geoffrus and realized there actually *was* a sound more jarring than third alarm.

"But I *assure* and *attest* that we have a *signed* agreement with the current Luxpadre and his Rainbow Men. Your help is not *required*, Renard."

Petronus recognized that name. Remus's son had been a Renard. And Remus had been a good friend to the Order over here. He heard a gravelly voice chuckle.

"Geoffrus, I do not *dispute* your contract. Nor do I offer myself for *hire*." The inflection of the voice, the way he emphasized key words, spoke of some kind of code, but Petronus could not parse it.

When the man appeared, Petronus was struck suddenly by how much he looked like his father: tall, lanky, with close-cropped salt-and-pepper hair and intensely blue eyes. The Androfrancine robes hung loose over his spare frame, and his high boots were worn from league upon league of Waste running. He clutched a long, slender staff in his hand, one end tipped with a fist-sized bulb. "You're Remus's boy," Petronus said as he stepped forward.

"You were my father's favorite Pope," Renard answered, offering up a yellowed letter.

Petronus took it and ran his finger over his successor's seal. He glanced at the words, knowing already that they said roughly the same as the letter he himself had provided the man's father. "He served the light well."

"We do our best." Renard looked at Grymlis and the Gypsy Scout lieutenant. "You are riding for the boy, Neb?"

Petronus shot a glance at Grymlis, then looked back to Renard. "What makes you think that?"

Renard paused before speaking, looking furtively around the camp. "He told me so." Petronus watched the man's eyes wander to the map peeking out from the lieutenant's leather pouch. Renard nodded to it. "I can show you where he is," he said, drawing a rolled map from his pouch, "but we do not have much time."

"They're cutting him, aren't they?" Petronus winced from the memory of his dreams.

Renard nodded, unrolling the map onto a flat rock. "They are interrogating him about your missing mechoservitors."

They seek to prevent the antiphon. Petronus wasn't sure how he knew this. He leaned over the map. "How far?"

"We're here," Renard said, dropping his finger. "They have the boy in an arroyo in these hills. They are running magicked patrols—but they're not using your scout powders. They've blood magicks, and in ample supply. I suspect an encampment someplace. Probably to the southeast."

Blood magicks. Petronus looked across to Grymlis's face and saw the surprise there. "An encampment of what size?"

Renard shrugged. "It's hard to say. But I've counted at least twenty of these runners, and only four of them are with the boy right now.

They use kin-ravens for communication and observation." He paused, and Petronus saw a hard edge in the man's eyes. "I suspect they already know you're coming—it would be impossible to hide a company of this size."

Petronus thought about this. Surely, the forces he and Grymlis marshaled were sufficient for four women, blood-magicked or otherwise. "If that is the case, why aren't they on the move?"

Renard shrugged. "They're far more mobile than we are, even carrying Neb. But I suspect there's more to it than that. I think either they have help on the way as well or . . ."

Petronus watched a dark cloud pass over the man's face. "Or what?"

Renard's look was grim, and he spoke in a low voice. "Or they know that they will have what they want from Neb and be gone before you get there."

The finality in the man's voice suggested a dark assumption. The boy's screams had been near to him for many nights, only to be suddenly gone. He tried to convince himself that no enemy would kill their source of information before confirming that whatever they'd learned was true. But if Renard was correct and there was an encampment of these foreign runners, they might already have the capacity to confirm the information quickly enough.

And it was hard to read the motives of this mysterious foe.

Of course, in the end, it didn't matter. Neb was in danger, and because of that, the light was in danger as well. Petronus saw it on Hebda's face, heard it in Hebda's voice, in his dreams of the man. He didn't fully understand the stakes but knew that they were high.

We must find Neb alive and before he has been broken.

He looked at Renard now and measured him. If the man was anything like his father, Petronus knew he could trust him. And according to his letters of introduction and credit, he'd served the Order for many years. "You mean to help us recover Neb?"

Renard smiled wryly. "Truth be told, I mean for *you* to help *me* recover him. You've no chance of it otherwise—and the lad is too important for anything to go wrong." Petronus saw the man's eyes dart downward for but a moment and followed them. The hands were moving just barely, and he recognized the words they formed. *The fate of your light rides on his success,* Renard signed. *Surely Hebda has told you this?*

He blinked, forgetting to sign. "You know him?"

Renard nodded. "I do." The hands moved again. *He assigned me to the boy's training.*

He forced his own age-gnarled fingers into an uncomfortable alphabet. *Training for what?*

But Renard ignored him. "I can get him out," he said. "I will need a dozen of yon Gypsy Scouts and magicks for myself and the boy." He looked to the lieutenant, his face sober. "You will lose men," he said, "but to take any more would leave you precariously shorthanded for your return to the Wall." The officer nodded, and Renard glanced at Petronus. "As it is, if they bring reinforcements to bear, they will likely run you down before you make D'Anjite's Bridge." The line of his jaw was tight. "You will not be able to hold your own against them."

Petronus swallowed. The bridge lay just four days behind them. That was not far at all. "We'll have to hold them," he said.

When he said it, he felt the full conviction of his words, and it gave him pause. He could remember meeting the boy, Neb, his hair freshly whitened by the Desolation of Windwir, his tongue commandeered by the madness of Xhum Y'Zir's spell. He remembered watching him move through that tragedy, watching it temper the boy's strength of character. Certainly he'd known the boy was odd. He still remembered the dream Neb had of the Marsh King riding south—a dream that came true, much like his dream of proclaiming Petronus's renewed papacy there in the ruins of Windwir. And he remembered with a stab of shame the day he excommunicated Neb from the Order so that Neb would not interfere with Petronus's plans to shut down their backward dreaming once and for all. He'd spent enough time with the boy to love him as if he were a son, but now something larger than those paternal feelings pulled at him like gravity.

We have to hold our own against them. Because saving Neb meant something far more vast than Petronus had realized, though he did not comprehend why it was so or how he had come to believe it so strongly.

The survival of the light depended upon it.

Jin Li Tam

Confident that she wasn't followed, Jin Li Tam slowed in her run. The magicks bent her stomach—it had been some time since she'd used them. And the heightened senses overpowered her. She could hear her heart pounding and could smell the frozen earth beneath the snow.

She'd found Aedric's note on her pillow—a message tied into a long strand of hair from her brush. Excusing herself from lunch under the pretense of a headache, she'd magicked herself and slipped out her window, careful to keep her feet within the footprints of others as she sped into the forest.

When she reached the designated place, she clicked her tongue to the roof of her mouth and heard Aedric's reply.

She felt his hand upon her shoulder. *Lady Tam.*

She took his hand and pressed words into it. *What have you found?*

I will show you. But go safely and silently with me.

Before she could reply, he'd looped a running line around her wrist and pulled it tight. She started to struggle but then thought better of it, seeing that it was a savvy decision on his part. He had no way of knowing her level of scouting experience. And after a year away from the powders, she might welcome the aid.

They ran the forest, zigzagging their way north and east, their feet whispering over the snow, here and there kicking up the faintest bit of powder. At key points, Aedric clicked his tongue and she heard the distant reply as posted guards acknowledged their first captain and queen's passing.

They ran for an hour before finding another path—this one bearing them eastward. As she stretched her legs, she felt Aedric picking up his own pace. When she found herself overtaking him, she fell back and matched his pace.

But not without first being certain he knew she could more than keep up.

They approached an open swath of land and Aedric slowed. They stopped at the edge of the forest, and she looked out on a clearing. On the far side, she saw the mouth of a cave.

She felt Aedric's hand on her shoulder again. *This is the bird station. We pulled back and waited. We didn't have to wait long. Watch.*

She crouched and watched. From deep in the cave, she heard a humming and hissing. It whispered like a beehive until finally, a clacking form stepped out of the cave, light hitting those parts of its dark metal surface not covered by its plain black robe.

The metal man raised a silver flute to its lips and blew, watching the skies with emerald-glowing eyes. The notes tickled her eardrums, but she felt them more than heard them. She was unable to take her eyes off the mechoservitor. It stood tall and thin, made of a dark iron-like metal pitted with time, and when it walked, it moved with a liquid grace that flowed across the snow.

She'd spent a great deal of time with Isaak and his generation of metal men. She'd also seen the previous generation—the one Sethbert had made sing while she and Rudolfo danced that first day they met. She saw similarity in all three, but this one—so much older than Charles's reproductions—was clearly superior in its design. It moved slowly, though she did not doubt for a minute that it could move faster than any magicked scout.

For a moment, she crouched and blinked, her mind spinning with this new data. She'd seen a few mechanicals left over from the Age of the Wizard Kings and from the shadowy times of Rufello during the age previous to their reign. But this even surpassed those imitations of the Younger Gods' handiwork.

The metal man tucked its flute into a pocket on the robe and turned back to the cave. Jin felt Aedric's hand upon her again. *It uses the whistle to divert birds. We're not sure how.*

She placed her hand upon his. *This explains how our codes continue to be broken.* Even now, Isaak's mechoservitors were creating new codes that were being deciphered just as quickly as they were issued.

The metal man paused at the cave entrance, then looked over its shoulder. When it spoke, its voice was melodic and low, though it carried easily across the distance. "Great Mother," it said, "you do not need to hide with the others. I have tea inside and would be honored if you would join me."

Jin Li Tam held her breath, unsure for a moment if the metal man had truly spoken to her or if it was some unexpected side effect of the magicks she used. The voice was so matter-of-fact, so casual.

An invitation for tea.

The metal man turned now, fully facing the line of trees where they hid. "Queen Winteria's vow certainly holds true here, Great Mother. Your safety is assured, and I'm certain you have questions about all you've read and seen of late." The metal man paused, as if in thought, then continued. "Your first captain and his men are not assured the same safety, I'm afraid, as they have no doubt already surmised."

She did not doubt the mechoservitor's words. Several times over the course of the past two years, she'd seen clearly that somehow she and Rudolfo and their child were excluded from the brutal violence that surrounded them. At least until the explosion—which clearly had not been driven by the Y'Zirites.

And the metal man spoke correctly: She was made of questions, and if he offered answers, it behooved her to seek them. Even if she suspected those answers, ultimately.

She started to stand, slipping the running line from her wrist, and felt Aedric's firm grip upon her shoulder.

She could feel the tension in the firmness of his fingers as they pressed words into her skin. *You can't possibly—*

She shrugged off his hand, her voice low and thick from the magicks. "I can," she said. "Wait here with your men."

She stood to her full height and strode into the clearing. Despite her magicks, the mechoservitor's head followed her as she went.

He sees past the powders. And as if to confirm it, the metal man spoke. "Great Mother, it gladdens me to see you after so many years of longing for your day."

She walked to him, no longer guarding her steps. "I am Jin Li Tam of House Li Tam, queen of the Ninefold Forest. Who are you?"

As she drew closer, she saw now even more clearly the effect of time on the dark metal surface, patches of spiderwebbed fungus, pockmarks and pits and faint scratches on the unfamiliar steel. The joints were less pronounced, and its form was more slender than the others. Its age was obvious, and she suspected strongly that she was witnessing a marvel from the oldest times—a leftover from the age of the Younger Gods.

"I am called the Watcher," the metal man said.

Jin Li Tam stopped before it. "What do you watch, Watcher?"

And at that, the metal man smiled, and it chilled her blood to see such raw emotion on a face that should not be capable of expression. "I watch all of you," it said. "But I have especially watched for *your* coming, Great Mother, and the coming of your son, Jakob." The Watcher turned and walked into the cave, the hum and buzz of his movement somehow soothing to her. "And in this particular moment," the metal man added, "I've a teakettle to watch. I put it on once I knew you were coming."

I was expected. Jin Li Tam looked over her shoulder. She could not see the Gypsy Scouts where they hid there in the shadow of the tree line, but she knew they watched her. And she knew that Aedric no doubt fumed at her decision.

He wasn't wrong to do so. Certainly her experience so far lent her confidence of safety in this place. Still, even now, she felt a kind of fear—one she'd not been familiar with previously.

A fear of the unknown.

With the sound of the Watcher already fading ahead of her in the narrow cave, Jin Li Tam brushed aside her momentary doubt and followed quickly after.

Rudolfo

Outside the cave, a low wind moaned through the canyon. Rudolfo sipped his firespice, feeling the warmth it made as it moved from his mouth to his stomach.

He'd taken to spending his days here near the ladder when he could, occupying a table in the corner of the cave. He found the low buzz of conversation and the steady whisper of the mechoservitors' pens strangely comforting as he read over reports that were days old before they reached him in the far north of his Ninefold Forest.

His own intelligence officers had been busy in the southern nations, but at each step, they were outcrafted by what he assumed must be the Y'Zirite resurgence's quiet operatives. They'd arrived at Lord Cervael's estate on the Emerald Coasts, tracing Jarvis through Rothmir to that place, only to find the minor noble missing. Rudolfo wondered if his wife would be called upon to execute this man as well, and found himself wondering if she would again do what needed to be done.

It alarmed him to discover that he was divided in his opinions on the matter. One part celebrated the swift and ruthless judgment; another knew that they could do this for decades and still be no safer for it.

Because the knives would simply beget more knives. It was a simple equation.

And yet, he thought as he took another drink, *I wish my hand were upon that blade.*

He heard a distant bell ringing from far below and pushed himself back from the table. One of the mechoservitors stood and went to the pulley crank, turning it with ease as it lifted a cage of tools and equipment for cleaning and inspection. After unloading it quickly, the mechoservitor lowered it and brought it up again, this time full of dirt-smeared packs.

Soon after, the first of Rudolfo's scouts appeared, climbing wearily over the lip of the shaft to strip down from their wet, filthy uniforms and wrap themselves in thick wool blankets.

Tyrus, a middle-aged miner from Rudoheim, was the last of the group to climb up. After he'd passed his satchel of papers over to the waiting mechoservitor and wrapped himself in a blanket, he approached Rudolfo.

Rudolfo pointed to the bottle of firespice and at the man's nod, filled a wooden cup with the thick liquor and pushed it to him. "How was this foray?"

Tyrus sipped the drink. "Good," he said. But something on the man's face and in the tone of his voice told Rudolfo that *good* was a relative statement in this matter. "We mapped another two hundred leagues farther south."

Two hundred leagues. That put them roughly halfway to the Seventh Manor—five days by caravan or two by horseback if the roads were reasonably clear. Rudolfo shook his head in wonder.

Tyrus nodded. "I've worked in the ground my whole life and never imagined there could be such a Whymer Maze beneath our forest." He took another drink and looked around the room, then lowered his voice. "But I do not think we're alone down there."

There it is. Rudolfo saw it in the man's eyes now. Fear like a low-grade fever burning behind those bloodshot whites, weighing down the brows and crow's feet around them. Rudolfo raised own glass to his lips. He felt the fire making its way into him. "The mechoservitors went west," he said, "but I don't think you are referring to them."

Tyrus shook his head. "No, Lord. I don't know what I'm referring to exactly. But we hear things. And we've seen boot prints that are not so very old."

Rudolfo felt his eyebrows raising. "Boot prints?" He was forming the rest of his question when a distant whistling from outside interrupted.

Faint and on the wind, he heard the strains of third alarm and watched as his men scrambled to arms. But even as they did, the noise of commotion grew in the canyon—muffled sounds of metal on metal, shouts and cries, and then suddenly, a storm spilled into the cavern.

It came twisting and writhing into their midst, a moving, muted cacophony of magicked and unmagicked forms locked in combat. He saw the bright-colored winter woolens of his soldiers, the darker colors of scouts who'd not yet had time to magick themselves, and the shimmer at the center that bespoke invisible aggressors.

Even in those first moments, as he tugged at a scout knife with his good hand, Rudolfo saw two of his men fall beneath blades he could not see, then be tossed carelessly aside as they bled out on the cave floor. The men in their blankets dropped them to stand naked and face the intruders with bare hands or knives they scrambled for in panic, and even as they did, the storm advanced into the room as tables were overturned and pages were scattered.

He heard a harsh but muted whisper in a language he did not recognize and watched as the closest mechoservitor was suddenly upended into the shaft, whistling and hooting as it plummeted below.

The miner, Tyrus, reached for a shovel, and lines of blood appeared on his flesh as his blanket was torn away. Invisible hands threw him up and into the rock wall, and when he fell, he did not move.

In the space of the time it took to blink, another three men fell.

Rudolfo moved forward only to feel an iron hand grab his wrist and twist the knife from him. A low voice, muffled by magicks, spoke in his ear. It was a woman's. "We do not war with you, Lord Rudolfo. Call off your men and let us pass."

The second mechoservitor spun, a dent appearing suddenly in the side of its head. One of its jeweled eyes guttered and then went out as it, too, was tossed into the shaft. This time, Rudolfo heard the distant crash of metal on stone.

Outside, third alarm grew louder as another wind poured into the cave.

The hand on his wrist twisted farther and then released when something heavy impacted the woman who held him, staggering her.

Rudolfo's foot lashed out, his heavy leather boot striking what he hoped was her knee. "You come magicked and in violence into my lands and tell me you do not war with me? Your queen has gone too far."

He saw the faint shimmer of his Gypsy Scouts as they moved into the room. But he knew they were no match for these invaders. He'd watched the enhanced strength and speed of the blood magicks tear through a room of armed men to assassinate Hanric and Ansylus, crown prince of Turam, at his Firstborn Feast. There was pain in the voice now when it spoke again. "We do not answer to Machtvolk house servants. Stand down your men in name of the Crimson Empress or watch her Blood Guard cut them down."

Rudolfo felt his scalp prickling with rage, but even as he opened his mouth, hands tugged him back and away from the magicked woman. "Stay clear, General," a voice hissed in his ear. "We'll take them."

Rudolfo struggled against the hands, and as he did, he watched his men fall. He heard the soft cries and grunts as his best went down beneath the whispering blades. The scout who had pulled him aside staggered into him, and Rudolfo felt warm blood that he could not see spatter his face as the man went limp and crumpled.

He tugged at his second knife with his good hand even as the woman's voice returned near his ear and her hands took hold of him. "Stand your men down and tell us where the other two metal dreamers are."

"We will not stand down," he said through gritted teeth. "Your Crimson Empress does not rule the Ninefold Forest."

"She will soon enough," the woman said. "We will find the Abomination's hand servants ourselves." She barked orders in a language he did not recognize and released him suddenly, pushing him back and away.

He watched what remained of his men as they disengaged, watched the small boot prints appear in the gathering pools of blood as the magicked force made their way to the lip of the well and its ladder downward.

The room became quiet but for the groans of the wounded. He heard his blood pounding in his temples and felt his body trembling. He took in the room at a glance, saw the crumpled forms of naked and bleeding scouts, their blankets cast aside in the fight. And he knew that among those bodies lay the magicked bodies of those men of his who pursued this Blood Guard into the cave.

It was the decision of a split second. He made it without thought beyond the need of satisfying the anger that blurred his vision.

Rudolfo saw the lever that locked the pulley and its heavy cage still in place and threw himself at it.

The ropes released, and the cage plummeted down.

Somewhere, far below, he heard a crash and a scream.

More men poured into the cave now, magicked scouts and unmagicked foot soldiers. Lysias came with them, his face red from exertion and his mouth grim.

Rudolfo locked eyes with the general. "Pursue them," he said. "Send a company if you have to, but find them and bring me prisoners."

Lysias nodded and started barking orders as men scrambled into the shaft and army medicos knelt beside the wounded.

Taking in the sudden carnage of the room, Rudolfo felt something break inside of him. He seized the edge of his worktable and hurled it over, no longer mindful of the pain in his arm. A flood of paper scattered the room, settling onto the bloody floor. His foot lashed out and caught the chair, sending it into a wall.

Blood for blood, he thought.

Then Rudolfo roared his wrath, silencing the rest of the cavern as all eyes went to their lord and general. And the anguish of that cry, echoing down the well and through the cave that led outside, was a sound that raised the hair upon even his own arms and neck.

"Blood for blood," Rudolfo said into the silence that followed.

Vlad Li Tam

They saw it on the horizon, and at first, Vlad Li Tam thought it must be a pile of white clouds. As they steamed closer, those clouds seemed more likely to be mountains or something like them.

Finally, the Moon Wizard's Ladder took shape ahead of them, and the vastness of it made him feel very small.

He stood at the bow with Obadiah and wished Baryk were here to see it. By now, he suspected the warpriest and the rest of the family aboard *The Serendipitous Wind* were three or four hundred nautical leagues northwest of them, moving slowly under sail toward the Divided Isle and the Entrolusian Delta that waited behind it. They would bear word to Rudolfo of their investigation so far and petition Charles, the Forest Library's arch-engineer, to see if the old Androfrancine might have another power source for their limping vessel.

Vlad Li Tam looked at the metal man. They'd spent many days together now, first in rough quarters they'd rigged for their guest in the boiler room before they'd determined which ship to send back. Then, later, after Ren had replaced the dead sunstone, they'd wandered the vessel together.

They'd spent the nights together in the bow, watching the d'jin—the light-bearer—moving ahead of them just beneath the surface of the water.

In all of it, they talked about the dream, though the mechoservitor still spoke cryptically and in riddles about it.

"It was not meant for your kind," Obadiah had told him at one point. "It was meant for the Homeseeker just as we were meant to prepare the antiphon for his coming. He will save the light."

Vlad Li Tam had met the boy Neb. He'd met him in the gravediggers' camp on the plains of Windwir. He'd seen him again in the crowded pavilion where Petronus had ended the Order by taking Sethbert's life without naming a successor. He seemed an unlikely Homeseeker. Vlad had heard bits of Marsher mysticism and still wondered how an Androfrancine orphan could fulfill their so-called prophecies of a promised home.

"You say the dream is not meant for our kind," he had said, "but Neb is our kind. And you tell me that I am called to the dream as well."

Obadiah's eye shutters had flashed open and closed. "The light-bearer calls you to your part in the dream, but it is not to be comprehended in a moment. It is arrived at with meditation and reflection. For me to expound upon it to you, even *if* I fully comprehended your role in the antiphon, would rob you of discovery."

"Did the light-bearer also call Neb to his own part in the dream, then?"

The metal man had shaken his head. "No," he said. "The dream was fashioned for the Homeseeker's advent." His voice became low, as if he spoke of something sacred. "It is his dream in the end. We are simply his abacus."

After that, they only discussed those aspects of the dream that Vlad could pull from the images that haunted those few hours he slept. Images of light dancing to a song beneath the water that grew more vivid the farther southeast they sailed. And something else—something dark and massive and hungry—that awaited in blue-green shadows and watched for his coming.

Now they stood together at the rail as the ladder took shape ahead of them. It looked nothing like a ladder, this massive ring of white stones standing high in the sky, each curving gently inward as they rose. Squinting at the top of it, lost in a veil of clouds, Vlad saw that the ends of the stones joined together. Something shimmered there, and it took him a moment to see it.

It was a massive globe made of a silver so bright that it reflected back the sky and clouds around it. It sat above the ring of stones, making it more like a gigantic cage that rose up from the sea, with gaps of leagues between each white stone bar.

"Gods," Vlad whispered.

"Yes," Obadiah agreed.

Vlad was so taken by the sight that he didn't hear his forty-eighth son approaching from behind. "We're ready to power down the ships at your word, Father."

He nodded absently, his eyes still locked on the ladder. Its sheer size boggled him, and he was struck by the unlikelihood of it, here in the heart of the Ghosting Crests, surrounded by wide open seas.

He forced his attention to the metal man. "You will know when it is time?"

Steam vented from Obadiah's exhaust grate, and he nodded. "Yes."

The metal man's memory was faulty on what exactly had happened—whatever had burned out its sunstone had also damaged its memory scrolls. But it was clear that at some point, as he and his metal brothers had approached the ladder, their power sources had begun to fail. His next memory was waking up in the boiler room to Vlad's questions.

Vlad looked back to the stones and the impossible globe that joined their upper reaches. "I wonder what we will find there."

Obadiah's ears tipped, and deep inside his chest cavity, gears spun and clacked. When he spoke, it was in a singsong voice, reedy and metallic. "You will find Behemoth, and he will take you into the basements of the ladder."

Behemoth. He felt sweat beads on his forehead at the word. Vlad's eyes narrowed. "But you do not know how or what it is I am to do there?"

The metal man shook his head. "We believed it was our part of the dream," Obadiah said, "but we were mistaken. The light-bearer chose *you* for this."

Again, images and sound washed him. The water swallowed him, warm and burning the open wounds that lacerated his skin. He clutched at his grandson as they plummeted, and he opened his eyes on light as the water around him filled with song. He felt his heart breaking from the power of it, and hands grabbed at him, pulling him up and away from the purest, truest love he'd ever known, though at the time he had not understood it to be so.

He shook the memory away, tasting the salt of water and blood in his mouth.

I have been chosen for this. He'd spent a lifetime in the shadow of the

Order, raised in the reason they espoused, though he could never quite revere their light with the same tenacious drive those robed and backward dreamers could. Certainly he grasped the Androfrancine need to control the flow of technology and magick, of knowledge and information. But it had never been an act of worship for him. It had been a means to an end. Still, he'd learned like most in the Named Lands to eschew mysticism and madness.

And now I hear prophecy from a metal man, Vlad thought. *I find dreams within a song. I chase ghosts in the water.*

Finally, he opened his eyes and glanced at Ren. "You know what to do when Obadiah gives the word."

The young man nodded. "We'll stop the armada and ready the captain's yacht under sail."

Vlad looked back to the great stone columns filling the horizon to the south of them. "It is impressive," he said.

Ren chuckled. "It is. But it looks like no ladder I've seen before," he said. "I wonder how he descended it?"

I wonder, too, Vlad thought but said nothing.

He'd seen the work of both the Younger Gods and the Older. But never anything of such scope. Of course, ancient texts he'd seen in the Great Library claimed that the Younger Gods had actually found the moon barren and white and lifeless—that they had made it into a garden.

And even Obadiah was a testament from their time, though the metal man was obviously a close approximation based on the reproductions of that ancient Czarist engineer, Rufello.

As the day crept on, Vlad was surprised to see his children and grandchildren gathering on the decks of the ships. He looked to the vessels to their port and starboard and saw it was the same there, as well. When the sun hung low in the sky, the silver globe burned red as the bloody sky.

Vlad watched as the water darkened and wondered if his dreams would tell him more when morning carried him to his narrow bunk for a few hours of sleep. He tried to imagine what it was that awaited him—this Behemoth Obadiah spoke of—and what it was that he was meant to do in the basement of the ladder. And most of all, he wondered when the light of her would rise so that his day-long need would subside. That ache that steadied him.

But when the lights did rise, blue and green beneath a moonless sky, Vlad Li Tam's breath caught in his throat. He heard the same all around him and could've sworn he heard it from the other ships from half a league away.

In the end, he could not help himself. He held back as long as he could.

Then Vlad Li Tam wept as a thousand, thousand d'jin swelled the sea around them, their song loosed upon the air.

Neb

The images floated and spun now faster than Neb could lay hold of them, and the pain from the blades settled into a dull ache. He'd stopped screaming, but it wasn't that he had nothing to scream for.

Instead, he bottled it and hoped to somehow turn it into strength.

Renard will come for me, he thought. *And Petronus, too.* Those realizations gave him focus. But still, he found now that it was easier to spin the dial faster rather than slowing it down when it came to the fleeting dreams, waking and sleeping, that he raced through beneath her knife, beneath the touch of that cold dark carving in her hand.

Something was happening to him, and he did not know what it was.

Her name is Shyla. The woman with the short, gray hair. He didn't know how he knew it and didn't know if it was even truly her name. But he heard it in her, and during yesterday's cutting, images of a vast hot desert and a silver, vacant throne draped in red robes flitted against his inner eye when her knife and her kin-raven touched his hot and bloody skin.

A new image seized him, and the surprise of it stopped him before he could spin it away. He stood on the deck of a ship with a metal man and a scarred and familiar old man with tangled red-gray hair. The cuttings upon him were like those of his thirty-second daughter and like the ones Neb knew now covered him.

That was not what surprised him, though.

It was the vast series of white columns rising up into a star-speckled sky and an ocean swimming with undulating moonlight where there was no moon to be found.

"It is the song," Shyla said, and Neb realized now that she was not speaking to him. She was speaking in the guttural language they'd been using among themselves.

She repositioned the knife, and he missed the beginning of the reply. ". . . Ladder?"

"It appears so," Shyla said, and he heard what he thought was fear in her voice.

He spun himself away, but not before the metal man met eyes with him. "Hail Homeseeker," he said.

"Take me back to the Moon Wizard's Ladder, Abomination," Shyla said.

Neb forced his eyes open and found hers. He tried to speak, but no words formed. He struggled long enough to push a dry croak through his lips, but it wasn't intelligible.

The knife bit into him again, and the kin-raven touched his blood. It was a dark place, warm and underground. A mechoservitor and an old Androfrancine moved through the passageways with a lantern.

Isaak. The mechoservitor stopped and turned. "Neb?"

But Neb couldn't speak. He simply spun and watched Isaak fall away.

"Avert your eyes, Homeseeker" the next mechoservitor said, looking up from the book it was eating.

He did, spinning now into a vast underground quicksilver sea with a large black stone floating in its center like the dark iris of a mirrored eye. Lying across it was a man he recognized, despite how much weight he'd lost or his haggard features.

He still could not find his voice, but his mind found words: *Brother Hebda?*

The man sat bolt upright. "You are learning how to manipulate the dream stone."

He'd seen his father in his dreams before, but he'd not been in these surroundings. He'd looked more like the man from his memory, only sometimes he was pale as a corpse with bloodshot eyes. This image of him felt different.

Dream stone. The black of it matched the black of Hebda's island.

He heard a whistle and the sound of oars. Neb turned and saw a longboat moving across the silver water toward them, a Gray Guard rowing.

Neb looked back to Hebda and stared into his eyes. He saw the fear there, and it stung him, though he did not know what his father was afraid of.

Then he left as Shyla started a new line of text using her knife as a pen.

He was in a valley hidden within a mountain, and at its center stood a giant scaffold.

Figures scrambled over the scaffold, and within it, a large object took shape. As they worked, they sang. And Neb recognized the song they sang.

"We have found them," Shyla said.

And when she said it, blood poured from her mouth, and her eyes went wide with surprise even as they glazed over.

Neb felt hands upon him and a voice near his head. "Hold, lad," Renard whispered. As he said it, the camp erupted in pandemonium. Neb heard the sound of fighting, the muffled sounds of magicked boots across the ground. The ropes that held him were cut away.

He felt warm water splashed against his lips. "Open," Renard said. But when Neb opened his mouth, he found it filled with bitter powder that he recognized. He felt the magicks taking hold, hot on his boiling skin.

Renard lifted him on his back. The Waste salts on the guide's robes burned him, and as the man staggered into a run that became a sprint, the wind cut him as deep as those silver knives.

Behind them, he heard the sound of muffled fighting. Renard ran them away from the camp, though Neb had no idea what direction. As they ran, the magicks that concealed him also began to work at his acuity. His sense of smell and hearing sharpened even as his stomach lurched at the nausea of the scout powders.

Something nagged at him as his focus gathered. Something was missing. Something terrible, and he could not quite place it.

But the farther they ran, the more he remembered the pouch and the silver crescent it contained.

I've lost the canticle.

"Go back," he tried to say, his voice rasping and quieted further by the magicks.

"We are not going back," Renard said. "Rest easy. We'll stop to bandage you up soon. We'll be to Petronus by tomorrow."

Neb kept his eyes closed and tried to lose himself in the rhythm of Renard's stride and the gentle draw and release of Renard's breath, the air filling with the scent of the root the guide chewed.

Somehow, he slept, and when Neb dreamed, he dreamed of an ocean shining like the moon and the song upon those waters.

Jin Li Tam

Jin Li Tam held the sweet tea in her mouth and tried to maintain her composure. The room was heavy with the thick stench of decomposing meat and bird dung. It was all she could do not to retch when she entered that space.

Still, she did not want her metal host to see this. And because the magicks that guttered beneath and upon her skin could not hide her, she forced herself to the same calm that she would show in any distasteful aspect of her father's work. If she could manage it beneath Sethbert's fat and sweaty face, she could manage it for this strange mechanical she suddenly found herself at tea with.

They sat at a table now, she with a cup and saucer and the metal man watching her take small sips. As they sat quietly, she took in the room. There were three workbenches—one covered in paper and pens and threads for the birds, and another covered in books in various states of binding scattered amidst loose pages and pens. Then, on the far wall, another workbench stood covered in vials and bottles, pots and pipes.

In the corner, a chimneyed furnace warmed the place, adding heat to the smell of dung and death.

There was no other furniture in the room.

"You write the Y'Zirite gospels?" Jin Li Tam finally said. She wasn't sure exactly how she found her words. The oddness of sitting to tea with a mechoservitor like nothing she'd seen before confounded her, gave her a sense so strongly surreal that she felt a level of disconnect from the moment.

The mechoservitor nodded. "I do. I provide oversight to Queen Winteria the Elder for education and religion as well." The metal man somehow smiled. "I hold thirteen percent of the Y'Zir Library in my memory plates. Part of my work here has involved establishing a network of Y'Zirite faith. I've spent half a century here preparing the way for the Crimson Empress, seeding our faith back into the land and reminding the Machtvolk of their true station. Their place in that faith."

Jin Li Tam sipped her tea again. "And monitoring our communications. Modifying them in some instances."

"Yes." The metal man nodded.

"And helping my family establish Rudolfo's Ninefold Forest as the centerpoint of the Named Lands."

"Yes," the Watcher said again.

Yes. And she was a part of that, arranged through her father to bear the Gypsy King an heir, a Child of Promise. She reached for the tea again, wishing the strength of its flavor would drown out the stench. She understood the reason for the smell of bird droppings, but the carrion smell made no sense to her until a dark bird hopped into the room. She recognized it immediately from her dreams, though up close the kin-raven seemed less fierce. It was still oversized, its feathers mottled and its eyes dead black drops of ink. It smelled like it had been dead for weeks.

She fixed her attention back on the mechoservitor. "You knew my grandfather, then," she said.

He nodded. "He took the mark with Lord Jakob on the Eve of the Falling Moon. I watched them weep for joy at what was coming."

The words drew her head up from her tea. "Lord Jakob was an Y'Zirite?"

The metal man's matter-of-fact tone surprised her. "Of course. It was a secret conversion. But all conversions were secret because of the children of P'Andro Whym. Those days are nearly past. We worship openly here in the Machtvolk Territories. Soon, the faith will spread and all may partake of her grace." The mechoservitor smiled again, and she was amazed at how the metal face could emulate such a human expression. "And one day," the Watcher said, "that grace will bring restoration."

Rudolfo's father had been a part of this. It went much deeper than she realized if the Ninefold Forest was complicit. She could not fathom Lord Jakob as an Y'Zirite. She'd heard stories of him, had read scattered bits of the history of his reign before her father's seventh son—Fontayne—cut his life short. Known for being fair and just, Jakob had ridden against the cult under an Androfrancine flag during a half-dozen resurgences. She thought about the book her father had taken from Mal Li Tam, her nephew. "Because my son and this Crimson Empress will somehow heal the world."

The Watcher looked at her cup, saw that it was empty, and stood to put the kettle on. He placed it on a small furnace and returned to his chair. "Yes, Great Mother. Their union will heal a world broken by deicide."

Their union. She had read over passages of the gospel they'd given her, seeing vague references to the Child of Promise as a bridegroom adorned for his empress. If she hadn't heard the singing on the day of her arrival here, she wouldn't have believed such a thing was possible. But the tears in those eyes and the reverence in those voices had told her that regardless of the plausibility, those Machtvolk believed.

As had her grandfather and her nephew.

As had Rudolfo's father, Jakob.

The prospect of it terrified her. It raised the question that she didn't know she wanted an answer for: *What if these beliefs are true?*

She shook it off. "I find this all hard to comprehend."

There was a quiet murmur deep in the ancient metal man. "You do not have to comprehend it to accept it."

Actually, she realized, *I do.* But she didn't say that. Instead, she put down her teacup and met those dark jeweled eyes with her own. "You know what is coming."

"I do," the Watcher said. "It is my great honor to have shaped it and watched it unfold for my soon-arriving lady."

Jin Li Tam remembered the note her father had left for her so long ago, during her brief stay in the papal summer palace. *War is coming.*

He'd certainly been referring to the resulting war that followed Windwir's fall. But now she could see the larger conflict. Years of damaged kin-clave and resources squandered in civil wars and minor conflicts, the loss of their Androfrancine shepherds and their war-making technologies and magicks, the creation of a strong army in the north, the return of blood magicks and Y'Zirite worship to their world.

This, she realized, was what the Androfrancines had been afraid of. Ironically, it was why they'd brought back Xhum Y'Zir's spell and the metal men capable of wielding it without being utterly destroyed by it.

The kettle whistled and the Watcher stood. He brought it to the table and filled her cup again. But this time, she did not touch it. She forced herself to breathe in the rancid air around her.

The metal man sat again before speaking. "I'm afraid I will need to return to my duties soon, Great Mother. But I am delighted for this time with you. I hope you will return to me when you can bring the child."

I could never bring him into this stinking hole. But she forced herself to smile, certain he could see it despite the scout magicks. "I will hope for that as well," she said, hoping this ancient wonder couldn't see through her lie as well as he did the powders.

She heard another hum and the softest of metallic clicks from deep within the mechoservitor. "I do have an uncomfortable matter to discuss with you before you rejoin your men and return to Queen Winteria's lodge."

She gave in, reached for the tea and took a long sip before setting the cup down again. "What uncomfortable matter would that be?"

The metal man sat up straight. She saw the liquid way in which he moved, heard the quiet whisper of the functions beneath his dark, pitted skin. "I have word from the regent that our Blood Guard hunt the Wastes for the Abomination's hand servants. We are fortunate to have caught the Abomination, but his metal disciples have proven more problematic. Their dream is dangerous, and they spread it as an infection among themselves."

Now there was no need to lie or to hide her surprise. "I do not know what you speak of."

The mechoservitor shrugged. "I suppose you do not. Still, the regent has requested that all mechoservitors remaining in the Named Lands be placed under my care until those in the Wastes are located and rendered nonfunctional. We do not want them contaminated by this anomalous scripting." His eyes went dull and then bright. "This includes the one chosen to bear the spell—the one your husband named Isaak."

She blinked her surprise. "What regent do you speak of?" *This is new.*

"The regent of House Y'Zir." He stood, and again she noted the way he moved as he walked toward the narrow corridor that fed back into the cave. "I would ask that you convey this word to Lord Rudolfo at your earliest convenience."

She found her composure again and stood. "I will bear the news, but I do not expect Lord Rudolfo will agree to this."

"His agreement is not required," the metal man said over his shoulder. "Only his obedience."

She followed him into the corridor, but instead of turning right and heading into the fading daylight where Aedric and the others waited, they turned left and moved deeper into the cave. As they moved, the carrion smell grew until her magick-enhanced sense of smell was overpowered and tears streamed from her eyes. It was dark, this space they moved into, but the dim light from the mechoservitor's eyes, coupled with her sharpened vision, allowed her to pick out two tables. Atop those tables were two stinking piles of skin and meat.

The metal man walked into the room as she waited. "I also assist Queen Winteria in the distilling of her blood magicks. A work that I find soothing." The mechoservitor stooped and lifted a folded stack of clothing and brought it to her. She accepted the bundle.

It took her a moment to pick out the rainbow colors of winter woolen uniforms, topped with leather belts, sheathed scout knives and carefully folded turbans. "Tell your first captain that he and his men may enter my cave to retrieve and bury their dead. But should they return beyond that, they will add their blood to my distillery."

She took the folded uniforms and turned woodenly without a word. She walked quickly away, moving from that darkness and toward the white light of a snowy afternoon.

When Jin Li Tam left the cave, she made herself walk in slow, careful steps. Already, the magicks were burning out in her, her head throbbing and her stomach clenching as they did. Still, she held herself erect and moved quickly through the field to where her men waited in the tree line.

"Lady Tam," Aedric said, his muffled voice afraid. "Are you—?"

But she interrupted him when all composure flew from her control. Falling to her knees, Jin Li Tam vomited, tasting the sour, sweet blend of tea and bile. Grabbing handfuls of snow, she rubbed it into her mouth and nose, hoping somehow it would scrub the taste and smell of death from her.

Petronus

They waited and watched eastward, their horses magicked for speed and stamina, stamping to gallop. The sun had risen just hours before, and already Petronus had the sinking feeling that things had gone awry. Grymlis sat beside him, shielding his eyes from the sun with a gloved hand.

"He's late," Petronus said.

"He's Remus's boy," the Gray Guard captain said. "I don't recall the father ever keeping to a schedule either."

Petronus swallowed his fear and kept watching. Nearby, Geoffrus and his men laughed and hooted among themselves until Grymlis withered them with a glare.

We should have ridden for him ourselves. Yet just in the past day they'd seen two kin-ravens against the cloudless sky. Renard had surely been correct: They could not have gotten close enough to extract the boy. And even Rudolfo's best were not trained for Waste fighting. Their scout magicks and knives were better suited for woodland combat, not the wide open stretch of rock and sand and fused glass that surrounded them now.

Still, under Renard's leadership, they at least had a chance.

It hadn't been so long ago that Petronus had faced a blood-magicked scout that night in his shack before his arrest and trial on the Delta. In the end, Grymlis and his men had saved him, but it had cost him some men. And he'd heard stories of the attacks on Rudolfo's Firstborn Feast and the other nations. The only weak spot in these blood magicks was the fact that they killed the bearer after roughly three days' time.

That did not appear to be the case with these runners. Not if Renard spoke true.

When Grymlis raised a finger and pointed, he followed it. There, on the horizon, he saw what he thought was a billowing swell of dust. Squinting, he picked out another just behind it—and behind that, another.

Any others were lost to distance and the play of sunlight over the blasted landscape.

"Now we ride," Grymlis said, urging his horse forward. Petronus did likewise, and the company fell in behind them.

Geoffrus and his band leaped to their feet, their teeth black from the root they chewed, but this time, they did not take the lead. Instead, they nestled themselves in among the galloping horses, stretching their legs into the run.

As they rode, Petronus kept his eyes upon the dust cloud and was able to pick out two more straggling forms behind. But even as he picked them out, another storm swept in from behind an outcropping of stone and one of the straggling forms went down. Another hesitated, just for a moment, and then sped up as another gout of dust rose up and cut the runner off.

They are pursued.

He saw Grymlis's sword out now, held low, though there were still many leagues between them and any foe. The hooves of his horse blurred as they moved over the ground.

They rode to intersect with the runners, and they rode in silence but for the panting of their horses and the muffled sound of magicked hooves striking stone.

But even as they galloped forward, Petronus watched another dust cloud fall into a blur of commotion.

We will not be fast enough.

The lead runner zigged south towards them. Grymlis adjusted their course, and Petronus followed. As they rode, Petronus grew aware of noise on the wind, and it took him a moment to place it. It was a song, faint and broken.

"Do you hear it?" he shouted across to Grymlis.

The puzzled look on the captain's face told Petronus he did not.

He cannot hear it. He has not been affected by the blood magicks as you have, Father. It was Hebda's voice, whispering between his ears.

Each word of that whisper was a hammer to Petronus's temples, and he winced.

Send Renard with the boy. The light needs you elsewhere.

The nausea set in, and Petronus's nose was suddenly filled with the scent of ozone and blood.

An image formed in his mind, and it wrenched him. He fell forward in the saddle at the sight of it—a hollow mountain far to the north, nestled in the Dragon's Spine. A scaffold draped in nets woven with evergreen branches rose up from the valley floor, and figures moved about, careful to keep the sun from reflecting off their metal surfaces.

He felt warmth in his beard and realized his nose had started bleeding at some point.

Shepherd them, Father. Wolves on the hunt.

He tasted the bile in his throat, the sour acid burning his mouth. And just as his equilibrium started to slide, the whisper receded and he clung to his horse, a cold sweat breaking out on his forehead.

When he had the strength, he looked to Grymlis and shouted over the sound of that song. "Our plans have changed," he said. "We ride north. Renard runs west with the boy."

Grymlis's face registered surprise. "Now?"

Petronus shook his head. "After we give him a head start."

The old Gray Guard nodded. "Aye," he said.

They rode wordlessly, low in their saddles and adjusting their course. Petronus wished now that he'd taken one of the swords they'd offered him, though he would've had no idea how to use it. He had been a fisherman, a statesman and scholar. Now, an exile back from the grave and possibly riding hells-bent for another.

When the lines of dust grew nearer, Petronus hung back and watched the others surge ahead. Grymlis and his small contingent of Gray Guard split away from the Gypsy Scouts while the Foresters magicked themselves from the saddle and leaped down to form a running perimeter.

Petronus heard Renard's shout and watched as the perimeter opened to let the magicked figure through.

"Hail, Father," the Waste guide called as he approached.

In that moment, Petronus felt the worry suddenly pull at him. "Do you have him? How is he?"

The pursuing Blood Guard struck the perimeter now, and horses screamed as they intersected with the mounted Gray Guard as well.

Renard's voice was heavy with exhaustion. "He's alive. He's wounded."

"We've new instructions," Petronus said. "You're to run him west." He paused. *Do I tell him the rest?* In the end, it was Remus's son. "We're riding north to tend the antiphon." He opened his mouth to say more, but Renard interrupted him.

"We've no time for long good-byes, Father," the Waste guide said. "I wish you good fortune."

Before Petronus could answer, the magicked man was running again, dust rising from his passage.

Petronus was turning his mount back to the battle when something solid hit him and his horse staggered. He felt hands he could not see grabbing at him, and the force of it toppled him from the saddle.

The world slowed down as he fell, and he felt the wind of rushing hooves as it blew his hair. His right leg caught in the stirrup and then released, the sudden jerking of the horse tumbling him out amid the other hooves.

When he struck the ground the wind went out of him and he gasped. The magicked runner pinned him. "You are the Last Son," a woman's muffled voice said. He smelled blood on her breath.

"I am Petronus," he said.

"You must stand down your men, Last Son, and give us back the boy."

Petronus did not answer. Instead, he kicked out and felt her move at the last minute to avoid his foot.

He heard a shift on the wind. *The song grows closer.*

Three of the Gray Guard dropped back and approached. When one leaned down, his eyes suddenly bulged as his throat opened. "I may not harm you, Last Son," she hissed. "But your mark does not protect anyone else."

He heard the song now pounding in his blood. It was so loud that it vibrated the ground and the scar at his neck burned. The woman who pinned him was suddenly gone as some greater force collided with them.

At first he thought it was a horse, but the dust storm that erupted around them registered finally. Another ghost—maybe one of Rudolfo's men—had tumbled her off of him.

The sound of the song drowned out the noise they made, but Petronus saw the dust from it, twisting and roiling around him in a circle. He scrambled back from them and waited for the storm to subside.

When it did, he heard a woman's voice. "I bring this for the boy," she said. "He is not finished with it yet." She pushed something into his hands and it vibrated there, the canticle so loud he felt it in the ground. Her voice was already fading when he opened the magicked pouch and the song reached a crescendo that made his hands shake. There, shining in the afternoon light, was a silver crescent shaped like a sliver of the moon, the continents, mountains and seas etched lightly into its surface.

He felt the heat of it in his scars.

Petronus dropped it back into the pouch and felt for its straps. He stood slowly and tied it to his belt. He climbed into his saddle and first looked back to the raging skirmish. Then, he looked to the west and tried to find the line of dust.

He hoped that Renard would bear the boy to safety if such a thing could be found.

And he also hoped that Renard was wrong about an encampment. They could not afford to face more of this Blood Guard. He did not fully comprehend what was happening—but he knew that the mechoservitors in their hidden valley were critical to something greater than he could comprehend.

It requires a response.

And his response was to ride for them with what few men he had, to somehow guard them like a shepherd from the ravening wolves that sought them and sought to snuff out the light.

He knew his paths would cross with the boy soon enough.

Until then, Petronus would also shepherd the dream.

Winters

Each morning, they walked deeper into the forest and Winters found herself wandering a Whymer Maze of questions that tangled her more and more with Ria's cryptic answers. Her older sister was far more forthright with the answers when it came to her vision for the Machtvolk and the Named Lands beneath the reign of the Crimson Empress.

But simpler matters, like where she'd grown up or how she came to share Winteria's name, were brushed aside with briefest mention. It was perfectly obvious that they shared the same parents. The more time she spent with her older sister, the more clear their similarity of appearance and even mannerisms were, but their beliefs were vastly different.

Today, they walked alone down an unfamiliar path. "You've stopped dreaming about the Abomination again, haven't you?" Ria asked as they paused to watch the sun rise behind them.

She means Neb. Winters looked from the smear of red on the white horizon. "I have. For three days now."

Ria smiled. "Good. Those are the hardest. Though the Home dreams are also difficult. I could show you meditations that have helped me with them."

I do not want help with them. She craved them. She longed for them. Though lately, the ones Neb screamed in felt like blades twisted in her guts, and the metal men that continued to devour her family's dreams devoured her each night, spitting her onto the top of the white tower. The dreams were definitely difficult, but she was glad they were back even though they were different.

"In time, the dreams will change," Ria said as she turned to walk. "You felt them change when Jakob was born."

She remembered. *Begone kin-raven. Your message is not welcome in this house.* It reminded her of the old blind prophet Ezra, and she realized she'd not seen him since her return. It was a question she nearly asked her sister but held back at the last moment.

While they walked the last league, Ria talked about the growing stories of the evangelists as they bore the message into the villages scattered around the ruins of Windwir. Traditionally, these had been protected by the Androfrancines, but after the last Council of Kin-Clave Ria had made it clear that those lands were now hers. They had just circled back and could see the lodge when a Machtvolk officer approached her.

"Queen Winteria, your man has arrived from the Emerald Coasts." Behind him, she saw Garyt ben Urlin's familiar face.

Ria smiled. "Excellent. I will begin my work with him later this morning." She looked at Winters. "I need to leave you now, little sister. But tomorrow we'll walk again."

Winters curtsied. "I will find my way back."

Ria smiled and looked to the officer. "Escort her, Captain, or have your man do it."

The captain inclined his head. "Yes, my queen."

But when he glanced to Winters, she saw something in his eye that caught her own. Her sister's voice distracted her. "You are still accompanying me to the mass?"

Winters nodded. "Yes. And I will see you in the morning."

Ria smiled. "Bring your questions."

"I will," she said.

After Ria had left, Garyt's hands moved. *The captain follows your dream.* He stepped aside, and the captain moved beside her.

"Walk with me, my true queen," the officer said, "and I will see you safely back to the lodge."

She took his arm. "I am dreaming again," she said.

"Yes. I took them down into the caves myself. There is more that you should be aware of," he said, his voice low. "The book has been disturbed."

Metal mouths chewing paper. "Yes," she said. She felt no surprise by this. And she knew by whom . . . or what. And she also sensed that it was important that she continue writing down the dreams just as she received them and making sure they were added to the book. Each day, she carried them in her gospel and left them on the rock at the edge of the clearing where she fought with Jin. Each day, they were taken by a magicked courier.

She glanced at the captain. "I think the book is safe for now," she said. "These disturbances are in my dreams as well."

His face flushed at a question he did not want to ask. At last he did, and the words tumbled out of him. "Do you think the Homeseeker truly will prevail?"

She looked at him, and she willed every stone's weight of conviction she could find into her voice. "I know he will." She met his eyes and was surprised at the faith and adoration she saw there. "The dream is true." But even as she said it, she did not know if it was true. She only wished it to be so.

She wasn't even sure that Neb still lived. His last dream had slipped quietly away.

Winters forced the memory of him away, feeling the knots grow in her stomach. She turned her thoughts instead to the Book. *There are metal men in my library.* She wondered what they were doing with her family's book.

And how had they come to enter the caves beneath the watchful eye of Ria's guards? What's more, where were they from? Rudolfo's library? She didn't think they were. In her dreams, these looked older than Isaak's generation, though not by much. And she couldn't imagine that the Ninefold Forest would place them here and not share that information with her. Still, she intended to find some way to bring it up with Jin Li Tam during their knife dancing later that morning.

They walked quietly, and as the lodge drew closer, they slowed. The captain inclined his head toward her, his voice low. "Is there anything else I can do to aid you?"

She looked at him again. *He sees me as his queen.*

And Winters smiled because she knew what to ask him for and knew exactly where he could find it.

"I need something from my former quarters," she said.

That afternoon, the voice magicks were underneath her pillow and Winters smiled again.

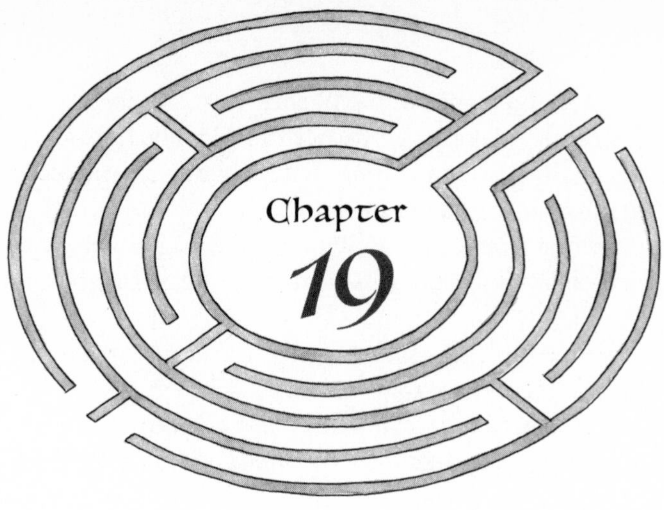

Rudolfo

Rudolfo rubbed ice water into his face and grimaced at the sour taste of last night's firespice. It wasn't the first night he'd drunk himself to sleep since the explosion and since coming north.

Or since my family rode east into someone else's care.

Jin Li Tam's most recent note had arrived last evening, outlining her experience with the ancient mechoservitor known as the Watcher, and some so-called regent's request that the library's mechanicals—and Isaak—be surrendered into Y'Zirite safekeeping.

He'd become angry when he read it and had poured another glassful of the strong liquor before fading to sleep.

Just a few hours ago. He blinked against the pounding in his temples and cupped more water into his hands, drinking it down. Outside, the camp stirred as mail was delivered, the couriers having plowed their way into the training camp.

And here, in his new quarters—a simple windowless wooden structure—Philemus and Lysias stood waiting for him with sober faces. He did not bother with his green turban of office. Instead, he shook the water from his hair and turned to them.

It cannot be good news. That was plain to see, and his first thought was to the prisoner they'd taken. He'd been quite surprised that she'd survived. If the wounds she'd taken being struck by the platform hadn't killed her, the blood magicks that burned through her system should have. But three days later, she'd been alive. Already, Lysias had logged hours interrogating her, sometimes with Rudolfo in attendance. And so far, that questioning had yielded nothing.

He looked first from Lysias to Philemus. "Sit," he said, gesturing to two wooden collapsible chairs. He walked to his worktable and sat in the chair behind it.

"I have word," Philemus said, "regarding our investigation."

Rudolfo felt his eyes narrow. "Of the attack?"

The second captain shook his head and glanced quickly at Lysias, who nodded encouragement to the man. "The Y'Zirite shrines, General."

He felt his stomach twist. "How many?"

"Three. Each within a similar grove." The man swallowed. "Each in use." He fumbled with a courier pouch, withdrawing a bundle of coded pages and passing them to Rudolfo.

Rudolfo took them and spread them out on the table. His eye went to the list of names first, and he scanned it quickly. "Are these what I think they are?"

Philemus nodded slowly. "We've observed each of them entering or leaving the groves. I've magicked scouts stationed at each."

Rudolfo heard the sound of papers rattling and realized it was his hands, shaking upon the table. He held his breath and willed the red haze to leave his vision. When his anger subsided, he found his next question waiting. "How many Y'Zirites in my Ninefold Forest, Captain?"

"Nearly two thousand, General."

Two thousand. He'd been worried about the Machtvolk evangelists while all along, Y'Zirites were already living quietly among them, worshiping in their hidden groves. Somehow, these seeds had been sown decades earlier, and he had to believe that it was somehow connected to everything that happened now. He'd seen the book that Vlad Li Tam's father had written. If he'd been a secret Y'Zirite or possibly even the author of this particular resurgence himself, it was certainly possible that others had made their way into the forests of the northeast. He looked from the Gypsy Scout to the Entrolusian general. There was more they weren't saying, and he could feel the weight of Philemus's dread in the room.

Rudolfo's fingers moved, fumbling into the hand language of his people. *What aren't you telling me?*

Philemus cleared his voice. "House Steward Kember is on the list, General. As is his wife."

Rudolfo felt his face flush. "Kember? You're certain?"

The second captain nodded slowly. "I am certain." His next words were a near whisper. "We think he may be one of their priests."

The air went out of Rudolfo, and he slumped in his chair. Kember had been like a father to him after his own had died. He'd been steward of the Seventh Forest Manor since Rudolfo was a boy—he and his wife and children had been an anchor to the boy king.

"This," he said in a quiet voice, "is unexpected."

"All of it has been," Lysias said. "From Windwir forward."

Rudolfo nodded and looked back to the papers. He scanned the lists and found his house steward's name. He also saw other names he knew—friends of his father's and mother's or the children of those friends. He had not imagined this path, and his mind—numb still from drink—worked hard to map a clear direction.

I wish Gregoric were here. This was one of those times that his friend would drop the title, call him by name and suggest the best course of action without Rudolfo's request that he do so. It was always a good path—though not always the one Rudolfo ultimately settled upon. But Gregoric was gone now these two years, dying on Rudolfo's back as they fled Sethbert's camp on the heels of the liberated mechoservitors.

He looked to the two men who sat near him. "What are your thoughts on this development?"

Philemus said nothing. Lysias looked to him, then fixed his eyes on Rudolfo. "They should be watched, certainly. A more conservative course of action may be to intern them until such time as we've learned more about any potential relationship they have with the Machtvolk."

Philemus scowled, and Rudolfo turned to him. "You have a difference of opinion?"

"We are spread too thin, General. I cannot keep the Gypsy Scouts tasked in this way. We're in the Wastes. We're underground. We're in the Marshlands and at the Wall. And now we're policing our own?" His face was red, and Rudolfo found himself growing angry at the man's honesty. "I've nothing left in reserve. Your resources, General, are spread too thin."

Rudolfo looked back to Lysias and found himself suddenly surprised by the question that leaped into his mind. His mouth opened to ask it of the old general, and then suddenly he closed it. Because he knew that if he asked, the old Entrolusian would rise to the work and they would be continuing a path he'd already started.

What would it take to create an intelligence division within this new army they built here in the north?

They made eye contact again, and he saw resolve behind Lysias's gray stare. *He knows what I'm thinking,* Rudolfo realized. But in the end he did not ask it. Instead, he closed his eyes. "Your concern is noted, Philemus."

He waited for a full minute, then opened his eyes. Both men sat still, their eyes still fixed upon him, and he felt naked beneath their stares. *They're waiting for me to say more.* But he couldn't find words that he could attach to the storm brewing inside of him. Clouds of despair, winds of rage and a downpour of sorrow tangled him, and the air of his inner landscape smelled like the wet iron of fear. "I will need time to form my thoughts on this," he finally said.

Philemus rose to his feet, but Lysias continued sitting. "I've another matter to discuss with you, Lord Rudolfo," the Entrolusian general said in a steady voice, his face a granite mask.

The prisoner. Rudolfo nodded. "We will discuss the Y'Zirite matter this afternoon, Captain."

Inclining his head, Philemus let himself out and closed the door behind him.

"What progress have you made with her?" Rudolfo glanced to the small Rufello chest in the corner. In it, they'd stored the woman's personal effects. Silver ceremonial knives and iron scout knives, a battered copy of the Y'Zirite gospel and a small bird carved from black stone that was somehow disorienting to the touch. That and the other items one would expect in a scout or soldier's kit, though each unfamiliar in their cut and make.

Lysias shook his head. "No progress. She's well trained, this one."

Rudolfo sighed. "Agreed," he said. "But trained by whom?" When the magicks had burned out and she'd become visible to the naked eye, she hadn't borne the characteristic face paints of a Marsher. Instead, her body bore other marks—symbols and runes he'd seen before, a latticework of scars carved into her flesh. It evoked memories of that island temple and his bride's father, Vlad Li Tam, stretched upon a rack with similar cuts in his naked flesh. And those times she spoke, she did so in a guttural language he did not recognize—though it was obvious enough from the way her brown eyes moved that she understood each question they asked her in turns.

"I don't think she's been trained by any we know of," Lysias said. "I think the theory of an enemy beyond the Named Lands remains our most reasonable answer."

Rudolfo stroked his beard. *The Crimson Empress . . . and her Blood Guard.* It was obvious to him, as well. They had seen the ships. And now a force that breached his borders with ease and used the blood magicks without ill effect to pursue the four mechoservitors with dark intent. They'd destroyed the two from his library on sight, and from what his men had seen of the wreckage below, they'd even stopped long enough to gut them utterly. These were the same who also combed the Wastes, and though Petronus's note requesting scout support had been carefully vague, Rudolfo suspected that the lad Nebios was caught up in this.

He also feared for Isaak now that he was somehow connected to this so-called metal dream. He only hoped the squad that followed after could hold their own against these women—he had no more that he could send.

"I concur," Rudolfo finally said. "Though I do not know how a power of this size could rise up in the wastes of the world."

Every child in the Named Lands knew that between Xhum Y'Zir's Seven Cacophonic Deaths and the Wizard Wars two millennia before that, most of the world was left a desolate and lifeless scar. The lands beyond the Keeper's Gate and the scattered islands of the Emerald Sea—according to the Androfrancine scholars who'd documented such things—were all that remained of a world that had once teemed with life.

Lysias shrugged. "I do not know either, but it seems true enough." His eyes met Rudolfo's. "Regardless, this is not the matter I would speak with you about."

Those eyes were hard again and narrow. Rudolfo found himself wanting to look away. "Yes?"

The old general paused, as if looking for the best words. "Philemus is correct—your resources are spread too thin. But there is more that he is not saying, either from respect or from hope that he will not need to."

Rudolfo felt something stirring in his stomach—some unpleasant emotion that he could not name. He could not imagine any of his men not speaking freely with him. His eyes narrowed. "And what is it he is not saying?"

Lysias's mouth was grim, the line of his jaw firm. His level stare burned into Rudolfo, and finally the Gypsy King looked away. When he did, Lysias spoke. "That you yourself," he said, "are now spread too thin, Rudolfo."

Rudolfo's eyes shifted back. "What do you—?"

Lysias leaned forward even as his voice dropped. "Your men need a leader. Not a drunk."

Rudolfo's mouth opened and then closed.

Lysias continued. "These two years have been hard on you. Great loss and great responsibility. And now great uncertainty. Until now, you've risen with strength to the challenge." The old man's brow furrowed, his eyes suddenly fierce. "Show me the general who routed my divisions at Windwir. Show me the man who snuck into my Overseer's camp to free his metal men."

Lysias stood. And his eyes held Rudolfo's once again. "Do not let loss or the fear of loss cause you to forget who you are, Rudolfo. You are too good a man for that."

Then, the general let himself out into the winter morning.

Rudolfo sat back in the chair and blinked, his eyes suddenly wet. He glanced to the half-empty bottle of firespice.

Then, he forced his eyes back to the report on his desk and bent his mind to finding a way through the thorny Whymer Maze his life had become.

Charles

After days of narrow passages zigging and zagging downward, they spilled finally into a wide cavern that stretched far beyond the reach of Charles's lantern.

He'd never dreamed such a place had lain beneath his feet so long. The caves and passages were man-made—or god-made—and seemed to stretch out and down endlessly. Certainly, time had done its work. They'd navigated their way around cave-ins and unexpected crevasses.

For the first few days, the prospect of it all was quite exciting. A vast new space to explore—and if it *did* hearken back to the time of the Younger Gods there was no telling what else might be found here. But now, he was ready for the sun again. He was even ready for the cold again. The deeper they'd gone, the warmer it had become, and the air was heavy and stale.

Charles held the lantern as high as he could and squinted ahead.

Soon, it would be time to stop and sleep again while Isaak stood watch over him. "How long have we been down here again?"

Isaak clicked for a moment. "Eleven days, six hours, four minutes and twelve seconds," he said.

Charles chuckled and stopped walking. "We should be looking for a good place to stop."

He wasn't as eager to stop in the open spaces, though he didn't know why. They'd been escorted to the last point Rudolfo's men had mapped, and then he'd followed Isaak's lead. The metal man moved with confidence, backtracking only twice when the passageways were blocked by collapses. And so far, though occasionally strange noises reached their ears, they'd encountered no one. Still, he slept while Isaak kept watch, usually in the corner of a narrow tunnel.

They moved out into the room, picking their way around the loose rocks and debris that crowded the floor. In the distance, dripping water sent its echoes across the stone and occasional breezes moved the heavy air around them, tickling the hairs on Charles's ears and neck. It was these rooms that disturbed him the most—vast in size and beyond his vision. Isaak set their course by his internal map, and Charles hung back from him. They moved at a quick but careful pace.

They walked an hour before they heard the commotion behind them. At first, after so long with nothing but ghost noises, Charles was uncertain of it. But then he heard a Forester whistle and a hissed command. "Douse that lamp."

He wasn't sure why exactly he trusted it, but he did. He closed the shutter on his lantern and then felt Isaak's hand close over his wrist. "We should move, Father."

They moved quickly away as the sound of commotion grew behind them.

Fighting. But who? The one sounded like a Gypsy Scout, and he wouldn't put it past Rudolfo to have them followed. But whom were they fighting with?

He couldn't wait to find out. He let Isaak lead him, his legs suddenly shaking from both weariness and fear. They moved quickly across the cavern and slipped into another narrow passageway.

As they walked, Isaak's stride became more confident, though Charles wondered at the route he chose. They were climbing now, then twisting and doubling back, moving quietly but quickly through the dark, their path barely illuminated by the mechoservitor's amber eyes.

Behind them, the sounds of fighting faded and finally, after what seemed like hours, they stopped for Charles to catch his breath and sip at one of the canteens that Isaak carried for them along with the rest of their supplies.

When Charles spoke, his voice was a whisper that echoed nonetheless. "I think Rudolfo had us followed."

"I am certain of it, Father," Isaak said. "It would be out of character for him not to. But it appears that they, too, were followed."

No, Charles thought. *We were.* But by whom? Someone obviously who was a match for Rudolfo's best, though he didn't imagine the Gypsy Scouts were well suited to tunnel fighting. Still, he'd heard determination and a healthy dose of fear in the voice that called out to him. He found himself grateful that they were between them and whatever foe pursued them, but he also felt a twinge of guilt for fleeing the fight.

Alongside that guilt, though, he felt his own fear—the one that whispered to him that they could not outrun whatever it was that pursued them through these tunnels. An old and unarmed man following a mechoservitor's dream.

After another two hours, they stopped again. As he leaned against the wall, Charles felt the heaviness first in his feet and legs and then upon his chest as he tried to breathe. The warm air combined with their forced flight left him wet with sweat, and he felt his heart pounding in his temples.

But even as he stopped and tried to control his ragged breathing, he heard something.

Only this time, he realized, it was from ahead of them.

"Close your eyes," he whispered to Isaak.

What little light they had vanished, and Charles sat with that darkness, cocking his head as he listened. Faint, but somewhere up ahead he heard voices.

Nearly a dozen days with no signs of life, and in the span of hours this place has become too crowded, he thought. And these voices were not even attempting to be quiet. He heard them growing in volume, and when the first, faint glow of lamplight appeared in the distance, he held his breath for a full minute before realizing that he gained nothing from it. Slowly the light grew.

Isaak's hand was back now, closing over his wrist with an urgency that surprised him. The metal man's gears clicked softly, and there was a hiss as steam released from his back. He pulled them back into a wide crack in the wall.

The voices were clearer now, and Charles was able to pick them out.

"There were four of them, for certain," one said. "See the footprints here?" It was a male voice. "They were traveling west." There was a pause.

Another voice spoke. "That damned behaviorist thinks they're in the Marshlands now."

Charles could hear footfalls now, and the light came into focus around two figures moving along the passage. "They most likely are. But I don't know what General Orius would have us do about it."

Orius. Charles felt his held breath go out of him. Orius was a familiar name. A tall man, a bit on the large size, with graying hair and an eyepatch as a reminder of some skirmish he'd nearly lost with a Marsher during his youth. When had Charles seen him last? Surely it was in Windwir's final weeks, probably in the Papal Offices. General Orius, commander of the Gray Guard of the Androfrancine Order, still lived.

He forced his attention back to their conversation. "—observe and assist quietly," the other was saying. "We don't have the resources for more than that. And he was very clear: We're to stay below and avoid being seen."

They were moving closer, and as they passed, Charles saw their uniforms and saw the scarves that denoted them as advance scouts. They didn't carry packs but did wear canteens and knives on their black leather belts. One held a map and the other held the lamp.

It means they're either not far from home or not far from camp.

For a moment—just a moment—Charles entertained the idea of stepping out of the shadows and introducing himself, demanding that they take him and Isaak to Orius. Just the notion that the man had somehow survived Windwir—and with at least some trappings of his Gray Guard intact—stirred up a need in him that unsettled him with its strength.

But he bracketed those feelings and let suspicion drive him. Behind them somewhere, the Gypsy Scouts had engaged or been engaged by someone or something. It was just as likely more of Orius's men, and if that was the case, Charles was not certain he could count on a warm welcome.

Still, Orius apparently lived and was pursuing the same mechoservitors that he and Isaak pursued. Gray Guard scouts wandered the Whymer Maze of caves and passages deep beneath the Named Lands. And behind him, Gypsy Scouts—or something worse if Rudolfo's men had not prevailed—followed after.

Not for the first time since descending the ladder—and certainly not for the last—Charles wondered if he would ever see daylight again or if he'd simply followed Isaak into a warm and winding grave, saving everyone the bother of finding a shovel for the work of burying him.

Closing his eyes, he held his breath and waited for the men to pass.

Then Charles gave himself back to Isaak's care and let his metal son lead him by the hand.

Neb

The nights were a warm wind and a hard ride upon the bony shoulders of the tenacious man who bore him. The days were a tossing and sweating in the grips of a fever that would not break. Underlying all of it, Neb heard the song fading and spun through dreams he could not comprehend beyond whispered noise and shifting light.

An ocean of moonlight and a white tower stretching far into the night. Metal men at sea and beneath the ground. All of these images danced together with scattered memories that intruded, unbidden. A pillar of fire in the sky as the pain of a city's death racked his body. Ships casting off the piers of Windwir only to burn as they sank. The weight of his father's arm around his shoulders in the park.

The images chased him into intermittent sleep, and only the briefest moments of clarity—moments he clawed at for purchase—visited him. Those were the times that he croaked out words too difficult to form in a mouth too dry to hold them.

Still, Renard ran and the smell of the root was strong on him.

He is overusing it, some vague inner voice told Neb. But his fevered brain would not unlock enough for him to remember what that meant.

"We're nearly there, lad," the wiry Waste runner told him between ragged gasps as they took water someplace west of D'Anjite's Bridge.

His mouth wet, Neb struggled for a word—a name—and found it. "Petronus?"

Renard shook his head. "Those plans changed some days ago." There was concern in the man's voice and upon his face, and Neb suddenly wondered how long exactly they'd been running without scout magicks. "You need more aid than he can offer, and his help is needed elsewhere."

Then, they ran again until the sun rose, red and angry, behind them to cast bloody light upon the shattered lands. This time, they ran into the day, and somehow Renard drew even more strength and stamina and speed from the root he chewed, pressing on through the shimmering heat.

They ran until a flash of silver brought the Waste guide to a sudden stop. Neb blinked and wondered if this was part of the dreaming, the small sparrow made of a silver so polished that it reflected its surroundings, nearly indistinguishable from the outcropping of rock it perched on.

"Brother Renard," the silver bird said, "our eyes are upon you now. North forty leagues and west one hundred. You will be met." It was a familiar voice he could not place, and it sounded far away.

"Reply function," Renard said, catching his breath, and Neb thought the bird cocked its head as if listening. "Message acknowledged. The boy is not well." He hesitated. "I suspect I'm not well, either."

And then they ran again.

The time passed and Neb lost all sense of it. As day became night, he saw faint splashes of silver moving quickly across the sky, and it seemed as if those fluttering wings moved between the throbbing stars scattered across the moonless canopy that covered them.

When the sun rose again, they stood in the center of a ruined city with the Keeper's Wall dominating their western horizon. Renard stretched Neb out upon the fused glass floor, and Neb groaned at the pain of it. The cuts that covered him had been a dull ache, but as the kallacaine wore off they became a blazing fire. And the pain-killing powders could not touch the fever or the deep ache in his bones. He shuddered.

He forced his eyes open and toward the man who'd carried him. Renard was bent over, his hands on his knees, gasping and choking for wind. A spasm took the man and he coughed, and Neb saw blood on his lips before he wiped it away with a shaking hand.

There was the faintest whisper of a breeze and a muffled voice materialized nearby. "You made it."

Renard continued coughing while he nodded.

Neb felt cool hands sliding beneath him—at least four of them—and he felt himself gently lifted and moved into a cloth hammock. "We'll carry him from here, Brother."

A finger moved along his lips, and when he opened his mouth, he tasted the bitterness of scout magicks. "Not long now, boy. But we need to hide you a bit longer."

It was the slightest dose—closer to the amount the Gypsy Scouts used on their new recruits to gradually introduce them to the powerful magicks. Still, Neb felt it take hold first in his stomach and then as a tingling upon his skin.

Once more they ran, and this time Neb fell into a deep and dreamless sleep.

Or at least it was dreamless for what seemed the longest of spans.

But somewhere in the midst of it, he dreamed their running had finally stopped and that he was borne through winding tunnels of rainbow-colored glass into a small cavern. There in the center of the cavern lay a hatch much like the one where he'd found the silver crescent and the dream it sang. And gathered around that hatch was a huddled squad of Androfrancine Gray Guard who looked up when he was carried into their midst.

And in his dream, that squad of soldiers parted to reveal a gaunt man with a worried face who leaped to embrace Renard and kiss him hard upon the mouth, then moved quickly to crouch at Neb's side.

"Oh my son," Brother Hebda said, tears coursing his cheeks. "What have I done to you?"

It was a good dream, Neb thought, though he did not understand it. Still, he smiled as sleep once more carried him into a dark and empty space.

Winters

Winters put down her pencil and started the work of collating last night's dreams into the pages of her leather-bound gospel. Outside, a steady snow fell and she could hear the wind as it moved over the eaves of Ria's large house.

There had been a message even this morning, shoved hastily beneath the door. *I'm sorry, little sister; I am required elsewhere.* Winters hadn't minded having her morning walk with Ria canceled again. The conversations were less and less helpful, and as much as she wanted to pay attention to Ria's words, to grab what insight she could from her sister's beliefs and somehow use it to aid her own work, she found that her mind wandered into the images that filled her inner eye each night.

She yawned, feeling the exhaustion that soaked her through and through.

The dreams were stronger now. Much stronger. Though Neb was no longer in them. She'd lost him days and days ago. Still, the metal men continued to share those dreams now in his place. They fed upon the Book, hidden deep in dark caves beneath her feet. They watched an ocean swell with moonlight and song beneath white pillars and a silver moon. They scampered across scaffolds draped in fishing nets and evergreen boughs.

They danced to the ocean's song in a circle at the top of the white tower.

And Isaak danced with them.

Winters put the final page into the book and then went to her wardrobe to pull out clean doeskin trousers and a thick woolen shirt. She stripped out of her shift and dressed quickly. The snow was too deep for knife dancing now in the clearing by the creek, and they'd taken to practicing indoors—though lately Jin Li Tam had been nearly as occupied as Ria. She'd gone off over a week ago with Aedric, and when she'd returned, her face was pale and her eyes were troubled. Still, the woman had said nothing of what she'd seen.

And Winters would not ask. After all, she herself had her own secrets. The voice magicks hidden in her room, the dreams she recorded and dropped daily for placement in the Book by those hidden loyalists within Ria's army.

She pulled two pairs of socks onto her feet, followed by a pair of sturdy boots, and gathered up the heavy parka and gloves that hung near her bedroom door. Then, she slipped into the hallway and made her way toward the entrance.

The captain of the watch stood by the door with a handful of guards. A lone Gypsy Scout stood nearby. The officer was familiar to her, and she smiled. "I am going to walk and meditate," she said.

The captain's eyes went to the book beneath her arm, and he nodded. "As you wish, Lady. I will find you an escort." He vanished down the hall, and Winters's eyes went to the Gypsy Scout.

He stood quietly apart from the others, the rainbow colors of his well-worn winter woolen uniform starkly contrasting against the new and ill-fitting dark uniforms of the Machtvolk. The scout returned her stare quietly, his brown eyes hard and his mouth a grim line on his unreadable face. She looked away and he started pulling on his coat and boots.

When the captain returned, a young guard followed behind him. "See her safely on her walk," the officer said. There was something in the way the officer looked at her that gave her pause, and she sensed unspoken words between the two of them.

She slipped into the cold predawn morning and noticed immediately the difference. This guard did not trail behind as the others had but stayed near her, just as Garyt had done. She set out for the trail, and when she staggered from the deepening snow, his hand shot out to steady her. When he gripped her shoulder she felt the words he pressed there.

Garyt has need of you at the door.

She looked to him quickly, then glanced to the Gypsy Scout behind them, wondering if he'd seen. Winters said nothing; instead, she turned in the path and made her way up the hill to what had once been her home.

She climbed in silence and finally saw Garyt's outline through the falling snow. The wind lessened its moaning, though she still felt the bite as it worked its way into the gaps in her clothing. Winters approached the soldier and immediately saw that something was wrong. Despite his best effort, Garyt's face was dark. He swallowed when he saw the book beneath her arm, then looked to the Gypsy Scout. "Whistle him in closer," he said. "Something has happened."

Until now, Winters had not needed the whistle Aedric had taught her. Puckering her lips, she blew three bars quietly and saw the scout pick up his pace to slip in next to her, hands upon his knives. "My lady?" he inquired.

Winters nodded to Garyt, who spoke in a low voice. "Our queen is needed elsewhere. I need you to be scarce until she returns."

The scout shook his head. "I am under strict orders. She doesn't leave my sight."

Garyt sighed and looked around again, his brow furrowed. Finally, he sighed. "Fine. But you observe only. You do not interfere or I will kill you myself."

The scout chuckled. "You might try, Marsh pup."

The guard's jaw was firm when he nodded. He turned to Winters. "You are required in the Cavern of the Book, my queen."

She started. "Required by whom?"

But Garyt said nothing. Instead, he turned and worked the locks in the door. Then, he cracked it open and gestured her inside. Passing his keys to the younger guard, he followed and motioned for the Gypsy Scout to do the same. Winters watched the Forester, looking for some sign of emotion upon his face other than grim resolution, but if he felt anything, he masked it well.

"We do not have much time," Garyt said as he took down a lantern and lit it. When it cast its light and made its shadows, he set out at a brisk pace, and Winters stretched her legs to keep up with him.

The caves were cold now, and she could smell the dust that had gathered in the months they'd lain unoccupied and under guard. They passed through the throne room with its wicker chair and its meditation bust of P'Andro Whym before slipping into one of the many narrow corridors that wound their way down into the deeper places.

Their footfalls echoed down the caves as they walked without talking. Certainly, the questions chewed at her as her mind spun the dials and worked the levers of this newest Rufello lock. But as they walked, a possibility began to dawn on her—one that she struggled to believe despite the truth her dreams so frequently carried.

What if they truly were here? She thought of those metal teeth working the paper amid the clack and whir of gears and memory scrolls, and then she knew of a certainty that she was on her way now to meet them. She turned to Garyt. "There are four of them . . . right?"

His brow furrowed, and he slowed in his pace. "How do you know this?"

Winters swallowed. "I've seen them in the dreams. Surely you've read them?"

He blanched and picked up his pace. "I would never do that," he said.

It made sense to her. Seamus, his grandfather, was of the older ways. A more brutal time, when any intruder caught in the Cavern, Marshfolk or not, would be hung. But she had granted Tertius, the scholar who'd tutored her, open access. And had even discussed the dreams openly with some of her Council of Twelve.

"I dreamed of them," she said again. "They wore robes and were eating the Book of Dreaming Kings."

Garyt did not answer.

They continued their descent in silence, the corridors twisting and turning as they went, the floors covered with thick rugs—plundered from border villages—now layered in dust. It evoked a homesickness in her that she had not expected, sharper because so far, nothing in her former homeland had been the same. The forests above them had filled with shrines and schools and uniformed soldiers. Her people followed a new faith. Everything else had changed, but her caves were largely the same as she'd left them. She suddenly missed a time she knew she'd never see again.

Winters sighed.

Finally, they approached the closed doors that marked the entrance to the Cavern of the Book. Garyt opened the door and motioned

Winters to follow him inside. She heard the Gypsy Scout step in behind them and close the door.

In the dark, beyond the reach of Garyt's lantern, amber eyes flitted open and gears hummed. The first of the mechoservitors stepped into the light. "Greetings, Winteria bat Mardic, Dreaming Queen of the Machtvolk," the metal man said. Behind him, three other sets of eyes opened as those mechoservitors also left the shadows to join him.

Winters looked around the room. The book still ran along its wall—volume after volume—and it looked the same as it always had. The latest volume lay on its side, and she saw familiar pages poking out. Garyt—or someone—had been putting them in for her each day.

"You are dreaming again," the metal man said.

She nodded. "I am."

There was a hiss as the mechanical released steam from its exhaust grate. "The Homeseeker has broken the tamps; the time for containment has passed."

She felt her brow furrowing. *Containment? Tamps?* "I do not understand."

"We are required to leave. The antiphon must be protected. But we will leave our brother here to receive your last dream." Here, one of the metal men inclined his head. "He will bear it to us across the aether, and we will share it with the Homeseeker."

Neb? She tried to force the panic from her voice. "Is he alive? Have you seen him?"

"We leave to seek him." The mechoservitor paused, its scrolls clicking. "We must show you something first."

Clanking, it turned and descended the gentle slope a few paces, reaching for the section of the book her father had added to. "Throughout each of these volumes, a page has been carefully removed from each king's dreams." He drew down a volume and handed it to her, a slender metal finger opening the book to a page.

Winters walked to him and leaned in to see more clearly. Barely discernible, she saw where an extremely sharp knife had left the faintest mark. "I see it."

The metal man continued. "These pages come from each king since the first dream. The Homeward Dream is in the blood of your line. The missing pages are the scripting of your final dream—the last lock of the tower. Do you understand?"

The tower. She saw it clearly, white and tall, overlooking jungle and sea. Her mind spun and she shook her head. "I do not understand. Who would remove the pages? What is this tower?"

The mechoservitor blinked, its eye shutters clicking open and closed. "Surely in thousands of years of dreaming you comprehend the tower?"

She shook her head again. "I've only recently started dreaming it. And I rarely comprehend the dreams—I simply record them, reflect upon them."

"The tower," the mechoservitor said, "is the hope of the light, and the Homeseeker's path is to restore it to your people. Without the final dream, the Homeseeker will fail. The tower will not be opened to him." She heard deep grinding in the mechoservitor's chest cavity and saw water leaking from the corner of its jeweled eyes. "If the tower remains closed, the light shall be lost. You must find the missing pages. You must dream the final dream."

I do not know how. She heard earnestness in the mechoservitor's voice, and her vision focused on one solitary, rusty tear that slid down the metal man's brass-colored face.

"We will show you," he said.

The metal man stepped forward, his hand out, and then paused. Cupped in the metal palm, Winters saw something small and dark—a stone, she thought, only carved. Garyt shifted uncomfortably and she looked to him. "I want to see," she said.

The metal man pressed the dark object against her forehead.

Four pairs of amber eyes opened and closed in unison, and she shuddered as a wave of nausea passed over her.

She opened her mouth to speak and suddenly felt the room slipping from her. Her knees went weak and she staggered.

Garyt reached out a hand to steady her, but already she felt her eyes rolling back in her head and heard the glossolalia, melodic and terrifying, as it poured from her open mouth. Her body fell back limp, and she became aware of other voices joining her.

Reedy and metallic voices rose in ecstatic utterance that blended harmonically with her own. The sound formed the notes of a song and she saw them again, encircled upon the tower with upraised arms. She and Neb stood weeping within the metal circle they made. Below them, the illuminated sea bubbled with each note. Above them, a brown and dying world filled the sky, hanging like a shameful scar against a tapestry of endless night.

This dream is of our home.

Then, as suddenly as it began, the vision ended and she opened her eyes.

"It is the Moon Wizard's Tower," Winters said in a quiet voice. She knew it, just as surely as she now knew that her sister would know exactly what had become of the missing pages.

And as one, the metal men nodded.

Jin Li Tam

Jin Li Tam drew in a cold lungful of air and rubbed the cut upon her arm.

She's getting quite good. This time, Winters had even managed to draw a bit of blood.

Now, the girl stood sheepishly by, her eyes worried. "I am so sorry, Lady Tam," she said again.

Jin chuckled. "You shouldn't be. You earned that blood." Even as she said it, she knew there was more to it.

I am distracted. And, she realized, something had changed in the girl. She had a ferocity about her suddenly that scared Jin a little. The girl's eyes, when she struck, had borne a striking similarity to her older namesake. She knew it had something to do with the events in the cave. Aedric's man had briefed her personally, though he'd not been close enough to hear everything that was said between Winters and the metal man. Something about a tower.

Between that and the message from home, she hadn't been fully focused. Though if she was truly honest, she'd not felt focused since she'd met the Watcher.

And the note from Rudolfo chewed at her. He'd not seemed himself. Gone now were the coded messages of inquiry after her well-being and Jakob's. The handwriting was sloppier, and he said very little but what needed saying and he offered no real news of events in the Ninefold Forest. She knew he was away from the Seventh Forest Manor but was not sure where.

It had dulled her wits, and now she had a healthy cut from it. *And she feels guilty for beating me.* Jin shot a glance at Winters and smiled. "I'll be fine," she said. "And I'd match you against *any* of Rudolfo's scouts."

She watched the worry melt from everywhere but the girl's eyes as she inclined her head. "Thank you, Jin."

She returned the nod. "You earned it," she said again. "Don't mistake my validation as a gift. It is a wage due you." One that stung, she realized as she stooped to scoop more snow onto the cut. She glanced up at the girl, then out to the Gypsy Scouts and Machtvolk guard who stood at the edges of the clearing. She lowered her voice. "I know about the cavern," she said in a low voice.

The girl's eyes moved away, and a blush rose to her cheeks. "I assumed Aedric's scout would tell you."

Jin wiped the snow from the cut and examined it again. The bleeding had stopped. "Do you know what they are doing here?"

The girl nodded. "I do," she said. There was hesitation in her voice. She looked around, and Jin could see that she was measuring the distance of the guards. "They are studying the Book of Dreaming Kings." The girl's eyes settled on the stump where their things lay.

Jin blinked. "What would they hope to find there?"

Winters met her eyes. "Our way home," she said.

There were other questions to ask, but this wasn't the time or place. And Winters's eyes told her that further answers might not be forthcoming. She also noticed the guards, now, and saw that they were edging their way closer. "Perhaps we will discuss this in more detail at a later time?"

Winters nodded, but Jin saw even in the nod that the girl intended to keep her secrets for now.

This is no time for secrets. She wanted to say so, but then thought of the Watcher in his cave—a mechoservitor like none she'd seen before, hiding here in the north. She'd not sought Winters out to share this knowledge with her. Neither had she told the girl about the metal men this Watcher and his regent wished to bring under their care to keep them from being exposed to the very mechanicals Winters had seen deep in the caves of the Dragon's Spine.

No, Jin had her secrets and must offer the same grace to her young friend. She forced a smile to her face. "I think we've practiced enough for today," she said.

Winters inclined her head yet again and then moved quietly off to the stump. Jin followed her, and they put their coats on in silence.

Quiet wrapped them as they trudged wordlessly up the trail that led eventually past the heavy doors set in the side of the hill. A light snow fell, adding a soft layer to the frozen drifts to either side of the trail. They were nearly back to the house when one of Ria's officers approached.

"Lady Tam?"

He looked weary, as if he'd been up all night, but he smiled. "The queen begs pardon and requests a word if the morning is not too cold for you."

"Certainly, Captain." She looked to Winters. "We'll talk later," she said. "Would you look in on Jakob?"

At the girl's nod, she turned to follow the captain. They climbed the trail behind the house, and she found herself hoping they weren't going to the shrine. Somehow, in her memory, the shrine had become tangled up in her recollection of the Watcher's cave. The smell of blood and decay choked her, and unbidden, the memory of the knife within her hand and its blade upon Jarvis's throat flooded her.

I did what needed doing. And yet. She was certain P'Andro Whym had something to say about that somewhere in his gospels. She'd killed before and it had not given her pause. Still, she'd never executed a man . . . and certainly never killed one who wanted to be killed.

And yet.

As they climbed, she became aware of noise on the hill. First, the sound of a pickaxe. Then, the ring of a shovel on hard earth.

When they crested the hill and moved behind the shrine, she saw Ria in dirty woolen trousers and shirt, her face red and sweaty from exertion as she leaned upon the shovel. Beside her, wrapped in a blanket, lay a body. Before her, a grave took shape in the frozen ground.

"Good morning, Great Mother," she said, smiling.

"Good morning," Jin answered. She looked from the body to the grave again. "You are burying Cervael?" She'd not known the minor Emerald Coast lord other than by reputation, but her father had. And when she'd learned of his role in the attempt on her life and the life of her son, she wondered if he'd have been so bold if House Li Tam had not been dismantled.

"I am. I had intended to offer you his life, but I'm afraid I became too engrossed in my work." She inclined her head. "My apologies."

She returned the nod, forcing calm to her face. "Accepted," she replied.

"But you will be pleased to know that our work with this lord has taken us to the root of the attack upon you and your family." The woman's smile widened, and above it, in those piercing brown eyes, she saw the same ferocity she'd just seen in Ria's little sister. "We are unraveling a network now that reaches even into Rudolfo's forest . . . and we know who has funded and fed it."

Jin Li Tam felt her eyebrows rising. "And you are confident that your"—here, she paused, looking for the right word and tone—"*means* of gathering this information is reliable?"

"Oh yes. Quite." She sighed, and for the first time, Jin realized the woman had been crying. She could see the white streaks upon her cheeks. "We were quite close in the end; he would not have lied to me." Their eyes met. "There's a bond that forms when we participate in another's redemption. The size of the bond is in direct proportion to the size of sin being atoned for." She moved the shovel. "I could have any of my men dig this grave and satisfy our people's custom. It is my right as queen. But I will bury him myself. Just as I cleaned him myself. I would have done the same for your father, had Rudolfo not interrupted my work there." She paused. "Because in the end, I loved him very much."

Jin hoped her revulsion did not show. She worked hard to keep her face an emotionless mask and reached for the first question that came to mind. "Who is responsible, then?"

"The order—and means—came ultimately from Queen Meirov of Pylos."

The words struck her like an open-handed slap. "Pylos?" That small nation to the south, nestled between the Entrolusian Delta and Turam, had suffered a good deal of late. Refugees had glutted her during the civil war to the east, and the collapsing Entrolusian economy had its impacts as well. But worse—far worse—Meirov's young son had been killed on the night that Hanric, Ansylus, and the others had been butchered by Ria's Blood Scouts. All part of an elaborate sacrifice that, combined with the torture and murder of most of House Li Tam, somehow created the blood magick that healed her son.

Not even a year ago, she'd seen the unhidden hatred upon that queen's face. But this response was unexpected. Jin closed her eyes, suddenly caught up in the sounds of screaming and panic in the library courtyard and the sight of bodies lined up beneath blankets just beyond the rubble.

"What will you do?" she finally asked.

Ria's voice was matter-of-fact. "I will call upon her to pay for her sins."

What if she doesn't wish to pay? But before she could ask the question, the Machtvolk queen continued. "There is no redemption for this one," she said. "She strikes too close to the heart of our gospel. All that remains is a lesson to be taught that others might understand the consequences of harming you and your son. I will call upon her to surrender herself at her border, and she will be quietly executed. Her body will feed the wolves."

"And if she refuses?"

Ria's eyes smoldered now, and Jin found herself wondering how the woman could move so quickly from ecstasy as she discussed redemption and her love of those who received it beneath her knife to such an obvious rage. Her voice was low now as she spoke. "If she refuses, then she will add the blood of her own people to that on her head."

And the tone with which she said it sent chills along Jin's spine. Their eyes remained locked for just a moment, and then the storm of fury was gone once more. Setting aside the shovel, Ria took up the pickaxe and hefted it. "I thought you should know. I would appreciate your discretion in this matter until my kin-raven arrives in Pylos."

Jin Li Tam inclined her head, already considering how she might code the message to Rudolfo. "Thank you."

Turning, she moved toward the trail. Her stomach knotted and clenched with the smell of death that she could not seem to escape. As she descended the hill, another sound reached her ears, the fall of the pickaxe keeping perfect time with it.

It caused another shudder and she shrugged it off, forcing her attention to the child she needed to feed and the message she needed to write.

Behind her, Ria's voice rose in a now-familiar song.

Petronus

The muffled sound of galloping hooves barely rose above the whispering night winds, and Petronus blessed the powders that sped and silenced them as they rode northward. They'd ridden hard for days, those that remained of them. He still flinched at what Renard's head start had cost them in lives, all for less than a handful of blood-magicked women. They'd lost a third of the Gray Guard and nearly a fourth of Rudolfo's scouts in that first skirmish. And the random patrols they'd encountered had drained off more men.

Still, they pressed on for the north, following Petronus's recollection of the map Hebda had shown him. The visions had ceased now, and a part of him felt their absence like a hunger, a hollow ache that he could not understand. Still, the headaches were gone and all that remained was the song.

He squinted, riding low in the saddle, and found the thread of music. Years of Franci meditation and conditioning had taught him how to call upon great focus when he needed to, and he'd summoned up every shred of that skill to quiet the canticle that played incessantly from his saddlebags.

On and on it played, and within the notes he heard patterns that he could not decipher. There were secrets buried in it.

And when the new moon rose, the song rose with it, sometimes even threatening the focus Petronus used to keep it from driving him mad.

A low whistle to his right brought his head up, and he looked to Grymlis. The old man bore a nasty cut now, red against his pale face and running from his temple along his jawline. One of the medicos had stitched it closed, but it would leave a scar after it healed.

"We can't push the horses much farther," the Gray Guard captain said. "They've only days left with these magicks in them."

Petronus nodded, feeling the solid strength beneath him as his mare labored. "We've only days to go." He swallowed against the discomfort of his next words. "I don't expect the horses to make it." He didn't say the other words. *I don't expect* us *to make it either.*

The kin-ravens were flying out of reach of sling and arrow, though the men did their best to bring them down when they saw them. And certainly between those strange sky-faring spies and the patrols that dogged them, he had no doubt they were pursued.

It was only a matter of time.

Grymlis said nothing for a moment, but Petronus felt his eyes upon him. Finally, he spoke. "This antiphon we're riding for," he said. "Is it worth the cost?"

Petronus wasn't sure how he knew it or why exactly he believed Hebda. Certainly what had happened to Neb was a part of it, though he didn't understand all of it. Somehow, the boy was tied into this along with the aberrant Marsher mysticism with its Home-seeking prophecies. Still, he did not have to understand it. When he looked at Grymlis, he felt the weight of his own words. "The very light depends upon this," he said.

Grymlis nodded. "Then we ride the horses into the ground for it, Father. And when they're gone, we run until our feet are raw."

What was that phrase Geoffrus had used back when they met and first discussed his contract? Yes, Petronus thought.

Time is of the essence.

Grymlis pulled ahead to confer with the Gypsy lieutenant, and Petronus settled into his saddle, once more relegating the song to a quiet corner of his mind that he rarely visited.

At sunrise, when they made camp, he fell fully clothed into his bedroll. They gave themselves four hours per day and one meal; it wasn't nearly enough, but already the Dragon's Spine, that vast, impenetrable range running west to east across the top of the continent, loomed before them.

We are close, he thought as sleep grabbed at him and wrestled him down into dreamlessness and song.

Grymlis's hand on his shoulder brought him up. Silently, the camp scrambled, and he forced himself alert. Grymlis's face was white and sober. "We've lost a patrol," he said. "We're leaving."

Petronus crawled out of his bedroll and started rolling it. "How long ago?"

"Thirty minutes overdue," Grymlis said. "On the eastern run."

They'd sent scouts to the four points of the compass, magicked and sweeping out by five leagues, white and brown birds rigged in belt cages to alert the camp should they encounter anything. Petronus rubbed his face. They'd not lost a patrol yet. "Should we investigate?"

Grymlis shook his head. "Our numbers are dwindling, Father. If you want anything left of us when we arrive, we ride now and we do not look back."

Petronus sighed and climbed to his feet. "I concur."

They were mounting up when the whistle of third alarm pierced the morning air. Petronus spun his horse to the east and studied the line of scrub and rock and fused glass there. There were figures moving toward them at an easy pace, and as they drew closer, he saw they were a tattered band. At least two of them were women, bound and walking in the care of cutlass-wielding guards. Another was indistinguishable until he realized it was a twisting and invisible mass tangled in what appeared to be a fishing net.

Already the Gypsy Scouts were fading from sight as they slipped from their horses, magicked to face the intruders. Geoffrus and his men stood aloofly by, watching with bemused interest.

The figure at the head of the party spread his arms wide, and both a white and a brown bird slipped from his hands to speed into the lieutenant's catch net. "Ahoy the camp," a voice cried across the distance.

Petronus blinked and felt his mouth go slack. The figures slowed but continued moving, four of them holding the net-tangled scout between them as they went. The women were dressed like the others they'd encountered—their dark silks torn and dusty. Their faces, like the faces of the others, were haggard, but they also bore a quiet disdain.

"Ahoy the camp," their leader said again, and Petronus knew him at once though he could not fathom how the man came to be in a vast and desolate waste, to stand here before him now. "We seem to have caught one of your fishes." There was a brief chuckle that sounded more like the bark of a seal.

Grymlis's sudden intake of breath told him that he recognized the man, too, and Petronus shook his head in disbelief. "How in the nine hells have you come to be *here*? You are a long way from home."

"That," the pirate Rafe Merrique said, "is a long and tragic tale indeed."

Vlad Li Tam

A warm wind pushed at his tangled red hair, and Vlad Li Tam brushed it from his face as he watched his raven approach low over the waters, bearing word back from the clustered remnants of his iron armada.

Even in the shadows of the Moon Wizard's Ladder, he felt the growing heat of another equatorial day. They'd steamed as close as they could without risking the power sources of their vessels and their metal guide, Obadiah. They'd seen the line quite clearly—for league upon league, the waters had swelled with the d'jin and their song, but two leagues out from the Ladder, the waters were suddenly devoid of life and light.

"The light-bearers know to stay back," Obadiah had said. And so, Vlad had ordered his vessels to do the same and to outfit the captain's yacht with a sail and a small company of his brightest sons and daughters. They'd spent several days now sailing about the pillars by day, sketching them and writing down the strange symbols they ran across on its ancient white surface.

Still, so far there had been no sign of an access point and nothing at all that might pass for the Behemoth Obadiah spoke of.

I do not know what is required, my love. Vlad closed his eyes, conjuring up the image and sound of her. At night, when they returned from their reconnaissance of the Ladder, he still stood at the bow of his ship to be near her, though he wasn't certain he could pick her out from the mass of light that undulated beneath the surface.

What had begun as bewildered awe had become willing curiosity that now gradually moved toward frustration, and it did not help that here, near the Ladder itself, his scars itched and burned more intensely. When his raven landed on the gunwale, he did not wait for his daughter to strip the message from its foot. He did it himself, his fingers fumbling with it.

Obadiah's careful script met his eye, and he read the note quickly before crumpling it and dropping it to the small boat's deck. He sighed, surprised at how much like a growl it was. "We'll work the perimeter of it again," he said.

"Father?" His forty-sixth daughter was at the rudder, and when he glanced to her he saw that she too had lost some of the wonder they'd first experienced. In the face of uncertain expectations, he was faltering in his confidence, and his children followed him.

"We sail the perimeter," he said again, turning his face back to the waters.

Again. There had to be something here. But not even the metal man and his dream had any sense of what was to happen. The coded messages within the canticle had borne the coordinates and vague warnings and prophecies—references to some great underwater beast that would carry them to the basements and make straight a path for the light-bearers.

They'd tried everything they could think of. Some of his strongest swimmers had dived the waters as far down as they could go, to no avail. One of the children had a flute and, with a rigged funnel and length of pipe, had played her closest approximation of the canticle into the water. Still nothing.

Wind caught sail, and the boat surged forward across the water, the waves slapping at it as it picked up speed. They would sail around the pillars until nightfall, and then, in the morning, they would pick it up again.

Eyes scanning both water and stone, Vlad sat silently in the bow.

It was just past noon, as they made their way along the backside of the Ladder, that the bird struck their catch net. The red thread upon its foot sent his children scrambling, and Vlad moved forward quickly to grab it even as a distant thunder reached his ears.

Cannon. There was no note upon the bird—just the thread—and he turned his head west, where his ships lay at anchor.

The Ladder blocked his view, but he found himself hoping fiercely that his captains would follow his orders. It wasn't so very long ago that most of his family had been taken—with relative ease—by ambush in unfamiliar waters. In hindsight, it terrified him how simple it had been.

Vlad shivered as sudden memory clogged his nose with the smell of death and his ears with the sobbing screams of his family as they cried out their last words to him.

Now, they knew better. For two millennia, the Tams had stayed ahead of their neighbors by learning and adapting to that path of change the Androfrancines preached about. The captains would err on the side of caution. They'd engage in defense and not wait to see how strong their opposing force might be . . . and they would not come looking for him. Not ever again.

They would divide what remained of the fleet and flee at top speed.

He forced his eyes to his daughter at the rudder. "Myr," he said in a quiet voice, "bring us in closer to the pillar."

She nodded and they moved into the shadows.

"Bring down the sail," he told one of his sons.

They huddled there, close up against the wall of white stone, and listened as the gunfire dwindled. Vlad nodded, keeping the worry from his face so that his children would not be alarmed.

"Good," he said. "They're fleeing."

But what were they fleeing?

He played out the scenarios while they waited. His children sat quietly, and he wondered how many of them did the same. They'd been trained from birth to observe everything, scrutinize all potentials. He'd already watched two of them inventory the contents of the yacht—their eyes darting to and fro as they calculated.

None of the navies of the Named Lands had sailed this far into the Ghosting Crests. Ships that did were seldom seen again. But there were others. He'd seen their vessels when they'd brought him to the island. And it stood to reason that somewhere out there in the vast ruin of the world, other survivors of Xhum Y'Zir's wrath existed. Tribes of maddened refugees who clung to their long-dead wizard gods, if the Y'Zirite resurgence was real and not just some concocted means to remove the Androfrancines and whip the Marshers—and his own father, it seemed—into a frenzy of faith.

A distant sound of bells and shouting reached his ears, and he looked south. He saw nothing, but the sounds of a ship reached his ears as it drew near.

He looked at the two children who'd inventoried the yacht. "What do we have?"

As they began listing off the items, Vlad smiled and watched the light of understanding grow in their eyes. He turned the bird loose with the same red thread tied upon its foot—now knotted with a coded message of distress.

Then, he and his children magicked themselves and slipped into the water, their shirts stuffed with everything they could hold.

Eight minutes after they'd first heard the approaching ship, they overturned the yacht and set it adrift with its oars, sail, and enough detritus scattered about to be convincing.

Then, Vlad Li Tam and his children treaded water and waited for what fish might take their offered bait.

Charles

Time in the Beneath Places blurred into a shuffling walk in the dark dimly lit by Isaak's eyes, and they slept in whatever nooks and crannies they could find. Charles felt his stomach rumbling and knew they must be close to their goal.

Water had been in good supply, but the rations they'd carried for him had given out days ago. The metal man had carefully calculated what food to bring, but changing course frequently to avoid pursuit had added time to their walking. Still, Isaak assured him they were near.

Their lantern had burned through their fuel as well, and Charles found himself hoping they'd stumble across more of Orius's men. The notion of surrendering to them appealed more and more to him.

Somewhere above them, an icy northern winter layered that part of the world with snow, but in the Beneath Places, warm breezes dried the sweat on his face as he leaned against the tunnel wall and caught his breath.

Isaak's eye shutters flickered. "We are close, Father."

Charles nodded. "I hope so."

For the first week, he'd felt the protest deep in his muscles and bones. Now, it was a dull ache, but he found there were still only so many leagues he could walk in a day. He questioned his judgment more and more with each step. He studied the metal man.

I am holding him back. But that was only partially true. Isaak could certainly move faster alone, but the strain it would place on his sunstone heart increased the risk of that fracture breaking open.

Charles slowed his breathing and closed his eyes, focusing on one of P'Andro Whym's meditations to center himself and slow his heart rate. "I am too old for this," he said.

Isaak's eyes dimmed momentarily, and his bellows wheezed. "You do exhibit outward symptoms of physical deterioration as a result of advanced age."

Charles's laugh was sharp, and it echoed through the cavern louder than he wished it to. "Thank you, Isaak."

When he'd caught his breath, they pushed on again, and three hours later they found themselves in an open space. Isaak guided Charles's hands and placed them upon a smooth, warm metal wall that curved. The dim light from the metal man's eyes revealed the rungs in the side of the shaft, and Charles felt something like elation growing in his chest. "Is this is it?"

Isaak nodded. "Yes."

They climbed in silence, Isaak following after. It wasn't said, but Charles knew it was for his benefit.

He is afraid I'll fall. And he was tired enough now to see the logic in it. Twice, the old man paused to catch his breath, heartbeat drumming through his body, loudest in his temples and accompanied by flashes of light that danced even behind closed eyelids.

But when they reached the top, a closed metal hatch met his reaching hand. Holding tightly to the rung to anchor himself, he pushed at the hatch and grunted. "I can't move it," he said.

He heard the bellows below and felt the warm rush of steam as Isaak released it through the exhaust grate in his back. Then, he heard the faint clicking of Isaak's internal workings. "I will need to open it."

A metal hand found his ankle, guiding the foot, and Charles moved to the side as best he could. Then Isaak was beside him and shoving a metal forearm upward at the hatch. Charles clung to the rung with one hand, leaning away to give the metal man room to work.

When it swung open, the mechanical scrambled up over the rim of the shaft. Still panting, Charles welcomed the hands that pulled at him.

These caverns were colder, and when he'd recovered from the climb, Isaak handed him a heavy wool sweater from their pack and they continued on. His stomach rumbled as they went, and he noticed that the metal man's pace had picked up.

After winding through a Whymer Maze of lefts and rights and tunnels that doubled back, ascending and then descending, they finally found themselves in a wider corridor. The air here was not as cold as where they'd been but wasn't as warm as the Beneath Places, either. And Charles could smell the faintest traces of kerosene in the air.

These caves are traveled more frequently. He'd known that many of the Marshers took to living underground. Some of the essays and notes smuggled out by Tertius during his time here had indicated that the Marsh King himself had lived in an elaborate series of caverns deep in the roots of the Dragon's Spine.

As they walked, the smell of kerosene fell away, and another smell—familiar as an old friend—came to him. He placed it instantly: It was the smell of paper.

They stopped as the floor began a slow descent downward, and Isaak released his hand, gently positioning Charles against the wall of the cave. He leaned against it and squinted.

This dark felt less oppressive, but still it disoriented Charles, and the dim amber light of the mechoservitor's eyes was not sufficient to show him his surroundings. "Wait here," the mechoservitor said in a low and reedy voice.

Farther ahead and down, Charles thought he heard the faintest rustling of pages.

He listened as Isaak moved away slowly, following the cave's gentle downward slope.

When Charles heard the other mechoservitor speak he jumped with surprise. "Greetings, cousin," it said. "I anticipated your arrival, though I fear you are too late."

A match flared, and a halo of candlelight illuminated a wall of books. The brightness of it after so long in darkness hurt Charles's eyes, and he closed them momentarily against the intrusion of light. When he opened them, he saw Isaak standing with a solitary, robed metal man that he recognized. "Hello, Father," the mechoservitor said. "It is agreeable to see you. But I fear my cousin has brought you into precarious circumstances."

Precarious circumstances. He chuckled. "I insisted upon coming."

The metal man looked from Charles to Isaak. "You should have prevented him, cousin. His kind is not made for this work."

Isaak shook his head. "He made us, cousin. He, too, serves the dream."

The eye shutters opened and closed rapidly. "Perhaps," the metal man said, "he does." He looked to Charles. "I am only concerned for your safety, Father."

Charles realized suddenly that he, himself, wasn't. He felt more a parental concern than any fear of personal danger. It hadn't been so in the Beneath Places, knowing that they were not alone in those dark places. But now that he was here, an optimism of sorts pervaded him.

And these children of mine would not let harm befall me.

"I appreciate your concern for my well-being," Charles said.

The metal man turned to Isaak, and Charles heard the high-pitched whine of scroll spindles as they spun. When the metal mouth opened, what came out was an unintelligible stream of numbers.

Isaak's eye shutters flashed. When he replied, it was a similar outpouring.

Charles vaguely recognized the code that passed between them as the same he'd heard from the moon sparrow, and he marveled at the ease with which they conversed in it. The fact that they used it at all added another meaning to the metal man's earlier words. *His kind is not made for this work.*

As they continued to speak, Charles took in their surroundings. The soft halo of light from the candle revealed a cavern that sloped downward in a spiral, its outer wall entirely dominated by volume upon volume of books. The Book of the Dreaming Kings, he realized: that massive, multitome collection of dreams reaching back to the first Marsh King who arrived to this temporary home with his Wicker Throne and his Firstfall axe. Several of the books were stacked on the table near the candle, and as the mechoservitors exchanged data, he watched Isaak lift first one and then another, opening to marked pages to study them briefly before closing them.

Finally, Isaak interrupted the other mechoservitor in midstream. "I think," he said, "our father should be consulted in this matter, cousin." He turned to Charles, not waiting for agreement. "Father, the Book of Dreaming Kings shows evidence of tampering with a precision beyond Marsher capacity. Pages have been excised, and in some instances, careful forgeries have been substituted. Besides a mechoservitor, what could do such a thing?" He extended one of the volumes.

Charles took the offered book and bent his eye to the page beneath Isaak's metal finger. But in this light, he couldn't make out any discrepancy. "A page is missing?" he asked.

"Many pages—pages vital to the dream—are missing," Isaak answered. "What besides a mechoservitor could accomplish this?"

Charles squinted at the page, tipping it toward the candlelight. It was indeed precise—such that he could not see it at all. He placed the book on the table and picked up another. On this one, he could barely see the faintest line where a page had been. "No technology that I am familiar with," he said.

"Then logic would dictate that it must be a mechoservitor."

The code started up again between the two metal men, and Charles replaced the book to pick up another. Once more it was barely perceptible, but a page had been carefully removed. And Isaak was correct—the only technology he was aware of that could do this with such precision and forge a suitable replacement was one of his mechanicals.

But the Androfrancines guarded their metal men well. Or at least they had before that first generation had been sent into the Wastes alone to create their hidden library. Still, if these were all united by their metal dream and the antiphon it required, it did not seem possible that one of their kind could do this.

He looked at Isaak, then remembered the metal man he'd rescripted to send east to the Keeper's Gate bearing his message for Petronus. "Could one of the others have been compromised somehow?" he asked. "Rescripted to remove the pages without the knowledge of the rest?"

But even as he said it, another possibility rose in his mind, and the thought of it raised both curiosity and fear. He remembered the drawings from Rufello's *Book of Specifications*, but more than that, he remembered the relics dug from the ashes of the Old World, the scant remains of Xhum Y'Zir's death choir torn to pieces and scattered across the Churning Wastes. They'd never found more than just trace evidence of their existence, and yet the decimated landscape of the Old World proved that they had once walked those lands and sung their spell for their wrathful master, carrying out his last terrible orders. The other mechoservitor's voice brought him out of his reflection, and he shook away the intrusive images of fire and darkness.

"All but four of my brothers are accounted for," the metal man said. "And those are far from this place."

Charles nodded. "I think," he said, "there is another possibility to consider."

And when he said it, it was as if one of those dials from that old inventor, Rufello, spun and clicked into place for him, unlocking a realization that made his legs weak. Carefully forged messages brought by quietly intercepted birds. Code after code broken without effort. Gospels produced and disseminated quickly in a corner of the Named Lands that had no presses and limited literacy.

It was said that in the days when the world was new the Younger Gods made metal servants for themselves. And the legends of the Wizard Wars spoke of the silver army that Raj Y'Zir brought with him when he fell. Charles had never embraced the metaphysical aspects of those stories but had understood like any good Franci that truth lay beneath myth. And he'd handled those blackened bits of metal, seen Rufello's sketches and notes.

He had taken those bits and those notes, and he'd created an approximation of something far more complex than his tools and technology would allow for. These creations of his—these children—had found a dream in the Wastes and now served it.

What, he wondered, might this other mechoservitor serve? It was not hard to guess, though he could not comprehend how it had come to pass without Androfrancine knowledge or intervention.

Charles closed his eyes against the images of fire and ash that pressed upon him and hoped that he was wrong.

Neb

He floated, suspended above the dream, and felt it moving over his skin, filling his mouth and ears and lungs, all the while the song vibrating the thick fluid that held him. He had no memory of being carried into this dark place, deposited with waters at first cool and then warm as his fever was leached away by them.

I am sorry for this deception, my son.

The words formed without voice, barely discernible above the noise of the song. Neb forced his eyes open, suddenly aware that he had no sense of up and down in this place. He moved against the fluid and felt a panic rising in him as the realization struck him that his lungs were full and his voice would not work against the thickness of the fluid that filled his mouth.

Be at ease, Nebios Homeseeker. Do not fight the pool.

The pool? Neb blinked.

I have bargained for you. Though there was no voice, there was still a pattern to the words, and it was familiar to him. *Be at ease and let the workers heal you.*

He tried to focus upon the words. The words were not Hebda's, or at least didn't seem like them.

A lethargy tugged at him, and he struggled against it though it felt he drowsed for a moment or two. When he felt that pull, he forced his eyes open, twisting and trying to move his hands and feet as he became gradually more oriented. He hung suspended in viscous fluid, the music washing through him. He could see a vague light, watery and silver, just beyond his reach.

You are whole now.

Neb focused his scattered thoughts into words. *Who are you?*

But the words were gone, and all that remained was the song and the dream. He floated above it and watched a line of men who ran and rode the Wastes, a familiar old man with a tangled beard riding at the front. North of them, a mountain rose, and within it, metal men clambered over hidden scaffolding. And south of them, women ran, their eyes sliding in and out of the aether as they cast about, stone carvings clenched in their sweating palms.

He felt them there and flinched, then realized they could not see him from whatever place he watched from. He watched for a moment longer, then rolled in the pool to face west.

He found Isaak first, and the others were near him, their dreams nearly touching, clicking and clacking as their memory scrolls spun. Just beyond them, he found the girl.

She stood high upon a tower amid a metal song, and he recognized the scene, shuddering at the memory of the silver knife and the small dark amulet against his skin, the lurching sensation of his mind being forced into the dream.

Now, there was no forcing—it flowed around him and he relaxed into it.

"This dream is of our Home," a woman said. The voice was low and murmuring, and it drifted out from a copse of trees in a warm jungle that smelled of flowers he did not recognize. He pushed a palm frond aside and saw the makeshift bed. He saw Winters there and a young man with silver hair that he vaguely recognized as himself. A fine sheen of sweat covered their naked skin and they lay together, tangled in each other and gazing up. Neb followed their eyes and saw the sky full of a moon impossible to fathom, brown and scarred and beautiful in its brokenness.

Slowly, that moon turned, and as it did, a familiar continent moved within his view.

Neb gasped from the surprise of it.

Still, it was clear to him. He saw the horn. He saw the massive scar that carved the Wastes asunder and the mountain ranges that walled off a sanctuary of green. And there, he could make out the Delta and the Divided Isle to the south of it. And the lush peninsula that formed the Inner and Outer Emerald Coasts.

Father?

Above him, the gray light grew, and he suddenly found himself rising. As if carrying him, the liquid bore him upward, and he rolled and choked as he broke the surface into a warm room that smelled of kerosene. Those waters—silver and thick, he saw now—carried him gently to a smooth metal shore, and when his naked flesh pressed up against it, he felt it was warm to the touch. He coughed, and as if helping him, the liquid silver rushed from his lungs, his nose, his ears, his mouth, rushed away even from his very skin to leave him dry upon the floor.

He rolled to his side and watched it chase itself back into the pool, then looked up and felt his jaw go slack.

Brother Hebda stood before him—certainly thinner than Neb remembered—holding out a thick robe to him. The man's eyes were red, underscored by dark circles of sleeplessness. Beside him, Renard watched with grim resolve upon his face.

Neb stared, his mouth opening and closing as he tried to find some coherent thought, some emotion he could lay hold of. All eluded him in this moment as he confronted a man he'd believed dead for over two years—a man he'd thought he'd killed by his own carelessness. He looked to Renard, took in the man's slow and careful nod, then looked back to his father.

"You're alive," he finally said.

"I am," Hebda said. His eyes had more to say, but his mouth was a firm, silent line.

Neb stood and took the robe, slipping it on and cinching its belt. When Hebda embraced him, wooden and brief, he accepted the embrace but could not feel it. He stepped back and took the man in again. "How is this possible?"

Hebda looked to Renard, and the Waste guide gripped the man's shoulder, answering for him in a sober voice. "Things are not exactly as they seem," he said. Behind him, a familiar man—another he'd thought dead these two years—entered the chamber, surrounded by a swell of gray uniforms. He'd seen the general in a dozen papal processions, standing beside Introspect in somber support.

"How is the boy?" Orius asked.

Neb stared at the Gray Guard and their general. He'd dreamed of the Androfrancines in another cave—one with a hatch and shaft much like the one where he'd found the silver crescent. He blinked as realization found him.

It wasn't a dream. He'd been carried underground by a Gray Guard led by his father.

"He's whole," Hebda said. "The bargaining pool restored him as we were told it would. Not even a scar."

Neb pulled up the sleeve of his robe, sudden memories of Shyla's knife upon his skin. The arm was unmarked, and when he opened his robe, he saw the same was true of his stomach and chest. He looked up. "Bargaining pool?"

I have bargained for you.

He suddenly felt the room moving, and as he sagged forward, Hebda and Renard both moved in to catch his elbows and steady him.

He turned to his father, letting him take some of his weight. His first question resurfaced, and when he asked it this time, his voice was a mumble. "How are you alive?"

"It's . . . complicated."

Neb heard something beneath the words and felt the first stirrings of an emotion. His legs found their strength suddenly, and he shook off Hebda and Renard as he staggered back. The heels of his feet hit the water line of the bargaining pool, and the men before him gasped.

He straightened himself, noting their fear. "It's an *uncomplicated* question, Brother Hebda."

The man's eyes held a plea in them. "Some of us survived the attack."

Neb shook his head. "I saw the Seven Cacophonic Deaths. No one survived but the mechoservitors."

"Some of us survived."

Orius sighed. "Tell him everything, Hebda." There was anger and sadness in the general's voice. "The time for secrets has passed, and the boy needs to ride with Sixth Brigade tomorrow if you want him to yon antiphon in time." The old man took Neb in with his one good eye. "Tell him everything," he said again.

Then, he turned and strode from the room, his guards falling in behind him as he went.

Neb's eyes went from the entrance back to his father. The man's face was pale. "Tell me, Brother Hebda."

But Neb already knew and felt that emotion twisting into something he could recognize and act upon. He felt it coil around the base of his neck. "I will tell you. Let's go back to camp and get you fed. We'll sit down and—"

Neb's voice slipped out low, nearly a whisper, but it sounded heavy in the room. "You knew," he said.

When Brother Hebda flinched, Neb saw the rest of it. The general spoke of brigades. There was a camp. They'd had time to hide themselves somewhere ahead of the spell. And that morning long ago, when they'd ridden out with their wagon supposedly en route for the Churning Wastes and his father had asked after the letters of introduction and credit . . .

"You knew, and you left me on that hillside. I didn't forget the papers." Now, his words marched out slow and sure as veterans coming home.

Hebda's eyes overflowed. "I argued against it, but he told us it had to be that way. He swore that you would—"

But in that moment, Neb had stopped listening. He surged forward quickly, so fast that Renard could not prevent him and Hebda could not escape him.

The sound of his fist against the man's face was a solid, meaty slap, and Neb felt the nose give way as red spray went up and out from it. He felt the power of the blow all the way into his shoulder, and as Hebda fell backward, Neb stepped over him and dodged Renard's grabbing hands.

"Neb—"

He heard his name but did not comprehend it. He felt rage washing through him, and he let it carry him like the silver waters of the bargaining pool had carried him. He slipped into the tunnel that Orius had used and followed it, changing course blindly at intersections, left here and right there, following patches of white moss that illuminated the ceilings and walls. He wandered for as long as the anger would bear him, and when it finally released its grip, he sat down against the wall.

He was in a large cavern lit high above by the mottled white moss.

A quicksilver lake reflected back the blotchy light, and at its center, floating like a black iris, Neb saw an island of familiar stone.

There, upon the shore, a rowboat sat empty.

He blinked, wondering at the new emotion that now filled in the hollow spaces that the anger had left in its wake.

Then, holding his head in his hands, Neb gave himself over to the grief of a betrayal he could not comprehend and sobbed himself into a dreamless sleep.

Winters

Cold morning air kissed the exposed skin of her face, and Winters blinked at it as the last of the moon vanished behind the mist-shrouded evergreens.

That moon dominated her nights and her days now, and she found her obsession with it alarming. At night, she stared at it, trying to pick out the Moon Wizard's Tower as the orb made its slow turn in the night sky above them. And by day, she mulled over what she had learned, savoring the return of a faith that said maybe—just maybe—the dreams would take them to this new home. Though how that was possible eluded her.

And the absence of Neb from those dreams frightened her as well.

In a few minutes, her sister would emerge from the lodge for their morning walk, and once again Winters would try to learn what she needed to. She had no sense of how to broach the subject of the missing pages with her sister. She'd considered magicking herself and searching the lodge and surrounding environs; but the scout powders would have been one more thing to hide in her room, and she had no training in their proper use.

She'd also considered bringing Jin into her trust, but something in that notion felt wrong to her. *It is not yet time for this much truth.* Though part of her thought perhaps Aedric and his men could find something.

Winters looked about at the gray morning. The shadows swallowed most of it, and hidden in them she saw movement. When Ria approached, it wasn't from the lodge after all but from behind it.

"Good morning, little sister," she said. Her smile was wide, but something lived beneath it that led Winters to believe it was forced. Behind her, a familiar figure followed—escorted on either side by a Machtvolk guard—and Winters's breath caught.

She'd not seen the Prophet Ezra since her arrival here, and though the man seemed even older than she remembered, he carried himself with stately grace. He smiled and turned his milk-white eyes toward her. "Greetings, Winteria the Younger."

She regarded him with level eyes, aware of the discomfort she felt. This man had lived among her people, teaching the Y'Zirite ways beneath her very nose, feeding the secret weed that had sprung up in the Marshlands. Certainly he'd not done this alone, but she'd heard him speak and knew the emotional power of his prophetic utterances. He'd played a key part in the loss of her throne. She forced herself to answer him, forced her sudden anger to the side.

"Greetings, Ezra," she said.

The old man inclined his head. "Your sister tells me that you are learning the faith. She says you carry your gospel with you everywhere and that your curiosity has no end."

She nodded, though she knew he could not see her. "I am learning it."

His smile widened. "You will enjoy the mass, then." His face darkened. "I'm sorry to miss it, especially with such notable guests in attendance at this first open celebration."

She'd seen the pilgrims arriving since her own arrival here, wandering in to stay with family or to bunk in the massive temporary structures that had been built to house them. Thousands would be in attendance at this most holy of Y'Zirite days, celebrating the advent of their wizard gods. She could hear the surprise in her voice. "You will not be attending?"

Ria interrupted, putting a hand on the old man's shoulder. "Father Ezra is required elsewhere."

Even as she spoke, more Machtvolk guards materialized out of the gray, leading horses with magick-muffled hooves. Ezra mounted and whistled. A dark shadow separated itself from the shrouded forest, and a kin-raven settled upon his shoulder. "I will inform you of her answer by the bird, my queen," he said.

Ria inclined her head. "Travel safely, Father, and preach well."

Whose answer? Winters wondered. *And where did the old man go a-preaching?* As they turned their horses south and picked up speed, she glanced at Ria. The troubled look on her sister's face told her it was a serious affair. Winters opened her mouth to ask about it, but Ria spoke first.

"She'll not bend her knee," Ria said. There was sadness in her voice. "Neither will she repent. She's already killed the bird I sent." She looked at Winters. "It will cost her far more than the sacrifice that drove her to such violence." Ria shuddered at her own words. Then, the woman tossed her braided hair over her shoulder and turned toward the path. "Let's walk," she said, "and talk of more hopeful things. Are you excited about the mass tomorrow?"

Winters fell in step beside Ria and tried to force enthusiasm into her voice and hoped her older sister could not hear her deception. "I am curious to see it."

Her battered gospel had very little to say about the Year of the Falling Moon, but over the course of their conversations she'd grown to understand it better. When humanity had twice stolen daughters from the Moon Wizard, in his grace he had descended to establish his just throne. He'd brought Shadrus and the rest of the Machtvolk with him, and they had served their Lord Y'Zir and the Wizard Kings that followed after.

Of course, P'Andro Whym had ended that rule on his so-called Night of Purging, and Xhum Y'Zir, according to the gospel Winters read, had ended the world because it was better to wipe clean the slate and start anew than for men—and women—to live without the oversight of gods.

It was a backward twisting of history through belief that frightened her. And how quickly her people had been seduced by it grieved her, though she could not blame them. They'd already had the metaphysical underpinnings of the Homeward dreams and largely lacked any exposure to the teachings of their Androfrancine neighbors. Winters had been fortunate that her father had seen the value of Tertius's lessons alongside the mysticism of her people's beliefs.

As they walked, she realized they were on the path behind the lodge now, climbing the hill. Their escort had fallen out of earshot, behind them, and Ria was speaking. Winters forced her attention back to her sister.

"It's been my favorite holy day since I was a young girl," Ria said. "The celebration of the mass followed by three days of feasting and gift-giving." She smiled. "Where I grew up, it was always celebrated openly."

This is new. Winters blinked. Until now, her sister had said very little about where she came from, and for the moment, she laid aside her questions about the missing pages. "Where did you grow up?"

Ria smiled. "Someplace far from here, little sister. Soon, I promise you, all will be known. But it is not yet time. We stand at the center of a web woven by many hands through years of quiet labor. And as desperately as I wish to bring you into my confidence, it is not for me to decide."

Winters tried to conceal the impatience in her voice. "I have so many questions, sister." The word tasted bitter in her mouth, but she saw Ria's eyes light up when she used it. For weeks, she'd avoided asking directly, but now saw a window she could crawl through. "Seamus told me that you died in infancy; yet you've come back from the dead. You speak of a place where the Y'Zirite gospel is commonplace and celebrated openly. I want to understand."

Ria placed a hand on Winters's shoulder. "And you will. But for now, I will tell you this much: You've seen the dead raised; my rebirth was not so spectacular as that. And it is a big world, after all, little sister, despite its many wounds and scars."

Yes. She remembered watching Petronus as he gasped and bled out on the floor of the pavilion on the day of Jakob's healing and Ria's declaration of herself. And though the world's barrenness was well documented it stood to reason that there would be other pockets of survivors from that Age of Laughing Madness.

They paused now at the door of the blood shrine, and a cloud passed over Ria's face. "I know we were to walk and talk," she said, "but it just isn't in me. Would you . . ." Her words trailed off as her brow furrowed. She leaned in and lowered her voice. "Dark days come. Sometimes even the purest love must lay axe to a dangerous root. Would you pray with me, Winters?"

She called me Winters. She couldn't remember Ria calling her that before, and some part of her noted it, cataloging it in her inner library. *She grows to trust me.*

And because she needed that trust for what was coming tomorrow, Winters nodded. "Surely I will, sister, though I do not know how."

"None of us," Ria said, "truly do."

They entered the anteroom of the circular building, and Ria closed the door behind them, leaving them alone in that warm and iron-scented space. She went to a small dark wooden box, ornately carved and attached to the wall. Opening it, she withdrew a silver knife. Then, the woman held open the inner door and nodded to Winters.

When she entered, she saw the altar at the center with its straps and buckles and catch-gutters. Wooden benches surrounded it in a rough circle, illuminated by guttering lamps.

Ria left the double doors open behind them and slipped past Winters to approach the altar. She knelt there, resting her knees upon purple cushions and her elbows upon the dark stone. Winters followed her and did the same.

"It is simple," Ria said, taking the tip of the knife and running it briefly across the palm of her hand. The blood welled up, and she squeezed it over the catch-gutter. Winters watched a few drops splatter, and when she saw that Ria waited, she bit her lip.

Trust. Summoning up every bit of strength she could muster, she extended her own hand and winced as her sister cut it open.

Then, she wrung her own blood onto the altar. "Like this?" she asked.

Ria nodded. "Yes. Now we beseech our empress to grant us grace for what is coming." There was darkness in her words now, and Winters nearly flinched from it.

"What is coming?" she asked in a small voice.

"Consequences," Ria answered. "Pray with me."

But when Winters prayed, it was not to an empress nor to any faith that required blood to be heard. It was to a white tower rimmed with singing mechoservitors and the song they danced to. To a boy with silver hair who had fallen into her dreams like winter snow, only to melt suddenly away.

It was a prayer to a pregnant moon now hidden by the gray of dawn, that it might rise soon to be her people's home.

And last, a prayer to the strength within her, that it would be sufficient for her to lead them there.

Petronus

As the sun crested the eastern horizon, it threw shafts of red light over the Churning Wastes. In the north, beneath the shadow of the Dragon's Spine, it was a cooler light, and Petronus's eyes had yet to adjust.

He lay stretched out on a ridge overlooking the valley below, with Grymlis and Rafe Merrique to either side of him. The massive dark metal doors set into the side of the gray cliff face told him all he needed to know.

If the visions are true, the hollow mountain lies somewhere behind that door. It stood tall as an Entrolusian bank, a half-dozen massive dials standing out from it, older even than Rufello's locks.

They'd made the best time they could, but the sudden addition of men on foot had slowed them down. And despite patrols, they'd been perpetually under attack from the south, losing nearly a third of their ragged company to the blood-magicked aggressors. And then, suddenly, the attacks had let up, though the kin-raven still kept pace with them as they rode and ran.

Rafe Merrique tapped his shoulder with the spyglass, and Petronus looked over at him, taking the glass in his hand. "How do we get inside?" the pirate asked.

Petronus put his eye to the lens and blinked as the terrain at the base of the door leaped into close focus. He steadied his hand and moved the glass up, taking in the metal and its massive locks. "I don't know."

"Maybe we knock," Grymlis said with a chuckle.

We need Isaak or one of his kind, Petronus realized. "You say four took your *Kinshark,*" he said, looking to Rafe. "We saw four others running west. Maybe there are others about." He thought about it for a moment. "But I don't think we have the luxury of time to wait for them."

Something was afoot. He knew it had to be, with the attacks letting up. And certainly, by now, their enemy knew their destination. The current of one strong river pulled them all to this place, and he knew the outcome would be conflict, even though he did not know exactly when that battle might arrive.

"But we should be ready," he whispered, and then started when he realized he said it aloud. The two men with him said nothing. He passed the glass to Grymlis. "Send in the scouts," he said. "We need to know every inch of that landscape."

Grymlis paused before raising the glass to his own eye. "Father, may I be candid?"

Petronus snorted. "When haven't you been?"

"Why are we here?" There was frustration in the Gray Guard's voice. "That door looks near impregnable. If your metal men and their antiphon lay beyond that door, an army could not dislodge them. What good is our ratty band?"

Petronus looked away from his friend and took in the scene below yet again. "I was called here," he said in a quiet voice. "Gods know why, but I was." He tapped the sack he kept near him now at all times, the roar of the song it held always at the edge of his mind. "Their response to this dream is the salvation of the light." Even as he said the words, he felt the power of them raising the hair on his arms. "They must not fail at this, Grymlis. I don't understand it, but I *believe* it."

The old man regarded him for a moment, then put his eye to the lens. "Then we do what we can," he said. "But," he added, "we'll do better from behind the door than before it, I'll wager." Then, he collapsed the telescope and passed it back. "I'll send the scouts in shifts."

They crept back from the ridgeline on their hands and knees by habit and made their way back to the makeshift camp at a quick walk. As a fresh batch of scouts applied their powders and vanished at a run, Petronus looked over what was left of their band.

They'd lost nearly half of the Gypsy Scouts and a third of the Gray Guard. Rafe's crew had fared best, but even they had sustained casualties. But they'd also managed to capture two of the strangely scarred women who hunted the Wastes for Neb and the mechoservitors.

He scanned the camp and saw them, bound to stakes in the shade of an outcropping of jagged stone. They showed no fear, looking bored as they sat silently in their tattered silk uniforms. Rafe had tried his hand at questioning them early after their capture but had gotten nowhere. And Grymlis's efforts during the short breaks in their forced march had yielded nothing, though the old captain assured Petronus that there were more *persuasive* techniques that could be employed with his leave.

He'd not granted it, of course.

One of the women saw that he was watching, and when her eyes met his, he saw disdain in them. It sparked an anger in him and he banked it, forcing the emotion out of his level stare. He walked to her slowly, his eyes never leaving hers.

"You are not afraid," he said, "because you know your people are near and you think they will save you."

"I am not afraid," she answered, "because I am already saved, Last Son."

Last Son. He'd heard this title before, though he did not comprehend it. Petronus crouched beside her, glancing to her companion where she sat testing the knots Rafe's men had employed. "Your notion of salvation leaves much to be desired."

She smiled, and when she did, the symbols carved into her face bent into a surreal mask. She lowered her voice. "I will offer you this once, Last Son. My sisters are coming, and when they do, you will watch them kill every person in this camp, dismantle each of the Abomination's metal hand servants before you are again set to your exile . . . alone." She looked away, across the camp, and he followed her gaze until it settled on Grymlis, where he stood conferring with the captain of the scouts. "You care for that one," she said. "You are friends. I've seen you talking to him." Her eyes returned to his, and he saw hard steel in the deep gray of them. "Bring me my dreamstone and I will see that he is spared the death that approaches."

Dreamstone. His mind flashed to the packs in his tent. He'd been through them a dozen times, setting out each of the items he found there and studying them carefully. Copies of battered, well-read gospels in an ancient script he could not read, spare clothing, mess kits and canteens, scout knives and ornate ceremonial cutting blades. And the carved totems—tiny kin-ravens made from a black stone that seemed familiar to him, though he could not connect to the hazy memory they referenced.

He stood slowly from where he crouched. "That," he said in a calm, measured voice, "is not going to happen."

"Then his death—and the others—will truly be on your head."

That may well be, he thought, as he turned and walked wordlessly away.

While the scouts ran their patrols and the sailors and soldiers established a perimeter, Petronus slipped back into his small tent. The woman's words stayed with him, and he reached for one of the packs where it lay beneath a gray wool blanket.

A sudden memory intruded upon him—a gaunt man stretched out over a black island floating in a quicksilver sea, dimly illuminated in the green light of phosphorescent lichen. He dug in the pack for the tiny statue, and when his hand closed over it, he thought for just a moment that he felt the slightest shock numb his hand and forearm. Withdrawing it, he held it to the light.

Dreamstone. He was not certain of its purpose, but a hunch grew in him. Could it be so simple? It would explain why she wanted it, certainly. He tightened his fist around it and squeezed, forcing his attention into the unsettling sensation that swept up from his hand to swallow the rest of him. The walls of his meditation slipped, and the song blasted out around him, so strong that his stomach lurched and his head threatened to explode. Biting his lower lip against the pain, he closed his eyes.

Are you out there?

No answer; just the noise of the canticle as its melody crushed him.

Can you hear me? He shifted his body on the bedroll where he sat, turning himself first westward and then north and—

He felt the shift and heard the dripping of water, the gentle wheeze of bellows in the dark as amber eyes came open.

The tamps have failed, Father. The aether is compromised. You must not be here.

"I am here," Petronus said. "I have come to serve the light." He paused, looking for more words. "I have come to assist in your response."

The eye shutters flashed. *It is not for your kind. The Homeseeker will—*

Petronus cut off the mechoservitor, his words sharp. "The Homeseeker is in the west with Hebda. I've brought men to defend the antiphon. I charge you to admit us."

The metal man clicked and clacked as gears and scrolls spun beneath its brass plating. Its head tilted. "You have brought the dream with you."

He nodded. "I have. It was taken from Neb and returned to me. I'm charged with its care."

Do not access the aether again, Father. We will come for you.

The eyes closed, and somewhere, far away and behind him, Petronus heard something. He turned south and felt the landscape rushing at him, bearing the distant and cold sound on strong, fast legs.

As he released the stone and slumped in his bedroll, Petronus knew that sound, and it chilled him.

It was laughter on the hot wind of the Churning Wastes, running north at breakneck speed.

"Come quickly," he whispered to the metal man he could no longer see. He felt something warm and wet in his tangled beard and tasted salt upon his lips.

Petronus wiped the blood from his nose, and the red of it on the back of his hand stood out, a prophecy of what swept northward toward them.

"Come quickly," he said again, and his voice was not even the slightest whisper in the cacophony of that swelling, roaring song.

Jin Li Tam

Jin Li Tam winced as Jakob bit her and shifted him against her breast, careful to keep her back to Aedric. These briefings after lunch had become more and more regular, though they'd largely curtailed the more blatant intelligence gatherings.

And the Watcher is what we need to know more about. But even as she thought it, Jin knew that they could not get close enough to that ancient mechoservitor to study it and parse its role in the current state of the Named Lands. It had played some part in her grandfather's and Lord Jakob's conversions to a faith thought extinct and carefully guarded against by the Androfrancines. Its forged notes and control of information by the birds was obvious now in hindsight.

"What more for today, Aedric?" she asked over her shoulder.

She heard the hesitation in his voice. "I've a note from Philemus. Lord Rudolfo is not well."

She bit her lower lip. "In what way?" But of course, she knew. She'd seen it in his messages.

Aedric said nothing, and Jin felt her eyebrow arching and let the irritation creep into her voice. "In what way, Aedric?"

"He is drinking. A lot. He does not sleep." He paused, then continued. "There is more. They've found shrines in the Forest. Rudolfo has the scouts compiling lists of Y'Zirite practitioners."

She had thought the words might surprise her, but she'd considered this possibility off and on since her meeting with the Watcher. This resurgence had decades of life here before Windwir's fall, but whatever came next could not do so with the Androfrancines watching.

She looked at her son's face. *We are a part of this.* Finally, she sighed. "What are they doing about the Y'Zirites?"

"For now, they watch them. Some of them are highly placed in Rudolfo's trust."

Jin Li Tam felt her heart sink and resisted the strong emotion that welled up in her. *I should leave tonight and return to him. He needs me.* And truly, she realized, the network that had plotted against them was now clearly dismantled with Jarvis and Cervael now cold in the ground along with countless others the blood cult had redeemed in their investigation. Perhaps it was time to put Ria's promise, sworn on her gospel, to the test.

Still, they needed to know more about this Watcher and what was yet to come. There was an army growing here, and soon thousands of Machtvolk would gather at midnight for the Mass of the Falling Moon. Jin felt the weight of something imminent growing in the air, and the voice of her father—a voice she often worked hard to deny—told her that she must persevere in this place.

She saw now that Jakob was finished, and she shifted him to her shoulder, letting his blanket cover her bared breast. She patted him. "I think we've been away too long, Aedric."

"Aye, Lady," he agreed. She could hear the worry in his voice.

"Still," she said. "He is Rudolfo. He will find the right path." She heard him moving toward the door, his feet whispering along the carpet. "Meanwhile, keep the scouts on the ready."

"We are always ready, Lady Tam."

She stood and walked to the door. "Thank you, Aedric," she said. "Go safely and hunt well."

"Aye," the first captain said. She opened the door and stepped partway into the hallway. She saw the Machtvolk guard nearby and called out to him as Aedric's magicked form slipped past her and moved the opposite direction.

"I am in need of more diapers," she said as the guard approached. "Would you ask the house staff to bring some?"

The guard inclined his head, and she slipped back into the room, closing the door.

She took Jakob to his crib and laid him in it. Then she went to the bed and stretched out upon it.

The whisper seemed a shout in the quiet of the room. "You are not meant to return to him."

Ria. Jin felt fear wash her colder than the icy streams that interlaced these foothills. She sat upright quickly and lunged for her knives. An invisible hand swept them out of reach.

"Hold, Sister," the muffled voice said, and she blinked.

No, not Ria. Someone else. She came to her feet and lunged forward even as the belt and its sheathed knives danced farther back, away from her. "I am not your sister," she said, her voice a hiss of anger. She put herself between the magicked woman and Jakob's crib.

The woman's voice was still low and calm. "Hold," she said, "and hear me. The message I bear you is the work of my life. What I have done, what I've endured, to reach this moment . . ." The words trailed off. "Hear me," she said.

Jin crouched by Jakob's crib, her eye upon the door and upon the belted knives that moved before her. She could just barely pick out the form of the shadowy figure that held them. "Speak."

"I'm glad it was you, Jin. Grandfather had several of us in mind, though he had no way of knowing who the task would eventually fall to. He left much to trust with the work he'd done in our father."

Jin Li Tam's eyes narrowed. "Who are you? What do you know of my family?"

"You do not remember me, but you know me," she said. "I have been gone for a long while." The knives lowered now and slid across the room beneath the bed. With the slightest wind, the magicked figure slipped close to her, and Jin saw a light green eye swimming in a latticework of scars—symbols framed by short red hair. "I am the thirty-second daughter of Vlad Li Tam."

Thirty-second? Her childhood had been riddled with loss. She could not count the aunts, uncles, brothers, sisters that did not come home from her father's work and his father's work before him. There had been many daughters born to Vlad's various consorts the year that Jin had been born. She'd naturally never known her mother, had been raised by her father and his siblings in the shadow of her aging grandfather. She'd grown up with those girls and had lost four of them before their training—their "sharpening" as grandfather called it—was completed.

"This is an easy claim to make," she said, "but not so easy to prove."

"Grandfather will prove it to you himself," the girl said. "Watch for his golden bird and listen carefully to it when it finds you. You must leave the Named Lands and fulfill the work you were shaped for."

The words were settling into her now, and as they did, more questions rose. "What work is that?"

"I do not know for certain," the girl said, "but I'm sent to assure you it must be done. The Named Lands are fallen and do not yet know it. The kin-wolves are at the fence, and the shepherds are crippled by their ravening. The antiphon will stand or fall as it will, Homeseeker willing, but what remains here will be lost utterly if you fail the work you were made for."

There was a knock at the door. Jin Li Tam opened her mouth to speak, but the magicked woman spoke first. "Come in," she said in a convincing imitation of Jin's voice.

The door opened, and a girl entered with a stack of folded cloth. Jin felt a cold hand suddenly on her shoulder and felt the words pressed there in the Tam subverbal. Jin read the words on her skin as she spoke. "Put them on the table."

And with the slightest rustle of wind, the hand was gone and Jin knew that this strange messenger had slipped from the room along with the servant.

But the words were in her skin still, and she could feel the weight of them.

Watch for the bird. When the regent bids you come, go with him. The boy will be safe in Y'Zir.

She felt those words and turned her eyes east toward Rudolfo. Surely it was yet another carefully laid trap. Some way of dividing the fold further, giving the wolves their run of the meadow.

She closed her eyes and called up the image of a sister just months older than her, stretched out upon the table, dead from the moonpox.

Ire Li Tam.

She'd seen much death. She'd seen the bone forests of Windwir and had lent her own hands and blades to the violence that had plagued them since. But never until Windwir had she seen the dead come back. And since then? Petronus, Jakob, supposedly Ria and now an older sister. The Y'Zirite gospel proclaimed the raising of the dead as a sign of a dawning age. She suspected this was true even while she maintained her skepticism of that faith.

It did not take faith to see the intricate web that was spun to remove the Androfrancines and pave the way for this resurgence.

The boy will be safe in Y'Zir.

The boy would, but she noted that the magicked messenger had not extended the same promise to her.

Looking to the face of her sleeping child, Jin Li Tam wondered exactly what she'd been sharpened for and what path lay ahead of her family. And when she wondered, it was about both the family she'd been born to and the one she'd made with Rudolfo and their son.

Neb

Somber guards shook Neb awake, and he let them lead him back to their camp through warm caves that twisted and turned as they swept farther down into the Beneath Places.

The Androfrancine camp was a massive cavern bathed in pale green light from a spiderweb of phosphorescent lichen and scattered with field tents and hastily constructed structures. Horses ate hay in rough corrals, and soldiers drilled in the wide open spaces.

Neb remembered Orius's order to Hebda and wondered how many brigades of Gray Guards they'd managed to hide away before Windwir fell. At least two from the numbers he saw here, possibly three.

The guards led him quietly across the camp to a simple wooden building. When they paused at the door, Neb heard low voices talking behind it as he raised his hand to knock. When he rapped lightly, the voices stopped.

"Come," he heard Hebda say in a congested voice.

He pushed open the door, and even the sight of his father was a cold fist in his stomach. He felt the sudden urge to turn and leave again, but the sight of the man, shoulders slumped where he sat on the edge of his bed, stirred something like pity in him. Renard sat beside him, holding the man's hand with a worried look on his face.

His eyes met Neb's first, and for a moment he saw anger there before it melted into something softer. When Hebda's eyes came up they were red. His nose was swollen and bruised, and the gaunt man looked away quickly.

Neb saw an empty chair, and without waiting to be told, he went to it and sat. He waited quietly, then finally, when neither of them spoke, he repeated Orius's order from earlier.

"Tell me everything," Neb said in a quiet voice.

Hebda nodded, and Renard squeezed his knee. "I'll be outside," the Waste guide said. He looked at Neb, and there was a hardness in his eye. "Don't hit him again," he said, "or you'll have me to deal with. I don't fault you your anger, Nebios, but there are many other shoulders at work here, each worthy of bearing the weight of your blame."

Neb nodded and waited until Renard slipped from the room.

After the door closed behind him, Hebda sighed. He reached into his pocket and drew out an ornate envelope made from a high-quality parchment. He handed it over, and Neb ran his fingers over the wax seal, feeling the crest of Windwir and its holy see beneath his fingers. "I was told to give this to you," Hebda said.

Neb broke the seal and drew out a carefully folded letter, the pinched script unfamiliar to him though the letterhead caused him to draw in his breath.

From the Office of Introspect, King of Windwir, Holy
See of the Androfrancine Order.

His eyes scanned the first line and narrowed. "It is addressed to me."

Hebda nodded. "It is."

He read further.

Grace and Peace to You, Nebios Homeseeker, for the cause of the light.
I beg your forgiveness of the man who bears this note, for his deception
of you was by Holy Unction and with his objections voiced clearly.
Two great sins have I committed without possibility of atonement:
First, I have condemned a city to die in the hope that the light
might persevere. Second, I condemned a boy to watch it die
that he might find his path.

Neb scowled and read the paragraph again, then continued. He stopped when the anger began to build yet again.

"How many people knew the city was going to fall?"

"Very few," Hebda answered. "We weren't certain ourselves until just four days before. But there had been rumors and fears for years before—it's what initially funded the research into the mechoservitors and the establishment of Sanctorum Lux.

Four days. "You had four days and you let every man, woman and child within Windwir's walls die in the Cacophonic Deaths?" Neb heard the disgust in his voice and made no attempt to soften it. "You had four days and you let Isaak sing the spell?"

Hebda shifted uncomfortably. When he looked up, his eyes were brimming with tears. He shook his head. "Introspect chose it. I watched him weep for his choice, and I wept with him. But he had to choose the city or the light."

Neb continued reading. A long and rambling confession with much reference to change being the path life takes and an admonition that he give himself fully to the mechoservitors' response and heed carefully the words of his father. He looked up to Hebda again at those words before continuing.

As a boy, I was asked by a Gray Guard if I would kill for the light,

the letter continued.

If you are reading this, you know that I have. I am bargaining
to save the light. I charge you under Holy Unction,
let not this sacrifice be in vain.

Bargain? Sacrifice? The room felt suddenly cold to him, and he forced his eyes to finish the letter.

He read to the end and looked up. "What bargain?"

He heard the voice again in the back of his mind. *I have bargained for you.*

Hebda nodded. "It is . . . complicated."

A thousand other questions crowded his brain, buzzing flies that eluded his voice. Finally, he settled upon one. "And Introspect ordered that I witness the city fall?"

A sob shook Hebda. "I protested it, but it was part of the bargain. We were told that it had to be so, that something in your blood would be activated by the spell or the desolation or both."

Neb recalled the day that his life had fallen away. He remembered being held, transfixed and cruciform, to watch the city swallowed by heat and fire. It had changed his hair from brown to silver-white and had left him without his own words for a time. Not long after, he'd fallen into the northern dreams of Winters and her people.

He looked away and then looked back. "You left me there. You rode out with me and left me."

Hebda shook his head. "We came back for you. But we underestimated Sethbert's eagerness to see his handiwork. His men arrived ahead of us. And once you were in Petronus's care, we were relatively confident of your safety."

Relatively confident. Another question jostled for position. "Why me?"

Hebda glanced to the door and then looked down. "It's what you were made for, Neb. Marsher mysticism aside, you *are* the Homeseeker. Tertius showed us that."

But the answer did not satisfy him. He took a breath, released it, then asked again. "Why me?"

Hebda sighed. "You've heard from Renard that your mother was one of his people?"

Neb nodded. He'd spent a month among them while Renard's leg healed, but the subject of his mother had not come up, and the Waste guide had warned him to let the dead stay a distant memory. And prior to meeting Renard, before his life changed on the plains of Windwir, he'd known better to ask about her of the one man who must surely know her. "I've heard it, yes."

Hebda nodded. "Did he tell you that she was his sister?" Neb's mouth fell open, and the gaunt Androfrancine continued. "I met her on a dig eighteen years ago. The Office often sent me east to observe the behavior of the nomadic tribal survivors in the Waste, and Renard and I had recently—" He paused, looking for the right words even as his cheeks tinged red. "We'd recently struck up a friendship."

He'd seen them holding hands, and he had a vague recollection of them kissing when they met in the caves back when the fever still racked his body from his infected cuts. He opened his mouth to ask another question, but Hebda kept talking.

"She'd been ostracized by her people—more mad than even the Age of Laughing Madness could accommodate." Hebda's eyes narrowed, and he chose his words carefully. "But she'd not always been so. She vanished from the village well one dawn and was found raving and mumbling just a few weeks later a hundred leagues to the west." He swallowed, and Neb saw the advent of uncomfortable words in the man's red eyes. "I met her a few months later and interviewed her. She claimed that mechanical men had taken her into the Beneath Places. She was great with child."

Neb blinked. "You're not my father." The words were a statement, not a question, and he watched Hebda flinch from them.

"Not in the biological sense. But I've loved you like I would imagine a father loves a son."

Neb's voice was cold and measured when he spoke. "By lying to me? By leaving me—intentionally—to watch everything I loved destroyed? By letting me believe you were dead when you were here the entire time?"

The tears spilled over. "I protested the path, but—"

"Do you even know who my father is?"

He felt that voice again, moving through the quicksilver to surround him. *I am sorry for this deception, my son.*

Hebda nodded. "They are coming to take you to him."

"Who is coming?"

But at that moment, the sounds of second alarm reached his ears from outside the closed door. Hebda stood, and Neb did the same. "Who is coming?" he asked again.

Their eyes locked, and Hebda's voice shook with emotion. "Nebios," he said, "I am truly sorry for the pain I've caused you. I only hope we chose the correct path. If we did not, then all is lost. If we did, then the light will live beyond us all."

There was a knock at the door, and when it cracked open, Neb heard the commotion outside. Renard poked his head in. "They're here for the boy," he said. "Orius is taking it about as well as we thought he would."

Hebda nodded. "It was never his to decide." He looked to Neb again. "If you succeed, I will never see you again. I'm sorry for the wrongs I've done you."

Neb looked at the man and tried to find some kind of pity or empathy for him, but there was nothing but distant echoes in the hollow space his heart had become. He said nothing and turned to Renard.

"Who is here for me?"

But even as he said it, he heard them coming. The whisper of their bellows and the dull clicking of their behavior scrolls buried deep beneath their metal skins. They moved with purpose, clanking forward wordlessly in the face of Orius's protests.

"He rides with the Sixth Brigade," the general said.

"It is not yours to decide," the metal man said. "Circumstances have changed; your army will not reach the antiphon in time. It should remain hidden."

There were three of them, dusty and battered, the remains of their Androfrancine robes torn and dirty from long running. All three looked up and raised their hands to him where he stood framed in the doorway.

"Hail, Homeseeker," they said in unison. "We've come to bear you to your father."

Neb did not look back. He bottled the remainder of his questions and gave himself to the mechoservitors. He did not ask for his pack or his clothing. He took nothing but the ill-fitting robes they'd put on him when he'd crawled from the bargaining pool.

And when they reached the edge of the camp and began to run through the tunnels, Neb ran with them, stretching his legs to keep pace with his metal escort. He pushed the image of Hebda's tear-streaked face away from him and forced emptiness to replace it.

He pushed his questions aside and clung only to the wordless rage that fueled his pumping legs.

Vlad Li Tam

When the dripping of the water awakened him, Vlad's first impulse was to find her. She filled his dreams with light and song, and he longed for her. She awaited at the prow of his ship; it was time to dress and go to her.

He sat up and started climbing to his feet before he realized he was no longer aboard his vessel.

I am not in my cabin.

Two nights here now. He forced himself back to the moldy straw floor and the tattered blanket they all shared during their sleep shifts.

Slowly, it came back to him.

There was a ship. The others had fled. They had magicked themselves and hidden in the sea near one of the Ladder's massive pillars until the new vessel stopped to search the water near their overturned yacht. They'd snuck aboard and mapped the vessel in less than a day. They'd raided the lifeboats for scout magicks and rations and had found a corner of the hold where they could sleep in shifts, unmagicked, while the others gathered what they could and kept watch.

Myr Li Tam's voice, muffled and low, drifted to him across the hay. "Father," she said. "Good morning."

He nodded. When the pouch of magicks materialized, he took it and applied a handful quickly, shuddering at the bitterness of the powders when he licked his hand. He felt them take hold of him and tried not to let her see the grimace on his face or notice that he'd broken out in sweat suddenly.

He knew it was the magicks. Chest pains and cold sweats were a sure sign that he'd passed the age of using them safely. Now, they would tear at his organs as long as he used them. And if he wasn't careful, his heart would fail him.

Still, he had little choice.

He inclined his head toward his daughter even though she could not see him do it. "Good morning," he said. "What do we know?"

"We're continuing to sail the perimeter of the Ladder," she said. "More vessels have arrived, and we've taken on passengers. Officers and a priest, by the looks of them."

One of the first things they'd noticed was that this was a uniformed fleet—a navy—though the markings were unfamiliar to him. These ships, though, were familiar.

He'd seen them at the Blood Temple.

Vlad forced his attention back to his daughter. "How many officers?"

"Three," she said. "Two women. High ranking; even the captain saluted. The priest was robed and hooded; male, I'm certain. And young."

Vlad felt the nausea hit him now, and his head started to pound. "Young? How can you tell?"

"Hands," she said. "And a certain swagger. Arrogance of youth."

Vlad smiled. "Good. Where are they?"

"They're in the captain's quarters. She is bunking with the XO and none too happy about it."

He nodded. "Good. Are we making any headway on language?"

"Very little, Father. It's nothing we've heard before. But we're taking down words as best we can."

He rubbed his eyes, feeling the stab of the magicks behind them. "What is there for me to do?" But he knew what she would say.

"Just stay nearby. Help us think. Collate the data."

Then, she handed him an apple and slipped away.

In the corner, nearby, he saw the faintest movement and realized it was the next recipient of the blanket, in from their work, with the magicks guttering their last. He stood and made way. Then, he found a place along the hull where he could crouch and munched his breakfast.

They wanted him to stay nearby, but they also knew he wouldn't. The visitors intrigued him. They were a constant tickle in the back of his mind as he started his day. He spent the first three hours listening to the reports his children and grandchildren brought back, adding his counsel and questions where it was appropriate, just as he had the two days before. His children had been diligent, too. They'd stolen what supplies they needed. They'd noted the uniforms and the scars that covered the bodies of their unwitting hosts. They'd named most of the crew and identified their shifts and now sought to learn the patterns they followed. And they'd inventoried nearly every space they could gain access to. Anything they learned, he scribbled onto tattered scraps of paper they'd liberated from one of their patrols. Then, they each took turns with the pages, committing the information to memory.

When Myr Li Tam came back from her patrol she went to him first.

He could hear the weariness in her voice. "Something is happening," she said. "The ship is being decorated, and the shifts are being reduced to minimum complement. The cooks are in preparation for some kind of feast—a day away, by the looks of it."

Some kind of holy day? It might explain the priest. He noted it as an option and then spent the next several minutes interviewing Myr about everything she'd seen on her last patrol. When he finished, he put down the stub of pencil. "I want to see these visitors," he said.

"I don't think it would be a good idea," she said. "It adds little value, and you are indispensable here." He could hear concern in his daughter's voice and could also hear the words she wasn't saying. *I cannot let you be captured again.*

He forced brevity in his voice. "Still," he said, "I want to see them."

Five minutes later, she led him by a silk string as they moved through the underbelly of the ship. Twice, they stopped while sailors moved quickly past, fetching various items from the hold. Then they were up narrow stairs and into the corridor that marked the passenger deck. Vlad heard bits of conversation and raucous laughter from behind the doors, and they stopped yet again as a door opened and a young officer moved away toward the stairs leading to the deck. Myr Li Tam got in behind him, taking advantage of his passage through the double doors, catching them easily as the officer pushed them closed behind him without looking back.

When Vlad reached the doors, she pressed words quickly into his shoulder. *We must take great care.*

He found her shoulder and gave it a reassuring squeeze. Then, they slipped out into sunlight and the smell of warm salt winds.

Vlad blinked at light so strong it brought tears to his eyes. Then, gradually, his surroundings took shape, but even as they did, his daughter tugged at the silk thread that connected them as they slipped quietly onto the deck. They made their way aft toward a red door that marked the captain's quarters, pausing and crouching in the shadow the sails made. The ship moved over the water slowly, and Vlad saw that other ships had indeed joined them—the beginnings of a sizeable fleet spread out in a broad formation that maximized their coverage of the waters within the circle of pillars.

They are searching for something, he thought. *Or perhaps waiting.*

Once more, Myr tugged at the string and they were scampering, breaking from one patch of shadows to find another. When they reached the red door, Vlad's chest felt like it had a wall of bricks stacked upon it, and he struggled to keep his breathing quiet.

Myr's hand found his shoulder again. *We can't afford to stay long.*

But he knew this already. The deck was too crowded, and the chances of them being stepped on or noticed as they passed through those inevitable patches of sunlight were simply too high. Sending out one at a time was risky enough, but two threatened their odds considerably.

And I am too old for this now, he realized. The powders gave him a strength and speed and stamina that his body could no longer control. And the constant focus on the pains in his chest robbed him of the focus a scout needed.

He gripped her forearm and pressed his own message into it. *We will not stay long.* But he did want a glimpse of this priest. He remembered the long dark robes of the cutters who had butchered his family before his eyes, and he had memorized the features of each during those weeks that he'd intended to build his pain into an army. Some part of his brain assured him that it was highly unlikely that one of those men would be the priest now behind the door they crouched near. But still, the line and trim of the ships and the uniforms of the men were familiar to him. And it could not be coincidence that these that had pursued and captured his family last year were once more pursuing House Li Tam.

He pressed his ear to the door and listened. He heard muffled voices and strained to pick out the words. A woman was talking now, her voice rising with frustration or impatience or both. When she finished, another woman's voice chimed in, this one quiet and measured. She talked for a while, and when she stopped there was silence for a full minute.

Then, the man spoke, and Vlad knew the voice instantly despite the unfamiliar language. His breath caught in his throat, and he squeezed Myr's arm harder than he meant to. He felt a rage building and very nearly missed the one recognizable word in a sea of gibberish.

Still, it registered.

Behemoth.

And the unmistakable voice that uttered it was that of someone he'd hoped was dead, though at some deep level he'd known he could not be so fortunate.

Still, he thought, if Mal Li Tam lived, it would give Vlad the pleasure of righting that great wrong.

After, of course, Vlad cut from his first grandson everything he knew about the Behemoth his love had sent him here to find.

Rudolfo

The stink of sweat and blood and urine overpowered the cold smell of snow and wood smoke as Rudolfo pushed through the gate to join Lysias and his men in the crude stockade they'd built.

Barring the gate behind him, he went to his stool in the corner and sat without a word.

His head pounded still, though it had been days now since he'd taken a drink, and he found himself breaking sweat every time he considered the bottles he'd had his men remove from his quarters. His eyes wandered every tent, every table for a drink that he knew he could no longer afford to take. The cost of it combined with his strong desire for it enraged him, the tingling in his scalp accentuating the hammers that pummeled his temples.

He quietly regarded the girl that Lysias stood over, listening to the general's quiet voice. Her lip bled where either he or one of his men had struck her, but her eyes held defiant resolve. Her tattered silks had been replaced with the oversized tunic and trousers of a Forest soldier, but now even these clothes showed the wear of her confinement.

Lysias glanced to Rudolfo and inclined his head. Rudolfo returned the gesture. Then, the general continued his quiet questioning, and the Gypsy King listened to the one-sided conversation and tried to keep his focus.

Three times, he found himself flinching at the sound of Lysias's fist as it lashed out. Once, his men had to step in and right her overturned chair from the force of the general's blow. And still, as always, the woman remained silent.

Finally, after two hours, Rudolfo looked up from rubbing his eyes. "This is not working," he said in a quiet voice.

Lysias looked to him, his eyes betraying his frustration at the tone of defeat in Rudolfo's voice. His hands moved in a subtle way, just out of the girl's sight. *Perhaps it is time for more extreme measures.*

Rudolfo looked at the woman. "I have considered this a great deal," he said slowly. And he had; he'd lain awake these last several nights considering both this and everything else that had transpired. The brutality of the sudden ambush by this Blood Guard, the reports of similar scouts running the Wastes. And it was obvious that someone was helping the Machtvolk build their own army and radically militarize and evangelize their territories while at the same time sowing discord in the nations to the south.

He sighed. "We cannot win here."

Lysias's face turned red with rage at Rudolfo's words, and when the girl chuckled, his fist lashed out, catching her jaw and overturning her once more in her chair. When the men moved in to pick her up, he waved them off and turned on Rudolfo. "Perhaps we should speak outside, Lord Rudolfo."

He dared his eyes to meet Lysias's and found a wall of gray steel there. "No," he said. He hoped his eyes were clear and strong, but he suspected strongly they were moist and red. "I will speak to her alone now."

"Lord Rudolfo, I cannot—"

Rudolfo let anger leak into his voice. "General, you are dismissed. Have your men fetch me this woman's kit. Find Philemus and instruct him to meet me in my quarters in one hour."

Rudolfo watched the older man force the anger from his face, but his eyes told him the anger would merely be banked for a later time. Lysias looked to his men, and with one last glare over his shoulder, he left with them and pulled the gate shut behind him.

Rudolfo regarded the girl where she lay, and when Lysias's man knocked, he stood and opened the gate, taking the pack before replacing the bar.

He walked to the girl and crouched before her. "We cannot win here," he said again. Then, he stood and wrestled her and the chair she was tied to back into an upright position.

Rudolfo returned to his stool and opened her pack. He'd been through its contents before. He'd spent many nights thumbing through her battered leather-bound gospel, testing the edge of her knives, smelling the contents of the small tin of cutting salts. He set these aside and then dug through her clothing and personal effects for the tiny kin-raven. When he drew it out and held it up to the lamplight, her eyes followed it and he saw hunger in them.

He smiled. "This interests you."

He watched as she forced that interest away. Dropping the stone into the pack, he held up one of the ceremonial knives. "Judging from your scars," he said, "this interests you as well."

Their earlier examinations had revealed that her entire body was a latticework of symbols cut into her by either this knife or one similar to it, all flowing out from the largest marking her skin bore—the mark of Y'Zir over her heart.

"I think," he said in a calm and measured voice, "that I understand this about you the most."

Something in her eyes changed for the briefest moment. He read curiosity there and continued. "I think these symbols are words—words about you or perhaps words about your faith. Prayers etched by sharp pain, salted that you not forget what you long for."

Because suffering teaches us how to remember.

He opened the tin and held it beneath his nose, suddenly transported back to the screams of Fontayne upon the cutting table as the Physicians labored for his redemption and the boy Rudolfo watched from his observation lounge.

He stood, placed the opened tin on the small table and lifted one of her knives. "I spent hours watching my father's Physicians at their work," he said. "I know most of the cuts that redeem." He brought the knife to his mouth and ran his tongue lightly along the blade, wetting it. "I know what parts of you that you can live without and just how long you can bleed." The memory was stronger now, his nose full of the smell of blood. She regarded him coolly as he dipped the blade into the finely ground salt. He continued. "I've watched them peel men and women like apples over the course of weeks, and I've watched them break from it, repentant and eventually atoned for."

He sat in Lysias's chair now, feeling the balance of the blade in his hand as he leaned close to her. His eyes held hers now, and he read nothing in them but mild curiosity. She was not afraid of the knife, but he'd known this the moment he'd seen her scars.

"Still," he said, "this does not frighten you."

He sat back and waited, raising his eyebrows as he toyed with the knife. He gave first one and then another minute of silence, listening to the ease of her breathing and keeping his eyes locked upon hers.

Finally, he leaned forward again. "I could let my men try other means—darker approaches—to loosen your tongue, but I'm not certain they would break you." Her eyes remained steady on his. "I think the only thing that you fear is disappointing your empress. Even if we broke your mind, broke your body, I don't think you'd ever give us anything useful under such coercion." He paused and watched her face. "Neither," he added, "would a gentler sowing produce a better crop, I'll wager."

When she spoke, her voice was raspy in the closed room. "You are correct, Lord. I will not answer your questions. I answer to a higher authority."

"Then why," Rudolfo asked, "am I keeping you alive?"

She smiled now. "Because you do not have the will to kill me nor the strength to break my faith."

When he moved, his own speed surprised him, as did the utter lack of any emotion in the act. He heard the whistle of her sudden exhalation and the slightest gasp as he pushed the knife into her heart. And when he twisted the blade, she cried out and her eyes went wide.

"You underestimate me," he said as she slumped forward in the chair, her mouth opening and closing as her legs and arms twitched and jumped against the rope that held her in place. He leaned closer still and placed his mouth near her ear. "Let us hope that your Crimson Empress does the same."

Then, Rudolfo let go of the knife and sat back to watch her die.

Charles

The white light of a winter afternoon, coupled with the blast of frigid air, brought water to Charles's eyes, and he blinked for a moment. The strong hand on his upper arm guided him quickly through the open door as he was passed from one Machtvolk guard to another.

He looked out over the snow-covered forest, his eyes taking in the smoke of a hundred fires and the scattering of buildings that punctuated the foothills of the Dragon's Spine.

If this doesn't work, he thought, *I could be dead by nightfall.*

He'd spent the first two days hidden with the mechoservitors and the book. He had met Garyt just hours after they'd arrived, when the loyalist guard brought the latest of Winters's dreams, adding them to the most recent volume of the Book of Dreaming Kings. And as soon as the man had left to find food and water for Charles, the old arch-engineer busied himself reading the book while the mechoservitors continued sharing data in code. That first night—or perhaps it was day—he'd slept with a full stomach from cold roast chicken and small potatoes fried in salt and fat with dried onions. The bread had still been warm and the water was ice cold and sweet.

In the morning, he'd made his decision. The mechoservitors had resisted, as he'd expected, but in the end they had no other choice but to let him go. They needed their missing pages, and they could not leave the cave. Charles would elicit help from Rudolfo's Gypsy Scouts.

Now, he stood outside for the first time in weeks. He felt the wind on his face and took in a great lungful even as Garyt pulled at him. "We need to move quickly," he said.

Charles nodded and followed the guard. The dirty woolen and fur clothes stunk in his nostrils and made his skin crawl. He tried to ignore both. He kept his head down, feeling the bits of wood in his beard as they tickled his neck. It had taken them an hour to get him ready, applying the mud and ash to every inch of his body and then dressing him carefully in the clothes Garyt had brought.

They walked past log structures that looked new, and immediately Charles noted the crowd. Through the trees, he could just make out the bright canvas of large pavilion-style tents—liberated he suspected from the papal summer palace. "There are a lot of people gathering here," he said in a low voice.

"Mass of the Falling Moon," Garyt said. "One of their high holy days. There will be a ceremony tonight followed by three days of feasting."

Charles smiled. *A good time to hide a crazy old man.*

They moved along the edges of the larger pockets of people, with Garyt steering them away from the uniforms that Charles saw interspersed among the crowd. They picked their way carefully across the more populated areas near the larger wood structures and climbed a trail that took them behind a round building made of stone. They left the trail when they were out of eyeshot of any others, and Garyt kept them moving quickly.

When they were deep in the woods, Garyt paused. "You're certain of this?"

Charles looked up. "I am."

He'd learned about the Watcher yesterday. He'd surprised the man with his question when the guard brought him a second meal. And Charles had known the moment he asked that the man knew something about it. Still, beyond eventually acknowledging its existence, Garyt had said very little else about it despite the questions. But he had finally agreed to take him to Aedric.

Not that Charles knew exactly what he would ask of the first captain of Rudolfo's scouts. The missing pages, according to both Isaak and the other metal man, were vital for the salvation of the light. Somehow, they had to wrest them from their mechanical guardian or—if fate was kind—search the caves that Garyt claimed it lived in while it was away on some other business. Charles hoped for the latter, because if they were truly facing one of those ancient artifacts from the days of the Younger Gods, the gypsy scouts would be no match in an open confrontation.

And Charles knew better than to believe it could be reasoned with. *Not a mechanical that operated on faith.* Of course, it wasn't so very different from his metal men and the dream they believed in and acted on behalf of.

He felt the strain of their quick walk in his legs now and noticed that the snow had let up. Overhead, beyond the canopy of frozen evergreens, he saw that the midmorning sky was clearing as northern winds pushed the clouds away. Even with all that time in the Beneath Places, his muscles protested the effort.

They'd not gone much farther when a low whistle brought Garyt to a halt. Charles started at the sudden sound and stumbled, catching himself. He looked around the clearing and saw the slightest shimmer, heard the slightest whisper of footprints as they materialized in the snow.

"Hail, Garyt," he heard a voice call out. "And you as well, Androfrancine, though you are a long way from home."

Charles noted that the direction of the words changed even as they were uttered. "Hail, Aedric. How are the others?"

"They bide well," he answered. "We'll see him safe back to your care, Garyt."

Garyt inclined his head and looked at Charles. "Be cautious, old man."

Charles nodded. "I will."

He watched the man jog south and west, then turned his attention back into the clearing.

"So." Now the voice was closer, and Charles could make out one eye, barely visible, just inches from his face. "Garyt tells me you are inquiring after a certain metal man."

Charles nodded. "It has something we require urgently."

"We?"

"I am here with Isaak," he said. "He is hidden with the Book of the Dreaming Kings. Pages have been removed from it with precision only a mechoservitor could produce. I'm told one lives in the woods and your men have encountered it." He paused as he realized what he was about to say. *Perhaps I do know what to ask of Aedric,* he realized.

"I need you to take me to it," Charles said.

"It is out of the question," Aedric said. "Aye, there is a metal man. It's been monitoring and altering our birds. It killed two of my men—cut them, bled them first and then sent their folded uniforms back with Lady Tam after serving her tea. She's left clear orders that we're not to approach the Watcher." He could hear awe bordering on fear in the man's voice. "It's like nothing we've seen before."

Watcher. Charles noted the name. "I need to find the pages it cut from the book."

"The Marsher book?" Aedric asked.

Charles nodded. "Yes. What they need from it is missing. Without them, they cannot complete their antiphon."

His own words surprised him. He heard faith there, and it frightened some part of him that remembered his vows as an acolyte of P'Andro Whym. *I shall eschew all but the light and trust reason as my truest guide.* And yet, some other part of him responded to the faith in his metal children and the risks they took for the dream they claimed to share. He did not know what the pages were for; he did not even know what the antiphon was, other than a response to their dream. But something in him cried out that it was true and that it was important for him to assist them.

Perhaps, he thought, because it was what fathers did to satisfy the hopes of their children.

"This is Marsher mysticism," Aedric said. He nodded to the northeast. "Yon Watcher is real and deadly. Evil, even, if such a thing may be. I'll not risk your life or the lives of my men for nonsense."

Charles felt the anger starting in his scalp. He tried to force it from his voice but was not successful. "It is not for you to decide, *Captain.* Bear word of this to Lady Tam. Tell her what I have told you. Do not tell her that only Charles asks it of her but that Isaak does as well, for it is his dream that these missing pages serve."

There was silence. Finally, Aedric spoke. "I will consult with Lady Tam. Wait here until I return."

Charles opened his mouth to protest, and a cold wind brushed his cheek.

He waited for a minute. "Hello?"

No answer.

After another five minutes, he found a tree and squatted against it, facing the direction Aedric and Garyt had run in.

As he sat, his mind played out every possible scenario he could envision with this Watcher, gathering questions as he went and turning them over and over like the dials and catches of a Rufello lock in his mind. How old was it? Had it truly fallen with the first Wizard King? Had it risen from some temporary grave in the Beneath Places? He sat and pondered until he grew numb from the cold.

Standing, he looked above and realized at least two hours had passed.

Where are you, Aedric?

The man should've been back an hour earlier. Unless, Charles thought, he'd been delayed. Or something had gone wrong. For a moment, he thought about making his way back to the gathering crowd. With all of the activity, he should be able to make his way unnoticed back to the double doors that led into the caverns. Then he remembered something.

No. I'll not go back.

Smiling grimly, Charles turned to the northeast and began walking in the direction Aedric had nodded. *Yon Watcher is real and deadly,* the first captain had told him.

Charles suspected that soon enough he would know this firsthand, and prayed that his children's faith would protect him in his hour of need.

Winters

The woman in the mirror surprised Winters and she stepped back, her mouth falling open. She'd never comprehended southern women and their vanities, spending most of her life dressed in ragged, cast-off clothing and rarely caring whether that clothing was meant for the body of a male or a female. Now, in the dress that Ria had left for her, with her hair carefully braided by hands more skilled than her own, she did not think it was truly her own face and body reflected back at her.

She turned, noting the way the soft fabric clung to curves she was only just becoming accustomed to, and then glanced to the dressing room door.

"How does it fit, Winters?" It was Ria's voice, sounding bemused.

She looked again at the long blue dress with its low neckline and laced sleeves. "It fits . . . well," she said.

"Well?" her sister asked.

Winters turned and opened the door. Ria wore a similar dress, only hers was in a deep burgundy the color of pooling blood. Her face had been painted in the Machtvolk custom, though tonight there were less greens and more grays and blacks and whites. Still, each color was laid to her skin with precision, interlocking with the others like pieces to a puzzle. The paints covered her face, her neck and even her cleavage, the colors darkening where they intersected with the raised scar tissue that peeked out from the mark of Y'Zir her dress mostly concealed. Her own brown hair was up, offset by a silver tiara that Winters had not seen before.

Ria stepped back to take her in and then frowned. "I could paint your face," she said. "There is still time."

Winters shook her head. "I'm certain you have better things to do with your time, sister."

Ria nodded. "I do. We've a special guest tonight that I should see to. Someone I hope will answer some of those questions of yours I've not been able to answer." She moved toward the door, her bare feet shushing the carpet. "Your boots and robes are by the main entrance. Meet Lady Tam and the others there at the fourth bell and my guards will bring you to me. We'll walk to the amphitheater together."

Winters nodded. She'd used it—or rather Hanric had—for those rare times that large groups of her people gathered. It was really nothing more than a valley nestled up against the mountain, the downward slopes logged of lumber, with the stumps left as places where people could sit. She'd seen them clearing the snow from it for days in preparation for tonight and knew that even now, bonfires were being set across its wide floor to provide at least some warmth for those able to huddle nearby. Most would rely upon their furs and the warmth of their companions.

Ria paused at the door and smiled. "I am glad you are here for this, Winters." Her eyes took on a concerned look. "I had thought when I returned to take my throne that I might lose a sister I had never truly had. I'm glad to be wrong."

Winters felt something cold in her stomach but forced herself to curtsy. "Thank you, Ria."

The woman returned the curtsy and let herself out. Winters forced herself to count to ten before she released her breath. "Pig shite," she whispered.

"I'm glad," a voice from the corner said, "you also see it as such."

It took her a moment to place it. "Aedric?"

The voice moved. "Aye."

She blushed. "How long have you been hiding in my room?"

The first captain chuckled. "I've kept my eyes averted, Lady Winteria. Rudolfo's scouts are gentlemen at the very least; we only look when asked to."

She felt the heat in her cheeks, nonetheless. She went to the dressing room and brought out its lamp, placing it on the desk. "I thought your secret meetings were exclusively with Lady Tam."

"We've a new development. One I am quite late returning to." The voice was low, muffled with the same magicks that concealed him. "Your sister isn't the only one with special guests. Charles and Isaak are here. I've left the old gray robe in the wood; he seeks pages missing from your Book and believes the Watcher has them."

"The Watcher?"

"Lady Tam will tell you more when she can. He's a metal man the likes of which we've never seen. A leftover of the Younger Gods, I'll wager, dug up from their graveyards beneath the ground. Charles and Isaak believe he's taken pages from your book. Pages required for their work of saving the light. Lady Tam sent me to inquire what you might know of this matter."

Winters was certain her face had already betrayed her. *Charles and Isaak are here?* And inquiring after the missing pages? She turned in the direction that Aedric's voice last came from and swallowed. "Yes," she said. "I know of it. It was what the other mechoservitors told me when Garyt took me to them."

"And these pages—do you say they are critical to save the light as well?"

She thought about this. "I do not know about the light," she said. "But I know they are the path Home for my people, Captain, and a part of the dream the mechoservitors serve, part of the dream *I* serve."

"The one that names your boy, Nebios, Homeseeker?"

She nodded. "Yes."

She heard Aedric sigh. "Then let's hope that even Y'Zirite metal men celebrate their so-called Moon Mass." His voice moved near now, and his face took shape before her, shimmering and faint in the lamplight. "I will do what I can to find these pages."

The sudden thought of a metal man attending the mass piqued her curiosity. Ria had mentioned a guest who could answer her questions, and she wondered if this might be that guest. She shook away the thought at Aedric's next words. "Open the door for me, Lady Winteria. It's time for me to go."

She did, stepping into the hall and calling out to a servant who was going someplace quickly, her arms full of coats. "When you are finished," she said, "I would like some tea, please." She felt the slightest wind on her exposed feet and ankles as Aedric moved away down the hall.

The girl nodded and continued on; Winters went back into her room and closed the door.

She walked to her bed and sat upon it.

Do I still want to go through with this? Charles and Isaak were here now. And Aedric was now involving his Gypsy Scouts. Still, the missing pages were only a part of what compelled her toward action tonight. She'd asked for her voice magicks before she'd even known about the final dream. She'd asked for them once she'd started dreaming again, once she'd seen the wrongness of the path her people were being led down.

She looked to her knives where they hung from their belts on the back of the wooden desk chair. Then, she looked back to the bed. She stood and then crouched down, stretching her hand underneath the mattress until it found the small phial. She held it and stared at it, remembering the last time she'd tasted the sour contents that fueled her announcement of ascension to the Wicker Throne. And later, those contents had let her preach her first War Sermon, compiled of glossolalia and the scattered images of her family's long Homeward dream.

Walking to the mirror, she saw her dim reflection now within it.

Such a girl now. No, she realized, a woman.

She'd much rather go to this in her ragged trousers and tunic, her hair braided in bones and sticks, her face washed with the ash of desolation, the mud of a land that rejected her people and cast them into sorrow. She'd rather face this moment with the knives that her friend had taught her to dance with.

She placed the phial between her breasts and pushed it to the right, adjusting both breast and phial until the one covered the other. She would have to find a safe moment to drink the magicks.

Then, she would have to find the words that needed to be said to her people and to the woman who had stolen them from her.

Wolves in the fold, Winters thought, and wondered if she would be as strong as the hero Jamael when the time came.

Jin Li Tam

The song rose in a cloudless sky the color of slate and speckled with the few swollen stars that were visible by day. Jin Li Tam held Jakob close, hidden in a sling beneath her fur robes, his tiny face peeking out. It was a cold evening, made colder still by the chills the Y'Zirite hymns brought to her skin. She glanced to Winters where she walked beside her and then to Lynnae on her other side. All three of them had been provided gowns and fur robes. They were walking now on wooden planks that had been hammered together to create a path above ground going muddy from those who'd walked it before.

They'd left the lodge in a large throng of people that she assumed were Ria's elite. Those who had helped her wrest power from her younger sister, those who had seeded the Y'Zirite resurgence in secret. She and her party walked close to the front, where the Machtvolk queen led the procession, accompanied by a robed figure who had joined them late as they gathered by the front door.

Now, they approached the natural amphitheater and Jin saw the light of a hundred fires and heard the hymn as it built to a crescendo. It was not the song she had first heard, but similar, and the words within it took her back to the war that had raged in her since the meeting with the woman claiming to be her sister.

When the regent bids you come, go with him. The boy will be safe in Y'Zir.

Her child was their messiah somehow, in conjunction with their Crimson Empress. The world's healing was in their hands, according to the gospels she'd read. And if the magicked woman in her room spoke true, somewhere beyond the Named Lands lay a place bearing the name of their faith—a place she was intended to go to with her son for some purpose yet to be revealed. Initially, she'd been convinced it was a trap. But the more she thought about it, the more she saw that it seemed the direction gravity pulled her toward. Truly, there had been a great conspiracy within the Named Lands, fueled and funded by a branch of her family with help from this Watcher. An enemy greater than these pulled the puppet strings, and the opportunity to get closer to that enemy was nothing to be taken lightly.

And there is no safe place in the Named Lands. Not unless she was prepared to live here with the Machtvolk. The conspiracy had done a good job of assuring that none of the nations of the Named Lands could trust her family or Rudolfo.

The music changed as they drew closer, and they carefully picked their way down a crowded slope, moving slowly. As they went, she felt tentative hands reach out to touch her, and she forced herself not to cringe from it. She brought her arms up over Jakob by instinct.

They reached the bottom of the slope and climbed wooden steps onto a platform where two dozen chairs sat in a ring around a large wooden cutting table. An elaborate system of catch trays was fastened to it, all feeding into a single pipe that fed a silver basin. Nearby, Jin saw a table with silver knives laid out upon it beside a bowl of white powder she assumed must be cutting salts. Over the past several days, she'd heard much about tonight's mass, but this was an unexpected aspect. Though in hindsight Jin wasn't sure why she'd not anticipated it.

Someone is going to be cut tonight.

They stood before their chairs. At first, she thought they waited for Ria, but she realized that the Machtvolk queen watched the robed man who joined them. When he sat, Ria did the same, and the rest of them followed.

Jin leaned forward, still unable to see the man's face, but she noted his hands. They were white and large, laced with scars that reminded her of the marks that her father bore, cut into him by Ria during his time in captivity. Whoever he was, he'd arrived late in the night and had been hidden away quickly. The shimmering forms that she glimpsed from the corner of her eye told her that he was accompanied by magicked scouts.

A handful of her own scouts had accompanied her, and she wondered how the others fared. She'd sent Aedric to Winters, and the fact that he hadn't returned told her that the girl had confirmed the missing pages and Isaak's need of them. By now, surely the first captain had reached the caves, gambling that its metal occupant was attending the night's event.

She looked around the crowd again. If the Watcher was here she could not see him; but there were thousands crowded into this space now, and if he was robed, she might never pick him out.

Still, she kept looking for him even after Ria stood and sipped from a phial she held in her ungloved hand. When she cleared her voice to speak, the sound of it rolled like thunder out over the valley and into the surrounding hills. "May the grace of the Crimson Empress be with you," she said.

Their response rose up, half a cheer and half a reply. "And also with you," a multitude of voices answered. One of them was the firm, confident voice of the robed man who sat near her.

"Behold," Ria said, "the falling moon!" As she said it, the first blue-green light of it rose up on the horizon. "Tonight, we celebrate the salvation it brought us in this—our first open celebration of the mass here in the land of our sojourn." She paused, the roar of her words echoing out into the forests for league upon league, blending now with the wild cheers of the faithful. Then she turned, pointing toward Jin. "And behold, even our Great Mother attends, bearing the Child of Great Promise."

The cheer was deafening, and she felt her face grew hot. Her eyes met Ria's, and behind the adoration she saw there was something else, something off-putting. Was it defiance? She couldn't be certain. Forcing her eyes away, she inclined her head.

Nestled close to her in his harness, Jakob laughed.

The Machtvolk queen spoke for nearly an hour, her voice rising in passion then dropping low and reassuring as she spoke of their home and their faith. Jin followed what she could but found herself focused instead upon the gathered crowds. Twice she saw uniformed soldiers wrestling individuals to the ground to drag them from the valley. And at least once, she thought she'd seen a tall, robed figure moving along the ridgeline above them.

She also watched the robed man, catching glimpses of a scarred jawline or of a crimson cuff beneath his fur robes. She could distinguish his voice from the others now, and it carried with it an accent she could not place at first.

It is familiar to me. Her sister Ire Li Tam had also spoken with an accent.

To her right, she heard Winters shuffle, and she glanced at her. The young woman's face was drawn tight, and she bit her lower lip with her eyes closed. *She looks pained. Or in prayer.*

Jin leaned over. "Are you okay?"

The girl nodded but did not speak.

They were singing again, and when they finished, Ria turned to the robed man. "We are honored by another guest," she said, passing over the phial to him. "He has come a long way to bear tidings of our empress. Tonight, he honors us by making the cuts of healing upon our proxy."

The robed man stood and cast off his hood to reveal a scarred and pale face beneath close-cropped silver hair. He looked first over the crowd and then turned to meet the eyes of the others he shared the platform with.

"I am pleased," Ria said, "to present to you Blood Regent Eliz Xhum."

The man stepped forward, and when he spoke, his voice was warm, inviting, even as it blasted out from him. "Greetings," he said with a wide smile. "It is good to see the Machtvolk on the edge of their new home." The crowd roared at this. He turned slowly as they did, and his smile widened even farther, though Jin was not certain how it could. "It is good to see you at last, Jin Li Tam, Great Mother of Jakob, our Child of Promise. I've awaited your coming for many years now, as have all of us in Y'Zir."

She met his eyes and found them disarming for that briefest moment before he looked away.

"I am honored to worship with you tonight," he said as he outstretched his hands. "And this mass shall be your last without a home. Even now, the places are set to the table and the feast is soon coming. Even now—"

But another sound interrupted him, and Jin looked to the right, startled by it. Another clearing of the voice like thunder, and she saw that Winters stood now, her face suddenly a hard mask.

"Oh my people," Winters cried out, "heed not the lie of wolves in our fold. The dreams of the House of Shadrus are clear. Our home is not *here* for us to take but rather"—she raised a finger and pointed to the sky—"it is *there* for us to seek."

Jin Li Tam followed her finger, saw the moon to which she pointed, and then looked back to the girl. Her hands moved quickly though Winters didn't pay her any mind. *What are you up to?* Already, uniformed men moved toward her, and Jin saw her own scouts slipping in closer.

Jin shot a glance to Ria and the regent. Ria's face was mottled purple in rage, but Eliz Xhum's face looked more bemused than anything.

"You surprise me, little sister," Ria said in a voice that dripped venom.

Winter raised her hands. "Hear me," she cried. "Our home arises, and our Homeseeker will bring us to it in the end. Do not lose your faith in our dream. Do not trade it for this late-coming lie." She held her copy of the gospel high above her head and then flung it.

Jin watched it as it tumbled out into the evening air to land within the closest fire. When it landed in the flames, she heard a thousand gasps.

Now, the approaching soldiers faced off with the Gypsy Scouts. Their hands were upon their knife handles as Jin Li Tam's fingers flew, issuing orders to them that they acknowledged with low whistles. "Stand down your men," she said over her shoulder to Ria.

"I'll not—"

But Ria's voice was cut off by the regent's. "Stand down," he said, and they did. When he spoke again, his tone was gentle. "Let us reason together," he said with a smile.

Jin Li Tam looked to the faith she saw upon Winters's face, bathed blue-green in the light of the moon, and then to the painted puzzle of Ria's face and the carved symbols that spiderwebbed Eliz Xhum's strong features.

Last, she looked to the face of her child, still laughing where he lay against her.

Whatever came next, Jin Li Tam doubted reason would have much to do with it.

Chapter 25

Neb

For the longest time, they followed warm and winding corridors that gradually descended farther into the Beneath Places. Neb's metal guides ran ahead, the breath of their bellows and the hiss of released steam playing counterpoint to the whir of their gears and the mechanical pulse of their pumping legs.

He ran behind them, surprised at how easily he kept up with them. The deeper down they went, the warmer the air became, and from time to time, the phosphorescent glow faded to leave them moving forward only by the light of their amber eyes in that dark place. Neb used the time to collect his thoughts, giving up on the notion of any answers from them when they ignored his initial questions.

Still hollowed by all he'd learned, he found a numb detachment ran with him. In the span of days, he'd found his dead father very much alive and had discovered through the man's tearful confession that not only had Windwir's fall been permitted, but that the man he'd believed his sire was not. True or not, it unsettled him most when he remembered the voice that vibrated through his body as he lay suspended in the bargaining pool.

In those moments, his detachment threatened mutiny.

What kind of father could anyone possibly find here?

Even as he thought it, the whispering started ahead as they once more passed through a broad cavern containing yet another silver pool—this one gurgling in a slow-moving current that fled away out of view. He strained his ears but could not distinguish anything intelligible. Still, the whispering grew in volume the farther they ran.

At last, it stopped when they reached a tall archway with a crystalline door set into it. The first mechoservitor placed a metal hand upon its crimson surface, and the door whispered open. A gust of hot wind escaped the space behind it, and a soft blue-green light poured out with it. The metal men inclined their heads.

Neb heard the quietest hiss, and the whispering started up again. As they stepped back, he stepped into the archway and took in the room behind it. It was another pool, one he recognized as similar to the one he'd awakened in, only this one was in a carved basin. At its center, hanging from a web of silver threads, hung a blue-green orb the size of a bull's head.

No, Neb realized, *not just an orb.* Legs unfolded from it—legs also silver and easily mistaken for part of the web it hung from. The light undulated, bent through the thick, glasslike construction of the crystal that contained it. The legs twitched and moved along the strings, and the whisper now was more obviously a song.

Neb's detachment failed now, and he felt fear grip him. He felt it like a cold fist squeezing his bladder, and as the spiderlike creature moved toward him, he stepped back. "What is it?"

A metal hand fell to his shoulder. "Wade in the waters," the metal man said. "You can only hear his voice if you are submerged in the pool."

Neb took a tentative step forward, then hesitated.

"This," the metal man said, his hand still firm on his shoulder, "is what the light requires of you, Nebios Homeseeker. A tremendous price has been paid to bring you to this moment. Do not be afraid."

He removed his boots slowly and pulled off his robe. Closing his eyes, he stepped into the pool, remembering the fear on the face of the Gray Guards when he'd nearly backed into the other pool. He felt the fluid moving over his feet, and the cool relief of it ran up his legs, soothing the ache from his run.

Yes.

He did not hear the voice as much as he felt it, and there was a calm in it that compelled him forward. He waded out to his waist and waited.

The silver legs unfolded, bearing the orb along the web as it moved closer to him. Smaller appendages—more slender than the legs—waved the air before it. Neb watched it approach. "Who are you?"

Come closer.

Neb took one step forward and then another. Now, the warm, thick liquid lapped at his chest. Beneath him, the floor of the pool felt spongy but solid. The smell of it was salty in his nose. He waited, watching as a tendril of webbing dripped from an orifice that appeared in the underside of the orb's silver chassis. The strand of web brushed the top of the pool, sending ripples out from the place it touched, and then the legs bore the orb along the line of the thread to hang inches above the pool and within reach of Neb.

He forced himself to stay put, feeling the vibration of the voice as it moved over his skin. *They named you Nebios.*

He closed his eyes and pushed his answer into a thought. *Yes. Who are you?*

He watched the light gutter and then pulse again through the thick crystal of the globe. *I am a ghost of the first people, those this world was made for.* A series of images came with the words now, and Neb found them disorienting. He saw a vast planet-sized garden, scattered crystalline towers reflecting back sunlight in the midst of orchards of fruit and fields of grain.

Neb's breath caught in his throat. "You are a Younger God."

I am the ghost of one. An echo left behind in hope with a pocket full of seeds. And in you, Frederico's Bargain is finally complete. The path is cleared to the tower, and you will take back what Y'Zir the Thief had no right to. You are Homeseeker and Home-Sower.

More images, stronger now that the silver legs stirred the pool, took shape behind his eyes. Neb felt the power of them on his skin. A white tower—familiar to him—rose up from the jungle and he stood upon it, surrounded by metal men and their song, a silver staff held high in his hand as the sea boiled beneath him.

He could hear the song in the air now even as he felt it moving through the fluid that pulled at him, and the gravity of it tugged him. At first, he resisted, but finally he gave himself to it, took in a great lungful of air, and immersed himself. He felt the pool shift and move about him.

Yes. Neb didn't know if it was his voice or the voice of the Younger God. Maybe it was both in unison. Regardless, he felt a splash as the globe dropped into the pool beside him.

I have bargained for you as I promised. You are the last of my seed and the last of our people. Last of the line of Whym and last hope of Lasthome.

The words tumbled through his brain, rocks tossed into a well. *The line of Whym?* How could that be? He tried to collect and focus his thoughts to ask, but that level of control eluded him.

Scenes shifted around Neb now, and they were impossible to discern, storms of light and sound that moved through his mind with an ache that made him groan. He opened his mouth and felt the thick fluid pushing its way into him. It moved inside him now even as it moved over him, and he lost his footing.

Silver legs reached out to steady him, careful in their grip. For a moment, he resisted and floundered. Then, he relaxed. *I do not understand.*

I am the ghost of Whym. Three sons have I sent out from the basement of the world; only one has returned for my blessing. And so I give it freely: dominion over what was made for you. Your awakening will be gradual and heuristic. You will learn the path by following it. You will follow the path and save our people.

The spider's legs were tightening upon his wrists and drawing him in. His eyes were closed against the warm pool, but he forced them open to see that the silver waters were now a brilliant blue and green. He wanted to resist but found that he hung limp as the quicksilver carried him. He felt the legs encircle him and felt the heat of the globe against his chest.

Then, those smaller appendages moved over his face, sliding into his nostrils and his ears and open mouth. When the pain came, it was instant and hot and blinding. He felt his body seize from it, and in the midst of the seizure, everything shifted to gray bordered by black.

As the world spun away, Neb heard and felt the voice once more. *I give myself for you.*

Then what had been light became darkness and what had been song became silence. Neb floated in it wrapped in a solitude deeper than he had ever known. And eventually, in the heart of that silence, a whispering arose. And in the core of that darkness, light bloomed and held.

When he emerged from the waters, the waters lifted him until he stood upon their mirrored surface. He ignored the empty crystalline husk with its limp silver legs. Instead, he fixed his eyes upon the metal men who waited on the shore. He knew them and he knew their song, knew the strands of it that connected them in the aether. He read the code in that canticle now and smiled at how simple it was.

"Time is of the essence," Nebios Whym said, and his words echoed through a room now lit only by the amber of their jeweled eyes. "The antiphon awaits."

Yes, a voice within him whispered.

Vlad Li Tam

The rocking of the ship and the rhythm of the words soothed Vlad Li Tam despite the nearby crowd of sailors. All hands were on deck now as his first grandson led some form of Y'Zirite service in the guttural tones of their language. There were songs, as well, and a long monologue with portions read from a black-bound book that Vlad suspected must be one of their gospels.

He found himself willing the service to continue, knowing that each minute that the lower decks were empty was time bought for his family to comb it for anything useful. The longer they were aboard, the higher the risk of discovery and capture. At some point, those stolen rations or tools or magicks would be noticed. They either had to take the ship—an unlikely feat—or escape it to something safer.

His grandson's voice dropped, and Vlad turned his attention back to him. The young man had raised his arms in supplication, a silver knife held high. The moon rose, and as it did, the waters took on an ethereal glow. Out on the waters, Vlad could make out other ships moving in slow, wide circles around them, and he noticed that they were now adrift in the center of the massive pillars. As the moon rose, he saw the light of it reflected in the silver orb that hung far above.

The setting, combined with the poetry of Mal Li Tam's voice, pulled at him. And from the looks of rapture on the faces of the crew, it compelled them as well. Two of them rolled barrels to the prow and another brought a plank. They laid the plank across the barrels.

What are they doing? But part of him already knew as his eyes followed the silver blade in his first grandson's hand.

He'd forced Myr to bring him back when the call had gone out for all hands. Even now, she sat beside him, huddled up against the rail, not far from the hatch that would take them back to the part of the ship they called home. He felt her fingers pressing into his skin.

Do you understand any of this?

No, he tapped. But it fascinated him. Certainly, he'd heard stories about resurgences. And his family was very involved in this particular resurgence, though obviously with a great deal of help from outside. Help from people who bore the marks of Y'Zir not just upon their hearts but upon their entire bodies. He had no doubt it was faith that drove those blades into their skin.

Mal Li Tam was pacing now and speaking with an impassioned voice. He paused and pointed the knife first at one man and then at another. He even pointed it briefly toward one of the women in the party. But eventually, it was the man Vlad recognized as captain that stepped forward and offered a one-word answer.

Then, he stripped down and stretched himself upon the plank as his men tied his arms and ankles so that he was firmly fixed to the table it formed. Deck buckets were passed forward, and Vlad suddenly felt a stab of tension in his shoulder blades as he watched Mal salt the blade and roll up the sleeves of his robe.

The moonlight danced over the captain's scarred body. He did not struggle or even cry out as the knife made its first pass. But by the seventh stroke, he wept and screamed and his men wept and screamed with him as his blood dribbled into the buckets through holes drilled in the plank. When Mal finished, he cleaned the captain's wounds himself and then kissed him on the mouth, uttering a loud proclamation with hands outstretched toward the crew.

Then, lifting the bucket, he pitched its contents over the rail. Afterward, he called out loudly, his voice booming out over the sea and Vlad recognized the word once more. "Behemoth!"

The young man waited, and the deck became silent.

Vlad held his breath. Mal Li Tam tossed back his head and laughed loud. The crew joined him and even the captain, tears streaming down his face. Raising his gospel in one hand and his knife in the other, the Y'Zirite priest launched into another long monologue and at the end of it, laid aside his gospel to take the knife to his own hand. He drew the gash deep and held it out for them to see. Then, he cast his eyes upward, and Vlad followed his gaze. The silver orb eclipsed the moon, and for a moment, it was a globe of blue-green water speckled with stars.

He stretched out his hand beyond the railing and squeezed his blood into the ocean with a cry.

Vlad felt a tickle along the back of his neck and realized when Myr squirmed against him that he held her arm too tightly. He released it.

Could it be so simple?

He heard it rising in the stillness of the wind, felt the faintest vibration of it in the deck beneath him as it moved through the deep waters. As it drew closer, it became a buzz and then a roar, and the sea heaved and bucked from it as it moved in a slow upward spiral toward them.

Already, Mal Li Tam was stripping off his robe and fixing the silver knife between his teeth. Around them, the crew raised a shout, and in the midst of that shout, Vlad made his choice.

With one hand, he slipped Myr's knife from her belt. With the other, he pressed words into her forearm. *See the others to safety. You bear my grace.*

It broke the surface off the starboard side of the bow, and he'd never seen anything like it. It was larger than a ship, long and made of a pitted metal that bent and flexed as it twisted through the water, gears grinding and shrieking as it moved. Dozens of jeweled eyes cast back the moonlight as it turned toward their ship.

Mal Li Tam leaped overboard from the prow with a loud cry.

Digging the edge of the knife into his own palm, Vlad Li Tam followed him.

Rudolfo

Rudolfo moved through the forest quietly, savoring the silence once he was far enough away from camp. Twice, he passed guard posts, whistling his intentions to them as he slipped by and into the deeper forest. At last, he reached a clearing with a tree he could lean against while watching the stars.

The meeting with Philemus had not gone well. He'd watched the man's face redden, and in the end Rudolfo had raised his voice to make his point clear. The second captain would follow his orders, but Rudolfo sensed a breaking point on the close horizon. The Gypsy Scouts were the pride of the Ninefold Forest, a fearsome fighting force, and reducing them to a type of state police did not sit well with anyone . . . especially among the officers. But word now sped south, and tomorrow, Philemus would follow the birds and return home to the Seventh Forest Manor. Tonight, Rudolfo needed to decide if he would ride with him. There was nothing here for him to do, and his epiphany held, the memory of it as fresh as the memory of the knife jarring his shoulder as he pressed it into the woman's heart.

We cannot win here. And still, he would find what path he could through what came. He had to. The face of his son, conjured up at each intersection, compelled him to find a way.

The forest was still but for the sound of overweighted branches losing their snow when the wind caught them just right. He stood and watched the moon and thought about the family that strengthened his resolve.

Over the past several months he'd found himself frequently asking himself what Jin Li Tam would do. And he'd grown accustomed to seeking her counsel late at night when they lay whispering in bed. Now, with her and Jakob so far away, he found he missed her words the most. The quiet and careful way she spoke them and the hard edge to those words when his stubbornness required it. Their pairing might have been a manipulation, but it was a formidable partnership nonetheless, and she'd proven this again and again.

We cannot win here.

The real enemy gathered strength and now made forays into the Named Lands with blood-magicked scouts who were capable of surviving the toll those magicks took upon their bodies. They were a hardy stock, well trained, and a brutal fighting force. And while this enemy built its own path, his own kin-clave to the south plotted against his family. His best intelligence couldn't touch the competence and ferocity of Ria's network, and his best ambassadors could not persuade even the opening of dialogue with any but Erlund, who was too distracted with political reform in the wake of his civil war to care much for what happened with the Ninefold Forest.

Rudolfo swallowed and wished for a moment he'd brought the firespice with him. He pushed the craving aside, alarmed at how quickly it had become a crutch he could limp along with.

The thought of limping brought Isaak to mind, and he wondered how his metal friend fared. By now, Isaak should be in the Marshlands with the others. Before Jin's coded note, Rudolfo had worried less. But knowing now that another metal man—this Watcher she spoke of—made his home there raised Rudolfo's hackles to third alarm. Whoever their enemy was, they did not want the mechanicals dreaming. And, more than that, they didn't want the Seven Cacophonic Deaths loose in the world. He did not doubt for a second that their call for him to release the mechoservitors into their care would ultimately lead to yet more light gone from the world.

Rudolfo sighed and tried to pull the stillness of the night into himself, tried to conjure images of his sleeping child.

He heard the man in the forest long before he saw him. The crunch of frozen snow, the labored breathing and the whispered curses were like shouts across an open plain.

Rudolfo remembered a time when Gregoric would follow him out into the woods. That first captain and closest friend always gave him plenty of time to think in the quiet, but inevitably, he turned up. That was a loss that still rode him hard.

Lysias broke into the clearing, bundled in furs and panting as he placed his boots in the prints Rudolfo had left behind. The old man looked around, clouds of steam rising from his mouth and nostrils as he caught his breath.

Rudolfo whistled low and the general turned. As the man made his way to him, he noted his posture and stride. Whatever anger he bore had been burned off by the quick-paced walk. He nodded to Rudolfo.

"You've found me," Rudolfo said.

"The snow helps." Lysias took the tree next to him and leaned against it, still gulping his air.

Rudolfo said nothing, giving the man time to gather his thoughts and slow his heart rate and breathing. He waited for five minutes, and then Lysias finally spoke.

"It is quiet here," the general said.

Rudolfo nodded. "It is good for thinking." He'd known since boyhood how to woo a crowd, but it was from the quiet, still places that he drew his strength and found his paths.

Lysias's eyes narrowed in the moonlight. "And what are you thinking?"

Rudolfo took in a deep breath. "I'm thinking," he said in a slow voice, "that no matter what we do, we're damned and buggered. We build our army too late for a hunter that has set his snares and harried his prey too long." As he released those words, he felt their power on the wind and felt relief from finally having said them. "We cannot win here."

Lysias nodded. "You may be correct."

"And I am thinking," Rudolfo said, "that it may have been a mistake, killing the girl."

The old general nodded again. "It may have been. I think I could've broken her."

Rudolfo regarded him. "Perhaps," he said, "but I think it would've broken something in you. Some actions we take can do that."

Lysias chuckled. "You underestimate me, Lord. Those parts of me were broken a long time ago." He was quiet for a moment. "Still, she is dead and that is an unchangeable fact." He looked back to Rudolfo, and their eyes met. "At least," he said, "you took action."

Yes. "I hope it was the right action."

Lysias shrugged. "It felt right at the moment?"

"It felt . . ." Rudolfo let the words trail out. His answer troubled him. "It felt satisfying."

"Perhaps it was what you needed to find your path again."

Perhaps it was. But another part of him rebuked that inner voice. He let the quiet settle in again.

The sound of the bird was loud, and Rudolfo heard its shrill cries long before it settled onto a fallen log in the center of the clearing. His hand moved instinctively for his scout knife as it flapped the ice from its wings.

It was larger than he'd imagined it would be up close. Its dead, glassy eyes stared, and even from a distance, he could smell the decay of it. The kin-raven hopped in place upon the log and opened its beak.

A voice leaked out. "Greetings, Rudolfo son of Jakob, lord of the Ninefold Forest. I am Eliz Xhum, regent of the Crimson Empress. Grace and peace to you from the Empire of Y'Zir." The voice paused, though the beak did not move. "Your father rejoiced at the coming of this day and bid me bear you his pride and love. He had longed to hold the Child of Promise in his arms but, alas, it was not the path set out for him."

Rudolfo felt the words even as he heard them. They were colder than the winter sky and sharper than knives. *My father?* He forced his attention back to the mottled dark messenger upon its log.

"I have been informed of the recent treachery against your family and can assure you that every step is being taken both for the prevalence of justice and the safety of the Great Mother and her Child of Promise. I regret the chaos and violence of the past two years and I regret the chaos yet to come, though I'm certain a time is coming when you will concur, as your father did before you, that this is essential for the healing of our world." There was a pause, and Rudolfo glanced to Lysias. The man listened intently with a look of understanding that grew to look more like alarm with every word. The voice continued. "My emissary will reach your western border by way of the Whymer Road in approximately one week's time. My eager hope is that they will be met with peace and welcome, and escorted safely to you that our strategy for a successful transition may be discussed. I look forward to our work together, Rudolfo."

The bird's beak closed, and Rudolfo did not hesitate. He drew his knife and flung it at the kin-raven even as its great wings spread. He'd not thrown in a goodly while, and he felt the strain of the sudden movement in his shoulder and arm. The knife went wide, missing by a span, and the bird lifted into the sky to shriek at him as it fled west.

Rudolfo cursed and walked to the log, recovering his knife. Lysias said nothing, and by the look on his face, Rudolfo could tell the older officer was trying to read him, to gauge this new information and its impact upon him.

My father. He did not believe it, of course. It wasn't possible. He'd watched his father ride out to put down resurgences in the name of the Pope. What was his role in this? The knots in his stomach were twisting now as his mind went back to the blood shrine they'd found in the forest. And the list of names, including some of his father's closest and most trusted friends.

Our strategy for a successful transition. He looked to Lysias. "What do you make of it?"

"Invasion," the old general said. "And he would not tell you so much if he did not know already that there was nothing to be done for it."

Rudolfo nodded. "I hope you're wrong."

But he did not believe he was, any more than he believed this sudden fear he felt about his father was somehow misplaced. It answered too many questions.

In that moment, Rudolfo wept, and he felt rage and despair rising off of him like heat from a banked fire.

Winters

Somewhere in the crowd, an infant wailed and broke the silence that had taken hold of them. Winters looked out over the mass of people who had gathered beneath the rising moon, took in the cutting table and then turned her attention to the man who had just spoken.

When she answered him, her voice rolled out for league upon league. "There is nothing reasonable about your faith," she said. "You impose it. You force your mark. You press your gospels into the hearts of small children and teach it to them as if it were certain truth."

As she spoke, a smile played at the corners of Eliz Xhum's mouth. Something bright sparked in his eye. "And how is that any different from your Homeseeking Dream? Were you not taught as a child that eventually this Homeseeker would arise? Did you not cover yourself with ash and mud to remind you of sorrow and loss during your sojourn between homes?" The regent spoke slowly, his magicked voice a gentle thunder in the winter air. "And beyond matters of faith, your Androfrancines—soulless offspring of that deicide, P'Andro Whym—did they not also teach their view of things as if they were certain truth? To children? And did they not hold hostage an entire population to their atheistic convictions and their worship of human knowledge, hoarding that knowledge to themselves in their walled city, doling it out or withholding it at their whim?"

Winters glanced to Jin Li Tam. The woman watched her, her eyes betraying concern, as she shifted Jakob in her arms. Winters turned back to the regent. "As to the Androfrancines," she said, "my people have resisted them from the time they arrived upon our lands. You know this." She looked to her sister. "And as to my faith . . ." She paused. *My faith.* It was indeed hers, and it stirred up a feeling in her even stronger than the feelings that Neb had stirred up in the days when their dreams had touched and they had touched within them. She met the regent's eyes. "My faith is built upon two thousand years of the Homeward Dream, passed down from father to son until at last, it came to me."

"And mine," Xhum said, "hearkens back to the days before, when the Moon Wizard Raj Y'Zir fell to live among us and teach us the love of a father for his child. But regardless, our faiths are not mutually exclusive, young Winteria. Indeed they are intertwined. You are young in your knowledge of Y'Zir, but there are many passages about the Machtvolk and their role. Perhaps this one will interest you." He looked from her to Ria, and Winters followed the glance and saw the worry upon her face. " 'In the Winter of Days, a daughter shall be born and named for the season of her arrival, and she shall call forth the true Machtvolk by blood in the shadow of the Deicide's pyre to take back that which was promised and heal that which was broken.' " It correlates with a passage from your own father's dreams that I suspect you have not read."

The words were unfamiliar to her. "I have read the Book of Dreaming Kings since my earliest recollection," she said. "I've not read any passage similar to that."

The regent looked to Ria again, and the woman smiled only slightly. "No, I suspect you haven't. But I digress. My point is that our faiths are built one upon the other. And more than that, they are intertwined one with the other."

She wanted to argue with him. She wanted to list the ways that they were different, but she saw clearly now that though he spoke of reason, there was no reasonable way to convey those differences. Her Marshers had skirmished with the Androfrancines and their neighbors, bellowing out War Sermons of a promised home as they did. They'd murdered for their faith even as surely as the Y'Zirites had. They'd raised their children in the certitude of those beliefs, baptizing them in mud and ash when they were old enough to walk. She swallowed, and her eyes darted again to Jin Li Tam. The Gypsy Queen's face was a mask, but her eyes bore both worry and curiosity.

Finally, she looked back to the regent and her sister. "Our faiths may be related, but they are not the same. And though parents may raise their children in the traditions they themselves were raised in, that does not make their belief necessarily compulsory."

The regent smiled. "Our way is not compulsory, though I think you believe for some reason it is."

Winters's eyes narrowed. "I know about the camps for those who dissent. I know about the children you are training on the blood magicks and the marks your priests cut over their hearts. I've visited the schools myself and heard your version of history."

The regent stepped toward her. "You believe the Y'Zirite faith is being imposed here. Very well. What assurance would you have from me that this is not the case?"

Winters looked out over the crowd. The gathered masses remained silent, and their faces were a kaleidoscope of emotion. Some were ecstatic, some frightened, a few even angry. *What would serve my people best?* "I intend to leave these lands," she said. "Your beliefs are an abomination to me. If you would assure me that your faith is not compulsory, then permit those of my people who wish it to follow me as I follow the Homeward Dream. Grant them the choice."

The regent and Ria exchanged glances. There was anger on the woman's face, though she tried to hide it. But Eliz Xhum simply nodded slowly as his smile widened. "That is something I could agree to," he said. "But I would ask something of you in return, Winteria the Younger."

Winters saw movement out of the corner of her eye, and when she realized it was Jin Li Tam's hands, she forced herself to glance slowly and interpret the coded message from her peripheral vision. *Be cautious here,* Jin signed. *Their bargains are never what they seem.*

She knew this. She remembered the look of despondency and hope on Jin's face when Jin watched Petronus killed and then raised, then begged for her son's cure from the woman whose magicks had been so compelling. Like this night, it had also been before a crowd. "What would you ask of me?"

"On the Eve of the Falling Moon," he said, "it is customary to select one to go beneath the knife that their blood might be given to the earth for our sins upon her." He reached behind him to a waiting guard and took a large burlap sack filled nearly to the brim with bits of parchment from the man's hands. "Honor us by drawing the name of our blood-giver, and you and any who wish to leave with you may do so. But you will leave in the morning and you will not look back." Ria's face was red, but the regent continued. "I promise it," he said, and his voice rolled out and away.

Winters looked at the sack and then looked out over her people. "It is by lottery?"

He nodded. "That is the custom. It is a great honor to be selected."

"To be cut upon in the name of Y'Zir?"

"Yes."

Winters looked to the cutting table and saw the knives lying upon a velvet cloth nearby. She'd seen the table in the blood shrine with its dark stains and knew that Ria had killed upon it. And she'd heard the stories from the Tam survivors of what that family had been subjected to upon that island. She'd dreamed of Neb stretched out and staked, writhing and screaming beneath salted blades.

Reaching out, she took the sack from Xhum's hands and held it. She drew in a deep breath, and when she spoke, she looked out over her people. "When I became queen, the charge of those who went before me was that I love my people as a shepherd and study the dreams for them that they might find a better home." She looked at Ria and her voice rose. "When I climbed the Spire and declared myself, this was the promise I bore in my heart." She lifted the bag of names, and as she did, she heard Ria gasp and then caught the momentary flash of rage on the regent's face. "I will not harm my people," Winteria bat Mardic cried out. "I will not let them suffer beneath your knife."

Then, she hurtled the sack of parchments down from the platform and watched the scraps of paper scatter on a cold wind that suddenly moaned around them.

The regent's voice betrayed impatience. "You are—"

But Winters interrupted him, her own voice sharp. "You will still have your blood, Eliz Xhum, and I will hold you to your promise."

She looked to Jin Li Tam, and when their eyes met, she knew the woman understood. The Gypsy Queen broke eye contact first, but not before Winters read the emotion clearly framed there.

She is afraid for me.

But in that moment, Winteria bat Mardic, Queen of the Marsh, was not afraid. She felt nothing but resolve. Fixing her eyes upon the moon where it hung high and inviting in the night sky, she walked to the cutting table and slowly started to undress.

Charles

The field lay shimmering white beneath the moon, and Charles squinted out over it to the hillside. Once the sun had dropped, the temperature had as well, and the freezing sweat beneath his clothing from hiking the snowdrifts added to the chill.

He'd come across the tracks hours ago and had known them instantly. The stride was far too long for any human, and the footprint was not dissimilar from those of his re-creations. The metal man—or Watcher, if that was its designation—had run this way, no doubt bound for the night's ceremony.

He'd retraced the prints with ease until the light went, mindful that his own tracks would give his path away as surely as the Watcher's had done. He'd pressed on into twilight, and when the dark settled in altogether and the moon rose, he found himself at the edge of the clearing.

He took a tentative step forward and then jumped when a voice of many waters roared out through the forest, resounding from the hills.

"May the grace of the Crimson Empress be with you." It was a woman's voice.

For a moment he thought he heard the distant roar of cheering, and then after more words, the woman launched into a discourse. Charles was familiar with voice magicks—they were distilled from blood and forbidden by the Articles of Kin-Clave, but the Marshers had never cared for, nor endorsed, those articles. They did not raise his curiosity nearly so much as the sermon she preached.

Like all acolytes, he'd studied the various resurgences that had sprung up. Most of the Franci behaviorists believed it was a holdover from the Age of Laughing Madness, much like the Marsher dreams his metal children now followed. But in the early words of the sermon that thundered out beneath the risen moon, Charles heard underlying structure supported by anecdotes and quotations from gospels and prophecies he'd never heard of.

This is something new.

Still, as much as he wanted to comprehend this change, he was not here to listen about the grace and love of Y'Zir and its Crimson Empress or its Child of Great Promise. He forced himself back to the line of footprints leading back toward the hill. He could not make out exactly where they ended, and so he put first one booted foot in front of the other and trudged out after them.

As he made his way across the snowfield, he stopped at the sound of a faint movement on the far side and heard a low growl. He'd grown up in the humid jungles of the Outer Emerald Coast and had spent his childhood paying more attention to the tools his father hunted and fished with rather than the actual work, leaving him less experienced in woodcraft. But this was not the high-pitched growl of a cat. More likely, it was a bear or a wolf.

Charles stopped and held his breath. When the growl drifted over the snow the next time, it was closer and circling him. Squinting into dim moonlight, he saw a form—no, *forms*, large and four-footed, approaching him.

Wolves. Only larger than wolves should be.

There were two of them, and even as he crouched and drew the hunting knife Garyt had given him to complete his Marsher disguise, he knew he'd be no match for what he suspected now hunted him.

He'd heard of kin-wolves, those rare leftovers from the days of the Wizard Kings, reduced to small but savage packs that roved the Churning Wastes and harried the Order's expeditions in that desolation. But beyond the studies, sketches and bones from the Office of Natural Science, he'd not seen one.

He waited and held his breath.

When something fast shot past his head, he flinched and fell backward even as the first shadowy form yelped. It took him a moment to make the connection. He struggled up out of the snow as a second and third bullet zipped across the open meadow to find their marks in their targets; then the kin-wolves were snarling and leaping past him.

A half dozen windstorms kicked up snow as another four bullets shot from magicked slings impacted. The volley brought one of the wolves down, and it thrashed and yelped as invisible blades from scouts on the run found it and carved it in a snow-swept dance.

A hand gripped Charles's upper arm to drag him back and away. When he offered momentary resistance a harsh voice whispered into his ear. "I told you to stay put, Gray Robe," Aedric said.

Charles felt the strength in the man's hand as Aedric pulled him backward through the snow, and the arch-engineer said nothing, simply watched and listened as Rudolfo's Gypsy Scouts did their work. The second wolf put up more fight but eventually succumbed to bullet and blade. When it was finished, Aedric's men clicked their tongues quietly against the roofs of their mouths to announce their status.

With help from Aedric's strong hands, Charles climbed to his feet, shaken. "Thank you," he said, the fear of it all suddenly settling upon him like clouds on the Delta.

Aedric's voice still held anger in it. "Do not thank me yet, old man. Just hope that what you and Isaak need so badly can be found in yon metal man's cave and that it is worth the lives of my men."

One of the scouts whistled for Aedric, and Charles walked with him, watching the prints from invisible feet materialize within the broken snow in an attempt to confuse his footprints. A match flared, and the light and smoke from it dimly illuminated part of a hand as a watch lantern was lit. Its lens of light was turned to the bloody ground, and Charles saw now the massive, dark-furred kin-wolves stretched out in death. The dark iron collars surprised him.

Aedric's voice was low and muffled by the magicks. "It seems our metal friend has set out watchdogs in the days since we've last visited him." He pointed to the bodies. "Take them up and bring them."

Then, by the light of the small lantern, Charles followed them to the waiting cave entrance, where they stood and listened. But the booming voice and its impassioned rambling about blood and life and empresses drowned out any sound that might've drifted back to them from deep beneath the ground.

"We go in carefully," Aedric whispered. His finger found Charles's chest and poked it. "You stay behind us until we know it's safe." He was quiet for a moment, then spoke again. "Feris, Grun, stay back here and guard our backs." Then, in afterthought, he added, "Skin these pups for me while you wait."

Charles blinked. "Why would you—"

But Aedric cut him off. "It is not your concern. You just worry yourself about finding your missing pages. You've only my grace because of the two queens who've granted theirs. This is madness, in my mind."

Charles waited until he felt the wind of them moving into the cave and then followed after. As they moved, slowly, he watched as the light fell upon the stone walls and tried to filter out the thick smell of dung and blood that choked him. When they reached the first room and its line of cages, they stopped again. Within the cages, birds of a dozen nations waited amid their stacks of papers. "In for a drachma," Aedric muttered before ordering his men to wring the birds' necks and gather up what intelligence could be found. "After tonight," he said, "our welcome will indeed be worn."

They only spent a few minutes in the cutting room, and Charles was glad of it, for that was the worst-reeking space. They left it untouched and moved into its simple working space with its tables of potions and powders, inks and papers.

Aedric's voice drifted across the room. "Tell us what we look for, Francine."

Charles went to the table of papers. "Parchment pages," he said, "handwritten and of varying ages." Of course, despite the potions the Marshers used to preserve the ancient tomes that held their dreams, some of these pages might not have survived their removal from the books. He only hoped that whatever they might find here would be sufficient for his children's antiphon to be successful.

Still, as they sifted through the room they found nothing that matched what they sought. They'd stuffed a sack full of the gospels they'd found, freshly transcribed and bound in leather, adding to that sack anything else Aedric deemed worthless to them. And just as they were finishing, one of the scouts whistled them over.

"There is a door here," a muffled voice said as a buckskin was lifted aside to reveal a small, dark door in the wall. The small dial betrayed a Rufello lock, and Charles pushed past the invisible scouts to kneel and look at it by the light of their lantern. He stretched out his fingers and felt the lock. It was one of Rufello's simpler models—one of the more common they'd found.

"I know this lock," he muttered. Many of the inventor's smaller locks had been designed with a master cipher known only to the Czarist engineer and coded into his *Book of Specifications.*

"Can you open it?" Aedric asked.

"If its universal release has not been reset, I can." He licked his lips. "Otherwise, we'd need Isaak or one of the others."

"We do not have that luxury."

Charles pressed his ear to the lock and shifted the dial, pressing at the buttons and levers set into the faceplate around it with careful fingers. When the first code brought about a quiet click inside the lock, the old man smiled.

"I have it," he said, and after he finished, he let Aedric pull him back so that they could cast their light within the chamber that awaited them when the door swung open on oiled hinges.

The familiarity of the room hit him first. It was nearly the mirror image of the same chamber in the northern reaches of Rudolfo's Ninefold Forest, a sealed hatch set in the granite floor and the walls lined with tables. Upon the tables, he saw the bent and twisted bits of wreckage so out of place here, though in hindsight it made sense.

"Gods," he whispered, walking into the room. He traced his fingers over some of the objects and drew up his memory of them and of the last day he'd seen them. There were tools and broken artifacts, scorched by the fires of the Seven Cacophonic Deaths. The broken wings of moon sparrows and the warped barrels of hand-cannons kept hidden in deep vaults, unknown even to the Pope. There were bits of metal scroll and broken pens for scripting them.

They're excavating Windwir, he realized as he felt his stomach sink. *They're excavating my workshop.*

But as staggering as that was, it was nothing compared to what he saw next, dead and looking nothing like the petrified remains they'd found in the deepest ruins of the Churning Wastes. This specimen lay stretched out, its eight large legs tacked to the wood of the table and its seedwomb cut open and empty. He stretched back his memory to his studies of this particular madness but could not remember just how many thousands of eggs each one carried. But he remembered how quickly they reproduced, and the knot in his stomach clenched even as he forgot to breathe.

"We need to leave," he said, and the panic in his voice made it shake. "Now."

"Gather what—"

"No," Charles said. "We leave the past in the past," he said. "We need to go now. We need birds to send to Rudolfo—as many as we have."

"What is it?" Aedric's voice now took on a quietness that Charles thought must be fear, and he was glad of it. *We should be afraid.*

But Charles didn't answer. Instead, he turned and left. He moved quickly through the caves, and when he broke into the fresh, cold air of the winter night he found the forest was full of screaming. He did not recognize the voice, but her agony filled sky.

Aedric caught up to him and spun him around. "You do not have the luxury of secrets or silence," he said in a voice now obviously afraid and angry about that fear.

Charles took in a deep breath and tried to force the screaming from his ears, tried to keep from screaming himself. "They're digging up Windwir," he sobbed. "And they've brought back the plague spiders."

Aedric said nothing, but Charles heard the gasps of his men. Every boy and girl learned about the Seven Cacophonic Deaths in ghost tales passed down around fires and in moral lessons from their parents. "Behave," they'd say, "or Xhum Y'Zir's death golems will find you." "Be kind to your sister, or plague spiders might visit their fevers upon her in the night." They were cruel admonitions that none would offer if they'd known what darkness truly lay within that spell that had decimated the Old World.

They took all of the birds they had between them, brown and white both, and as three of the scouts worked their ink needles and pulled black threads from their scarves of rank, the others laid a fire to the sack of gospels and what parchments Aedric deemed unhelpful for intelligence.

Then, the sack of documents that remained vanished into a magicked cloak. Three of the ghosts pulled away, and when they returned, Charles felt Aedric's hand upon his shoulder.

"We've not found what you sought, but perhaps what you did not seek will be worth this incursion. This Watcher will not be pleased by this."

No, Charles thought, *but truly the time for secrets and silence* has *passed.* He said nothing.

"I am sending two men back to our borders. If the birds do not reach Rudolfo, at least these men might. And I'm going to ask Lady Tam strongly to bring our stay here to a close immediately."

Charles nodded. "That is wise, Captain." *And I should leave as well.* But despite what they found here, what they had *not* found here still held him to his work. The missing pages were not here. They were either with the Watcher or—and more and more, Charles feared this—they'd been destroyed as soon as they were pulled from the books. Regardless, he knew now that he had to consult with Isaak and the other metal man before he proceeded. "I'll need to return to the Book of Dreaming Kings."

"I will see you there," Aedric said.

The screams were growing weaker now, and Charles hoped whoever twisted beneath the Y'Zirite knife would die soon and be far from the salted pain that racked them.

The fire burned there at the mouth of the cave, its smoke lifting in a narrow trail that blurred the moon. They stood around it in silence, and then, at the last, Aedric himself folded the bloody kin-wolf hides and left them in the mouth of the cave.

Charles watched flames lick parchment and knew that this gesture would be just a raindrop upon an ocean of need. He also knew there would be ripples from it, and he wished he could gauge just how far those ripples would spread.

Closing his eyes and praying to gods he did not believe in, Charles turned and walked into a forest of screams, the ghosts around him whispering across the snow and the ghosts within him whispering along his spine.

Jin Li Tam

The screams at last were weakening, and for the thousandth time, Jin Li Tam forced her face calm and forced her hands to her sides. She'd identified at least six knives and two pouches of scout magicks she could have taken and had calculated at least four paths to the cutting table and three possible routes off the platform and into a crowd that might hide her and the girl.

Of course, she'd done this after handing Jakob over to a distraught and weeping Lynnae, bidding her bear him back to their rooms in the hope that the screaming would be muffled there. Ria had shot her a questioning glance that had gone sour when she saw the rage in Jin's eyes.

The Machtvolk queen made her way over to her to take the seat that Winters had vacated to take her place upon the table. "I know our ways seem strange to you, but this is truly a great honor my little sister has taken upon herself. And for you and your son to be present for it is the fulfillment of two millennia of longing."

Jin Li Tam had bitten her tongue and tasted her lie. "The voice magicks frighten him," she said simply, and then forced her eyes back to the girl upon the table until Ria finally returned to her own place to take up her silver axe with a smile.

Courage, she had willed her eyes to convey to the girl, but Winters had stopped seeing anything many cuts ago.

Now, it seemed the regent's work was drawing to an end. Her screams quieted as the knives moved slower and more slightly over her skin and as the voice magicks burned themselves out. Jin found herself wondering just how far away her screams had been carried.

With careful fingers red with Winters's blood, Eliz Xhum reached up now to untie her hands one at a time. Then, he untied her feet and gently rolled the girl onto her back. Jin saw the whites of her eyes, and her moan was the sound of thunder. Once again, she found herself nearly losing her composure and still was not certain she did the right thing.

She makes her own path, and I must respect it. She was fairly certain that the cutting was not a part of Winters's plan, but the girl had shown some premeditation in smuggling the voice magicks into the gathering and making her loud proclamation. And she'd kept it to herself.

Certainly, Jin realized, they both had their secrets. Aedric had sought her out regarding the missing pages from the book, and she was confident that Winters had known of this as well. She wondered if the girl had picked up the subtle message she'd intended by sending Aedric to her to confirm that fact. And she wondered how Aedric and Charles fared and if, as she suspected, the Watcher had left his cave to watch this first open mass in the Named Lands.

She did not subscribe to the Marsh dreams herself, though she took it more seriously now that she'd had time to get to know the girl.

And now I know just how seriously the girl takes it.

The knives were down now, and the regent was reaching for buckets of steaming water and clean white rags, laid near the table where Winters stretched out naked and bleeding.

Something broke in her, and the rage could no longer be contained. She stood and pushed her way to the front as he squeezed out the excess water, a smile of pure love upon his face.

"No," she said in a loud voice. "You'll not touch her again." She doubted it carried very far, but it carried far enough. He straightened and turned to her as she approached, and whatever he saw upon her face took his smile away.

"Great Mother," he began, "it is customary—"

But she interrupted him. "I will tend her. You've done enough." Then, she poured every bit of the rage she felt into her eyes and watched him blink at what he saw. She walked to him and snatched the cloth away before he could object.

The words of her sister—if indeed it was her sister—suddenly reasserted themselves, and she could not fathom why under any circumstances she would go with this man. She forced the thought aside and pushed past the regent to stand near the girl. He looked from her to Winters, then nodded slightly and returned to his seat.

She leaned over the girl, taking in the smell of her blood. "This is going to hurt," she said as she lifted the cloth.

The girl fidgeted and croaked; it took Jin a moment to recognize the word. "No." Then, the girl mumbled words she could not make out.

She does not wish to be washed clean of this.

She bent her head closer. Behind her, Ria was on her feet and inviting others to stand as another Y'Zirite hymn rose up into the night. It was a song about kin-healing, and despite the noise of it, she could just make out Winters's whispering.

"And she shall call forth the true Machtvolk by blood," the girl muttered, and Jin Li Tam understood. Let them see her, naked and bleeding for them. This blood purchased exodus for those who chose it.

She rose up and turned to the regent. Their eyes met. "You will honor your promise?" she asked across the platform, her voice drowning in song.

"Yes," he said.

Then she turned back to Winters. "Can you walk?"

The girl struggled, and Jin took hold of her arm to help her up. Her hand slipped over the blood and Winters gasped, but she rolled and sat up on the table. Jin cast a glance to her neatly folded dress and furs, but knew that anything she put over the girl would simply add more pain to what she'd already faced. Instead, she tried to find a part of her body that had not been cut and helped pull her, sobbing, to her feet.

"Lean on me," she said, "as best you can."

Together, with slow and measured steps, they crossed the platform, and Winters cried out softly with each step, though Jin knew she tried not to. They would leave this place, and when they were alone, Jin would wash the true queen of the Machtvolk clean of the blood and see her to Lynnae's care for the treatment of her wounds.

When they climbed down from the platform, she guided the girl onto the wooden boardwalk and noted the wash of emotion upon the faces of those they passed. Some wept in ecstasy and others in sorrow. Some averted their eyes in shame and others gazed upon her in pride.

They shuffled their way out of the crowd, and when they were safely into the forest beyond the gathering, Winters slumped against her and nearly fell. The girl was of small frame, but the dead weight of her staggered Jin, and she held her for a moment.

Then, she felt a hand upon her shoulder and looked up into the face of a weeping young Machtvolk soldier. She'd seen this one before, guarding the door that led into the abandoned throne room and the caves that wound their way down to the Book of Dreaming Kings.

The young man scooped the girl into his arms, and Jin heard the sorrow catch in his throat as Winters cried out at his touch. "I will bear you, my queen," the young man said in a voice that stumbled with emotion.

Jin inclined her head. "Thank you."

He returned the gesture and then set out down the wooden boardwalk in the direction of Ria's lodge.

Jin paused before turning to follow him. The night was filled now with song instead of screaming, and she looked back in the direction of the singing.

This must be ended.

She did not know now how that could happen exactly. It was a vastly larger proposition than she had conceived when she'd first seen the beginnings of this resurgence last year. And she'd had no suspicion that anything could be darker and more frightening than the pillar of smoke and fire on the day that Windwir fell. But that pyre, it seemed, had only been the beginning of a darkness she could not comprehend and could not bear to be a part of.

The last thing she noticed, gleaming wetly in the scattered moonlight that penetrated the evergreen canopy, was the footprints in blood leading backward along the way that they had taken.

"We walk a path of blood," Jin Li Tam whispered, and as she said it, a shudder ran its course along her body, like the kiss of a silver blade over a cold and salted wound.

Neb

An unsettling calm flooded him, and Neb looked down to where he stood upon the silver pond before looking back up to the waiting mechoservitors.

He could feel their song now vibrating up through his feet, and he could hear the whispering of their processing scrolls in the aether.

And from where he stood, he could sense a myriad other vibrations in the strange waters.

You stand upon the veins of the world. They are yours to command now, something whispered within him. *And the aether is yours to walk, but you will need assistance there.*

He cocked his head. "Father?"

I am with you, Son, but only for a short while. I cannot follow where you must go. A strong sense of urgency flooded him, and he felt the pull of his inner eye eastward across the aether. But whatever lay there was out of reach.

Neb walked to the waiting mechoservitors, and as he did, they both knelt. He took his robe from them and clothed himself. One reached within a pouch to withdraw a small object and hold it out to him in a closed metal fist. "I've held this for you, Lord Whym," the mechoservitor said, its voice reedy.

When the small black bird fell into the palm of his hand, the world shifted and Neb fought the vertigo that seized him. His mind flashed back to his last encounter with it, lying naked and staked in the Churning Wastes while the Blood Guard took their knives to him and pressed a similar bit of carved stone into his skin. Now he saw the meaning of it.

The stone extends my sight within the aether. They'd used it to find the location of the antiphon.

Yes. Once more, the whispering of his father's ghost.

Neb felt the slightest tingle beneath his scalp, soft fingers on his brain, pulling at him, and he gave himself to it. *This is how you look,* the whisper continued. And Neb understood, bending the lens of the dreamstone east.

He found Petronus first. The old man stood at the foot of a tall door, surrounded by a ragged group of Gypsy Scouts, Gray Guard and sailors looking out of place. The song poured out from the old man.

No, he realized, it poured out from the pouch the old man held.

Neb smiled. "You hold the dream, Father Petronus."

Petronus jerked alert and looked around, his eyes wide.

"Do not be afraid, Father. It's only me."

His voice was incredulous. "Neb?"

There was a low rumbling, and Neb saw that the gate was slowly swinging open. And though he could not see behind the gate with his eyes, the aether showed him. A single metal man dressed in Androfrancine robes worked the large wheel that opened the way to them. Beyond him, others took down the scaffolding and camouflage to reveal a large metal vessel that was tethered to the ground. Overhead, the moon filled the small circle of sky visible from the bottom of the hollow mountain.

Amber eyes turned upon him. "The antiphon is ready for you, Nebios Homeseeker, son of Whym."

But before he could speak, those ghostly fingers were in his mind again, pulling him away, and he looked south to see a storm of wind that raced across the shattered plains, raising clouds of dust. *Time,* his father's ghost told him, *is of the essence.*

"But how will I—?"

The ghost anticipated him. *You will swim the veins. I will show you.* Already, the fingers were back, and Neb felt as if parts of his mind long left dark were suddenly lit, though poorly. He saw the veins and the pools they linked to, a world shot through with silver, and he knew that it was made for him. He held dominion over every aspect of it, and it served him with gladness. The vast network of pools were his for traveling if he bent them to his will.

He was before Petronus again as the man and the others moved quickly into the large cavern behind the door. "I will be to you soon," he said, "but they will be to you sooner. You must hold the gate against them."

Petronus opened his mouth to answer, but before he could, a scream rose from the west so loud that it blotted out the song. The old man's eyes went wide and Neb faltered. He lost hold of the aether and found himself suddenly pulled back to the cave and the mechoservitors who still knelt before him.

The scream was still with him even in that place, and the sound of it raised the hair on his arms. There was familiarity in the shrill cry, and the power of it drowned out all other sound within the aether.

He released the stone and fell to his knees to bury his face in his hands and somehow rub the pain from his skull.

You are new to the dreamstone, the whisper told him, *but with time you will learn how to control it.*

He couldn't find his voice. Instead, Neb poured focus into his own thought. *Who is it?*

It is irrelevant; time is of the essence. The antiphon awaits.

But the familiarity of the voice chewed him, and with shaking fingers, he reached out again to take up the carved kin-raven.

Her scream flooded him when his fingers closed around the stone. Closing his eyes and gritting his teeth, he forced himself to steer into the scream and follow it west across the aether. What he saw broke him, and his own cry joined hers.

He knew her instantly, stretched out upon the table, and the shock of seeing her there blinded him momentarily to the massive crowd that watched. He saw the lines of words upon her bleeding skin, saw the strong, sure hand that wielded the silver knife, and it summoned a memory of pain and despair. He felt the bite of the hard ground in wounds now healed, felt the burn of salted blades upon the softest of his skin, and heard the questions incessantly asked as the kin-raven was pressed to each wound.

Neb blinked. "Winters," he whispered.

Their eyes met for the briefest moment before her back arched and she screamed again. The man who stood over her wore a red robe and set to his work with a quiet smile. Now Neb took in their surroundings and saw the gathering. He saw the platform, saw Jin Li Tam as she whispered with a woman he did not know before handing a baby—Lord Jakob, he realized—over to her. Another woman, one who could be an older twin to Winters, stood by watching the man at his knife work.

Abomination.

It was a metal voice that filled his mind, overpowering even the screams.

Neb looked around and singled out a lone robed figure on a hillside. "Who are you?"

I am one who watches. Your woman is beneath the knife. Come and save her, I bid you. There was a tone of amusement in the voice. *Surely your baptism has revealed your heritage. Surely you have now attained dominion over the ancient ways.*

Come and save her, Abomination.

Neb saw the distant flash of jeweled eyes from beneath the cowl.

Do not listen, the ghost of his father whispered.

But Neb did not know how to do that. The sound of the screams tore at him from the inside, wrenching a sob from him even as he pulled back from the aether.

"Time is of the essence," he told the metal men. "I must leave you now. Join Rudolfo in his work. He will hide you among the others."

He turned to the bargaining pool and stepped out onto it, willing its silver water to bear his weight. He clutched the kin-raven in his fist and felt the veins of the world shifting and whispering beneath his feet.

He looked first east to the pool buried deep beneath the antiphon, then looked west to find the pool closest to Winters.

All will be lost, the voice inside told him, *if you do not reach the antiphon.*

He heard the truth in it, though he also knew from the canticle that played among his abacus, his metal servants, that only part of the antiphon was truly complete. Silence to the south told him that his abacus had failed there, that Frederico's kin had yet to attain the staff. And in the midst of the madness to his west, a dream could not be found.

He felt the weight of it, but a greater weight settled upon him, and it surprised him after so long away from the girl.

"No," Neb said, "all will be lost if I lose *her.*"

Then, he bent the fingers of his mind west and pulled at the vein that would carry him there. Light swallowed him as he descended suddenly into the pool and rushed at him, roaring, as he shot west, now blue-green lightning in a twisting stream of silver.

When he stood at last upon the pool he'd called for, he stretched out a hand over it.

"Clothe me," Nebios Whym cried out, though he was uncertain why he did so.

The blood of the earth heard him and gave itself to him, rising from the pool to enfold him in its embrace. It crept over him, into his ears and nostrils and mouth, and he pulled it in to himself with a reflex he did not know he had.

He felt strength flooding his body even as the makers and workers within that fluid shored him up and fit his hands for war. He felt his mind clearing, felt the gentle rhythm of his breathing as it steadied.

He stared down at his hands and flexed them. The sheath that encompassed them flexed as well, fluctuating between a bright white that blinded and a silver so pure that its intensity reflected his surroundings and bent light around him.

He took the dreamstone from his pocket now, letting his fingers brush its dark surface. Winters's screams still flooded the aether, and he winced as he turned in the direction they came from.

Two leagues hence he knew a ladder and hatch awaited him. Beyond that, the woman he loved and must soon leave lay writhing beneath knives his own body remembered too well.

"I am coming," he whispered to her where she lay stretched upon the table.

He ignored the metal laughter that tickled in the back of his brain and, instead, gave himself over to the surge of strength within his legs, the sudden sureness of his feet in dark places, the sweeping song that filled him up to overflowing and threatened to burst his heart.

Vlad Li Tam

A wall of water struck him and then lifted Vlad Li Tam up, bringing him down hard, and he moved into a breaststroke in the direction of Behemoth. The sea was hot enough to burn him, and his nose stung from the briny steam that lifted from it.

What in hells is it?

It thrashed the waters, and as a wave lifted him up, Vlad saw that the beast—something like a snake—had turned in their direction, its maw grinding open. Ahead, Mal Li Tam swam for the open mouth, and Vlad tried to recall what Obadiah had told him about Behemoth.

He will take you into the basements of the ladder.

His first grandson spilled over into the gaping mouth and vanished.

Vlad felt the strain in his chest as he swam for it. He did not know what lay in the basements of the ladder, but he knew that the dream required it and that the d'jin had brought him to the dream and to this place. He swam and felt his muscles straining.

When the next wave raised him up, he was nearly upon it. And then when it dropped him, he found himself tumbling into a metal mouth lined with algae and sea moss. He caught at it with his hands to slow his fall, but the water pushed him deeper in, and the slick sides of the inner mouth afforded him no grip. Vlad felt himself tumbling and then felt his fall slowing as the beast leveled out.

At one point, he thought he brushed up against a soft, yielding form that flinched at his touch, but then he fell away from it and found himself suddenly caught by a pocket of water. His fingers were still curled tightly around the handle of his knife, and when his feet pushed against the soft, slippery floor, he kicked against it gently and let that kick carry him to a surface that was not far out of reach. Even under the hot water, he could hear the loud grind and clank of Behemoth's machinery, and when he found the warm, brine-thick air, he drew it in quietly.

There was a faint glow to the algae that cast eerie light upon the large chamber he found himself in. Several spans away, he saw his grandson crawling onto a metal platform as a new sound joined the dull roar that enveloped them—a high-pitched whine.

The water level started dropping.

Vlad took stock quickly. He had his knife and he had the advantage of the scout magicks for at least another handful of hours. But his grandson had years, and more than that, he seemed to have some sense of what he was here to do. Even now, the young man was walking along the far metal wall, and Vlad watched him stop to work the wheel of a large hatch. When it swung open, red light poured out from it, and Vlad watched as Mal Li Tam disappeared into it, pulling the hatch closed behind him.

He made his way to the platform and climbed onto it, walking to the hatch. He could feel his years now in his muscles and joints as they protested with each step, and he forced his breath in and out slowly as he lay his ear to the warm metal door. Beyond it, he heard nothing but the sounds of massive gears and the shifting plates of the segmented metal snake.

As a Tam, he'd had special dispensation from the Pope and had seen many of the mechanical wonders of the Old World and the older world that lay beneath the ruins of it, but he'd seen nothing like this. He'd thought his iron armada or their mechanical men to be a great wonder, but this Behemoth was like nothing he'd imagined, and he suspected that this was merely the anteroom.

He counted to a hundred before he put his hands upon the wheel and turned it slowly. Then, cautiously, he pulled open the hatch enough to look inside. A long corridor stretched out, and it moved and twisted even as the beast did. Its walls were lined with doors, illuminated dimly by red jewels set into the ceiling. At the far end, a door stood open where Mal must've gone, and Vlad quickly slipped into the hallway and pulled the hatch closed behind him.

He felt the pressure shifting around him as the beast descended in a wide, slow spiral, and somewhere behind him, the whining suddenly stopped. Yet even as Behemoth moved, he found his feet steady beneath him and he made his way slowly up the hallway.

He was halfway down the shifting corridor when his grandson appeared at the end. He walked easy, standing tall with his knife dangling loosely in his hand as he went. He left the door open and tugged at another. This one did not open and the young man moved to the next, gradually working his way back toward Vlad.

He could not imagine what might be behind the doors but was certain it wasn't worth being discovered, despite his curiosity. He could visualize bunks and passenger cabins, supply rooms and galleys in this most unusual machine, and he wondered if somewhere within this metal serpent there also lay a pilothouse or if, like the metal men, there was simply a cavity filled with scrolls that spun out a scripted response that had been etched into it millennia before by whomever had crafted the mighty mechanical.

Vlad found a corner of the corridor with less light and huddled in it, mindful of the puddle his wet clothing created. At the far end of the corridor, Mal Li Tam opened another half dozen doors, disappearing into each for minutes that seemed like hours.

Just stay to your end of it, Vlad willed. Then, he turned himself to thought.

She had brought him to the ladder with some urgency, and he suspected now that the timing of his arrival was intended to coincide with the full moon. And certainly, it seemed that his family's blood played into it as well. But what of the strange ceremony aboard both the ship he had fled and, he assumed, the other ships that were gathering there? Was this some new aspect of those dark blood magicks this resurgence had brought back? And what was his d'jin's role in it?

He collated the data and stored it with the rest he'd mined in the time since he'd first read the slender book that he'd taken from his grandson.

As they descended, the corridor shuddered, and Vlad heard the deep groaning of the metal even as he felt it beneath his feet and the red lights flickered and dimmed. He watched the jewels and found himself wondering what powered the large machine. Surely not the sunstones that drove his armada or the metal men. The waters around the Ladder killed those ancient power sources, if Obadiah's experience rang true, and whatever it was that tainted this part of the Ghosting Crests also held the d'jin at bay. Thousands of the rare sea lights, including the one he specifically followed, were waiting at the edge of a perimeter only visible because of their presence.

The machine lurched and shuddered now, and Vlad pressed his back tighter against the wall he crouched against. His grandson was moving toward him again, and once more Vlad calculated just how long the powders would hold. He'd remagicked before returning to the deck with his daughter Myr maybe two hours earlier, leaving him nearly twice that remaining. They would gutter and spark for thirty minutes before finally burning out, but if he kept to the shadows . . .

Another groan, and the vessel shivered again, its descent leveling out before it shifted and rose and then stopped.

Mal Li Tam poked his head out from an open door and came into the hallway with deliberate steps. He moved quickly down the hall, and Vlad found himself holding his breath, gripping his knife tightly, as the young man approached.

I could kill him now and be done with it. The naked back was to him now as Mal worked the hatch, and Vlad saw at least three paths that would leave the boy bleeding out his last. He was under no illusions that it was exactly how things would play out at some point between now and the first moment his magicks began to gutter—he could not afford to lose the one advantage he held. But for now, he restrained himself. Still, each time he imagined the scenario—the knife blade slipping between his grandson's ribs or sliding across his throat—a warm satisfaction flooded him, fueled by the memory of his children's screams.

Mal left the hatch open when he passed through, and Vlad counted again silently before he followed.

Behemoth's mouth gaped open now, and faint light filtered in the massive pool it created. At the edge of it, near a row of metal teeth the height of a man, Mal paced and looked for a place to climb. Vlad moved slowly through pockets of shadow, eyes never leaving his prey, and when the young man scrambled up over the teeth and into the dim light beyond, Vlad moved faster, the sound of his feet in the water masked by the grinding and clanking of the mechanical, though even now those noises were subsiding.

He reached the edge of the mouth and leaped to catch the top of a massive tooth, and despite the scout powders, he felt the exertion in his muscles and in his chest. Pulling himself up with a muffled groan, he stretched himself out over the top of the teeth and held himself in place so he could look around.

Behemoth rested now in a dim lagoon lit poorly by more of the red jewels, casting the dark water in a rust-colored light. It had brought itself to a stop, open mouth pressed close against a stone pier.

This is the basement of the ladder.

The sound of footsteps echoing through the chamber turned his head, and he saw Mal climbing a staircase cut into the far wall. Sighing, Vlad pushed himself up and scrambled onto the pier, trying to control his breathing as he went.

He pulled himself up and turned back to Behemoth where it lay stretched out. The size of it daunted him, and even as he watched, he saw steam venting from it as its gears wound down, and he imagined it sleeping here, waiting for the appointed time for its appearance.

Called forth by blood.

Shivering suddenly, Vlad set off at a brisk walk toward the stairs and soon found himself climbing. He slowed when his ascent stitched his side and threatened his breathing, pausing here and there to listen for the bare slap of Mal's feet on the steps above him. When he reached the top, he saw another open hatch and found himself reeling from a kind of vertigo when he passed through it and found himself surrounded by water, above and below and around him. It was a corridor of crystal that stretched out across an expanse to end at another hatch.

Mal Li Tam worked the wheel of it and then slipped inside. Vlad followed carefully and quickly after.

He followed his grandson for what seemed hours, up stairs and down ladders, through crystal corridors and red-lit chambers with purposes now lost to time. Finally, as his scout powders showed their first sign of guttering and burning out, he passed through another hatch and came to a sudden stop.

This chamber was also crystalline—vast and round—and hanging in the center of it, suspended by silver wires thick as palm trees, was a massive and dark orb. A circular staircase led up from the bottom of the round chamber, stopping at a platform just beneath the stone, and already Mal was taking those steps two at a time.

This is what he seeks.

And Vlad knew that it must be the same for him, though he did not comprehend what it was exactly. Still, with the younger man's sudden burst of energy he felt his own sense of urgency grow.

He felt heat just beneath his skin as the scout magicks guttered again, and he tightened his grip upon the handle of the knife. He moved as quickly as he could without making sound or wind, his feet whispering across the floor and then upon the stairs.

Mal had reached the platform now, and from Vlad's new vantage point, he could better see the orb that hung above them. At first, he thought it was fractured, but as he drew closer he saw that the glass was shot through with silver veins. Already, his grandson had dropped his knife and was climbing up into the thick wires that supported it, moving along the dark surface of the orb.

Vlad reached the platform, scooped up the knife, and leaned back to watch the young man climb.

What is he doing?

Mal Li Tam stood upon the top of the orb now and laid both of his hands upon something that protruded from it. Vlad heard the youth grunting as he tugged on it, and when it began to give, it slid out of the stone with a sound that was nearly music. As he withdrew it, the veins of silver dissipated, and even below on the platform, Vlad felt a tickling in his ears as something, somewhere stirred to life with the faintest vibration.

It built, and he realized that as it did, the light in the room grew. When the long, slender staff was completely free of the stone, Mal Li Tam extended it upward with both hands with a loud cry. The light radiating from the stone's core reflected white and hot from the surface of the silver staff, but an even greater light, from beyond the crystal room, rose to cast its eerie reflection.

The room itself began to move, the stone rotating with it as the wires that supported it whispered and sang. Vlad placed his back to the railing and crouched, trying to keep his focus on the movements of his grandson as Mal made his way down, the silver rod clenched tightly in one hand.

When his feet are on the platform I will strike.

But the rising light pulled at his eyes, and as it did, he found tears welling up again at the beauty of what he saw. Blue-green light from all sides drove away the shadows as d'jin filled the sea beyond the crystal vault. Writhing and twisting, they danced through the waters, and the vibration in his ears became a familiar song even as the knife within his hands became an antiphon of its own—a response to that song that he would soon give.

One d'jin, larger than the others and moving with a fluid grace he knew very well, separated itself from the others and descended into the silver veins, flooding the glass stone and transforming it into a blinding moon.

Mal's feet dangled over the platform now, and Vlad held his breath.

When those feet touched down, Vlad Li Tam smiled and let loose his fury, bathed in the light of a love he could not comprehend, knife-dancing to a song that required his response.

Petronus

They moved through the caves at a rapid walk, often reduced to single file as they followed their metal guide. Petronus walked at the front with Grymlis and Rafe Merrique, while the others spread out behind them.

The metal man had said little since admitting them, despite Petronus's attempts to engage it, and now he'd left the mechanical to its secrets, focusing instead on his unexpected encounter with Neb in a waking dream that left his nose bleeding and his skull pounding. The boy was nothing like the orphan he'd found in Sethbert's camp two years ago. There was a confidence and strength about him even beyond what he'd attained in the grave-digging of Windwir, and along with that confidence and strength, there was a hard edge and a sadness. It didn't take much Franci behaviorist training to see it or to speculate as to what kinds of events might have brought it forth in him.

Just his time under their knives would be enough to change him forever. But Petronus suspected more than that had altered the boy. Beyond the cutting, there was the reason behind it—his role as the Marsher Home-seeker, something that until a few weeks ago Petronus had disbelieved.

Until I was pulled into the mythology myself.

And now, he could not help but believe that he stood upon the precipice of something of vital importance, though he had no real information to prove it was so. And equally, he believed that it was likely he and this ragged group of men he led would not survive to see the antiphon do what it was made for.

Still, he knew they would give their lives for it.

Ahead of them, a dim light grew, and when they spilled out into the open, Petronus saw that it was the moon, high and full above the mountain. It washed the valley with blue-green light, reflecting off a large metal mass he saw there.

He'd seen it hidden with evergreen branches upon a massive series of scaffolds those times he'd seen this space in his dreams, but now he saw it standing free of the scaffolds and open to the night.

No, he realized, not standing. *Floating.* Easily the size of one of Tam's vessels, made of a burnished gold, the ship hung tethered to the rocky ground. A large door in it stood open, and metal men hauled sacks and crates of supplies along a gangway.

Petronus blinked, taking in the image and recognizing it.

"Gods," he whispered. "Do you see it?"

From the corner of his eye, he saw Grymlis nod. "Aye, Father."

He'd seen the drawings—those fragments they'd been able to find in Rufello's *Book of Specifications.* It was that old Czarist engineer's greatest accomplishment, blending ancient sciences and magicks with those considered modern when he served the czars. As a boy, *Felip Carnelyin's One Hundredth Tale* had been one of his favorites, though much of the story had been lost over the millennia that had passed. Still, Petronus had no doubt what he saw. It clicked into place the last of this lock's cipher, and he understood.

It is the ship that sailed the moon.

Somehow, the metal men of Sanctorum Lux had reconstructed it here, in secret, and even now Petronus saw they prepared it for flight.

He forced his feet to their work again and moved out of the cave and into the open air, allowing the men behind him to fan out. He wondered how many of them would recognize what hung suspended in the air before them, chained to the ground as it hummed and sputtered.

He felt a metal hand upon his shoulder, and he tore his eyes away from the ship to take in the metal man before him.

"Father Petronus," the mechoservitor said, "you should not have come."

His eyes slid past the amber eyes to the vessel beyond. *It is larger than I imagined.* Swallowing, he forced his eyes back to the metal man. "Hebda told me I was needed here."

"He and his kind have been interfering a great deal of late."

His kind. "Still," Petronus said, "we are here. We will see your antiphon safely into the air." He could not take his eyes off of it, and quick glances to his left and right told him that it was the same for his men as more and more of them filed into the open space. "When do you launch?"

The mechoservitor's eye shutters flashed open and closed as steam released from the steam vent. "When the Homeseeker instructs us to."

Neb had told him earlier that he would come soon, though Petronus was not sure how that could be possible, nor how the boy would wade through the small army that even now was gathering at the gate. Another voice spoke up to his right as Rafe Merrique stepped forward. "I don't suppose," the pirate asked, "this Homeseeker will instruct you regarding the return of my vessel?"

The metal man regarded him, and when it spoke, the tone was measured and matter-of-fact. "I regret the loss of your vessel in its service to the light, Captain Merrique, but I would be unkind if I failed to point out that it is unlikely you or your men will have use of it given your choice to come here."

The pirate's chuckle was pained, and Petronus winced at it. They'd talked enough in the quiet hours before dawn to know that none of their group expected to survive their latest venture, but he couldn't blame the man for hoping. Now, Rafe Merrique spoke with a flourish. "Then I shall hope that she served you and the light well."

Again, the mechanical was blunt. "The vessel was functional. But a misinterpretation of our role in that aspect of the dream has cost us your vessel along with two of our brethren and a combined fourteen percent of the holdings of Sanctorum Lux."

Merrique opened his mouth to speak, but the mechanical was already moving away, back to the line of mechanicals as they loaded the ship. His jaw went firm for a moment, and that was the only outward sign of the man's anger.

Petronus turned and took in the last of their company as it emerged from the cave. The men that staggered out into the moonlight were a brooding, weary bunch, carrying only their packs and weapons. They'd sent their extra gear, and that of the horses that had survived, away in the care of Geoffrus and his men, knowing even as they did it that the horses were as likely to be eaten as cared for . . . if the Waste mongrel and his band weren't taken by the Y'Zirite forces first.

Grymlis took a step closer and lowered his voice. "What are your orders, Father?"

"We hold the gate until the ship is up." Certainly, they couldn't hold it forever. At some point, their enemy had to find a way around the Rufello locks. But if Neb came soon and the locks held long enough, they could hold the cave. In the end it would be only a matter of time before the Y'Zirites reached them, and Petronus was under no illusion over how it would go for them. Certainly, he himself was set apart from the promised violence—his role as the Last Son of P'Andro Whym assured his survival, according to the Blood Guard Rafe had captured, now buried in shallow graves just beyond the gate. But he also knew that he would take his own life, no matter how abhorrent that was to him, before he went into their custody.

"Establish a line in the caves and work it in shifts," he said. "Mandatory rest for the others; I want them hydrated and steady. Neb said he would be here soon."

When Grymlis spoke next, Petronus heard the awe in his voice and noted that it was barely a whisper. "And where do you imagine Neb will be going?"

Petronus met his eyes and then looked up to where the moon hung in the sky above them. He did not say it; he did not want to. Many Androfrancine scholars disputed the accuracy of *The Hundredth Tale,* claiming it to be a story twisted by mythology and mysticism. But the vessel was here—or one much like it—and there were just as many scholars who believed Rufello's science had once guided a Czarist Lunar Expedition so many millennia before and that it was possible, just possible, that the disaster of that expedition had eventually brought about the Year of the Falling Moon and the wizard who fell.

Grymlis followed his eyes, saw the moon, and then nodded. "We hold the cave until the ship is up."

Grymlis moved off barking his orders while men scrambled and Petronus pulled aside to think. He had a list of questions longer than his leg but knew this was not the time to ask them. Still, his mind required that he order them, and he was setting himself to that work when the ground shook and a distant rumble tickled his eardrums.

He looked up quickly and saw that Grymlis had stopped, midorder; then the orders came faster and the men who'd been pitching their bedrolls abandoned them, took up their weapons and sped into the cave. The metal men stopped along the line, looking in unison toward the cave entrance before starting up again as one and moving their supplies aboard at increased speed.

Petronus made his way to a white-faced Grymlis, certain his own face was pale as well. "We've underestimated them."

Grymlis nodded. "We have. They've brought blast powders to the door, I'll wager."

Rafe Merrique joined them, drawing his cutlass and testing its edge with his thumb. "Then let's hope this so-called Homeseeker comes quickly."

Petronus looked one last time to the ship and to the moon that hung above it. Then, without a word he entered the cave to join his men in their last work upon the earth.

Jin Li Tam

They laid Winters out on a bed that had been stripped down to a simple cotton sheet, and as Lynnae set to tending the girl, Jin Li Tam pulled aside with Garyt.

There were white paths upon his painted cheeks from the tears he'd cried, and Winters's blood dried upon his hands and uniform. Jin could read the despair upon him and understood it at once.

He loves her. She doubted that he knew he did, but she could read it plainly upon him, and she remembered the ache of that kind of love, remembered its own genesis between her and Rudolfo in what seemed a lifetime ago. She put a hand on his arm. "She will be fine," she said. "Scarred but fine."

He nodded, and when their eyes met she saw more than his anguish; she also saw his rage. "Why did she choose this? Any of a hundred of us would have taken the knife in her place."

Jin looked at the girl. She was moving in and out of awareness now that the kallacaine was taking hold, and her body flinched at Lynnae's sponge as the woman cleaned her wounds and applied her ointments and powders. "I think she saw it was her place to do this for her people, to show both the faithful and the unfaithful among them."

He nodded and looked to the door, then back to her. "There is much work to do," he said. "There will be people gathering at dawn to leave with her."

Yes. But how many? Jin was uncertain, but despite Winters's choice she suspected the numbers who actually chose to leave their hearth and home to follow the girl would be low. But she also suspected, just as strongly, that it would only be a beginning. What they had witnessed this night would stay with her people, and over time, more would trickle out as the reality of what they saw settled into their hearts.

She looked to the young Machtvolk guard. "What will *you* do?"

His answer did not surprise her. "I will stay as long as I can," he said. "I will be her eyes and ears here."

She nodded. "I would have you bear word to Aedric if you see him." Now she chose her words carefully. "Tell him that our stay here is finished and to prepare his men for travel."

"Aye, Lady. I will tell him."

She thought again for a moment. "Bid Charles and Isaak the same. They would be wise to leave by the way they came."

He nodded again. "Aye."

She studied the man. "And the Ninefold Forest is ever your friend, Garyt. You bear my grace and thus Rudolfo's as well. If you have need, get word to him."

He inclined his head. "Thank you, Lady. I fear that what we need may be out of his reach to give us." He laid a hand upon the door latch and paused. "Bid my queen good health and safe journey," he said.

Then, he slipped from the room.

He'd been gone less than five minutes before the sounds of third alarm grew beyond their window. It started in the distance and moved through the forest, a growing clamor that soon enveloped the lodge as she heard the running footfalls of soldier and servant alike. Jin went to the window and watched as squads formed up in the yard. She watched a handful of men drink down phials of blood magick and warble out of sight as they ran eastward.

There was a knock upon the door, and Jin turned from the window. "Come in," she said.

The door opened, and Ria stepped into the room, her face washed in rage and worry. Behind her, still in his furs from the walk back, stood Regent Eliz Xhum. "How is she?"

The concern in the woman's voice angered Jin, but she forced that anger from her voice, though her words were still frosted. "She will be fine." She nodded toward the window. "What is happening?"

Ria scowled. "Our perimeters have been breached. And our—"

But she was cut off by a booming voice out of the east that shook the glass and raised the hair on Jin's arms and neck.

"I come for Winteria bat Mardic, true Queen of the Marsh," the voice cried out. "Where is she?"

She knew that voice, though she did not know the magicks that propelled it; there was a clarity and power in it beyond the blood-distilled voice magicks she was familiar with. She saw light moving toward them now and watched the Machtvolk scramble toward it. She heard the cries and grunts of those who found what they sought and then saw the light grow until it took the shape of a man.

His run slowed to a walk as he entered the clearing, and Jin blinked as she recognized the voice, though the man it belonged to looked nothing like the boy she'd last seen so many months before.

Neb?

But not the Neb she'd last seen the night of Jakob's birth. He burned with a hot, white light now from his toes to the tips of his hair, and his eyes were the color of the moon as he strode roaring into the clearing. His silver robe caught the wind and flowed out behind him as he went; and as Ria's men closed in, he swung his fists like clubs and scattered them like kindling. When the invisible wall of blood-magicked scouts pressed in, he tossed them into the trees, where they thrashed and fell.

By the time they were on their feet, he stood upon the porch. "I have come for Winteria bat Mardic," he bellowed out again, and then he was in the lodge, roaring down the hallways.

Jin Li Tam looked to the girl. Her eyes were open now at a voice she also recognized, and she wrestled against Lynnae's ministering hands in an effort to sit up. "Neb?"

Jin glanced at Ria and saw her face grow cold at the name. Her voice was low when she spoke. "Lord Xhum," she said, "I think it would be best to remove you to a remote location."

The regent smiled. "Nonsense. Let the Abomination come. The faithful have nothing to fear from him."

The sound of fighting in the hallway intensified, and then suddenly, the regent and Ria were pushed aside as the room filled with light.

Up close, Jin could see now that a fine sheen of silver flowed over the young man, rippling and moving with him at each step, giving off a heat of its own. He pushed himself into the room, oblivious to all but the girl stretched out upon the bed. He went to her and fell to his knees, a single sob racking him as he did.

He laid his hands upon her stomach, his fingers outstretched over her wounded skin. "Be whole," he whispered.

The silver shifted on his hands, and veins of it appeared on the surface of her skin as her body stiffened. Slowly, before their eyes, the wounds began to close, and as they did, he looked up to finally take notice of the room. His eyes locked with Jin's, and what she saw in them chilled her, not because she'd never seen such rage—she had seen such many times—but because they were alien eyes now, inhuman and distant as stars. "Who did this cutting?"

Xhum stepped forward. "I did, Abomination."

Neb was on his feet now and turning toward the man.

He intends to kill him. And a part of her knew that she should let him, that much of the evil that had come and that would yet come traveled with this man. But another part heard the words of Ire Li Tam, heard the passion and conviction of them, and could not risk that perhaps the woman was right, that the true end to this lay in Jin accompanying the man and waiting for her grandfather's golden bird.

As Neb closed on the regent, she stepped between them and raised her hands to place them against the young man's chest. She felt the heat of the quicksilver skin he wore and felt it yield at first and then resist her touch. "Nebios," she said.

Neb stopped and seemed to notice her for the first time. "Lady Tam," he said. "Stand aside."

"Yes, Great Mother," Eliz Xhum said. "Let him pass. I do not fear death at his hands."

Jin shook her head. "No, Neb. She took the cuts willingly."

Neb looked confused for a moment, and Xhum spoke into that confusion. "Yes, Abomination, it is true. She asked for my knife upon her skin. It was such soft skin, too, and her cries of pain were beautiful, were they not?"

Neb pushed at Jin, and she felt the strength of him but forced her feet to stand their ground. "No," she said again in a quiet voice.

"I think," the regent said, "you should kill me for what I've done. Your demon's bargain in the Beneath Places should let you easily rip me limb from limb. Do it for what I've done to your woman. For the two hand servants whose heads decorate pikes in the lemon orchard outside my palace gates. For the dreams my Watcher has burned and the staff my high priest has taken." He chuckled. "Or do it for the vessel that my Third Desert Brigade will soon dismantle and bury, the heads they'll collect in that hidden place." The chuckle became a laugh.

"Kill me for whatever reason you choose, but know that in the end, the Child of Great Promise is upon the earth and the throne of the Crimson Empress is established. You and your kind are obsolete now, and the tower shall remain closed to you."

Jin felt Neb pushing against her, and for a moment she thought he would simply move her to the side and fall upon the man. But something stirred behind him, and she saw Winters rising, still naked, scarred, and half covered in blood. The girl took three steps and laid her hand upon Neb's shoulder.

"Do not listen to him, Nebios Homeseeker," she said. "Do not let him distract you from your work with the pettiness of this transitory sojourn." She paused, her voice shaking. "I am dreaming again, and I have seen our home. I have seen us singing upon the tower, and I have watched you raise high the staff of Y'Zir and boil the lunar seas with life. You are Homeseeker and Home-Sower."

He turned to her, and Jin saw as he did that his eyes for just a moment were the brown she remembered them to be. But it was only for a moment. Then, a loud and metallic voice from outside shook the windows yet again.

"Abomination," the Watcher cried, "I hold your final dream and bid you come take it from me."

Neb looked to Winters, and Jin saw the pained look that crossed his face. And it was easy to read the root of it, because at the metal man's words, the girl's eyes had faltered.

Jin felt the ice in her stomach, moving out and into her spine. "It is a ruse, Neb. Do not—"

But already, the young man was pushing past them and out into hallway. Already, he built speed and knocked easily aside those who stood in his way.

Jin looked first to Winters and saw the fear that paled her face. Then, she looked to the regent and saw the wide smile that grew upon his. When their eyes met, the smile widened even farther, and Jin had to look away so that he would not read the hatred in her own.

Outside, she heard the tremendous crash of metal colliding with metal, and Jin Li Tam staggered when the ground shook from the force of it.

Charles

The screaming had been over for nearly an hour when the shouting began. Charles heard it and suspected half the Named Lands heard it as well.

They'd been moving more slowly, Charles's muscles protesting a hard day's walk. He'd tried to block out the screaming by thinking about everything he'd learned. The thought of plague spiders harvested from Windwir terrified him. He suspected that those ruins were rife with the leftovers from the Seven Cacophonic Deaths that had brought down the city. He was amazed when he thought of how fortunate Petronus's gravedigger army had been. Digging in the ground there was bound to uncover all manner of evil.

He'd set himself to compiling an inventory of other possible threats and made good headway on it until the shouting. This was a man's voice, bellowing after Winteria, and it was louder even than the voice magicks.

Aedric whistled them to a stop. They were quiet for a moment, until the voice started up again. "I'd swear that was Nebios," he said.

Charles remembered meeting Isaak's Homeseeker in passing, thinking him to be an odd choice of messianic figure. He'd been in the Churning Wastes, and as far as he knew, the boy remained there.

They started moving again, and when the second voice—this one metallic—roared out into the night he stopped again and replayed the words.

I hold your final dream and bid you come take it from me.

The resounding crash that soon followed shook the ground. Charles felt Aedric's hand upon his shoulder.

"I don't know what's afoot," the first captain said, "but it's not safe here. We need to get you back to your cave."

They pressed on amid the shouting and the sounds of battle, moving north along the base of the Dragon's Spine. When the chaos to the south shifted in their direction, Aedric sped them up or slowed them down. Charles heard the sound of trees falling and from time to time saw the snow shaken from them and stirred up from the forest floor.

How can a man be any match for that machine? The question perplexed him. He could think of no magick—neither blood nor earth—that could make this boy Nebios a match for such as the Watcher. And yet he seemed to hold his own. The scientist in him wished he could see the battle, and there were moments when he thought he saw glimpses of moonlight flashing on silver and bursts of white, fast-moving light, but it was impossible to distinguish one form from the other, and they moved with such speed that it was far easier to see the aftermath of where they'd been.

They were moving now through the recently dispersed gathering, and the Gypsy Scouts fanned out, still magicked, as Charles took on the semblance of a lone Machtvolk traveler. He could see the door ahead, though there was no guard apparent. But others gathered here—a crowd of Machtvolk with frightened faces, some carrying children and others with hand wagons and packs. Charles couldn't gauge the numbers, but they appeared to be growing as others joined them from the surrounding forest.

He approached the door and felt Aedric's hand once again. The Gypsy Scout's voice was a whisper. "You would do well to leave this place, old man, by whatever way you came. I am recommending to my queen that we do the same. We don't have the strength to take whatever last dream this Watcher holds. Perhaps the boy does, but I'd not wager on it."

As if in answer, the sounds of battle shifted, and Charles saw them break from the forest—an ancient metal man that moved with fluid grace and a being of silver light. They were surrounded by Machtvolk soldiers who fell like paper men when they found themselves within the fray. The rolling, tumbling, kicking mass moved toward them, and then a metal blow connected and the silver being was tossed easily to land in their midst.

Neb was on his feet quickly, his face fierce and his teeth bared. He glanced at Charles and then launched himself back across the clearing to collide with the Watcher. Charles tried to measure the man's speed even as he tried to comprehend the skin of white light that enwrapped him, but he couldn't, and he left off trying as a hand settled upon his shoulder. He looked up and saw Garyt, covered in blood, standing beside him.

"I need you back inside the cave," he said. "You need to talk some sense into them."

Charles saw now that the door was cracked open, and behind it he saw the dim glow of amber jeweled eyes. He looked next to the gathering crowd and saw that a few of them stared, squinting into the shadows to see what manner of creature might lurk behind that door.

"We're away to our queen," Aedric whispered. "Heed me and flee this place with your metal men while the way is open."

Charles nodded and let Garyt lead him by the arm until they pushed through the door and closed it after them.

Isaak and his cousin stepped back, both venting steam at the same time. Charles was less able to read the older model but saw the signs of distress in Isaak's posture.

"Father," Isaak said, "it is agreeable to see you. Did you find the missing pages?"

Charles shook his head. "I did not." *But I found other things.* Still, he did not say so.

The older mechoservitor's eyes shuttered. "Then it falls to us to help the Homeseeker take them from our wayward cousin."

Outside, Charles could still hear the roaring and crashing as the fight moved through the forest. And he could hear the cries of Marshers when they were unintentionally included in that conflict. "You are no match for him," he said. "You were designed for scholarly pursuit."

Isaak's tone was somber. "Before that, we were designed to bear the spell. We were made as weapons."

The shock of those words forced his eyes to Isaak's. *He can't mean that.* Charles had seen Petronus's notes, the scraps of evidence pointing toward limited deployment of the spell to defend against invasion, but the way in which Isaak said it made his stomach clench. He smelled hot metal and looked for his words carefully. "Whatever your dream is worth, Isaak, it is not worth *that*."

Isaak shook his head. "No, Father. Never that. And our predecessor was designed with the same protections as we were. Our kind is built to survive the spell."

"Then what would you do?"

Isaak said nothing but exchanged a glance with the other mechoservitor. "We have calculated seventeen possible strategies between us."

Charles blinked, suddenly realizing that whatever sense Garyt hoped he'd convey to them, he would ultimately not be successful. They were not waiting for his permission. But what then?

"I wanted to see you first," Isaak said. "We calculate an eighty-three percent chance of one or both of us being non functional at the conclusion of this matter." His memory and processing scrolls spun as steam released from the grate in his back. "The odds are higher for me given the condition of my power source. I have accessed your papers on sunstone technology and have familiarized myself with the various stages of failure."

Charles found himself surprised by the sob that shook him. He suddenly saw Isaak stretched out, broken and dead, upon his table as he labored to bring him back, the sharp smell of grease and ozone flooding his nostrils, and the hollow resolve as he scavenged parts from his other children to save this one in particular. "You cannot go out there, Isaak."

"I must," he said. "The antiphon is ready, and time is of the essence. But I have words for you first."

Charles shook his head. "I do not want your words. I am Charles, arch-engineer of the Androfrancine School of Mechanics and Technology. I command you to remain with me, Isaak. Acknowledge my command."

Isaak placed a metal hand upon his shoulder. "The dream commands me, Father. My love for you seeks your blessing that I might follow it."

My love for you. Charles felt the words moving through him, weakening his knees and shaking him to the core of his soul. He felt the tears now, and he resisted them. "You do not need my blessing."

"I crave it. But I also crave your safety, Father. Though it is not a son's place to command a father, I would bid you stay hidden among the Machtvolk until you return to Rudolfo's care. Your knowledge and skills are necessary for the library to prosper."

Charles shook his head again. "Do not do this, Isaak."

Hot water leaked from a tear duct that Charles himself had carefully re-created from Rufello's notes. "I must follow the dream, or the light will be lost."

"Then do so without my blessing," Charles said, hearing the bitterness in his voice.

"I will," he said. "I must."

Isaak's other hand was up now, both of them settling over Charles's shoulders as he gathered the old man into his arms. The old man was reminded of the embrace he'd seen Rudolfo give the metal man before they'd entered the Beneath Places. He let Isaak pull him in and finally raised his own arms to return the embrace briefly.

"Come back to me when you are finished," he whispered.

"I will do my utmost, Father."

Charles nodded and sniffed, suddenly embarrassed at the emotion he knew must paint his face. He looked to Garyt and saw the young Machtvolk look away, also uncomfortable.

Then the door was open and the two mechoservitors were speeding across the snow, sure-footed, as they raced to join their Homeseeker.

Charles watched them go, feeling both powerlessness and pride as they followed their faith in the moon's whispered song. They did not need his blessing, not any more than Isaak had needed Charles to install the dream scroll in him. But regardless, just as he'd needed to give his metal son that dream, he also needed to relinquish him to serve it.

Because love offered asks its blessings and love returned offers those blessings freely.

"Bless you," he said quietly. Then Charles turned away and buried his face in his hands so that Garyt would not have to see him weep.

Winters

Winters packed quickly, her mind still foggy from the kallacaine she no longer needed. Her encounter with Neb had left her shaken.

No, she realized. *Terrified.* The first time she'd seen him, when she was tied to the table and beneath Xhum's knife, he'd seemed more himself, though he was taller, more hollow-eyed than she'd remembered. And she'd not yet gotten used to the length of his hair. But at least she'd recognized him.

What she'd seen when he burst into her room was not the boy she once kissed in Rudolfo's Whymer Maze. She'd not recognized him at all but for the voice. He had been something terrifying and ancient—a man wrapped in light and power with rage in his eyes. She had no doubt he would have killed the regent if she and Jin hadn't interceded.

Maybe I should have let him.

She shook away the thought and tried to focus on the packing. She'd already dressed for rugged weather. They would go due southeast as quickly as they could. She'd pondered taking her people through the Beneath Places, but she still held out hope that the system of underground passages was unknown to the Y'Zirites and the Machtvolk. Better to keep it secret for as long as possible.

And the rest of my people need to see our exodus. She had purchased that with her blood, along with those people who joined her. Those who chose the convenient lie would die in the land of their sorrow. She and those who followed her would follow the Homeseeker and return to the birthright of Shadrus.

Neb. The boy she'd led into her camp two years ago, the young man who'd stood with her at Hanric's Rest, had been gentle though old for his years. But the man she'd seen today had no gentleness in him.

When he'd laid his hands upon her and healed her wounds, even that act had a fierceness about it. And even now, she heard the thunderous crashing of him as he fought the Watcher in the forests. At first, she'd tried to pursue him, to persuade him to flee. But Jin had caught her arm, and the look in her eye had been enough to stop Winters.

It hadn't taken much. And she understood why now: Neb—the Homeseeker her people had longed for these two millennia—frightened her. He had become something unexpected. So in the end, she let him go and trusted that he would find his way to the new home they were promised, that he would make a path that she and her people could follow. And whatever magicks fueled him now, she hoped they would somehow help him wrest from the Watcher that which had been cut from her people's book so that the tower could be opened.

But her hopes felt flat now.

No, she realized, it was not hope that had become flat. She knew he would do what must be done.

It was the love. He'd burst into her room, with his wild eyes and unruly hair, and she'd seen nothing in him familiar or beloved remaining from the time before he left for the Churning Wastes.

She sighed.

When the regent had requested audience with Jin shortly after Neb raced bellowing from the lodge, Winters had returned to her own room to pack. People were already gathering, she'd been told, at the door that had once led to her throne room and living quarters. She would join them and lead them.

She took another look around the room. She'd packed everything that might be useful, fitting it into a scout pack that one of Aedric's men had provided. She had socks and spare clothes, paper and pencil, and last, she strapped on her knife belt and took comfort in the blades upon her hips. She'd learned the dance with Jin thinking that she might take back her people by the blade, but in the end, it was someone else's knife that gave her those people who were truly hers.

There was a knock at the door, and before she could speak, it opened. Jin stood framed in lamplight, and Winters forced a smile.

"May I come in?"

Winters nodded, and the tall woman slipped into the room. She held Jakob in one arm, nestled to her shoulder, as she pushed the door closed behind her. Jin nodded to the pack that sat on the bed. "You're ready, then?"

"I am." Winters frowned. "They're still fighting."

"They are. They're moving northeast, though. You'll want to steer clear of them."

She's not coming with me. Winters wasn't sure why she'd assumed that the woman would, but she had. "You're staying, then?"

Trouble passed through Jin's eyes, lingering only for a moment. She shook her head. "I'm not staying either. Can we sit?"

Winters went to the bed and moved the pack, sitting where it had been. Jin took the desk chair, turning it with her free hand so that it faced Winters. Then, she sat slowly, careful not to wake Jakob.

After they were both sitting, Jin met Winters's eyes. "We've had our secrets, you and I," she said, "and I think it's time for us to trust." Winters opened her mouth to answer, but Jin continued. "The regent has asked me to bring Jakob back with him to Y'Zir. He is citing tonight's event as one of several indicating that it is not safe in the Named Lands for his Great Mother and Child of Promise."

Winters felt her eyes widening. "You're going with him?"

Jin nodded slowly. "Three nights ago, a woman claiming to be my sister appeared in my room and told me that Eliz Xhum would bid me come with him and that I should go. She told me that my grandfather's golden bird would find me and tell me why."

"And you believe her?"

"I don't know what to believe," she said. "But I've seen miracles I never imagined I would see, and for whatever reason, my family is swept up in this—both my family of birth and my family of choice. Some paths can't be escaped from," she said, "and some shouldn't be." She glanced at Jakob as she spoke. "I believe he will be safe there. And my eyes and ears could be useful to us." She paused. "I think my father was more right than he knew: War *is* coming, and this unknown empire is a superior force."

Especially with the discord and devastation sown here. The southern nations were in disarray, recovering from assassinations, civil wars, the loss of their economic and moral center with the loss of the Androfrancines.

Jin continued. "I am sending Aedric and his men with you. I've not told him yet that I'm not coming. He will be angry. And Rudolfo will be even more angry, but I bid you tell him for me that I will see Jakob safely back to his care, and if I can, I will return to him as well." Here, her words failed and her eyes fled from Winters. The woman's mouth pursed for a moment, and then her eyes returned. "Tell him that I love him and that he bears my grace above all others but the son we have made."

Winters nodded, stunned at the finality she heard beneath the woman's words. *She doesn't think she's coming back.* "I will tell him."

Jin inclined her head. "Thank you." She stood. "The scouts will go with you and keep you safe. The regent assures me that his promise will be honored, that you and those who wish to leave are free to do so."

Winters stood, too, suddenly awkward in this moment, feeling the weight of a good-bye she did not want to give. Instead, she stepped toward the woman, stretched up on her tiptoes and kissed her on the cheek. Then, she kissed the top of Jakob's head. "You have been mother and sister to me, Lady Tam. And friend."

Jin looked surprised at the affection, and Winters felt the heat of her blush as it moved out from her ears and face and down her neck. "Rudolfo would say you are a formidable woman, Winteria bat Mardic. I value the friendship dark circumstances granted us." She smiled, reached out a hand and touched the girl's cheek. "I hope your boy finds his way to the home you seek and that he takes you there soon."

Winters wanted to open her mouth and protest, to say he was no longer her boy, to confess that he had changed, that she had changed and that because of those changes, love had fled. But she did not. The time for all secrets, it seemed, had not passed.

So she watched and said nothing as Jin Li Tam inclined her head one final time and left the room. After she'd gone, Winters wiped from her eyes the unwelcome tears that had sprung up there.

Then Winteria bat Mardic strapped on her pack and left to find her boots, her coat, her people and her path toward home.

Neb

Neb heard the sound of the tree cracking as he struck it, then held his breath as he fell with it. His skin prickled with heat as the silver fluid that somehow encased him absorbed the force of his impact.

Blood of the earth made to serve me. And how was it that he knew? He shook away the thought and pulled himself up from the snow, turning as he did. The Watcher bore down on him and would have reached him again, but Isaak intersected with it, tumbling them both away from Neb. The other mechoservitor joined in, hands and feet flailing for purchase on the Watcher's ancient, pitted metal surface.

They had joined the fight how long ago? He'd lost track of time, but it felt like hours ago. The two metal men, at first, had seemed to turn the tide, but the Watcher adapted quickly and now held his own against the three of them. Neb had managed to turn the battle north and east, away from the more populated area. It wasn't until now that he realized he was also moving them toward the Watcher's cave.

And toward the bargaining pool that lies beneath it. He'd found the cave after climbing the ladder and opening the hatch. He'd seen the cutting room and the blood-still along with the bird station. It had been recently ransacked, and a pile of gospels still burned just outside the entrance beside two bloody but neatly folded kin-wolf skins.

I am slowing down. He was winded, now, too. The silver sheath that swam over his skin seemed sluggish, and his muscles were beginning to ache. Its brightness vacillated, moving between white and gray.

You are losing your strength, his father whispered. *It will burn out soon.*

Yes, Neb realized. He'd first felt it when he'd healed Winters. And now, with each blow the Watcher landed—and each blow Neb returned—the blood of the earth burned hotter over his skin.

He forced his attention away from his father's whispering and back to the Watcher. The metal man flowed in combat, moving with far more grace and precision than Rufello's re-creations, brought back to life by the Androfrancines.

It was taking a toll.

Even now, Neb watched as the Watcher's fist came down on Isaak's companion, shattering a jeweled eye and denting the metal skull. As it reeled away, Isaak threw himself at it only to be tossed easily aside.

"Abomination," the Watcher said, "do not make me dismantle your metal playthings. I hold the final dream." He chuckled, and it was colder than the winter's night they fought in. "Come take it from me."

And Neb knew it then of a certainty: *I can't.*

The blood of the earth was failing. It would not sustain more than a few more impacts before it burned off utterly. Without it, he would be broken like kindling over a metal knee. And the mechoservitors were no match for their older cousin.

I cannot beat him.

No, his father answered. *You cannot.*

Neb dodged north just ahead of the Watcher's charge.

What do I do?

The image of the bargaining pool flashed before his inner eye. *You are the Homeseeker, Nebios. Leave this to your hand servants and go to the antiphon. Time is of the essence.*

He'd forgotten about the antiphon, and he cursed. He squeezed the kin-raven in his fist, feeling the bite of it in his palm. "Petronus," he said.

The old man looked up from where he crouched in the cave. The song flooded the cave, drowning out the sounds of the fight that raged there. There were bodies piled, both magicked and not, as they fought in the dark. "Neb?"

"How do you fare?"

The old man didn't answer the question, shouting one of his own instead. "Where in hells are you? We can't hold out much longer."

Behind him, Neb heard the crash of a metal man colliding with the Watcher. "I'm coming," he said.

No, the Watcher whispered, *you are not.*

When the metal mass struck Neb from behind, it felt like a building falling upon him, and he fell to the left, careening into an evergreen, hearing it crack as it dropped its load of snow upon them. The breath went out of him, and for a moment he felt the bite of bark in his cheek and saw bright flashes of light. A metal fist connected with his other side, and then a metal foot lashed out to catch his thigh.

The two mechoservitors fell upon the Watcher. The ancient mechanical shrugged off one, but Isaak clung to it, tugging at the Watcher as his gears groaned. The steam poured from his back and from gaps that were opening in his joints and from the tear ducts beneath his eyes. Neb heard a high-pitched whine from deep inside Isaak's chest cavity.

He pulled the Watcher away and threw him.

Then Isaak looked to Neb. "You must listen to your father," the metal man said. "You must leave this to us, and if we fail, you must find another way into the tower."

Neb saw the Watcher lifting itself from the snow and glanced again at Isaak and his companion.

Then, he turned and ran north and east as fast as his feet could carry him. The blood of the earth that wrapped him felt the pull of the bargaining pool and poured the last of its strength into him as he flew over the snow.

"Coward." Neb heard disdain in the metallic voice, but he pushed it aside and poured his attention into the run.

Isaak was right. His father was right. It was past time to leave. More than that, he realized, it might've been a mistake to come here. He'd gained nothing, really, other than alleviating Winters's pain.

And seeing her again. It was hard to believe a year had passed between them, most of that time spent beyond one another's dreams during his time in the Churning Wastes. When he'd seen her both with the kin-raven and there in front of her, she'd looked different. She'd grown taller, her body taking on the curves of a womanhood she grew awkwardly into. But what had changed most about her was her eyes. They were darker, sadder, and when she'd first opened them upon him when he'd burst into the room, he'd seen something else in them that unsettled him now.

She was afraid of me.

Neb couldn't blame her. The events of the past year—the past two years, really—had changed him into someone else. And now, his true parentage and the legacy that came with that had changed him even further.

A realization struck him, and he found himself suddenly choking back a sob as he pushed his feet harder to carry him even faster. *I don't know if I am even human.*

He heard another collision of metal behind him, but no matter how badly he wanted to cast a glance over his shoulder, he resisted the urge. Instead, he squeezed the kin-raven.

Isaak?

The metal man was in the aether, the song playing around him. *Yes, Lord.*

Are you okay?

There was no answer at first. *I am functional for the time being.*

He reached for the other, his stomach lurching as he looked into the aether and ran at the same time.

Isaak's companion was no longer with them.

Neb saw the meadow ahead and the last traces of the fire that marked the cave's entrance. He raced over the wide open space and willed the dark opening to swallow him. He slowed slightly as his eyes, enhanced by the quicksilver, adjusted to the diminished visibility. Still, his feet flew as he pushed his way back into the cave, to the small door he had smashed open when he'd first arrived in this place.

He reached the shaft and climbed down, pulling the hatch closed over him even as he heard the sounds of fighting in the caves he'd just left.

He took the rungs as quickly as he could and heard the hatch torn open overhead as he went.

The sheath of silver hummed now, and the heat of it was unbearable upon his skin. He could smell the hairs on his arms and legs and head as they started to singe from it, but he pushed himself even harder, taking the twisting passage of the Beneath Places farther down. His own footfalls were quiet compared to the metal ones that followed him.

He returned to the aether. *I am nearly there, Isaak.*

But Isaak didn't answer. The Watcher did. *You are going nowhere, Abomination. The tower will remain closed and the antiphon will—*

Neb roared and left the aether behind. Two more turns and the room would open to him on the right. As he rounded the corner, he saw the glowing moss that marked the ceiling and saw the shimmering pool. This one was larger than the others, a river feeding in and out from it, a thick vein carrying the blood that sustained a world and served the Younger Gods it was made for.

"Clothe me," Neb cried out as he entered the room.

Nothing happened.

He opened his mouth to utter the command again.

It serves you, his father said, *but it does not necessarily obey you. It knows what your body can and cannot sustain.*

Will it carry me? He moved toward the pool now, suddenly aware of how tired he was, how sore he was.

It will.

Metal hands laid hold of him then, lifting him back and away from the pool, tossing him easily into the stone wall. The last of the silver burned out with the impact of it, and Neb groaned as he fell to the stone floor. Another metal hand gripped his ankle, and he felt it break beneath that viselike strength.

"Your time upon this earth has passed, Abomination."

Neb twisted onto his back and looked up. A metal fist rose, and in that instant, he squeezed the kin-raven again. "Isaak!"

There was a whir and a high-pitched whine that hurt Neb's ears. When the mechoservitor burst into the chamber, he saw in that brief moment that smoke—not steam—poured from gaps in his plating. Isaak's jeweled eyes guttered, and his chest cavity glowed white-hot as he hurtled himself at the Watcher with a feral cry that sounded like steel grinding on steel. The room filled with the smell of ozone. With both metal arms locked tightly around the Watcher, Isaak's momentum carried them forward and into the pool. Neb kicked himself back with his good foot as the two mechanicals tumbled into the thick quicksilver, thrashing as they sank beneath the surface.

He rolled over onto his stomach and crawled to the edge of the pool. *Isaak?*

A single word found him. *Flee.*

Then, a white light built at the heart of the pool, and the floor began to move—first a tremble and then a wild shaking. There was a loud roaring noise from beneath the surface, and the bargaining pool swelled upward and outward, a sudden hot and rising sun contained within it as it did. Neb felt his hair catch fire even as the pool fell back in on itself. Boiling silver rained down even as the ground continued shaking, and he heard the crack of stones breaking in deep places.

A compulsion seized him, and he thrust his hand into the hot mass of liquid. He felt the fire of it travel up his arm, and he screamed the anguish even as he uttered the single word that went out from him and into the blood of the earth.

"Isaak," Neb cried out, and the word rang loudly in the room with a tone of command that surprised him.

The ceiling fell now, large chunks of rock splashing into the pool or landing upon the cracked floor. Fissures deep below had opened, and already the pool was draining as the quicksilver followed gravity and the path of least resistance in the aftermath of the explosion.

Neb pulled himself out onto the boiling surface, feeling the heat of it as it burned what little remained of his robes. He willed it to bear him, and he gave himself to the network of veins that flowed east, letting the hot light swallow him, leaving only his screams behind to mingle with the sound of stone upon stone as the caves collapsed.

When Neb felt the metal hands upon him, he kicked and thrashed against them, unable to see in the dark place he found himself in. But the hands were cool and they stilled him.

"Lord Whym," the metal man said, "the antiphon awaits you. I will bear you to it."

He felt himself being lifted and felt his awareness graying. He heard the quiet whisper of moving gears and spinning scrolls as the metal man moved quickly through the dark cavern. His hand throbbed from where he'd thrust it into the boiling pool, and he felt the kin-raven still clutched in it. With his last conscious thought, Neb cast about within the aether.

"Isaak?"

But there was no answer as the gray became a dark that swallowed him. And this time, when Neb dreamed about the moon, the Watcher waited for him there, laughing down at him from the pinnacle of a tower that remained closed to him.

Vlad Li Tam

The old man danced with abandon and poured his body into the blade. Three times he sliced, three times he punctured, the faces of his children flashing across his inner eye as he brought edge and point home to his grandson's flesh, a steel traveler too long on the road. The young man's surprised cries were the welcome of an innkeeper and the wideness of his eyes, a lantern-lit window.

As he danced, he laughed low and savored the jarring of his arm and wrist each time the knife found purchase.

When he finished, Vlad Li Tam wiped his grandson's blood from the knife and stooped to recover the shining staff. The boy tried to move, his mouth opening and closing and his chest whistling from the wounds that punctured his lungs. Vlad stepped carefully around the pooling blood as he moved back and squatted on his haunches to watch.

Mal Li Tam's eyes rolled, a mumble on his lips that gradually took form. "My . . . last . . . words."

Vlad shook his head, never looking up from the staff. "Lord Tam hears the last words of his kin. You are not my kin."

More muttering, and in the wet-sounding words, Vlad thought he heard something about love. He scowled and was not going to answer, but suddenly words found him as image after image of his family upon the cutting table flashed before his eyes. "What would you know of love?"

The voice was a whisper, and Vlad leaned forward to hear it. "Everything I've done, I've done for love."

He felt the anger first; then it resolved into something calm and quiet. He did not know if it was the exhaustion and last dregs of the scout powders that made him so or the hypnotic way that the blue-green light danced the room, bent through crystal and water. Regardless, he sighed. "Perhaps you have," he said. "And perhaps you've loved the wrong thing."

Then he stood, placed his foot on the neck of his fallen grandson, and let his full weight settle upon his heel as he crushed the boy's windpipe.

Child of Frederico.

It was a woman's voice. He heard her clearly above the moving crystalline room, and the radiating stone hummed. Vlad looked around, feeling gooseflesh rise on him. Then, he realized he was not hearing the voice with his ears.

It spoke again. *My love.*

He looked to the d'jin that throbbed and twisted, captured in the stone. When he found his words, they were a whisper. "Is it you?"

She continued, as if she hadn't heard. *You have drawn the Moon Wizard's staff from the heart of the ladder and can now make right that which he has made wrong. It must return to the tower before Lasthome falls or the Continuity Engine of the Older Gods will fall with it and the light will be extinguished. Seek the heir of Whym and place the staff in his hands; he will know by his birthright how to wield it. Find Shadrus's children. Bid them follow the song home.*

Vlad stretched out a hand toward the stone. It hung above him just out of reach, and for a moment, he was tempted to tap the stone with the staff he held. But something in him resisted.

Use the staff to aid you; but use it with care. For the tools of the parents are not made for the hands of their infant children.

He recognized the quote but had thought it was P'Andro Whym's, possibly from one of the earlier gospels. Another question arose and he asked it, though by now he suspected perhaps this wasn't a conversation as much as it was words rehearsed and now reproduced. "Who are you?"

Frederico's Behemoth will bear you to the Barrens of Espira. I have hidden my father's spellbook there. The staff will lead you to it. It too must return to the tower and be locked away in the Library of Elder Days. My family stole both when they took the tower and raised their fist against the Engine of the Gods.

There was a pause, and it was so long that Vlad thought perhaps she was done speaking. When the voice returned, it was quiet and low. *My love has called you forth and will continue with you, Child of Frederico. We have bargained in the Deepest of Deeps that the light once more be sown in the darkness that contains us all.*

One of the silver lines broke free and moved, slow as a python, and its tip touched the end of the staff. Light moved through it, and he felt the steel grow warm in his hands as it vibrated. The surprise of it caught him off guard, and when he tried to release the staff, he found that his fingers would not move. The vibration increased as the rod burned first white, then blue, then green.

But it wasn't only the staff the light penetrated and suffused. He felt it moving over his skin, then moving into it through his pores and beneath his nails, entering him through his ears, his nose, his mouth and every other orifice on his body. Stronger than the heat of the guttering scout magicks, it crawled into him from the point where the tendril touched the staff, and he resisted.

Another silver vein detached itself and encircled his waist, anchoring him in place as his scars began to itch and then burn. He opened his mouth to cry out and swallowed it as yet another and then another line reached and pulled at him.

Vlad felt himself lifted up and carried closer to the glowing stone and the d'jin—the light-bearer—that blazed within it.

She fills it like she fills my heart.

Yes, the voice said in his mind. *And I power the ladder even as my love powers you.*

The room spun faster now, and Vlad heard the song beyond its crystalline walls reach a crescendo as a sea full of d'jin danced in the waters above and below him.

He opened his eyes against the light. "Who are you?" he cried.

I am the Moon Wizard's daughter, the voice whispered in his mind. *I am Amal Y'Zir, beloved of Frederico, the Last Weeping Czar.*

And then that light became darkness, and when Vlad Li Tam awoke, he lay in the belly of a metal serpent that ground and clanked its way across deep waters. He lay still and clutched the shining staff, taking his breath slowly like kallaberry smoke as his tears dried, the memory of a song echoing in his ears and the sharp ache of love in his very bones.

Petronus

A momentary quiet fell upon the caves, and Petronus closed his eyes in the dark, drawing in a deep breath. He could no longer count the hours or the dead, though he knew there had been plenty of the one and too much of the other.

Most of Rafe's crew and Grymlis's Gray Guard had fallen early. A handful of Rudolfo's scouts somehow held fast, their bodies fortified by scout magicks and the black Waste root, knife-fighting as low whistles counted off their kills in the narrow tunnel. Still, their numbers were dwindling and their lieutenant was down, lost somewhere in the pile of bodies, magicked and unmagicked, that made the floors first slick and then sticky with blood.

When Neb had spoken to him in the aether, they'd just fallen back for the third time. Now, they were far enough back that he could smell the pine trees and sage in the valley where the antiphon stood. Grymlis crouched next to him, and Petronus could smell the sweat and blood on him.

"What do they play at?" the old captain muttered.

"Nothing good," Petronus offered.

Where is the boy? Certainly, there were many unanswered questions, and Petronus wasn't convinced he would be alive long enough to get those answers. Once the scouts fell, along with the last of Merrique's more skilled fighters, he intended to reopen the scar on his neck and let his blood join that of the others who'd given themselves for the light. The Y'Zirites might not be permitted kill him because of his role in their gospel, but he did not doubt that they could visit a worse fate upon him. It was bad enough to be a miracle for their blood-loving faith.

And I've already lived longer than I should. He shuddered at the memory of Ria's knife and wondered if his resolve was such that he could carry it out himself.

"I'm going forward," Grymlis whispered. "Wait here."

Petronus shook his head. "I'll go as well."

Slowly, they picked their way forward until a low whistle stopped them.

Rafe Merrique's whisper was loud in the darkness. "They've pulled back," he said, "and not because we were routing them."

Petronus squinted ahead into the darkness. "How many men do we have left?"

"Less than ten," Rafe said.

Gods. They'd been whittled down. "How long do you think we can hold the cave?"

"Once they start up again? Maybe thirty minutes. But—" The man interrupted himself. "Our metal hosts are back."

Petronus heard the whir and clack of approaching mechoservitors. Three had moved into some deeper place within the caves over an hour ago, and now he saw their jeweled eyes moving toward them like three pairs of fireflies, bobbing with the perfect rhythm of their stride. The amber light dimly illumined the enclosed space, and he saw they ran single file with the middle bearing a body in its arms.

The body groaned, and as they approached, Petronus smelled burned hair. "Neb?"

They slowed. "We have the Homeseeker," the first said. "Lord Whym is wounded but functional."

Lord Whym? Petronus blinked.

The boy stirred, and Petronus saw that most of his hair had been burned away from his naked body. His closed fist looked blackened and smelled of burnt meat. He moaned again.

Father.

The voice was a whisper in his mind, and as quiet as it was, Petronus felt his temples pound and his stomach seize from it. "Neb. We can't hold them for long. Do what needs doing."

We've failed. Isaak is dead. The dream is lost. The staff is lost. There was despondency in the words as they dropped into Petronus's mind.

He did not know how to respond. So little of any of this made sense to him after a life spent resisting metaphysics and mysticism. And yet he felt in his very bones that something far greater than himself—far greater even than the Androfrancine Order whose foundation he'd loved so much that he'd been willing to euthanize it when it could no longer serve the light effectively—worked its way out in these metal men and their response to the dream. Even now, the canticle played on in the pouch he carried, a twisting and turning song of codes within codes that he could not hope to comprehend.

He swallowed and pulled the pouch from his shoulder. "I do not pretend to understand what is happening," he said, "but you've not failed yet, son, if you still live. Too much blood has flowed to bring us to this moment. You will find another way. Go and do what needs doing for the light." He handed the pouch to one of the metal men. "He'll be wanting this back."

The mechanical took it. "Thank you, Father Petronus."

Then, the mechoservitors were moving again, back into the valley where the vessel awaited.

They'd been gone only minutes when the sounds of snarling and howling reached Petronus's ears. He'd heard it before during his time in the Wastes, though distant, and every time it ran long nails of dread along the slate of his spine.

Kin-wolves. But these were not far off and in the open. These growls echoed through the caves, growing louder and louder as they sped toward them. When they intersected with Rudolfo's men, he heard a cacophonic choir of muffled shouts and feral yelps. Then, he heard the savaging and felt the air rush out of him.

"Hold the cave," he bellowed, his voice ringing out over the din.

A voice was in his mind again, but this one was not Neb's.

No, it said. *Fall back with your men to the ship.* The power of it set his nose to bleeding and his ears to ringing.

He winced. *Who is this?*

I am called Whym. Parent of P'Andro and T'Erys. Parent of Nebios.

"Gods," he whispered.

Yes, the voice answered. *Fall back with your men to the ship. I cannot go with him. You will accompany my son and save what may be saved of us.*

He heard the wolves in the caves, heard the cries as Rudolfo's men paid for each span of rock they held, and looked in Grymlis's direction. Then, once more, the man who did not believe in faith took a leap of it.

"We need to fall back to the ship."

The old captain snorted. "Not a likely scenario."

Petronus closed his eyes. Dreams. Voices. A ship that sailed the moon, restored and even now rumbling to life behind him, its own growl louder than the wolves that savaged his men. "Fall back," he said again.

Rafe chuckled. "You mean to take us to the moon, then?"

Petronus gave the whistle himself at Grymlis's hesitation. The old captain followed it up with a shout. "Fall back!"

They moved backward at first, listening to the sounds of fighting as the scouts fought in retreat. But when they heard the first of the kin-wolves break the narrow line, they turned and ran.

Petronus felt his heart pounding in his head as he went. He and Rafe were nearly neck and neck, with Grymlis just behind. He felt the slight wind of movement but could not tell how many scouts ran alongside them. Certainly not all, because the sounds of fighting continued behind them.

A gray circle of light took shape ahead of them as they approached the entrance of the valley, and the howling behind them increased as more kin-wolves flooded the caves. In the dim predawn light, Petronus felt a large mass of stinking fur lunge past, ignoring him entirely to nip at Rafe's heels. The pirate went down, and without thinking, Petronus thrust his short sword into the kin-wolf. The beast yelped as the Gypsy Scouts added their invisible blades to its hide.

He reached out and caught Rafe, dragging him from beneath the thrashing kin-wolf and back to his feet. Now, they were in the valley and saw the ship looming over them, its gangway down and its large hatch open as the mechoservitors as one released the chains that held it down.

Something growled deep in the vessel, and it shifted upward momentarily before hovering in place. Overhead, the moon was gone now, and the last of the night stars were fading as the sky moved toward morning.

Another wolf hurtled past, this one racing for the closest mechoservitor. It leaped, bringing down the metal man only to yelp when the metal hands closed upon its neck to snap it with mechanical precision.

The other metal men fanned out at the base of the gangway as more kin-wolves poured from the cave.

Petronus ran, his chest aching from it, and he felt the ghosts that ran alongside of him. Ahead, Rafe reached the bottom of the gangway and paused. "Get aboard," Petronus shouted.

The last two of Rafe's men were there now, too, helping their captain aboard, and Petronus was nearly there himself when he heard Grymlis cry out.

He stopped and turned.

The Gray Guard lay on his stomach, two kin-wolves worrying at his legs as the last of Rudolfo's men, unseen and barely heard, moved about them, their knives drawing lines of dark blood upon dark fur in the predawn gloom. Petronus glanced back to the unmoving metal men where they awaited.

"Help us," he said.

When they didn't move immediately, he cursed and ran back. Three other kin-wolves had joined the skirmish, and another two had sped past Petronus, oblivious to him.

He reached Grymlis and swung his short sword at the closest wolf. It yelped, snapped at him and turned, yanking the blade from Petronus's fingers. Grymlis had flipped onto his back, but his flailing and kicking had slowed.

Petronus grabbed up the fallen soldier under his arms and pulled at him, putting his full weight into dragging the man free from the wolves. He tried not to notice the blood that soaked the man's shredded gray uniform, focusing instead on moving them toward the waiting gangway behind them.

The wolves closed, and the last of the scouts danced backward beside him as he pulled his friend. One grabbed at the tattered remains of Grymlis's boot, nearly pulling Petronus over as the old captain cried out.

Then, metal hands were upon them, lifting them, and they were on the gangway. The vessel groaned again and shifted, but the sure-footed mechanicals carried them aboard, kicking at the wolves that tried to pursue.

The last moments were a blur. Petronus found himself in a large metal room stacked with crates and sacks bearing the Order's seal upon them. He lay propped against a metal wall across from a crystal porthole, cradling Grymlis against him as the gangway was brought in and the large hatch was closed. Inside the ship, the growl was nearly a roar, and he felt the room shake and then sway.

He clung to Grymlis and glanced quickly around the room. One of Rafe's men tended wounds he could not see on the last three surviving Gypsy Scouts while another tended Rafe. The mechoservitors had vanished up a ladder into some other part of the ship, and there was no sign of Neb.

"We made it," Petronus whispered.

Grymlis mumbled something, his voice thick. He'd lost a lot of blood. Petronus felt it warm on his own hands, seeping through his own clothes. He leaned his ear in close to the working mouth but could not distinguish the words.

"Rest easy," he said, then looked across the room. "I need a medico over here."

Grymlis muttered again, and this time he heard names in the muttering. Lysias. Resolute. "I can't understand you," he said.

He felt the hand, weak, upon his leg. At first, he thought the old man simply squeezed it, but his mind put together the words he was pressing into his thigh.

I helped Lysias kill Resolute. Tam forged a note for us.

It was a confession, he realized, and he knew why now. "We do what we must to serve the light," he said. "I killed Sethbert and ended the Order." He thought for a moment. "What was it you used to say to the orphans you recruited? That it is easier to die for the light than it is to kill for it?"

And now, he held his dying friend in the belly of a ship that bore them slowly upward. Voices that called him out to serve. Dreams that pointed the way in whispers he could not comprehend. Promises of home and promises of violence. These all moved across his inner eye, going back two years to the pillar of smoke that marked Windwir's grave.

Petronus looked up and saw the bloody sky of another sunrise over the Churning Wastes.

"Look Grymlis," he said. "We're flying."

But Grymlis had already flown, and Petronus hoped his friend would find home and light awaiting him in whatever place he landed.

Weeping, he lay still and watched the porthole as the sky shifted from red to black. When they came to take Grymlis away, he let them, his eyes never leaving the expanse of night they now flew.

Rudolfo

A cold wind whistled outside as Rudolfo sipped chai made over an Androfrancine camp furnace. Sleep had eluded him, and he'd eventually given up his cot to spend the night going over reports that he'd been too drunk to read the first time they'd crossed his worktable. As he read, he'd packed those that needed to be packed into his administrative chest and fed the rest into the furnace, watching the fire gobble down the words. Once he'd finished that, he'd laid out traveling attire—doeskin pants, a heavy wool shirt, a coat made from beaver pelts that had been a gift from one of his house stewards, and his green turban of office. He laid his father's knives and knife belt next to the clothing.

Then he'd packed the rest of his things. After, he put on the chai and settled into his chair with a copy of the Y'Zirite gospel.

Two years. Where had he been riding when his life had changed so irrevocably? He frowned and stared at the lantern. Paramo. They were turning toward Paramo, where he'd hoped to bed down with a log camp dancer or two and enjoy a Second Summer night of drinking wine from freely offered navels. That was when he looked up and saw the pillar of smoke upon the sky. He remembered that Gregoric, who never flinched at anything, went pale at the sight of it.

"I miss you, my friend," he said as he lifted the chai mug to his lips. "I wish you were here now." Still, he wondered now if even Gregoric would be daunted by all that had transpired.

He'd given the orders yesterday. Philemus already sped south for the Seventh Forest Manor. The second captain would follow those orders, though Rudolfo knew that trust was strained. He'd written the edict himself, carefully and in four drafts, having Lysias read each. It grieved him to write it, and a part of him knew that it was not the right path; but another part recognized that sometimes, when only wrong paths were left, one chose the best wrong path available and hoped a right one would emerge eventually.

Before, he would have felt he shamed the memory of his father. But now, he questioned that man he'd revered for so very long, and feared that if he were brave enough to exhume the corpse and if time were kind enough to have left his body intact, he would find a mark over the man's heart that would break his own.

He thumbed through the pages of the book, his eyes settling on a passage about the Child of Great Promise and the healing of the world. He'd read the gospel through several times, each time gleaning more from the patchwork words of Xhum Y'Zir's seventh son, the one-eyed Wizard King, Ahm. What he took most from it was how carefully it was woven with just enough truth to foster a sense of trust, enough fancy to stimulate imagination and enough personal application to engender a sense of belonging and commitment. It delivered purpose. He could see why the Androfrancines, focused upon the light of human achievement and knowledge, would resist and suppress this. Making each and every individual potentially an important contributor in a faith that promised healing to the world—particularly in the midst of cataclysm and upheaval—was a potent elixir for the disempowered, disenfranchised and disillusioned.

But how different is it from Winters and the Homeward Dream of her people? He wasn't certain, at the root of it, that they differed much, though her people's faith had no gods to speak of. Their Homeseeker, if he understood it correctly, was more a servant than an object of worship. Still, it was no coincidence that the one people who had room in their hearts for a faith were the first to openly declare their commitment to Y'Zir.

If it had been left at that, this would all be simpler. But it hadn't. There were secret shrines, even in the Ninefold Forest, and even his own father had been a practitioner, it seemed.

Rudolfo sighed and sipped his chai. He tried to conjure the smell and smile of his infant son to comfort him, the softness of his bride's cheek and the fierceness in her eyes. He'd sent the bird yesterday, calling them home. Something dark crept toward them—he heard its footfalls in the changing times—and he knew now that he could not truly protect anyone whom those forces wished to harm. And he also knew now of a certainty that those dark footfalls intended grace for his family, not harm. While others fell, the Ninefold Forest thrived. What the Androfrancines once hoarded and kept hidden, the Forest Gypsies now rebuilt and made open.

The words had ridden him hard of late. *We cannot win here.*

Still, he would try. He would resist. But he would not bend his knee; he would not bare his heart.

Hefting the gospel in his hand, he weighed it carefully and wondered how many other gospels there were, how many prophecies and psalms, and how many more were coming.

Rudolfo took a deep breath, held it, and gently placed the book into the furnace. He watched long enough to see it catch fire. Then, he stood and dressed carefully, quickly, and slipped outside into the gray light of morning.

The stars were guttering and the moon was down. To the east, pink tinged the peaks of the Keeper's Wall. He walked alone at a brisk pace, climbing the ridge until he found a place where he could watch the sunrise.

He could not watch it without thinking about her and the first time they'd met. In those days, he'd been more interested in pleasure than love, but something in her had struck him and struck him hard.

A sunrise such as you belongs in the east with me.

It had been a blow to him and to that fledgling love when he learned it had been engineered by her father, followed soon after by the announcement that she carried his heir. And the day that he'd watched his son, Jakob, emerge from her was a day he could never forget. Those first weak cries changed his life, and he'd wept and laughed at the wonder of it all.

Learning yet later that the betrothal and heir were part of a larger scheme had not shaken him as much, though now it did. Still, the why of it was not nearly as important, regardless of the knives and blood of the Y'Zirite faith that overshadowed his son.

Because, Rudolfo realized, he is *my* child of promise first and foremost. A promise that his line would continue even in a world vastly changed from the time he first saw the pillar of smoke against the sky. A promise that life and light could emerge from death and darkness.

Yes, he thought. It would be good to have them home.

The sun rose now and smeared the sky red.

Rudolfo watched it and squinted at a star where no star should be.

No, not a star. It was light reflected upon something golden and distant, rising above the Keeper's Wall and moving slowly up and away.

What strange bird is this? Rudolfo wondered.

He watched it until it vanished from his view, and then he climbed slowly down the ridge beneath a sky that promised no snow at least for this day but offered no promises at all for the morrow.

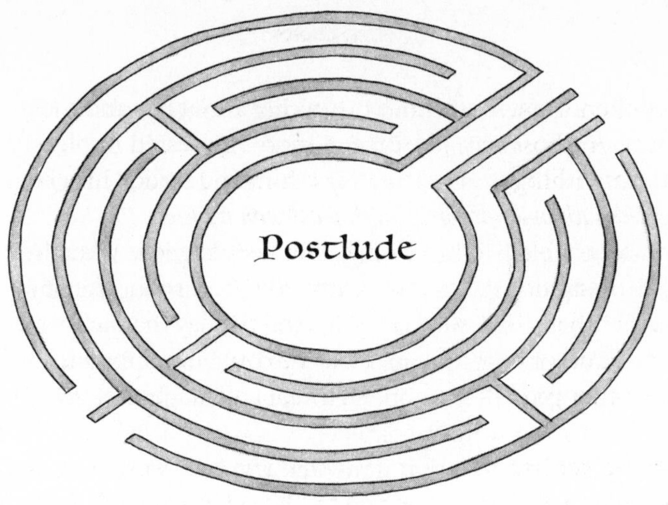

Jin Li Tam stood at the rail and held Jakob close to her chest as the moon rose over the Named Lands. The gentle rocking of the ship lulled her son but did nothing to settle her own restless heart.

She and Lynnae had packed after seeing Winters and her ragged band of Marshers off in Aedric's care. The man had refused to meet her eyes as he left, and it grieved her still, knowing that Rudolfo's rage would be even greater than his captain's.

When she and the regent had finally left, it was without fanfare and with a small escort.

They'd ridden hard, Jakob swaddled and slung against her as they galloped magicked horses down from the mountains, across the plains of Windwir and into the lower nations of the Named Lands. During those long days in the saddle, she'd learned what she could of the regent and his forces, even picking up smatterings of the guttural language they spoke quietly among themselves.

Part of her restlessness was what she'd seen on that ride. The mounds of earth and snow where teams of Machtvolk and other robed figures excavated the desolate city, their shovels and pickaxes digging up artifact and skeleton alike. But that was not nearly as unsettling as what awaited farther south.

Pylos had brought the bile to her throat, but she'd held it in despite the lurching of her stomach. At least someone had cleared the highway ahead of their horses, stacking the bodies of those who'd tried to flee off to the side to make way for the riders.

She'd lowered her eyes, knowing the truth like a blade on her skin. *Every man, woman and child killed for Queen Meirov's sin.* And the queen herself—or at least her head—now decorated a pike in the courtyard outside her palace, if Ezra's report to Regent Xhum was accurate.

Jin suspected that it was.

Now, as the moon came up, clouds drifted in to blot out corners of the sky, veiling stars that throbbed in the cold night. She found herself looking first to the southwest, where she'd spent her youth learning from her father how to be his daughter and his spy. Then, she looked to the north, where one day, two years earlier, her life had changed suddenly into something she would never have imagined.

Mother. Queen. Wife. These were not roles she'd asked for or particularly wanted, and yet now, she could not fathom relinquishing them. Gifts given in the midst of desolation. Gifts, she realized, carved from the manipulations and machinations of her family in service to a dark gospel.

And now, in some ways, it felt as if she gave those gifts back.

She closed her eyes and tried to bring up Rudolfo's face, tried to find the memory of his hands on her and hers on him, but found now that all had fled. In its place lay the hollow, dead eyes of Pylos and the gnarled hands grasping against whatever fell sorcery had decimated that nation.

What kind of magick visits plague with such careful discrimination? Across the river from the highway, life on the Entrolusian Delta seemed business as usual, though there were more soldiers at the river crossings.

She shuddered the memory away and opened her eyes at Jakob's sudden laughter.

There, perched on the railing of the ship, was her father's golden bird. Last she'd seen it, Isaak had restored it and caged it in his office in the basement of the new library. Before that, she'd seen it delivered to the forest in a wagon with other artifacts and books from her father's library.

She looked around to be certain no one was in eyeshot and then looked back. Its beak opened, and the voice that leaked out was one she'd not heard in many years.

"I do not know," her grandfather's voice whispered, "which of you will be the one Vlad sends to Jakob's son. Ire. Jin. Gwen. But whoever of you hears this message, heed me well. I am a foolish old man, and my transgressions are multitude. My greatest folly was bending my knee to the resurgence, though at the time I thought it the only path left me. Their path is the path into darkness and an end not only to the light but also to life. If my greatest, fondest hope is true you are now en route to Y'Zir, and when you arrive you will do what you are made to." The voice paused. "It falls to you, under the protection of your role and the role of your son, to end this madness. It falls to you, Granddaughter, to kill the Crimson Empress."

There were no other words, no blessings bestowed. The bird simply lifted from the rail and bent its way north and east in a direction she knew well.

Long after it had gone and long after Jakob had settled into sleep gentled by the waves of the Emerald Sea, Jin Li Tam, Great Mother to the Y'Zirite Child of Promise, watched the northeast and wondered how desolation could find someone a home they never expected, and how love of that home could drive one to leave it behind.

The boy will be safe in Y'Zir. Her grandfather had offered her no such assurance. But she'd heard the songs and seen the look of adoration in the eyes of the Y'Zirites; she'd read the passages and heard the schoolmistress expound upon them with her own ears. He would be safe, but what kind of life awaited him in Y'Zir if she failed?

And why did I choose this path knowing the risk I take for this child who is my very soul? The answer arose within and brought a sudden sob to her shoulders that she forced aside.

"Because I am my father's daughter after all," Jin Li Tam told her sleeping son.

Then she watched the waters for a long while until clouds choked out the moonlight and a cold rain baptized her for that dark work ahead.

Acknowledgments

This is my third time out and I'm even more mindful that it does, indeed, take a village to produce a novel. There is a long list of folks I'd like to thank for helping put *Antiphon* together and into the world.

Like *Canticle* before it, this one was marked by loss with the passing of my father (just thirteen months after Mom) when I was roughly halfway through the drafting of the book. But this particular book was also marked by gain in that my daughters, Elizabeth and Rachel, were born just as I reached the finish line.

First and foremost, I'm grateful to Jen for the partnership and encouragement—and for the gift of two little Incentive Factories to keep me grinding out the words. Thank you, darling. And thank you, Lizzy and Rachel, for giving me added drive. It was fun editing this book while holding you in my other arm.

Also big thanks to the rest of the J-Team: John, Jay, Jerry, Jean Ann—you are great friends who keep me honest and hard at work.

I'd be remiss if I didn't thank the West Clan for all their support both in general, and also specifically when the girls were born. Those two weeks of help got the last of this book written.

There is an even longer list of other friends who've come alongside and helped me push these last several months. Just to name some: Aimee, Amy, Aliette, Alessa, Rodger, Mary, Lee, Other Lee, Robert, Scott, and Pierce. There's a much longer list that I could recite; apologies if I've left anyone out.

I'm also grateful for my agent, the thirty-second daughter of Vlad Li Tam finally debuting here on these pages. Like the Other Jen, I made you taller, Jenn, and made you bad-ass with a knife. It's a small token of my gratitude for all you've done.

This truly couldn't happen without the fine folks at Tor. Their faith in these books is a great encouragement to me. Big thanks to Irene, Melissa, Patty, Alexa, Kyle, and all the other hands who've helped along the way.

I especially want to thank Beth Meacham. Beth, you are a wonderful editor and a lovely human. We work well together. Your support most recently through the death of my father and the birth of my daughters is a great gift in my life, and this book would not be here if it weren't for your constant, caring approach to your writers.

And last but not least, thank *you*, Dear Reader. For those of you who've written via email or looked me up on Facebook, thank you. Your kind words about the series so far really do help me stay at the keyboard to lay down the next bits. I'm pleased that you've joined me here in *Antiphon* and I look forward to seeing you in *Requiem* really soon.

Until then, magick the scouts.

War is coming.

Ken Scholes
Saint Helens, Oregon
January 3, 2010

About the Author

Ken Scholes is a winner of the Writers of the Future contest with short stories appearing in various magazines and anthologies since 2000. *Antiphon* is the third volume in his Psalms of Isaak series.

Ken grew up in a small logging town in the Pacific Northwest. He has honorable discharges from two branches of the military, a degree in history from Western Washington University, and is a former clergyman and label gun repairman. Ken lives near Portland, Oregon, with his wife, Jen West Scholes, and their twin daughters, Rachel and Elizabeth.

Ken invites readers to visit his website, www.kenscholes.com.